THE DEVILFISH STRIKES AGAIN!

As the *Koji Maru* rocked in the grasp of a massive swell, the fishing master raised his camera to snap off the first frame. Cursing in pain, he reached out to divert the spotlight to illumine the sea off their starboard side.

What he saw almost made him forget the agony of his bruised torso. Quickly approaching from the sea was a frothing line of turbulence that preceded the appearance of what appeared to be a monstrously huge manta ray with two distinct horns protruding from its rounded gray head. The crazed creature was on a collision course. There was a bone-jarring concussion followed by a moment of confused blackness. The next sensation that the Sendo was conscious of was the icy grasp of the sea. A passing buoy allowed him to keep his head above the water. With his camera still strapped tightly around his wrist, he watched his fatally wounded ship slip beneath the waves, its doomed crew trapped in a tangle of ink-soaked drift nets and debris.

ECOWAR

RICHARD P. HENRICK

HarperPaperbacks
A Division of HarperCollinsPublishers

This is a work of fiction. The characters, incidents, and dialogues are products of the author's imagination and are not to be construed as real. Any resemblance to actual events or persons, living or dead, is entirely coincidental.

HarperPaperbacks   *A Division of* HarperCollins*Publishers*
10 East 53rd Street, New York, N.Y. 10022

Cover illustration by John Berkey

First printing: October 1993

Printed in the United States of America

HarperPaperbacks and colophon are trademarks of HarperCollins*Publishers*

❖ 10 9 8 7 6 5 4 3 2 1

This story is dedicated to those brave, seagoing eco-warriors, who have devoted their lives to fight for the preservation of our planet's endangered oceans. They are the true heroes of this tale.

The earth mourns and withers.
It lies polluted under its inhabitants;
for they have transgressed the laws,
violated the statutes,
broken the everlasting covenant.
—ISAIAH 24

BOOK I

TRAIL OF THE BEAST

*In that day the Lord
with his great sword
will punish Leviathan.
And he shall slay the beast
that is in the sea.*
—Isaiah 27

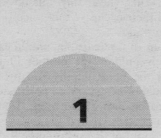

1

November 2, 1974—Southwestern Pacific Basin

The mother blue whale and her six-month-old male calf swam steadily southward. Their four-thousand-mile migration had begun in the warm, tropical waters near the equator, where the calf had been born.

By the time they reached the Antarctic ice shelf a month from now, the calf would be weaned. Meanwhile the forty-seven-foot-long, twenty-ton infant would continue to feed on its mother's rich milk. Over two hundred pounds of the nourishing fluid passed through his hungry lips each day, causing the calf to gain nearly seven pounds of body weight an hour.

Throughout this seven-month period of extended nursing, the mother blue would fast. With her sleek, eighty-two-foot-long body now weighing a mere one hundred tons, she would soon teach her son how to utilize the fringed, brushlike baleen that hung from his upper jaw to catch krill. These tiny, planktonic crustaceans would provide their exclusive diet once they reached the polar feeding grounds.

With visions of the feast that would calm the ache in her empty belly guiding the mother blue's stroke, she emerged from the black depths and broke the water's surface. Her dual blowholes were positioned side by side, on the forward portion of her back. Immediately after these cetacean nostrils cleared the water, they shot up a single, slender spout of fine spray some fifty feet skyward. Her calf joined her on the surface, and together they greedily filled their immense lungs with fresh air.

A series of intricate one-hundred-decibel blasts of sound was the mother's signal that it was time to return to the protective depths. Almost reluctantly the calf took one last fond look at the powder-blue sky above before resealing his blowhole and arching his neck downward. Viewed from above, the youngster's enormous blue-gray back looked like an island in motion as he rolled slightly on his side then disappeared with a final salute of his raised fluke.

In a nearby part of the Pacific, the French attack submarine *Agosta* silently hovered some seventy-five feet underwater. Inside the vessel's cramped operations center, Ensign Jean-Louis Moreau, the *Agosta*'s junior-most officer, sat at the sonar console monitoring the sub's hydrophones. The strange cacophony currently being conveyed through his headphones mesmerized the recent naval academy graduate, who couldn't help but voice his amazement.

"It's like something from another world, Commandant! I've got increased biological activity on the thirty-hertz band. It's almost deafening, and seems to fill the seas around us."

The slender, bald-headed officer Moreau addressed stood behind the sonar console. With a practiced ease,

Captain Michel Baptiste clamped a set of auxiliary headphones over his ears. This allowed him to tap into the assortment of strategically placed microphones in the sub's bow. Much as he expected, the headset conveyed a somewhat familiar chorus of deep, guttural cries, which caused the *Agosta's* commanding officer to grin thoughtfully.

"They're whales all right," Baptiste reflected aloud. "Enjoy this aria of the deep, Ensign. It's a song few humans have ever heard firsthand."

"I never dreamed that they could produce such a wide variety of noises," Moreau remarked as a particularly complex series of high-pitched cries streamed through his headphones. "Could they be talking to each other, Commandant?"

"Our scientists still don't know the answer to that question, *mon ami*," answered Baptiste. "Although, in my opinion, this racket has to have some sort of purpose. My best guess is that they're communicating in some primal fashion. And we can't understand them because man isn't intelligent enough to crack the code."

Jean Moreau looked up from his console and searched his commanding officer's grizzled face. "The thought of those creatures out there having a language of their own intrigues me, Commandant. I wonder what species of whale we've chanced upon?"

Baptiste met his junior officer's inquisitive blue stare and replied while removing his headphones and turning for the nearby periscope well. "Why don't we see for ourselves, *mon ami*?"

Baptiste addressed the helmsman, who sat facing the dials and gauges in the compartment's forward bulkhead. "Bring us up to periscope depth, Chief."

The helmsman verbally acknowledged the order and gingerly pulled back on the partial steering column he gripped between his knees. In response, the boat's bow angled upward.

At the proper depth, Baptiste activated the periscope. It rose from its storage well with a hydraulic hiss, and he wasted no time snapping down its dual handles and peering into the eyepiece.

The calm surface of the sea greeted him. It was a spotlessly clear day. The midafternoon sun commanded the sky, and Baptiste instinctively blinked when a wave gently slapped up against the extended lens, momentarily veiling his view.

To check for possible surface obstructions, he initiated a hasty 360-degree scan. Only when he was certain that no other vessels were in sight did he focus his search on the waters directly south of them.

"I've isolated the whales on the lateral array, Commandant," Jean Moreau announced. "They appear to be gathered some three hundred feet below us, on bearing two-two-zero."

Baptiste turned the scope to the west. Another swell momentarily swallowed the elongated lens, and the *Agosta*'s commanding officer muttered, "They'll be back to the surface to breathe soon enough. Then we'll have a proper look at those boisterous, seagoing rascals."

A full thirty seconds passed before Moreau relayed the next sonar update. "The whale songs continue to emanate from the water below, though the frequency range has narrowed to twenty hertz. I wonder how long they can remain submerged?"

"Patience, *mon ami*," advised Baptiste, who remained glued to the eyepiece. "Though his home is exclusively in the sea, leviathan is a mammal, and as such shares one important trait with man—namely, the need for air. Our whale friends will rise again, and then we'll be able to determine their exact species."

Jean Moreau absorbed this thought while pressing his right headphone against his ear and turning up the volume gain. "We seem to have lost them!" he shouted, his eyes desperately scanning the waterfall display of his sonar screen.

"Perhaps they're broadcasting below twenty hertz," Baptiste suggested.

"The screen is blank, Commandant," returned Moreau. "One moment they were singing away so clearly, and then, in midnote, complete silence, as if they disappeared off the very face of the earth."

Baptiste was preparing to leave the scope to check the sonar console himself when a rippling disturbance broke the surface of the ocean. A line of frothing seawater fringed a monstrously large, slate-gray back that seemed to go on and on for all eternity. Enchanted by the incredible sight, Baptiste looked on in shocked silence as the newcomer released a single, pear-shaped spout high into the cloudless sky above.

"Thar she blows!" he cried mockingly.

Baptiste's delight was doubled when yet another whale, noticeably smaller than the first, surfaced. It, too, spouted, and the veteran mariner noted the relatively small, nubbinlike dorsal fin that graced its lower back, and its massive tail fluke.

"They appear to be blues," he observed. "*Mon Dieu,* the incredible size of those graceful brutes!"

"I've got them on sonar," said Moreau. "There are two distinct sounds. One is high-pitched and shrill, like the mewing of a cat, while the other has more bass to it."

"So far I see only a pair of them," said Baptiste. "We've most likely chanced upon a mother blue and her calf. I've read that the blue whale is the largest animal ever to roam the planet. Even the greatest dinosaur couldn't rival it in size. What a pity that such a magnificent creature has been hunted to the verge of extinction."

The periscope was filled with the arched back of the calf as it followed its mother into the depths.

"*Au revoir, mes amis,*" whispered Baptiste reverently, backing away from the periscope to rejoin Moreau at sonar. "Listen closely to their sad, lonely song, Jean-Louis. You could very well be the last man on earth to enjoy the privilege."

Moreau nodded solemnly and reached out to

increase the volume gain of the *Agosta*'s hydrophones. The haunting song of the whales intensified, and the young ensign from Toulouse found himself feeling a new respect for these gentle denizens of the deep. Yet his thoughts were cut short all too soon by an alien, chugging sound.

"Surface contact, Commandant!" he reported while redirecting the angle of the sub's hydrophones. "I've got a single vessel, bearing one-five-zero, maximum range."

Without a moment's hesitation, Baptiste raced back to the periscope. His scan quickly centered on the southeastern horizon, where a small black dot representing the approaching ship was just visible in the distance.

The sonic signature of this vessel continued to take shape on sonar, where the innocent song of the whales was all but forgotten. Jean Moreau applied the skills he had learned in the classroom to determine the contact's exact range. The *Agosta*'s active sonar sent a powerful acoustic pulse streaming out into the surrounding waters from the sub's bow-mounted transducer. By timing the Doppler shift in the return signal, the new surface contact was precisely pinpointed. In a combat situation, utilization of the active sonar mode would be avoided whenever possible, since the acoustic transmission would give away the submarine's position as well.

Once the exact range was determined, Moreau shifted his attention back to the boat's passive sonar. This system relayed the sounds received by the sensitive listening devices strategically placed along the *Agosta*'s hull.

He started off with a broad-band scan. Their target was a noisy one, and Moreau had little trouble isolating the signature of the approaching surface vessel from the sounds of the surrounding seas.

Once the signature was locked in, he carefully analyzed it with the narrow-band processor. In such a way, he was able to determine the contact's unique sonic footprint. The console's waterfall display showed the footprint's entire frequency range, while his headphones relayed only that portion of the spectrum audible to the human ear.

Moreau inched up the volume gain and listened to the surging, cavitational hiss of the contact's single prop screw, which was badly nicked and thus "singing." The diesel power plant turning the prop was definitely not built for stealth. It produced a resonant, deep-throated growl, indicating that the throttle was being run wide open, with no concern for the resulting racket.

"I've got a clear visual on the contact," Baptiste reported from the extended periscope. "It's a small, rust-covered trawler with a tall observation mast set forward of the bridge and funnel. There's a single gun mounted on the prow that appears to be loaded with a harpoon."

The mere mention of the last object caused Moreau to look up from his display screen. "Could they be after the whales?"

"It sure looks that way," answered Baptiste, a hint of displeasure in his voice. "Are our whale friends still in the vicinity, Jean-Louis?"

With a flick of his wrist, Moreau readdressed his console, isolating the hydrophones beneath their bow. The incessant whine of the approaching trawler faded from his headphones, to be replaced by the now-familiar but still unearthly cries of the two blues.

"The whales continue to sound close by, Commandant," said Moreau.

"For the sake of those magnificent creatures, pray that their dive is a long one, *mon ami,*" said Baptiste, whose amplified periscope view showed a pair of scraggly sailors anxiously posted at the trawler's harpoon gun.

Moreau's face winced in concern when his headphones went unexpectedly silent. A quick check of the waterfall display showed that the song of the whales had once again fallen beneath twenty hertz, the limit of man's audible range. The last time this occurred, the blues had surfaced. He wasted no time voicing his suspicions.

"I believe they're returning to the surface, Commandant."

Michel Baptiste instantly decreased the lens magnification of the periscope, allowing him to carefully scan that portion of the sea lying between the *Agosta* and the approaching trawler.

Much to his disappointment, dual, pear-shaped spouts of water broke the ocean's surface. "The blues have indeed surfaced, and now they're in for it, Jean-Louis. Divert the passive sonar feed into the public-address system, and come have a look for yourself."

Moreau addressed his console, and as he pulled off his headphones and stood, the control room filled with the haunting cries of the whales. By the time he joined his commanding officer at the periscope, the trawler's distant throbbing whine could be heard as well.

Both men were slight of build, with almost identical five-foot, eight-inch frames. They could easily pass for father and son, only Baptiste's shiny, bald skull and tight, leathery skin setting them apart. No height adjustments were thus needed to the periscope as Moreau grabbed the handles and peered into the eyepiece.

The sea was eerily calm, with only an occasional swell rippling its glassy surface. Less than three thousand yards away, the trawler could be seen approaching. Moreau studied the vessel closely, estimating the ship's length at 175 feet. It sported a black hull, a sharp, curving bow, and a low-lying white superstructure amidships, with a single funnel aft of the bridge. This funnel appeared to be the only portion of the vessel not in need of a good coat of rust primer.

By increasing the lens magnification tenfold, Moreau centered his inspection on the part of the ship forward of the bridge. A narrow catwalk led to the prow. Bisecting it was a tall mast, topped by a crow's nest. A single sailor was stationed here, his gaze locked on the sea immediately before them.

The harpoon gun was situated on the prow itself. It

was a formidable-looking weapon, capped by a razor-sharp tip and manned by two burly individuals in stained yellow oilskins. They, too, had their gazes focused forward, and Moreau decreased the lens magnification to inspect these same waters.

A slender, fifty-foot-high spout pinpointed one of the blues, halfway between the *Agosta*'s extended scope and the advancing trawler. Another thin column of watery spray spouted close by. This one extended only half as high, and Moreau knew it belonged to the calf, whose high-pitched, catlike cries continued to sound from the compartment's elevated speakers.

"Well, Jean-Louis, what do you see out there?" asked Baptiste.

Moreau answered while watching the mother blue undertake a series of shallow dives. "The larger of the whales looks to be almost as long as the trawler. My, the incredible size of that graceful brute!"

"Have they acknowledged the presence of their human adversaries as yet?" continued Baptiste.

"I'm afraid not," said Moreau, who readjusted the angle of the lens to include the trawler. "They don't seem to be making any effort to escape. And if they don't sound soon, I fear the worst. The trawler is less than a thousand yards away from them, and continues to quickly close."

Baptiste momentarily replaced Moreau at the scope, and the junior officer took this opportunity to focus on the strange mixture of sounds emanating from the compartment's intercom. Filling the control room was the gentle mewing of the calf, the deep, soothing cowlike bellows of its mother, and the steady, grinding, alien hum of the ship sent to hunt them down.

"The harpooners are readying their weapon!" Baptiste noted. "Yet the whales continue to spout, completely oblivious to the danger hovering so closely above them. If only we could warn those blues of their predicament."

Moreau had been wishing this very thing. Feeling

frustrated and impotent, he could only stand there and listen to Baptiste's sad commentary.

"It looks like those bastards are trying to isolate the calf!"

The intercom speakers filled with the distinctive throbbing rumble of the trawler. Like an onrushing locomotive, it rose in volume, until it all but overrode the confused squeals of the young blue.

"Dive, *mon petit*," urged Baptiste. "Sound to the depths, for your very life!"

Moreau found himself silently channeling his will outward to implore the calf to follow this course of action. His pulse quickened, and as he attempted to visualize the life-and-death struggle taking place outside the *Agosta*'s hull, a bloodcurdling screech was relayed through the hydrophones. A muffled explosion followed, sending Michel Baptiste reeling away from the periscope.

"*Non,* it can not be!" he shouted, his voice heavy with rage.

Moreau was quick to replace him at the eyepiece. Filling the lens was the surfaced, madly thrashing calf. A portion of harpoon shaft protruded from the creature's back. Copious amounts of blood poured from the wound, staining the surrounding sea a sickening shade of red.

One only had to listen to the squeals relayed through their hydrophones to share the young blue's pain. Moreau noted that the persistent growling throb of the trawler was no longer audible. He decreased the scope's lens magnification and saw the reason for this. The rust-speckled platform of death lay still in the water, less than thirty yards from the injured calf. A group of seamen could be seen on its angled prow, pointing toward the doomed whale, satisfied smirks on their faces.

"Why aren't those bastards pursuing the mother?" he somberly questioned.

"Why waste the petrol?" answered Baptiste. "*La mère* will not abandon its progeny. And the whalers are playing on this unselfish loyalty to lure it to an easy death."

The tormented cries of the calf noticeably lessened. Blood continued to gush from its wound, yet it no longer thrashed about in agony. Rather, it lay unmoving, its spirit gone.

On the prow of the trawler, several of the sailors could be seen anxiously pointing to the nearby waters. Moreau scanned these same seas, and all too soon he viewed for himself what had gained their attentions. Just as Michel Baptiste had observed, the mother blue had returned to her injured child, with a mighty spout and an angry slap of her immense tail fluke.

The *Agosta*'s control room filled with an anguished bass cry. There was a weak, scratchy, high-pitched response, followed by a gut-wrenching bellow from the confused newcomer.

Tears of compassion cascaded down Moreau's cheeks as he watched the mother blue gently nudge the calf with the rounded tip of her flat head. A series of deep, guttural blasts of sound touched Moreau deep in his heart. In that sad, magical moment, the barrier to interspecies communication was momentarily surmounted, and the young Frenchman clearly understood the whale's tragic plight.

The arrival of another harpoon cut short the mother blue's mourning. Moreau watched in horror as the lance ripped into the mother's back. Seconds later the grenade in its explosive warhead detonated. An ear-piercing cry of anguished pain was followed by the arrival of yet another harpoon and another sharp explosion.

A bloodred spout poured from the mother blue's blowhole, causing the whalers still gathered on the trawler's prow to raise their arms in celebration. Infuriated, Jean Moreau backed away from the periscope and addressed his commanding officer.

"*Mon Dieu!* Why does man do such a horrible thing?"

"For pet food, lipstick, lubricant, and lamp oil," spat Michel Baptiste. "Such a waste can never be excused!"

Shocked into speechlessness, Moreau locked gazes with his veteran shipmate. Together, they listened to the final death throes of the largest animal ever to make the earth its home.

2

The Present—Virginia Key, Florida

This morning's bike ride was like a dream come true for Dr. Peter Kraft. Seven months ago a simple spill from this very same bicycle had landed him in the hospital with a fractured hip and a broken femur. Emergency surgery was needed to repair the break, and he left the hospital three days later, with a stapled-shut, seven-inch-long scar lining his upper right thigh. This hid a pair of permanent stainless-steel implants that were screwed into the fractured bone to assist the healing process.

For three long months he wasn't allowed to put any weight on his leg. Getting a sound night's sleep was all but impossible, and he found his movements confined by a wheelchair and walker. Late in the spring he graduated to crutches. And at long last he was allowed to take his first tentative steps.

Summer found the forty-three-year-old marine biologist

building up the strength in his leg through long walks on the beach and frequent swimming. Yet it wasn't until the arrival of the fall equinox, three days before, that his physician gave him the okay to resume bicycling.

Before his accident Kraft had been an avid bike rider. On his day off he could easily handle a fifty-mile jaunt, and completed his fair share of centuries. He also biked to work. Of course, his condo on the southern tip of Key Biscayne was less than five miles from Virginia Key, where the institute on whose staff he served was located. Thus the ride barely caused him to work up a sweat.

He was both excited and a bit nervous as he prepared himself for this morning's commute. It felt good to put on his bicycle gear, which included a helmet, spandex shorts, a backpack, and gel-filled gloves. He had cleaned up his ten-speed the night before, and climbed up onto the seat somewhat shakily. Fortunately traffic was at a minimum as he pulled out onto Crandon Boulevard, and his anxieties were all but forgotten by the time he approached the Rickenbacker Causeway leading to Virginia Key.

It was a glorious autumn morning. The air was fresh and mild, full of the scent of the sea and the adjoining mangrove swamp. A good portion of this swamp passed on his right. Much of the older growth had been decimated by Hurricane Andrew, which had ripped through the area in the summer of '92. Yet since that fateful night, Mother Nature had already taken root anew, in the form of new growth to replace the old.

A gull cried out overhead, and Kraft looked up into a deep blue sky, interspersed with floating tufts of gossamer clouds. His love of the outdoors was one of the primary reasons he enjoyed bicycling, and he silently thanked God for giving him a second chance.

The road sloped slightly upward as he began to pedal over the causeway leading to Virginia Key. The uphill climb caused an unfamiliar ache to course down his right thigh, and he cautiously shifted into a higher gear.

A wide, blue channel of swift-moving water passed below. A lone sailboat was tacking out into the open Atlantic, the luffing sails flapping in a stiff, onshore breeze.

As he reached the causeway's midpoint the chrome-and-glass spires of downtown Miami sparkled in the distance, on the far side of Biscayne Bay. Appearing much like the fabled city of Oz, the colorful cityscape glimmered like a jewel, lit by the tropical, midmorning sun. Kraft would never tire of this magnificent sight.

A slight downward slope led him onto Virginia Key. He braked and glided past the entrance to the Key's Coast Guard station. On the opposite side of the roadway was a low-lying complex of modern, concrete structures, surrounded by a barbed-wire-tipped, chain-link fence. With a quick glance over his left shoulder, Kraft maneuvered his bike into the left-hand turn lane. He had to wait for several cars to pass before crossing the road and entering a narrow driveway guarded by a security kiosk.

Kraft braked to a halt alongside this structure's open doorway, which was topped by a sign reading, WELCOME TO THE RICKENBACKER INSTITUTE OF MARINE SCIENCES— AUTHORIZED PERSONNEL ONLY. A single uniformed individual, with a bulging potbelly and a thick mop of dark, curly hair, stood inside, clipboard in hand. Kraft couldn't help but smile as the guard's brown eyes opened wide in surprise upon identifying him.

"Dr. Kraft?" The watchman was astonished. "Is that really you on that bicycle?"

"That it is, Gustavo," the blond-haired marine biologist answered with a playful wink. "I'm having trouble believing that this day has finally arrived myself."

The guard's pleasure as he left the kiosk and offered Kraft a warm handshake was obvious. "It's so good to see you getting back to normal again, Doctor. After your accident, I didn't know if you'd ever ride to work again."

"To tell you the truth, neither did I," Kraft replied, while unconsciously massaging his right thigh.

"Does it still hurt much, Doctor?"

"Nothing that I can't learn to live with." Kraft abruptly changed the direction of their conversation. "So tell me, Gustavo, how was the fishing this weekend?"

The watchman shook his head and grinned. "The bonito were running just like you said. We pulled in so many that my arms and shoulders are still smarting. I left a couple of fillets for you in the commissary freezer."

"I appreciate that, Gustavo," Kraft replied after looking down at his wristwatch. "By the way, is the boss here yet?"

"The director arrived about a half hour ago. He was on the phone when he pulled in, and didn't acknowledge my wave."

"Some things never change," said Kraft as he prepared to continue his ride. "Keep your cool, Gustavo, and thanks again for those fillets."

The security gate swung open and Kraft guided the bicycle over a large parking lot, packed with automobiles. He crossed the narrow alleyway between the institute's administration building and library and emerged onto a flat, two-acre clearing, where several water-filled holding tanks were situated. The largest of these had seven-foot walls, and when Kraft spotted a familiar blond-haired figure working on an upper catwalk, he braked to a stop and dismounted.

A latticed steel stairway led him up to a narrow platform surrounding a pool of crystal-clear water. The blonde, her back to him, was in the process of cleaning the sides of the tank with a nylon brush on a long, aluminum pole. She was dressed in a tight blue tank suit, which more than adequately displayed her tanned, fit body.

Mary Walker was one of his hardest-working research assistants. She had arrived at the institute two years before to take an introductory course in marine biology and had been with him ever since.

Kraft was about to raise his voice in greeting when a

series of excited, high-pitched squeals sounded from the water. It was obvious that the pool's occupants had spotted him, and he watched as a pair of sleek, gray bottlenosed dolphins raced to the side of the tank beside him. Both dolphins curiously poked their smiling faces out of the water and addressed him with an animated burst of clicks and whistles.

The racket was enough to gain Mary Walker's attention, and she turned, surprise lighting up her freckled face. "Good morning, Dr. Kraft."

"Good morning, Mary," said Kraft. Then turning to the water: "And good morning to you, too, Dolly and Matilda."

Once again the dolphins chattered noisily, prompting Kraft to remove his backpack. He extracted a large thermos, twisted off the lid, and grasped the tails of two dead mullet that lay inside. "Don't worry, girls, I haven't forgotten your Monday-morning treat," he teased. "But first you've got to earn it."

The marine biologist raised his free hand and made a tight fist. This visual cue was all the dolphins needed to submerge and begin quickly circling the tank. After two times around, they plunged to the bottom, then rocketed upward, simultaneously breaking the water's surface and leaping high into the air in a graceful, perfectly formed arch. They reentered the water with barely a splash and shot back to the side of the pool, where Kraft delivered their treats as promised.

"I gather from that gear you're decked out in that you rode your bike to work," Mary Walker observed. "Congratulations."

"Thanks, Mary. When my surgeon gave me the all clear to cycle the other day, I knew it had to be now or never."

"Was it scary riding again?" she asked.

Kraft answered while reaching up to remove his helmet. "I'd be lying if I said it wasn't. It's going to be a long time before I can leave the memories of my accident behind. But I guess this morning's ride was an important first step."

"I'll say it was," said the research assistant. "It seems like just the other day that you were scooting around the grounds in that wheelchair of yours. You've certainly come a long way since then, and all of us here are very proud of you."

"Don't forget, I couldn't have made it to this point without your support. Remember that day you helped me climb the steps of this very tank with my walker. How I wanted to give up, halfway to this platform, but you wouldn't hear of it."

Mary fondly smiled. "I've got to admit that I had an ulterior motive in getting you up here. You see, I told Dolly and Matilda that you were on your way up to visit, and I couldn't disappoint them. They missed you terribly as it was, and if you didn't show up that afternoon, they would have been absolutely impossible to work with."

At the mere mention of their names, the dolphins squealed out in delight and began a spirited backward tail walk. It was Dolly who followed with a double forward sommersault while Matilda leaped high into the air and smacked into the water with a playful belly flop.

"Hey, girls, save some of that energy for this afternoon's test," admonished Kraft.

"So you're still going on with it," Mary said, her tone serious.

"That's an affirmative, kiddo," Kraft replied. "I'd like to get started later this afternoon, right after my budget meeting with Dr. Kromer."

"My offer to take your place still stands," she added.

Kraft's handsome face filled with his most diplomatic smile. "What, and me miss out on all the fun? Besides, my girls aren't about to let me down, are you?"

Looking down to the water at this point, he held his left hand overhead and made a rapid circular motion. The dolphins took their cue and began circling the tank with a jetlike swiftness. 'Round and 'round they traveled, their ever-pumping, tapered flukes and streamlined bodies slicing through the water at a speed close to twenty knots.

Only when Kraft clapped his hands overhead did the dolphins break off their blind pursuit. Smiling admiringly as they arched through the air in a final jump, he waved good-bye and shouted, "See ya' in a couple of hours, ladies!"

After leaving his research assistant with a mock salute, he carefully made his way back down the stairway. He grabbed his ten-speed by the handlebars and walked with it beside him.

Kraft's hike took him past a seawall, where the glimmering waters of Biscayne Bay slapped up against a formidable, man-made barrier of stone and wood. Adjoining the seawall was a wooden pier. Its main slip was presently vacant, the institute's thirty-eight-foot capture boat currently in the Dry Tortugas monitoring the region's sea-turtle population.

Directly opposite the pier was a twelve-by-two-hundred-foot circular channel of water, spanned by a wire-mesh bridge. Yet another of his research assistants stood on this bridge with a large, metal bucket at his side. Andy Cummins was a graduate student at the University of Miami. He was taking a little time off from his dissertation for some hands-on experience.

"You have my permission to give them all the seconds they want this morning, Andy," Kraft greeted as he engaged his bike's kickstand and climbed up onto the bridge.

Cummins was pulling the blood-soaked back half of a bonito out of the bucket. He spoke while tying a stout hemp rope around the creature's tail. "Would you believe that I can't even get a nibble out of them. I'm hoping that some of these freshly caught fish that Gustavo dropped off appear a bit more appetizing."

Kraft watched his assistant dip the bonito into the waters below. It didn't take long for the first of the channel's inhabitants to swim by. The ten-foot hammerhead shark swam under the bridge and passed the bait without so much as a second look.

"Well, I'll be." Kraft was dumbfounded by this unusual behavior.

In an effort to stir up some excitement, Andy yanked on the rope and slapped the surface with the jagged bonito. A pair of tough-looking makos swam by, completely oblivious to this ploy.

"I hope they're not saving their appetites for brunch," Kraft remarked. "Pour in the whole bucket, blood and all. If that doesn't draw their attention, nothing will."

Cummins did as ordered, and the cut-up bodies of three large bonitos splashed into the channel, along with a good deal of deep red fish blood. A lone trailing mako appeared, and swam directly through the swirling, bloody mass of debris. The ten-foot-long, five-hundred-pound predator seemed to sniff the water curiously with its pointed snout before abruptly turning and circling the bait.

"You certainly got his attention," Kraft said to his bearded assistant. "Now if only he'd use that mouth of his."

No sooner were these words spoken than the mako snapped open its massive jaws and ripped into the bonito with a vengeance. Seconds later a pair of hammerheads joined the mako, and soon all of the channel's five sharks were in a violent feeding frenzy.

Kraft's relief was noticeable as he watched Cummins deposit the bloody contents of another pail of fish scraps into the frothing water. "I feel better already," he said facetiously. "Stuff 'em good, Andy."

"Don't worry, Doc. Once they get started, nothing can stop them."

"For my sake, let's hope that's not the case," replied Kraft. "The test is on for later this afternoon. Terri will give you an approximate start time, and then you can coordinate the dolphin transfer with Mary."

"Will do, Chief. Hang loose. And by the way, congrats for surviving your bike ride."

"Thanks, kiddo. Now, if I can just survive my budget meeting with the director!"

Kraft took a last look at the feeding sharks before leaving the bridge and continuing on foot to the administration building. With his bike close at his side, he crossed an open plaza, filled with palm trees and picnic tables, and entered an underground tunnel. The concrete floor of the tunnel sloped slightly downward and led him to a large, double-paned observation window set into a white-tiled wall. This portal provided him a fish-eye view of a huge aquarium that contained a living coral reef and its inhabitants.

Though he was already late, he couldn't help but stop and admire the reef's colorful inhabitants. A trio of glimmering silver-and-blue angelfish swam by, followed by a family of brown wrasse, several grunts, and a massive, sluggishly moving grouper. His gaze was locked on the graceful movements of a young stingray when a concerned female voice spoke from behind him.

"Thank God you're here, Peter. Dr. Kromer has been asking for you all morning."

Kraft turned and set his eyes on the pert, smartly dressed figure of his administrative assistant. Terri Jackman held a mug of coffee in one hand and a leather portfolio in the other.

"How was the bike ride?" she asked while handing him the coffee.

Kraft took a grateful sip from the mug before answering. "As you can very well see, I survived. In fact, I hardly feel it in my legs, which means that I wasn't in such bad shape after all."

"I still think you're making a big mistake riding again," Terri said as she brushed back her brown bangs. "Next time you might not be so lucky."

It was obvious that they had had this conversation before, and Kraft diplomatically changed the subject. "So what's new in the world of marine biology?"

Terri took this as a cue to switch to business mode. "Dr. Kromer is waiting for you in the conference room. His meeting with the regents has been moved up to eleven A.M., and he needs your budget projections at once."

As she led Kraft away from the observation window down the tiled hallway, she continued. "Commander Lawrence called, and I told him to be here for the test no later than three. He'll be bringing along an associate from NOSC and an official navy photographer."

An elevator conveyed them to the floor above, where they entered a carpeted hallway, whose walls were lined with various species of stuffed marine life.

"Will our esteemed director be joining us tankside?" Kraft asked as they passed a magnificent blue marlin.

"If he does, it will be under strong protest." Terri halted and looked Kraft straight in the eye. "Peter," she continued. "Dr. Kromer remains firmly opposed to your participation in the test, and for once I completely agree with him. The risks are far too great."

Kraft calmly finished his coffee before responding. "Your concerns are noted, but my decision stands. I'm the one who dreamed up this project, and I'll be the one to see it through. Discussion ended."

With his bike still at his side, Kraft moved to a door at the end of the hallway. As he removed his backpack and stuffed his helmet and gloves inside, Terri caught up with him.

She pulled a folded newspaper from inside the leather portfolio and handed it to him. "I just pray that your pigheadedness doesn't cost you an arm, leg, or even worse."

"Don't worry, kiddo. My ladies won't let me down." Kraft looked at the newspaper and asked, "What's this all about?"

Terri pointed to a story on the front page. "I thought you'd be interested in this article in the *Herald*. It seems there's been another sighting."

Kraft glanced down and read the headline: SEA MON-STER AGAIN SIGHTED BY JAPANESE. As he skimmed the article Terri provided a brief synopsis.

"Like last week's report, the discovery took place near the Kuril Trench. Yet this time the fishermen who spotted it swore that the creature was over a hundred feet wide, with the saucerlike shape of a manta ray."

Kraft chuckled skeptically. "So much for the sea serpent they reported seven days ago." Handing back the newspaper, he added, "Someone's been sipping too much sake."

Expecting just such a comment from him, Terri replied, "I wonder if you'd have had the same reaction to the report of the first coelecanth pulled from the waters off South Africa."

"I'll hold back any further judgment until I see the first pictures of this so-called monster. Until then, I rest my case. Anyway, right now the only monster I'm concerned about is waiting for me behind this door. Would you mind stowing my bike and backpack for me, kiddo? And then I'd appreciate a prayer. Science and budgets just weren't meant to mix."

Terri smiled sympathetically and took hold of Kraft's ten-speed while handing him the portfolio. "You'll do just fine, Peter. And besides," she said with deliberate irony, "just think what you'll have to look forward to once the director is through with you."

Kraft grunted and reached for the doorknob. "For some strange reason, I'd rather take my chances with the sharks!"

3

The Sendo, fishing master of the *Koji Maru*, was a grizzled veteran with dark, piercing eyes and the shoe-leather-tough, sun-dried skin of a lifelong fisherman. Born on the northern Japanese island of Hokkaidō, he first went to sea at about the same time he learned how to walk. True to the tradition of his ancestors, he grew up with a single goal in mind—to become one day the Sendo of his very own fishing boat.

The opportunity arrived on the eve of his fiftieth birthday. So as not to disappoint the corporation that employed him, he made sure to operate his vessel with ruthless dedication, which earned him and his nineteen-man crew their fair share of record catches.

Their current prey was squid. The rubbery, ten-armed cephalopods were a staple foodstuff, and it was said that the Japanese consumed them like Americans ate hot dogs.

For a month now they had been fishing the waters above the Kuril Trench, halfway between Hokkaidō and

Russia's Kamchatka Peninsula. During previous excursions, they had never failed to fill the hold with their desired catch. Yet for thirty long days and nights their drift nets had been bringing up everything but squid. They had found untold numbers of drowned dolphins tangled in the nets. And who could count the numerous sea turtles, birds, sharks, and other trash fish they had managed to snag.

The Sendo assumed that the squid were farther north, in the cooler waters above the fifty-degree-north latitude line. Unfortunately international agreements drawn up to protect the North American salmon kept them from fishing here.

Cursing his government's weakness in negotiating this ridiculous treaty, the Sendo knew that he had little choice in the matter. The *Koji Maru* would have to move farther north. Otherwise he would have a certain mutiny on his hands.

There could be no denying the crew's restlessness. They were demoralized and edgy, their nerves raw from long hours of work and nothing to show for them. There was talk of numerous bad omens, and even rumors of sea monsters in the area.

In an effort to have done with these foolish grumblings, the Sendo decided to cross into the forbidden northern zone. They would fill their holds quickly and return to Hokkaidō as conquering heroes.

For an entire day they traveled northward at flank speed. The sun was just about to touch the western horizon when the Sendo finally ordered the engines to halt. He then proceeded to personally bless the net with sacred sake before ordering it to be deployed.

It took four hours to get all of the net in the water. Altogether they used eight separate drift nets. Each was three miles long and created a barrier thirty-five feet deep, fitted with corks on the top and weighted line on the bottom. The mesh itself was four and a half inches wide, composed of a light, translucent, monofilament fiber, whose tough, synthetic base was virtually indestructible.

It was long after midnight when the Sendo climbed onto the elevated bridge and sounded two piercing blasts on the ship's air horn. He then activated the bridge's powerful spotlight, and within minutes the crew, in black boots, yellow oilskins, and white helmets, had gathered at the stern. From the transom, a pair of rollers were activated with a grinding mechanical roar, and the first section of net plopped onto the deck amidships. Tangled within it was a trio of drowned white-sided dolphins, a dead swordfish, and dozens of expired yellowtail—but there were no squid.

His heart heavy with disappointment, the Sendo instructed his men to throw the dolphins overboard. The swordfish and yellowtail would be kept for future consumption. In the past, these waters had swarmed with squid, and he wondered if their luck had indeed gone bad. He turned to the small Shinto altar positioned beside the radar screen, and was about to petition the gods yet again for favor when an excited shout rose from down below.

"Ika! Ika!"

The rousing cry of squid caused the Sendo to glance back to the boat's stern. Here the bridge spotlight illuminated the second of their nets, in whose ink-blackened mesh squid hung like thick bunches of grapes. The Sendo clearly saw that they were good-sized specimens, some two feet long and weighing a good five pounds. One of the fishermen picked one up by the tail, and jet-black ink squirted from its tubular mantle while the suction-cup-filled tentacles madly whipped about in a vain effort at escape.

To celebrate properly, the Sendo popped a cassette tape into the stereo, and the lively, new-age pop sounds of Himekami's *Moonwater* blared forth from the *Koji Maru*'s loudspeakers. Then, to document this harvest, he pulled out his 35mm camera, its compact frame protected by a specially designed, waterproof casing, and began snapping off pictures of his crew in action.

It was during this frenzy of activity that the *Koji Maru* unexpectedly lurched to a sudden halt. The Sendo was forced to reach out to the bulkhead to keep from tumbling over, and he quickly lowered his camera and peered down at the fantail. "What in the hell has happened down there?" he cried.

The assistant engineer screamed out a reply after a hasty examination of the boat's transom. "The third net has snagged the prop, Sendo-san. Shall I send a diver over to untangle it?"

"That could take hours," answered the Sendo. "Cut the net loose and be damned with it. And then get on with the retrieval of the remaining one."

Though necessary, this was a bad choice for the veteran mariner. A good two miles of the third net still remained at sea. Aside from the fact that it would be a virtual wall of death for any sea creatures unfortunate enough to become entangled in it, the drift net would be very expensive to replace. He thus made absolutely certain to take plenty of pictures to document the loss.

While the Sendo raised his camera the *Koji Maru* was rocked by a massive swell. Again he reached out to the bulkhead to steady himself. The sacred sake decanter tumbled off the altar and smashed on the deck behind him, and he himself crashed into the annunciator, badly bruising his arthritic hip. He cursed in pain and reached out to shift the spotlight to illumine the sea off their starboard side.

What he saw there caused him to forget the agony that coursed through his bruised torso. Quickly approaching the boat from the sea was a frothing line of turbulence, preceded by what appeared to be a monstrously huge manta ray with two distinct horns protruding from its rounded gray head. The crazed creature was on a certain collision course, and the terrified Sendo instinctively triggered the emergency radio transmitter and raised his camera in an effort to get the incredible beast on film.

There was a bone-jarring concussion followed by a moment of confused blackness. The next thing the Sendo was conscious of was the icy grasp of the surrounding sea. A passing wooden plank allowed him to keep his head above water. With his camera still strapped tightly around his wrist, he watched as his fatally wounded ship slipped beneath the waves, its doomed crew trapped in a tangle of ink-soaked drift nets and other debris.

4

The autumn sun had long since reached its zenith. Billowing gray clouds were ominously gathering over Biscayne Bay, hinting of a possible late-afternoon thunderstorm. No strangers to such a tropical atmospheric event, a collection of curious students and researchers gathered alongside the institute's shark channel. On the wire-mesh bridge, where a portable hydraulic lift had been positioned, Terri Jackman and Mary Walker anxiously looked toward the tunnel leading to the administration building when Andy Cummins pointed out two newcomers emerging from it—a man with neat silver hair dressed in a pinstripe suit and a younger blond man in a black wet suit.

Dr. Charles Kromer, the institute's director, appeared unusually glum as he followed Peter Kraft to the shark channel. After they climbed up onto the bridge, Kraft greeted his three wide-eyed associates.

"'Afternoon, kids. Is everything set?"

"We're ready when you are, Chief," answered Cummins.

Kraft looked to Mary Walker. "How are the girls?"

"The transfer went smoothly," she answered. "But they definitely know that something out of the ordinary is about to come down."

Dr. Kromer scanned the faces of the dozen or so onlookers gathered at the edge of the channel. "Where's Commander Lawrence and his group?"

Terri Jackman held a cellular telephone at her side. "We just got word from Gustavo that they're on the grounds. They should be joining us any moment now."

Andy Cummins reached down and picked up a five-foot-long, polelike object, which he proceeded to hand to Kraft. "Here's your bang stick, Chief," he said casually. "It's loaded with a fresh twelve-gauge shell."

Dr. Kromer winced at this news. "Damn it, Kraft. I still think this whole test is too dangerous!"

Peter Kraft responded to this outburst while calmly making sure that the bang stick's safety was engaged. "Just look at it this way, Charlie. If something should happen to me, you can always use my remaining salary to help balance the department's budget."

The arrival of a trio of white-uniformed naval officers cut short the director's reply to Kraft's sarcastic comment. Leading the group was Commander Michael Lawrence, a tall, dashing-looking forty-year-old, assigned to the Naval Ocean Systems Command in San Diego.

"Sorry we're late, folks," he apologized sincerely.

"Don't worry about it, Commander," returned Dr. Kromer. "I was just giving Dr. Kraft here one more chance to reconsider his decision to participate in this afternoon's test."

"The navy is still more than willing to take over the project and conduct the preliminary test with our own personnel," Lawrence offered.

"Why waste the additional time and funds?" retorted Kraft. "Besides, the risks on my part are minimal."

"As you wish, Doctor," Lawrence said, watching as Andy Cummins helped Kraft buckle on a back harness and attach it to the hydraulic-lift cable.

"I've invited Lieutenant Phil Spratley from NOSC along as a witness," added Lawrence. "His cameraman, Ensign Baumgartner, will be recording the event for posterity."

The two officers nodded in greeting, and the shorter of the pair produced a compact, hand-held video camera. He aimed the lens at Kraft and followed the wet-suited marine biologist to the edge of the bridge.

Peter Kraft was in a world of his own as he peered down into the waters of the channel and watched a nine-foot mako swim by. The shark appeared to ignore the humans gathered above him, and smoothly cut through the water with a pair of remoras attached firmly to its gill slits.

"Let's do it," said Kraft, his mouth unnaturally dry. "Andy, crank up the lift and put me in the water as gently as possible. Mary, stand by the gate release and let the girls loose on my command."

Cummins activated the hydraulic hoist. As the lift cable tightened, Kraft momentarily looked to his left and met his research assistant's worried glance. He managed a confident thumbs-up and, while tightly grasping the bang stick in his other hand, began the short trip to the water below.

It was cooler than he expected, and had an unpleasant claminess to it as it seeped into the open seams of his wet suit. For some reason, the theme music to the movie *Jaws* sounded in his head, and he fought the urge to curl up his legs beneath him. Feeling as if he were beginning a bad dream, he anxiously scanned the water for the first sign of the channel's inhabitants. Tentatively he slapped the surface with his free hand while doing his best to ignore his racing pulse and the tight knot of fear gathering in the pit of his belly.

The director's strenuous objections clouded his

thoughts, and for a brief second he wondered what the hell he was doing here. Yet such doubts swiftly vanished when a dark gray triangular fin broke the water directly before him.

"It's the mako, Doc!" Andy Cummins warned from above.

Kraft tightly grasped the bang stick as the shark swam by him and made a broad, circular turn. The fin was only five feet away now, and Kraft had seen enough to know that he had definitely caught its interest.

"Okay, Mary," he shouted. "Send in the cavalry!"

This was all the blond-haired research assistant had to hear to engage a flat steel lever, causing the tubular steel grate on one of the channel's holding pens to snap open. On the opposite side of the bridge, Dolly and Matilda shot out into the water and dived into the green depths.

Fifty yards away Peter Kraft intently watched the fin of the still-circling mako. The shark was less than two feet away when it abruptly turned and headed straight for him. Kraft had been anticipating the aggressive move, and without bothering to arm the bang stick, he utilized the weapon's blunt tip to poke at the shark's head. This desperate move temporarily warded off the attack, though as the mako retreated, its rear fin knocked Kraft's weapon from his hands. The bang stick went sinking to the bottom, and as the shark began to circle once more, Kraft hastily scanned the surrounding waters.

"Dolly, Matilda, where the hell are you?" he called.

"That does it," the director shouted from above. "Cummins, pull him up this instant!"

The graduate student reached out to trigger the hoist lift's engage switch. Yet it was the excited voice of his blond-haired associate that kept him from pressing it.

"Hold on, Andy," Mary Walker cried. "Here they come!"

All eyes were on the two sleek, submerged creatures quickly approaching Kraft from the bridge. The mako continued to circle fearlessly. And this time, when it lunged toward the defenseless human, its eyes rolled back and its massive jaws opened wide.

Because it was at the top of the food chain and feared no other creature in its watery realm, the mako was caught completely off guard by the bruising blow from Dolly's snout that struck directly on its sensitive gill crease. Matilda followed with a powerful punch to the shark's exposed gut, and the mako reeled around in pain and beat a hasty retreat to safer waters.

Relief etched Peter Kraft's face as the two dolphins surfaced beside him. They poked their smiling faces out of the water and greeted him with a chorus of animated squeals and whistles. To the applause of the human onlookers, Kraft reached out to hug his rescuers.

"Girls, I knew you wouldn't let me down," he said, smiling.

Dolly and Matilda reacted with another burst of noisy chatter, and Kraft looked up to address his co-workers on the bridge. "I told you it would be a piece of cake. Call 'em back to the holding pen, Mary. And Cummins, get me out of this infernal place!"

Mary Walker blew into a dog whistle, which sent the dolphins sprinting back to the holding pen. Meanwhile Kraft climbed onto the bridge, where Commander Lawrence addressed him while helping unhook the hoist cable.

"Good job, Dr. Kraft. When your dolphin training program is properly applied, U.S. Navy divers will never again have to worry about being the victims of shark attacks."

Lieutenant Commander Spratley also offered a handshake. "As a fellow marine-mammal trainer, I must say that was a wonderful display, Doctor. I've got to admit that I didn't envy you when they dipped you into that water. And I speak for all of NOSC in praising you for a job well done."

"I second that, Peter," added the director. "Even though I still think the risks were far too great."

Kraft was returning a relieved smile from his administrative assistant when Commander Lawrence asked him a question. "Dr. Kraft, before you go and pop the champagne, may I have a word with you in private?"

"Sure, Commander," Kraft replied. "Just let me get out of this wet suit, and I'll be right with you."

Terri Jackman had thoughtfully remembered to bring along a change of clothing, and Kraft excused himself to adjourn to the nearby, pierside rest room, where he dried himself off and changed into his bicycle shorts and a *Save the Whales* T-shirt.

He joined the distinguished senior naval officer at a picnic table on the wooden dock beside the sparkling blue waters of Biscayne Bay. The clouds continued to gather above them, and as Kraft sat down opposite Lawrence he heard the distant rumble of thunder.

"Dr. Kraft, I truly appreciate your contribution to our marine-mammal program. It took a lot of guts to go into that shark channel. Although I'd like to have further tests done at once, I've just been tasked with a priority investigation that I'd like your assistance with."

"How can I help you?" asked Kraft.

Lawrence pulled a folder from his briefcase and handed the marine biologist a stack of eight-by-ten-inch photographs. The first of them showed the stern deck of a fishing boat, where several fishermen, apparently Asians, dressed in black boots, yellow oilskins, and white helmets, were lashing together the pieces of an immense, nylon drift net.

"This picture was taken this morning, aboard the *Koji Maru,* a Japanese squidder based on Hokkaidō," Lawrence explained. "The ship was working the northern sector of the Kuril Trench when it was struck from below and sank. All hands were lost except for the vessel's captain, who is responsible for these remarkable photographs."

The second photo was a bit more difficult to figure out. Kraft supposed it showed a bubbling, rectangular expanse of seawater, caught immediately amidships. The shots that followed supported this supposition. They showed an immense, phosphorescent, saucer-shaped object with two hornlike projections rising from the bubbling froth. The last blurred photo caught the mysterious object as it smacked into the side of the trawler. Kraft expressed his amazement with a startled grunt.

"These pictures have yet to be made public," Lawrence went on. "They were developed only hours ago, and faxed to me from the USS *Enterprise*. It was one of the *Enterprise*'s choppers that pulled the *Koji Maru*'s sole survivor from the sea."

Kraft shook his head skeptically. "Does this have anything to do with the sea-monster sightings that have been in the newspapers lately?"

Lawrence replied without blinking. "I believe that as an authority on marine life, you're in the best position to answer that question, Doctor. Because with this tragic incident, we've progressed way beyond a mere sighting. Could the object in these photos really be a living creature?"

Kraft sorted through the series of photographs once more before answering. "It certainly resembles a manta ray, especially those two horned projections. But for it to actually be responsible for sinking a ship, it would have to be unbelievably immense."

"Preliminary photo analysis shows it to be over one hundred feet wide," Lawrence informed him.

Again Kraft shook his head in wonder. "If it's a ray, it's the grandfather of them all, the likes of which has never been seen before by man."

Lawrence made certain to meet the marine biologist's gaze before continuing. "How would you like to be the one to track it down and reveal it for all the world to see?"

Kraft was amazed. "You've got to be kidding me."

"Doctor," said Lawrence, "I can assure you that the U.S. Navy is taking this sighting most seriously. In fact, I can have you on a C-5A out of Homestead within the hour. Tomorrow at this time you'll be on Hokkaidō, where a 688-class nuclear-powered attack submarine has been reserved as your personal laboratory."

The reality of the commander's words finally sank in, and Kraft spoke while allowing his gaze to return to the photographs. "Commander, even though in my heart I still don't believe in sea monsters, if what you say is really true, you just made yourself a deal."

5

When Lieutenant Brad Bodzin received the orders sending him to the isolated, northern Japanese island of Hokkaidō, he wondered what he had done wrong. He had been previously stationed in San Diego, where he was a sonar instructor at the antisubmarine-warfare school. Except for a single DWI charge, his record was spotless, and try as he could, the thirty-three-year-old Texan failed to figure out how he had incurred Command's wrath.

He had arrived in Japan three long months ago. It was his first visit to the Far East, and he had to admit that when the C-130 touched down at the Sapporo airport, he found the mountainous landscape breathtaking. Unfortunately the navy allowed him precious little time for sightseeing, and the very next day a Seahawk helicopter arrived to convey him to his new duty station in the island's extreme northeastern corner.

He would never forget the moment he laid his eyes

on Rausu, the tiny, primitive fishing village that would serve as his new home. Most of the villagers were Ainu, the indigenous Caucasoid people of this region. They had little contact with the outside world and lived as their ancestors did, with few modern conveniences, almost completely dependent on the sea for their livelihood.

Now that fall had arrived, even the weather in this godforsaken spot was getting hostile. This morning Bodzin had taken the Hummer into town to pick up some groceries. The naval installation he was assigned to was located on the very edge of the Sea of Okhotsk. As he left the Quonset hut that was his living quarters, an icy Siberian gale was blowing. The howling wind almost knocked him off his feet, and he gratefully scrambled into the mud-splattered utility vehicle to begin his drive.

A perilously narrow dirt road took him east over the barren, rock-strewn hills of the Shiretoko Peninsula. Fifteen minutes later he pulled into Rausu. The village overlooked the Nemuro Strait and was little more than a collection of small, plaster-walled hovels surrounding a rickety wooden pier. Rausu had a single general store, and it was to this structure that Bodzin headed.

The wizened, gray-haired proprietress had little English and addressed Bodzin as "GI." The Texan's Japanese was as limited as her English, and he called her "Mama-san." For the most part, they communicated with grunts and gestures. And in such a manner he was able to purchase the morning's groceries. Since his last visit the weekly supply ship had arrived, and he returned home with several cartons filled with canned soup, cornflakes, rice, and a treasured supply of apples. He also stocked up on whatever produce was available, as well as milk, eggs, and of course the town's staple: fresh fish.

What Bodzin really missed was some good ol' Texas barbecue. Only the other night his dreams were of juicy brisket, tangy beans, ice-cold slaw, and a couple of Lone Star longnecks to wash it down. Yet such visions only served to torture him, and he knew he'd better not dwell on such mouth-watering thoughts if he wanted to stay sane.

As he guided the HUMVEE back over the peninsula, he counted off the hours until his long-anticipated leave would begin. Tomorrow at this time he'd be packing his duffel bag for a week's stay in Tokyo. Though the capital city was certainly no Dallas, it provided all the conveniences of a major city, and probably even had a couple of barbecue restaurants. Then there were the hot spots that Chief Avila had told him about. No stranger to Asian duty, the veteran master chief mentioned a particularly friendly hostess bar in the fabled Ginza nightclub district. The girls there were as hot as the Texas sun, he said, and had a particular affinity for American sailors.

It was a little after 11:00 A.M. when he arrived back at base. A remote-control device opened the gate of the security fence surrounding the seaside compound. Strategically placed video cameras followed him as he braked beside the central Quonset hut and stepped into the icy wind. He hurriedly unloaded the groceries and, after accessing the four-digit security code into the doorway's keypad, quickly entered.

A plywood barrier separated the actual living quarters from the central kitchen. Bodzin stowed away the perishables in the refrigerator and, with an apple in hand, proceeded to the hut's far wall. He addressed yet another keypad here, and the door to a modern elevator hissed open before him. The blue-carpeted lift conveyed him to the heart of the installation, some three hundred feet below ground level.

The door slid open, revealing a brightly lit, equipment-packed room, about the size of a three-car garage. Mainframe computers lined the walls, alongside a complex communications terminal and several softly buzzing electrical transformers.

At the room's center were three dark gray consoles with glowing cathode-ray tubes set into them. Two of the consoles were currently manned by the room's sole occupants. Master Chief Adrian Avila sat in the middle position, with Seaman First-Class Michael Fox on his left. Both wore headphones, their eyes riveted on their individual display screens.

Bodzin knew in an instant that something unusual was occurring. Their installation's sole purpose was to monitor a series of strategically placed hydrophones that were anchored to the floor of the Sea of Okhotsk. Known as the SOSUS system, the arrays of powerful microphones listened for passing ships and were especially designed to pick up the sounds of submerged submarines. Assuming it was just such a vessel that had caught his co-workers' attention, he hurried over.

"What's so interesting, Master Chief?" Bodzin took up a position directly behind the wavy-haired, tattooed veteran.

"We just tagged two submerged contacts transitting the La Pérouse Strait, sir," answered Avila. "I've got Fox doing the signature ID as we speak."

Bodzin glanced over to the fair-haired, crew-cut sailor at Avila's side. The burly youngster was busy at his keyboard and shouted out excitedly when his display screen began filling with data.

"Bingo! Computer shows a sixty-seven-percent probability that our lead bogey is a diesel-electric-powered, Romeo-class attack sub. And get this—I show a seventy-three-percent probability that the contact right behind it is a Xia-class nuke!"

Genuinely astounded by this news, Bodzin leaned over to check the youngster's monitor. "This is incredible," he muttered. "What in the hell are the Chinks doin' this far north?"

"The way things look, they're runnin' for the shelter of the open Pacific," Avila answered. "Array Bravo just triggered, and indicates that our targets are headed due east, smack toward the Kurils."

Bodzin rushed over to the vacant console and queried the data bank for a map of the region. He barely had time to settle himself into the upholstered chair when a detailed chart popped up onto the screen. It showed the eastern coast of China, extending northward past Korea as far as Sakhalin Island.

"They must have traveled by way of the Korea Strait," he said. "But why risk running the entire length of the Sea of Japan when they could have just stayed south and merely transitted the Ryukyus?"

"I wonder if this has anything to do with that freighter we tagged earlier," said Avila.

Bodzin looked to his left. "What freighter are you talkin' about, Chief?"

Avila met the young officer's inquisitive stare. "Shortly after you left this morning, we monitored a surface contact penetrating La Pérouse, on the same course those subs are currently taking. Since the computer couldn't ID it, I took the liberty of querying our Jap hosts. A JMSDF P-3 got a definite visual, and they were able to tag it as the *Star of Linshu,* a twenty-thousand-ton, PRC cargo vessel registered in Qingdao. And brother, were the Nips ever glad that I brought their attention to it."

"Why's that?" asked Bodzin.

Avila grinned. "It seems this same freighter had a run-in with the JMSDF only last spring. The Japs caught it dumping a full load of industrial waste into the waters a scant fifty miles southwest of Kyushu. That's prime fishing grounds, and boy, were the Japanese pissed."

"I can't blame them," returned Bodzin.

"You know, Lieutenant," interjected Seaman Fox, "perhaps the Chinks are tryin' the ol' end-around play, with the *Star of Linshu* set to do its dirty deeds up north this time."

"You could be onto something, sailor," said the chief.

Bodzin's main concern remained the two Chinese submarines, and his glance returned to the map that still lit up his display screen. He returned to his keyboard, and the broad overview of central eastern Asia was replaced by a detailed bathymetric chart of the narrow strait of water lying between Hokkaidō and Sakhalin to the north. This all-important choke point was the only opening to the Pacific, with the other accessway far to the south.

With a practiced touch, he gradually expanded the chart eastward, until it included the Kuril Island chain, the last barrier to the open seas. Utilizing the cursor, he underlined the dark blue trench of water that followed the island's north-south meander.

"What manned platforms do we still have out there, Chief?" he asked while intently scanning the screen.

"As far as I know, the *Chicago* and *Louisville* are it, sir," said Avila.

"I've got a feeling that the bubbleheads on those pig-boats are going to be awfully busy this afternoon," returned Bodzin.

"It's funny." Seaman Fox spoke now. "But with all of this activity, the mornin' has just flown by. I sure wish every day was this excitin'."

"Son, you should have been around here ten years ago when the Ruskies were still alive and well," Avila said. "The waters up here were just crawling with Soviet warships, and we had over twelve full-time sonar analysts working this installation."

"I didn't realize you had duty up here before, Chief," said Bodzin.

Relishing the spotlight, Avila stretched his muscular arms overhead. "Not only was this my first official stint after graduating ASW school, but I arrived on the eve of an incident that almost ignited World War III."

"What was that?" asked the wide-eyed young Seaman Fox.

Avila hesitated a beat before responding. "As fate would have it, I had my very first watch on the night KAL 007 was shot out of the skies above Sakhalin. Talk about activity! These waters were jam-packed with warships, especially when it was learned that the 747's black box was somewhere out there on the bottom of the Sea of Okhotsk. I personally tagged a representative of every damn attack sub in the Soviet Pacific Fleet. Needless to say, we had a good number of our own subs out there scouring the seafloor with their active sonars, and how they ever kept from tanglin' with the Reds is beyond me."

"Was the black box ever found?" asked Bodzin.

"I heard tell that a Soviet mini-sub yanked it right off the seabed not far from this very coast," Avila answered. "That was recently confirmed when Boris Yeltsin presented the cockpit voice recorder to the Koreans in an act of goodwill. Interestingly enough, the recorder's tape wasn't included in the transfer, and we're still lacking certain proof that the Russians did indeed shoot down an innocent jetliner."

The chief's recollections were abruptly cut short by a piercing electronic tone. Spurred into action by the alarm, Seaman Fox attacked his keyboard and determined the sound's source.

"We've got a main-systems failure!"

"Activate the backup link!" ordered Bodzin.

"Can't do, Lieutenant," replied Avila, who had already embarked upon this very course of action. "I'm showing that the entire data link has been severed."

"Shit!" Bodzin cursed as he reached out for the red telephone handset in his console.

A direct satellite uplink would connect him with the Pentagon situation room in far-off Washington, D.C. As important to the nation's defense as the air force's highly publicized early-warning satellites and NORAD radar sites, SOSUS was a vital trip wire. With the demise of ICBMs and manned bombers, strategic attack from beneath the seas was a greater threat than ever. Positioned in various choke points throughout the planet's oceans, only SOSUS could give advanced notice of a massed seaborne nuclear assault. Thus the integrity of the entire network was critical, and any breakdown was taken most seriously.

With his eyes glued to his flashing monitor screen, Brad Bodzin isolated the last known positions of the two suspected Chinese submarines as he waited for the uplink to be completed. The mere idea of these unpredictable vessels this far north continued to bother him, and he wondered if they could be a hint of things to come. Such an attack was his greatest fear, and the Texan all but forgot about his long-anticipated leave in Tokyo, his thoughts instead focused on his sworn duty to defend his country.

6

Fifty-seven nautical miles due east of the island of Hokkaidō, the USS *Chicago* sliced through the black depths, 180 feet beneath the Pacific's surface. Manned by a crew of fourteen officers and 135 enlisted men, the *Chicago* was a Los Angeles–class attack vessel. In June 1988, the sub had left Norfolk, Virginia, and arrived in her new home port of San Diego, California, where she had been based since.

With a length of 360 feet, the *Chicago* was longer than a football field. When submerged, it displaced some 6,900 tons, with all of its great bulk propelled through the water by a single S6G nuclear reactor. This power source gave the boat virtually unlimited endurance and provided enough energy to operate an advanced BQQ-5 sonar suite and PUFFS fire-control system.

Unlike earlier vessels of the Los Angeles class, the *Chicago* was the first to be outfitted with a vertical launch system. Located between the bow sonar array and the forward end of the pressure hull, it allowed the sub to carry a wide assortment of offensive weapons, including the Tomahawk cruise missile, the Harpoon antiship rocket, and the dual-purpose Mk48 torpedo, which was launched from four midship torpedo tubes. Altogether, this layout was the state of the art in high-tech fire-control design, creating a deadly force against enemy submarines, surface ships, and even distant land targets.

Of all the sub's operational systems, none was as important as sonar. When submerged, sonar provided the eyes and ears of the immense warship, guiding it safely through the depths and determining the presence of other vessels. Thus the men trained to operate the complex active and passive sonar systems were among the most essential members of the entire crew.

Petty Officer Matt Cox was the current sonar watch supervisor. A former all-state high-school quarterback from Missouri, Cox was only a year out of sub school, but he already displayed the quick intellect and compassion of a natural leader.

Well into his first watch of the day, Cox was perched on a tall stool in the sonar compartment, adjacent to the control room. The size of a large walk-in closet and packed with equipment, this room was fondly known as the "sound shack." Directly behind him sat three co-workers; all wore headphones and were focusing on a trio of glowing CRT screens. The screens showed a visual breakdown of the variety of sounds being conveyed by the *Chicago*'s hydrophones. They were accessed by manipulating a thin black joystick mounted into each console, and by addressing a square keyboard positioned beside the monitor.

"I've got a new contact off our port bow," announced the young sailor seated on Cox's left. "Designate Sierra seven, biological."

"Good work, babe." Cox reached up to speak into a microphone that hung from the ceiling. "Conn, sonar, we have a new contact, bearing three-two-zero, designate Sierra seven, biological."

"Sonar, Conn, designate Sierra seven, biological, aye, sonar," said a scratchy voice from the compartment's intercom speaker.

"What do you make of the contact, Algren?" Cox spoke to the sailor who had initially reported the contact.

The neophyte sonarman hesitated a moment before responding. "The way they're chattering away, I believe that they're shrimp, sir."

Cox isolated this characteristic sound on his headphones, and a fond grin turned the corners of his mouth. "I don't know about you guys, but I like my shrimp fried, with plenty of cocktail sauce on the side."

"Sounds like someone's gettin' a Big Mac attack," observed "Marvelous" Marvin Johnson, the technician seated at the middle console. "Hang in there, bro. We've got less than an hour to go, and I hear Mallott's servin' burgers for lunch."

"Shit, you mean turkey burgers," returned Cox. "I don't care if they are good for ya. I'd like some good ol'-fashioned red meat for a change." He looked over to the studious, bespectacled technician seated to his right. "What do you think of Mallott's new health menu, Specs?"

The newest member of their team, whose nickname referred to his wire-rim glasses, failed to respond. His attention was locked on his monitor screen.

"Earth to Specs. Earth to Specs," Cox paged jokingly.

When this failed to coax a response, he gently put his hand on the technician's right shoulder. "What's so fascinatin' out there, Specs?"

"I can't really say for sure," the soft-spoken technician answered. "But I somehow get the feeling that there's something out there in our baffles."

This observation immediately gained Cox's full attention and he quickly scanned the sailor's CRT screen. "How long have you been monitoring the towed array?" he asked.

"I've been on it ever since we passed the SOSUS array, sir," said Specs.

Cox looked at his wristwatch and fought to contain his displeasure. "That's a good quarter of an hour ago, sailor. Why didn't you call out your suspicions back then?"

"I'm s-sorry, Mr. Cox," stuttered Specs. "But my suspicions are based more on a hunch than on anything else."

"That makes no difference," Cox said. "In this game, your hunches are just as important to me as a solid active return."

Softening his tone a bit, he added, "Strange as it may seem, simple intuition has saved many a bubblehead from getting deep-sixed. Science can't explain it, but the facts are there all the same. And to show you how important we treat a man's hunch, I'm gonna ask the Conn to clear our baffles. And then we're all gonna listen real close for any unwelcomed visitors out there."

Back in the captain's stateroom, the request to clear the *Chicago*'s baffles was relayed via intercom by the boat's current officer of the deck. Commander Mac McShane was taking a catnap when the OOD's call arrived, and he okayed this routine request without so much as a second thought.

As he placed the intercom handset in its cradle beside his bunk, he yawned and glanced up at the instruments mounted into the nearby bulkhead. With a single glance he was able to determine that the *Chicago* was at a depth of 180 feet and was traveling at a speed of seventeen knots. Their course was almost due north, though this would shortly change as the *Chicago* initiated a tight 160-degree turn to check the sound-absorbent cone of water that lay at their stern.

The deck was just beginning to cant over to starboard as he scooted out of his rack and slipped on his rubber thongs. Once more he yawned and, while scratching his beard-stubbled jaw, decided that a shave was in order.

He crossed over to his Pullman-style head, dressed only in white scivvies and a crewneck T-shirt. The deck was steeply angled by the time he reached the sink, and he waited for the course change to be completed before activating the hot lather machine.

A quick scan of the mirror displayed a familiar square-jawed mug, which was looking more like his father's with each passing day. They shared the same dimpled chin, high angular cheekbones, and thin aquiline nose. Like the previous three generations of McShanes, Mac also had a full head of straight black hair and bushy eyebrows that capped a pair of deep, sea-green eyes. His forty-three years of life were revealed by the lines etching his upper cheeks and the gray that speckled his short sideburns.

The *Chicago* soon returned to even keel, and Mac soaked his face in warm water. He then covered it with hot lather and began his shave, using the new Sensor razor his son had given him for his last birthday.

At ten years of age, Mac Jr. was growing up to be quite the little gentleman. Back home in San Diego, he thrived on soccer and baseball, and even his school studies were finally coming along. It seemed only yesterday that the boy was experiencing the emotional troubles that had plagued his early childhood. He was hyperactive with a short attention span, and even had a bed-wetting problem.

Of course, all of this was aggravated by his father's navy career. Gone a good six months of the year, Mac depended upon his wife, Nancy, to pull the boy through. An elementary-school teacher by profession, Nancy had the patience that Mac lacked, and never gave up on their son. She showered him with attention and was always there with a kind word and a helping hand. And sure enough, he responded, and by his ninth birthday the worst was over.

After he completed scraping the thick, white lather from his face, Mac brushed his teeth, gargled, then dressed in a clean, dark blue set of coveralls, cotton socks, and leather walking shoes. Thus attired, he sat down at his bulkhead-mounted desk to do some paperwork.

He was well into a review of the latest crew proficiency report when his growling stomach indicated that it was lunchtime. The wardroom was located on the deck below, and Mac proceeded there with his usual quick, urgent stride.

The melodious strains of Richard Rodgers's *Victory at Sea* soundtrack greeted him as he entered the wardroom. Five of the sub's officers had already arrived and were well into their meals. Mac took his customary place at the head of the table while an alert orderly ducked into the galley for his food.

"We didn't think you'd be joining us this afternoon, Skipper," said Lieutenant Commander Phil Moore, the slim, immaculately groomed Afro-American seated on Mac's right.

"To tell you the truth, XO, I wanted to give one of Mallott's turkey burgers a try," returned Mac. "What's the prognosis?"

The *Chicago*'s executive officer wiped off his mustache with his napkin before replying. "I've certainly had worse, though they're a little on the dry side."

"That's because of the lack of fat," interjected the balding officer seated directly opposite of Mac, on the far end of the rectangular table. "Load 'em up with condiments, and there's no way you can tell it's not beef."

This comment came from Lieutenant David Walden, the boat's supply officer, who was better known as simply Chop. Walden was the only non-nuclear-trained officer on the *Chicago,* and was known for his perpetual smile and easygoing personality.

"I just wonder what the enlisted men are going to think about this meal," offered Lieutenant Vic Bradley, the boat's weapons officer, or Weaps for short.

Beside Bradley, the navigator Len Matson consumed his meal with gusto, stopping only long enough to voice his own opinion. "I agree with Chop. If nobody told me, I'd never know this wasn't hamburger."

This generated a skeptical grunt from Lieutenant Paul Ward, their tight-lipped engineer, who toyed with his partially consumed ground-turkey patty with a knife and fork.

Mac's curiosity was fully aroused by the time the mess attendant returned with a plateful of food. He had to admit that it certainly looked appetizing enough. His quarter-pound burger lay on a freshly baked bun, next to a healthy serving of fried potatoes and a mound of coleslaw. Taking Chop's advice, he went heavy with the condiments, covering his patty with lettuce, tomato, relish, and steak sauce.

All eyes were on the head of the table as he took his first bite. He thoughtfully chewed and nodded admiringly.

Another individual was watching from the galley peephole, and he burst into the wardroom just as Mac swallowed. "Well, Captain, how do you like it?" It was the *Chicago*'s chief cook and bottle washer, Chief Petty Officer Howard Mallott.

"Mighty tasty, Mr. Mallott," Mac commented as he prepared for another bite.

This brought a wide smile to the cook's pudgy face, and he excitedly wiped his hands on his stained apron. "I knew you'd like it, Captain. And not only does it taste good, it's good for you. Now try the fries."

Mac picked up one of the golden-brown potato wedges and examined it closely. "You're not going to tell me that this is also a turkey by-product, are you, Chief?"

"Of course I'm not, Captain," returned Mallott. "But the good news is that those potatoes aren't fried at all. They've been oven-baked, in a light coating of canola oil. And that's nonfat mayonnaise in the coleslaw."

Mac looked at his XO and winked. "Not only is *Chicago*'s crew the most proficient bunch of submariners in the fleet, but they're the healthiest as well."

The wardroom filled with laughter, and Mac took this opportunity to sample both the fries and the slaw.

"You've got a real winner here, Chief," he said. "I want you to give the XO a complete nutritional breakdown of this meal. I understand that COMSUB is going to be passing down some strict new dietary restrictions shortly, and you're right on the cutting edge. Good work."

Beaming from the compliment, the portly cook turned and headed for the galley. "Thanks, Captain. And wait until you taste the dessert—strawberry-rhubarb cobbler, with nonfat yogurt à la mode."

With Mallott's departure, Mac went to work on his meal. The intercom rang while he was chewing a mouthful of slaw, and Phil Moore alertly picked up the nearest telephone handset.

"XO, here . . . I understand, Mr. Cox, and apologies aren't necessary. Call in the next watch and grab some chow. And remember, in this business you can never be too cautious."

Moore hung up the handset and pulled a battered corncob pipe from his pocket. No one on board had ever seen him light up this pipe, and true to form, he merely put its scarred bit between his lips and looked to his left.

"And just what were the results of the baffle check?" asked the captain.

"Negative, Skipper," answered Moore. "And the thing is, Petty Officer Cox and his boys really didn't have any substantive reason to ask for the check in the first place."

Mac replied after swallowing down a potato wedge. "From what I've seen of the kid, Cox knows his stuff. As long as he thought that the check was warranted, it's okay with me. And you never know, they just might have tagged *Louisville* sneaking up for a cheap shot."

"Do you really think that's a possibility, Skipper?" asked Moore. "After all, their patrol grid is a good fifty miles north of us."

"Never take Tim Lucas and that band of pirates of his for granted, XO," warned Mac. "That SOB would drive *Louisville* straight up to the gates of Hades just for the thrill of it."

Moore chuckled and looked across the table to the navigator. "Lieutenant Matson, just in case the *Louisville* is indeed laying a trap for us, I want you to pull all the charts of the central Kuril Trench area. We've still got a good twelve hours until we're scheduled to rendezvous with them, and I want you to know those bathymetrics like the back of your hand."

"Aye, aye, sir," snapped the navigator.

The "Theme of the Fast Carriers" was playing in the background as Mac completed his meal and laid his napkin on the table. This was the sign for the orderly to serve dessert. The piping-hot cobblers arrived as promised, and over coffee the captain revealed the afternoon's schedule.

"As previously discussed, we'll be undergoing another fire drill in the reactor compartment at 1430. This time I want to see some real improvement. Mr. Ward, you have my blessing to come up with a humdinger of a casualty. Afterward I want a full debriefing here in the wardroom, with all department heads present."

Any further instructions on Mac's part were cut short by a polite knock on the wardroom's closed doorway. A lanky sailor in blue denim dungarees nervously entered and sheepishly addressed the captain while handing him a folded piece of paper.

"Sir, this priority-one dispatch just arrived for you from COMSUBPAC."

Surprised by this news, Mac unfolded the message and quickly read it. He reread it again slowly, then handed it to his XO. "What do you make of this, Phil?"

Moore absorbed the dispatch's contents and voiced his opinion. "Sounds like the *Chicago*'s got herself a new mission."

"What's coming down, Captain?" asked Chop.

Mac looked directly at the supply officer. "You'd better make room for one more passenger, Chop, and a civilian at that. Hopefully he'll be able to explain what this whole damned thing's about, once we pick him up off the Hokkaidō coast in two hours' time."

7

Dr. Peter Kraft peered out the helicopter's Plexiglas hatchway at the rugged landscape some ten thousand feet below. To the constant thumping roar of the Sikorsky Seahawk's rotors, he studied a range of steep snowcapped mountains that extended all the way to the southern horizon.

"That's the Hidaka-Sanmyaku range, Doctor," explained the chopper's air tactical officer, who practically had to shout to be heard. "They roughly cut southern Hokkaidō in half, and include several active volcanoes."

The ATO handed Kraft a thermos cup full of coffee, and doing his best not to spill it, the marine biologist nodded in thanks. "How much longer until we reach our destination?" he asked.

"We should be touching down in Kushiro in another fifteen minutes," answered the ATO. "Are you sure I can't get you something to eat? I believe I can dig up a couple of peanut-butter-and-jelly sandwiches."

"This coffee's more than adequate," returned Kraft, who felt more fatigued than hungry.

"As you wish, sir," said the young sailor. "Just holler if you change your mind."

Kraft watched as he crossed the equipment-packed cabin and disappeared into the cockpit. Returning his weary gaze to the window, he stifled a yawn, then took a long sip of his coffee.

The last twenty-four hours had been occupied with this exhausting trip, which took him halfway around the planet. His death-defying exploits in the shark channel seemed to have taken place a lifetime ago. Yet it was only yesterday afternoon that the NOSC commander had offered him this strange assignment.

Barely giving him time to return to his condo and pack, Commander Lawrence personally drove him to Homestead. Terri Jackman accompanied them, and together they cleared his upcoming work schedule for the next week. She left him at the airfield with a textbook she had managed to pull from the institute's library. It was aptly titled *Monsters of the Deep,* and Kraft had begun reading it once he got settled into the immense Lockheed C-5A Galaxy transport that was to be his home for the next twenty hours.

The first leg of the flight took them to San Diego, where they took on additional freight. Then they proceeded to cross the entire breadth of the Pacific, stopping for a single in-flight refueling along the way.

From his seat on the plane's upper deck, Kraft immersed himself in his book. It proved to be a light, somewhat entertaining study of the many mysterious creatures haunting the earth's oceans, with detailed chapters on whales, giant squid, and even sharks. He especially enjoyed its coverage of prehistoric sea creatures, which included several excellent photographs of a wide assortment of fossilized remains. The book also had a segment on lake monsters, and since Kraft had once traveled to Loch Ness in the Scottish Highlands in search of Nessie, he read this chapter with particular interest.

It ended with a chapter on the coelacanth and other ancient creatures, once thought extinct, which had managed to reach the nets of modern fishermen. Nowhere in the book, however, was there mention of giant manta rays. But, after all, Kraft reminded himself, the oceans were vast, covering over seventy percent of the planet. With trenches deeper than Mt. Everest was tall, the seas still held their fair share of mysteries, and man knew more about the surface of the moon than about the floor of his own planetary home's oceans. Remembering this, Kraft mentally prepared himself for the unexpected.

Never one who could sleep while airborne, he managed only the briefest of naps. He tried his best to consume a tasteless MRE, and satisfied his tastebuds instead with endless cups of hot, black coffee.

Midway through the flight, his right leg had begun to throb painfully. His thigh muscles were tight with the need to exercise, and Kraft did his best to stretch them by exploring the giant aircraft. He paced the upper deck and found a large section of unoccupied seats positioned aft of the wing. A ladder led him down into the cavernous cargo bay. Over two hundred feet long, it was packed with supply-laden pallets. A catwalk bisected the compartment, and he walked its length, passing tons of crated spare parts, ammunition, food, and even a small helicopter. After a quick trip to the cockpit, he returned to his seat, thankful that their destination was rapidly approaching.

Less than an hour later the C-5A had touched down at Sapporo. This was Kraft's first visit to Hokkaidō. He had previously toured Japan's southern islands during an international fishery symposium that had been held in Osaka.

From the airport, Kraft could just see Sapporo's modern skyline and the snowcapped mountains to the west and south. This would be as close as he would get to Hokkaidō's capital city, as a shiny white Seahawk helicopter with U.S. Navy markings waited on the adjoining tarmac to convey him farther eastward.

His current means of transport was certainly less comfortable than the aircraft that had flown him over the Pacific. It was noisy, drafty, and constantly leaked smelly hydraulic fluid from the maze of pipes and hoses that lined its ceiling. Yet the one thing it offered was an unobstructed view of the spectacular landscape below.

Unlike the crowded island of Honshu to the south, Hokkaidō was sparsely populated. The few towns they had passed over were little more than tiny villages of the most primitive kind. Most were situated on the winding banks of the Tokachi River, whose twisting path they had been generally following since leaving Sapporo.

As Kraft took his last sip of black coffee, the throaty grind of the chopper's engines seemed to deepen. They appeared to be steadily losing altitude, and as he gazed out the window he viewed a particularly craggy stretch of terrain. Long tendrils of steam rose from dozens of volcanic fumaroles here, hinting at the area's geological instability.

The helicopter continued to drop, and Kraft looked to the south, where Hokkaidō's coast met the surging Pacific. Even from this lower altitude, the vastness of the sea was all too apparent. He knew that somewhere out there, beneath the surging whitecaps, the vessel that he had traveled these thousands of miles to rendezvous with was waiting.

What would the crew of the USS *Chicago* think of the unusual orders that he carried with him from southern Florida? Surely this would be an unprecedented mission for them—a nuclear-attack submarine asked to track down a sea monster. Well aware of his own continued skepticism about the mission, Kraft could hardly imagine how a shipful of hardened navy veterans would react.

On the coastline below a rail line was visible as well as a good-sized settlement, which was much larger than the others they had flown over. It was obvious that this seaside community was their goal, for the helicopter continued to descend, until, hovering directly over a circular clearing at the village's northern outskirts, it began to set down with a deafening racket. Still not certain exactly where they were, Kraft watched as the ATO emerged from the cockpit.

"We're here, sir," he reported as he made his way over to the cabin's main hatch.

"This is Kushiro?" Kraft asked.

The ATO nodded that it was and popped open the hatchway. Outside, the rotors continued to spin madly, their whopping sound intensified. "Watch your step," warned the ATO. "And keep your head down, sir. I'll be right behind you with your bags."

Careful not to put too much weight on his right leg, Kraft climbed out of the hatch. He hunched his shoulders and quickly made his way to the edge of the concrete clearing. The swirling rotor wash made it difficult to stand, and he protectively squinted as the ATO joined him with his duffel bag and briefcase.

"Good luck, sir," offered the young airman.

"Thanks for the lift." Kraft watched the ATO rush back to the helicopter, which wasted no time returning skyward. He was enjoying the return to relative quiet that followed its ascent when a female voice spoke out behind him.

"Dr. Peter Kraft?"

He pivoted, and set his eyes on an attractive Asian woman in her midthirties. She had just emerged from a black Toyota Land Cruiser, and was dressed in designer jeans and a heavy, cable-knit sweater. Brushing back her bluntly cut black bangs, she held out her right hand in greeting.

"Hi, I'm Tammy Noguchi, with the U.S. State Department. Welcome to Kushiro."

Kraft accepted a warm handshake, liking this young woman instantly. "Thanks," he said while searching her dark eyes. "This might sound a bit strange, but I thought that my next mode of transport was supposed to be submarine."

"It is," she replied, reaching out for his duffel bag. "Though it's going to take a short automobile ride to the pier and a quick boat ride to get you to that sub."

"I believe that I can handle that, Miss Noguchi. Lead on."

Glad to be free from the noisy confines of the helicopter, Kraft gratefully climbed into the Land Cruiser's passenger seat. In a matter of minutes they traversed the entire town and reached the central pier. During this brief ride the personable Ms. Noguchi revealed that she worked for the U.S. Consulate office in Sapporo, where she held the position of senior translator. Because the navy had no personnel assets in this relatively isolated portion of Hokkaidō, she had been asked to relay Kraft to the rendezvous site and to hire a boat. The latter, a compact, white harbor launch, was tied to the dock's last slip. They parked beside it, and Tammy led the way down to the water.

"My orders are to accompany you out past the breakwater," she reported, joining him on the boat's open deck. "That's where we're supposed to meet the submarine, at two P.M. sharp."

A quick check of the time showed that they had less than ten minutes to get out to sea, and Tammy spurred the captain on with a rapid exchange of fluent Japanese. The emaciated, chain-smoking mariner listened to her, politely bowed, and signaled to his sole deckhand to release the mooring lines. Then, with the boat's diesel engine sputtering away in the background, they slowly crossed the harbor, heading for a relatively narrow seaward opening cut into the protective, rock breakwater.

A rising swell announced their arrival into the open Pacific. A cold wind blew in from the north, and Kraft found himself chilled and a bit queasy.

They appeared to be headed toward a bobbing red mooring buoy that was anchored to the seafloor for the use of vessels too large to enter the harbor. Two o'clock arrived and they tied up to this buoy. Wondering how long he could contain his nausea, Kraft desperately searched the southern horizon for any sign of the submarine.

"Are you sure we're in the right spot?" he asked.

Tammy answered him while scanning these same waters. "The captain says that this is Kushiro's only deep-sea mooring buoy, and that's where I was instructed to bring you. Maybe the navy won't be able to make it this afternoon."

No sooner were these words spoken than an expanse of frothing water appeared a good hundred yards off their starboard bow. Kraft was the first to spot it, and as he excitedly pointed out the bubbling disturbance, the black sail of a submarine rose from the depths and towered above them, followed by a sleek hull of incredible size. As Kraft met the astounded gaze of his attractive escort, his own expression was awestruck.

"I never realized a submarine was so huge!" she exclaimed.

The captain of the launch didn't seem the least bit impressed. He calmly instructed the deckhand to untie the mooring line and expertly guided his fragile craft toward the newly arrived giant.

The submarine's forward access trunk popped open at about the same moment that two sailors appeared on top of the sail. While they scanned the approaching launch with their binoculars, a trio of their shipmates climbed up onto the forward deck from the open trunk. They carried a mix of paraphernalia, including a rope ladder and several large, rubber bumpers.

Kraft had been worrying about how he was going to make the transfer to the submarine, and what he saw did nothing to ease his anxiety. Apparently the launch would maneuver itself beside the mammoth warship, and Kraft would board the sub by grabbing hold of the ladder that the sailors were draping over its rounded side. Of course, the agitated state of the sea only increased the difficulty of the transfer as did the injured state of Kraft's right leg.

The captain of the launch displayed excellent seamanship as he made good his approach while the submariners prepared the bumpers. Kraft noticed that every member of the deck party was wearing a bright orange life jacket.

"You know, those life preservers don't look half-bad," he whispered to his State Department escort. "Are we carrying any ourselves?"

"Hold on, Doctor, and I'll check," she replied.

Tammy addressed the deckhand in rapid Japanese and received an abrupt negative nod, which Kraft took to be the answer to his question.

His suspicion was confirmed when Tammy hopefully asked, "Can you swim, Doctor?"

The marine biologist smiled and replied sarcastically, "I never planned to live long enough to collect my pension anyway. Thanks for getting me this far, Miss Noguchi."

He took a series of deep breaths and bravely walked over to the amidships rail, where the transfer would take place. From the exposed wheelhouse, the captain spewed forth a torrent of indistinguishable words, which Tammy just as rapidly interpreted.

"Doctor, he says that you must time your step over to the submarine to coincide with the arrival of the next swell."

"That sounds easy enough," Kraft lied.

Sensing his unease, Tammy added, "If it's any consolation, I used to spend my summers in Redondo Beach working as a lifeguard. If you should miss that step, I'll be right behind you."

"Don't worry," Kraft said. "I'll get over to that sub if I have to fly. Thanks again!"

She left him with a warm smile, and he ambled up to the now open rail and stared out at the approaching submarine. They were less than five feet away from the immense vessel, and he could clearly see the faces of the awaiting deck party, only one of whom was dressed in officer's khakis.

This balding figure displayed an easygoing manner as he glanced down at Kraft. "You must be Dr. Kraft. I'm Lieutenant Walden, the *Chicago*'s supply officer. Do you think we could get you over here on the next set of swells?"

"I'm on my way, Lieutenant," Kraft replied.

Before he had time to change his mind, the launch bobbed upward and Kraft bravely stepped off the gunwale. As he reached out to grasp the submarine's rope ladder, his right foot slipped, and he momentarily found himself hanging solely by his arms from the ladder's nylon crosspiece, his legs dangling between the sub's hull and the bobbing launch. A cramp tightened the muscles of his right thigh, and as he looked down to try to hook the ladder with his left foot, the launch crashed into the sub's rubber fender, only inches away from him. The nylon rope bit into the tender skin of his palms, and just as he was about to let go, a pair of brawny hands grabbed him by the shoulders and lifted him up onto the submarine's deck.

Kraft took a moment to catch his breath and watched his baggage being safely transferred. He managed to return his State Department escort's wave of good-bye before turning when a concerned voice addressed him.

"I hope I didn't hurt your shoulders when I grabbed you, sir." The speaker of these words was a good-looking, muscular young sailor, with bright blue eyes and a spiky crewcut.

"The hell with my shoulders," returned Kraft. "Damn it, son, you just saved my life. What's your name?"

"Matt Cox, sir. And you're welcome to join me and my boys in the *Chicago*'s sound shack anytime you'd like."

"Sound shack?" Kraft was baffled.

"That's what we call the ship's sonar compartment, Doc," Lieutenant Walden interjected. "And by the way, let me be the first to officially welcome you aboard the USS *Chicago*."

Kraft replied while accepting the officer's firm handshake. "That was quite a dramatic entrance on my part, Lieutenant. But at least I made it in one piece."

"If you'd like, feel free to call me Chop. Hell, everyone else on board does."

The launch was well on its way to rounding the breakwater when the supply officer beckoned Kraft toward the open access hatch. "Have you ever visited a 688-class attack sub, Doc?" he asked.

"I'm afraid I haven't."

"Well, no matter," continued Chop. "Let's get out of this infernal wind and go down below. I'll help you get settled."

A narrow steel ladder led Kraft into the darkened bowels of the vessel. Careful not to reinjure his throbbing leg, he cautiously stepped off the final rung and found himself in a rather spacious corridor. There was a strange smell in the air; as the supply officer joined him he asked, "What's that funny scent—machine oil?"

Chop grinned. "That's amine, Doc. It's an ammonia derivative used in the ship's air scrubbers. You'll soon enough get used to it."

He pointed forward, toward the sub's bow, where several men were gathered in a brightly lit room. "Doc, that's the control room. Before I can give you a tour of it, we need to get you fitted with a TLD. If you'll just follow me . . ."

A stairwell took them to the deck below, where they headed aft, down a long, well-lit corridor. They passed a sailor working a paper shredder, a small copier, and a bulletin board holding the plan of the day. To the left was an open doorway marked WARDROOM, which turned out to be a wood-paneled compartment dominated by a large, rectangular table, at which a single dungaree-clad sailor was seated, making notes on a legal pad. As they entered he quickly rose to his feet.

"Pills," said Chop to the boat's medical corpsman. "This is Dr. Peter Kraft, *Chicago*'s newest passenger.

While you're taking care of business, I'll stow away his gear. What bunk do we have him in?"

"Bunk two, in the nine-man berth," answered the serious-faced corpsman.

Chop left the wardroom, and Kraft was given several forms to fill out. The TLD turned out to be a small, gray plastic device that he was instructed to clip onto his belt.

"What exactly is the purpose of this device?" Kraft asked, as he laced the TLD through his belt loop.

"I take it that you're not a medical doctor," said the corpsman.

Kraft shook his head. "Actually I'm a marine biologist."

"Have you been exposed to any ionizing radiation lately?" the corpsman wanted to know.

"This past winter I fractured my hip, and since then I've certainly had my fair share of X rays."

The corpsman wrote this information down on his legal pad, then handed Kraft a sealed packet, holding a quarter-sized circular Band-Aid. "At the end of your cruise I'll analyze your TLD to determine if you were exposed to any ionizing radiation while you were with us. Are you susceptible to motion sickness, Doctor?"

"To tell you the truth," Kraft admitted, "I'm feeling a bit nauseous right now."

"Then open up that packet and put that adhesive patch on your upper neck, behind your right ear," the corpsman instructed.

No stranger to Transderm Scope, Kraft did as ordered while the corpsman excused himself to make a copy of his driver's license. There was a growling venting noise in the background and a slight flutter of air pressure in his eardrums, followed by a barely noticeable downward tilt of the deck, which indicated that the submarine was returning to its habitual medium. Intrigued, Kraft took this opportunity to examine the wardroom.

A dozen sturdy chairs surrounded the central table, with an upholstered blue booth lining the far bulkhead. A television monitor was set into the wall at one end of the table, along with a CD player and a VCR. At the opposite end was a long aluminum counter beneath a sliding window. Kraft supposed this was the entryway to the kitchen. Directly behind him, a mounted plaque showed a large wave, cut in half by a submarine whose length was formed by the letters spelling CHICAGO. Beneath this were the words WINDY CITY, with SSN 721 right below. When Chop returned, he explained that this was the ship's seal.

The supply officer then guided Kraft out into the hallway and led him past the officers' quarters. There were six cramped cabins in all, holding two bunks apiece. All were currently empty, and held individual laptop computers on the bulkhead-mounted desks.

At the end of the corridor was the officers' bathroom or, as it was better known, the head. Chop gave him a quick lesson in flushing the toilet, which necessitated the use of a long, steel lever to open a ball-cock drain, and then the turning of a valve to set off the rinse cycle. He also demonstrated the use of the shower's water restrictor and showed him where the squeegee was kept.

Kraft's berth was off an adjoining corridor. Unlike the rather spacious officers' cabins, this cramped, dimly lit space held three tiers of three bunks apiece. His bunk was immediately inside the sliding doorway, on the middle level. He noticed that his duffel bag and briefcase lay on top of the narrow mattress when Chop switched on the fluorescent light that was mounted into the wall directly above the pillow.

"You'll find adequate space beneath your mattress to stow your clothing," Chop explained. "At the foot of your bed is a small locker. Use it to keep your personal belongings and toiletries. Since this bunking compartment was originally designed to hold computers, it's several degrees cooler than the rest of the boat, so I gave you an extra blanket. Also, here's a welcome-aboard packet. Inside, there's a schematic of the boat, pertinent data explaining its history, and a card listing the officers and chief petty officers. You'll also find the meal schedule inside."

Chop looked at his watch and added, "Dinner will be served in the wardroom at 1700, in another three and a half hours. And don't be afraid to bring along your appetite. I understand that we'll be having roast turkey and all the trimmings this evening."

Kraft replied while stifling a yawn. "Sounds good, Chop. Do you mind if we postpone that tour you promised me until after dinner. I could sure use some time to myself to get properly settled."

"I thought that might be the case," said Chop. "Go ahead, unpack and relax. And if you need anything, just ask one of the crew where to find me."

Grateful for some time alone, Kraft began unpacking his duffel bag. So rushed were his initial preparations that he really wasn't certain just what he had managed to stuff inside it. With a bit of effort he lifted up the mattress and stowed away eight pairs of Jockey shorts and an equal number of white cotton socks, the extent of his available clean underwear. He also emptied into the shallow storage space a set of gray sweats, a green turtleneck, three denim work shirts, and a pair of khaki trousers. Realizing that he had forgotten pajamas, he pulled down the mattress and unpacked his toiletries.

Once again he was aware that the deck was tilting forward as the sub descended. This time the angle was a steep one, and he tightly gripped the edge of the bunk to keep from falling over, then decided to try to make it up onto his mattress. It took several awkward attempts before he finally succeeded.

With just enough room to turn onto his back, he pulled the curtain shut and placed his briefcase on his stomach. Though he had every intention of sorting through the packet of orders that Commander Lawrence had given him, his fatigue finally caught up with him.

Soon, the gentle rocking motion of the *Chicago*'s hull lulled him into a deep, dreamless sleep.

Captain Mac McShane scanned the control room from atop the elevated platform beneath the dual periscopes. To his left, two seated planesmen gripped their steering yokes, their gazes fixed to the various gauges and dials set in the bulkhead before them. Between them, Chief of the Boat Joe Hoffler occupied the diving officer's position. The barrel-chested COB had a fat cigar clenched between his lips as he double-checked the complicated console positioned on his left. The chief of the watch was responsible for monitoring the status of the sub's vents. The column of green lights displayed on this console indicated that these critical openings to the sea were currently closed, and it was here the boat was trimmed and its ballast controlled.

Behind the captain, the navigator worked with his team at the navigation plot. To McShane's right was the vacant fire-control console and the doorway to the adjoining sonar room.

Despite the fact that they had successfully attained a depth of 150 feet, there was a certain tenseness in the air. Mac could see it in the drawn faces of his men and the surprising lack of small talk. Well aware of the reason for this anxiety, he watched as their supply officer entered the control room.

"Captain," Chop greeted with his usual relaxed manner, which seemed out of place at the moment. "I've got our passenger settled in. I suppose you're gonna want to meet him and see what our new orders are all about."

"Whatever these orders might be, for the moment they're on hold," returned Mac. "A couple of minutes ago we received an urgent transmission from COM-SUBPAC, tasking us with a priority-one assignment."

Before the captain could explain what this new duty was all about, the XO rounded the navigation plot and addressed him. "Skipper, I've got a positive verification on those new orders. It indeed appears that the entire Kuril line is down."

Chop appeared confused, and it was the captain who straightened him out. "We've got a SOSUS array breakdown, Chop. Until the system goes back on-line, the National Command Authority is relying on us and the *Louisville* to run picket duty along the Kuril Trench."

"Sounds bad," Chop commented.

"You bet it is," said Mac. "Though it's damn fortunate that we were in the neighborhood."

"What portion of the trench will we be patrolling?" asked Chop.

Mac looked over at his XO while answering. "We've got the southern quadrant, while *Louisville*'s been sent up north. And since the Pérouse Strait is in our sector, you can bet the farm that we'll be seeing all the action."

"Skipper," said the XO, "I'd better visit the sound shack and explain our new assignment."

As Moore disappeared into sonar Chop spoke again. "What are we going to do with our passenger, Captain?"

Mac looked at his watch and grunted. "Bring him to my cabin in another hour. I'll check out his orders and explain our current situation. And as soon as this crisis is over, we can get on with whatever NOSC is asking of us. By the way, what's he like?"

"He seems nice enough, sir. I understand that he's a marine biologist and that this is his first sub embark."

"Well, he certainly picked a rotten time to join us, Chop. I sure hope he won't be bored while we're on picket duty. Who knows how long it might take to get that SOSUS system back on-line. Until it's fixed, or we get some relief out here, the *Chicago*'s got only one mission, and that's to patrol the southern quadrant of the Kuril Trench."

8

Peter Kraft's sound sleep was broken by a gentle hand shaking his shoulder. His eyes popped open, and for one confusing moment he didn't know where he was.

"Hey, Doc, it's Chop," whispered the supply officer.

Kraft looked into the man's eyes and yawned. "Hello, Chop, is it time for dinner already?"

"We've got a couple of hours yet for chow, Doc. The captain would like to see you."

Still a bit groggy, the marine biologist sat up abruptly and cracked his head on the bunk above in the process. This painful encounter served to awaken him fully, and he cautiously scooted off the mattress onto the deck below.

"Crawling in and out of your rack will take a bit of practice, but you'll get the hang of it soon enough," Chop belatedly informed him.

Kraft rubbed his bruised forehead. "I sure hope so, my friend. Do I have time to wash up and grab a cup of coffee?"

"You bet," Chop answered. "And while you're in the head, why don't you change into this poopy suit that I brought you. I believe I got the size right, and it will certainly be more comfortable than those civvies you brought along."

Kraft had already seen several sailors dressed in similar blue coveralls, and he readily accepted the offer. They fit perfectly, and he emerged from the head looking like a typical submariner in a uniform that included a set of golden dolphins on the left side of his chest and an embroidered patch version of the USS *Chicago* seal that he had seen in the wardroom on the opposite side.

Chop, who was waiting for him outside with a mug of coffee and his briefcase, appraised him. "Now you're lookin' like a real live bubblehead, Doc."

A short climb took them to the deck above and the closed cabin door of the captain. Chop knocked several times, and a rough voice from inside said that they were free to enter. Inside, they found two seated figures huddled over a detailed chart. Kraft admired the square-jawed, rugged handsomeness of the elder of the two and the way his deep green eyes lit up upon spotting him.

"Ah, Dr. Kraft, at last we get to meet," he said with a cool smile. "I'm Mac McShane, the CO of this pigboat. I sure hope that our esteemed supply officer has been taking good care of you in my absence."

"Chop has been the perfect host," Kraft replied. "In fact, I already feel right at home here."

"You certainly look the part," said Mac. Then, referring to the balding sailor seated opposite him: "Doctor, I'd like you to meet Lieutenant Len Matson, our navigator."

Kraft accepted a simple nod from the navigator as the captain continued. "I'm anxious to hear more about the mission that brings you to the *Chicago,* Doctor."

Taking this as their cue to leave, Lieutenants Matson and Walden excused themselves. With his coffee mug in hand, Kraft accepted the captain's invitation to sit down on the chair the navigator had previously occupied. He positioned his briefcase before him and listened to the *Chicago*'s CO get down to business.

"The orders I received concerning your visit were extremely sketchy. I was only told that you were a civilian tasked to NOSC, and that we were to provide whatever assistance you desired for the completion of your mission."

Kraft was surprised at the sketchiness of the captain's knowledge. "Do you mean to say that they didn't even tell you what my mission concerns?"

"That's affirmative, Doctor."

Kraft felt uncomfortable with this news, and reached into his briefcase and pulled out the order packet Commander Lawrence had given him. Inside was a sealed envelope addressed to Commander McShane's eyes only, and copies of the photos that Lawrence had shown him only yesterday back on Virginia Key. "I hope the contents of this envelope with your name on it will further explain things," he said.

McShane quickly tore open the envelope and removed a three-page document. As he proceeded to read carefully Kraft sorted through the photographs, mentally preparing himself for the captain's reaction. Several minutes passed before McShane finally spoke.

"This is absolutely incredible, Doctor. Are those the photos of this supposed sea monster?"

Kraft handed him the stack of photographs and watched the captain carefully examine each of them. "Well, I'll be," he said. "Will you look at the size of that brute!"

"Preliminary photo analysis indicates it to be a good one hundred feet in diameter."

Mac shook his head in wonder. "I didn't think a ray could grow that big."

"Neither did I, Captain. And to tell you the truth, I would never have believed it if I hadn't seen those photos myself."

"This photo sequence is simply amazing." The captain shook his head again. "Those horns of his look like quite an effective ramming tool."

"The horns of a devilfish are cartilaginous," Kraft explained. "And with a species of that size, they'd be extremely dense and unyielding."

"Devilfish?" Mac repeated.

"Merely another name for the type of manta ray this creature resembles."

"The name certainly fits it, Doctor. And just knowing that it's haunting these waters gives me the creeps. NOSC seems to have a pretty accurate idea of where this incident took place. We should be able to isolate the location on this chart of mine."

Mac circled the latitude and longitude coordinates that were included in his orders. He then grabbed a clear plastic ruler and studied the bathymetric chart laid out on the table. It didn't take him long to encircle a deep blue portion of the Kuril Trench on the extreme northern edge of the chart.

"As fate would have it, this incident took place just within the confines of our current patrol quadrant. Unfortunately, at the moment, I can't give you one-hundred-percent cooperation in hunting this creature down."

"Why's that?" Kraft asked.

Mac pointed at the chart and outlined the north-south meander of the Kuril Trench. "Doctor, do you know what SOSUS is?"

Kraft nodded. "Several years ago I provided NOSC with a pair of working dolphins to assist navy divers during the installation of the SOSUS network monitoring the Florida Straits. I was given a fairly intensive briefing at the time, and am well aware of the SOSUS network's importance to our national defense."

Mac appeared relieved to hear this. "We could sure use those dolphins now, Doctor," he said. "Because sometime within the last couple of hours, we lost our

SOSUS coverage of the Kurils. Until we get it back on-line, *Chicago* has been tasked with picket duty, our primary target being potential enemy submarines. Though I'd love to work with you in tracking that monster down, right now I'm afraid that your mission will have to be placed on the back burner."

"I understand, Captain," Kraft replied woodenly.

Once more Mac sorted through the photographs that had been taken by the *Koji Moru*'s only survivor. Quick to see the disappointment that etched his guest's expression, he attempted to offer some encouragement.

"Of course, just because we've been tasked with an alternative priority assignment doesn't mean that we can't be on the lookout for any other seaborne visitors that might cross our path. We'd better get you down to the sound shack so you can explain to the boys in sonar just what they should be listening for. Then I'd like you to brief the boat's department heads. Brother, I can just picture their faces when they learn that we've been ordered to track down a friggin' sea monster!"

Kraft grinned. "If they share my initial reaction when I read about the sightings, they'll think the whole thing's insane."

"You know, Doctor"—the captain spoke as if he'd just realized something of major importance—"there's absolutely nothing in my orders about what *Chicago*'s supposed to do if we should manage to tag the damn thing."

Kraft reached into his briefcase and took out a padded envelope containing a hand-sized, jet-black ammunition clip. A bit awkwardly he removed one of the sharply pointed bullets from this clip and handed it to his curious host.

"These are specially designed 5.56-millimeter shells," he explained. "They're fully compatible with the M-16A1 rifles I'm told you carry aboard ship. With NOSC's assistance, we initially developed this shell to effectively track large migrating fish and marine mammals. Encased in the bullet's soft tip is a miniature, battery-powered, ultrasonic homing beacon that's triggered upon impact. A reduced powder load vastly decreases normal muzzle velocity, resulting in little injury to the desired target. So with your assistance, I hope to tag the devilfish with one of these implants so that its movements can be tracked should it impose a further hazard to surface traffic."

Mac whistled appreciatively. "*Chicago*'s sure gotten its fair share of unusual assignments before, but this one beats them all."

"I hear you, Captain," Kraft said. "And I truly appreciate your candor. When the navy came to me yesterday and showed me those same pictures, I must admit that I was very dubious about the existence of such a creature. But I quickly changed my tune when they asked me to drop my current research program and accept this new assignment."

"May I ask what you were working on?"

"Of course you can, Captain. For the past year I've been training a pair of bottle-nosed dolphins to protect a human diver from shark attack."

"Sounds intriguing," said Mac, whose curiosity was cut short by the ringing intercom. He picked up the nearest handset and spoke into the transmitter. "Captain, here."

Kraft watched the senior officer's expression change to one of concern as he listened to the voice on the other end of the line.

"I understand, XO, and I'm on my way." Mac hung up the handset, stood, and gestured for his guest to join him. "It seems that sonar has just tagged an unidentified submerged contact approaching us from the west. There's a good chance it's another submarine, so why don't you join me and watch my men in action."

"I'd enjoy that," Kraft said as he followed his host into the passageway.

They turned to the right and entered a hushed, dimly lit compartment that Kraft supposed was the sub's control room. It took several seconds for his eyes to adjust, and he sensed rather than saw a good many men anxiously gathered in the equipment-packed space that was about the size of a three-car garage. They passed by the two seated sailors manning the helm, and the ship's current OOD, who stood beside the central periscopes orchestrating the action.

"We're continuing on course zero-four-five, Captain," the officer of the deck reported. "Our depth is one-eight-three feet, at eighteen knots."

"Very good, Mr. Bradley," Mac replied, as he continued on to an accordian-style sliding doorway marked SOUND SHACK in red stenciled lettering.

Gathered inside the narrow space were five individuals. Three were seated, facing glowing CRT screens, while the other two stood directly behind them. Kraft recognized Matt Cox, the young sailor who had saved him from falling overboard during the transfer. Beside Cox stood a tall, slender black man, an unlit corncob pipe clenched between his lips, who greeted them.

"Our unidentified submerged contact has just turned into a multiple, Skipper. We believe we've got two submarines out there, at a range of twenty thousand yards, on bearing two-eight-zero."

"Good work, XO," Mac replied. "Do you think they know they have company out here?"

This time Matt Cox answered. "I seriously doubt it, Captain. They're churnin' up the depths somethin' fierce, and with all that racket they're producin', they'll never be able to tag us."

Kraft took a seat on the vacant ledge immediately inside the doorway beside the first console. He watched the captain fit on a pair of headphones and close his eyes in concentration. Several hushed minutes passed before he removed the headphones.

"That sure is an unusual signature. What does the computer have to say about it?"

"Unusual ain't the word for it, Captain," Matt Cox said. "Because Big Brother shows there's a fifty-three-percent probability that one of those contacts is a Chink Xia-class boomer."

"And the other?" Mac's voice revealed that he was clearly surprised by this information.

"It appears to be a diesel-electric," the XO replied. "Most likely she's one of their new Romeos on escort duty."

"What the blazes is a PRC ballistic-missile submarine doing way up here?" Mac asked. "They're thousands of miles north of their authorized patrol zone, and as such are in direct violation of the Vladivostok Strategic Missile Accord."

"They sure picked a hell of a time to try to run the Kurils, with SOSUS down and all," said Matt Cox.

Inspired by this comment, the XO pulled his pipe from his mouth and pointed its stem toward the senior sonarman. "You could be onto something, Mr. Cox. Is their presence out there just a coincidence, or could the Chinks somehow be responsible for the SOSUS line's unprecedented failure?"

All of this was getting a little too complicated for Kraft to comprehend. He watched the captain put one of the headphones up to his ear and say, "I sure hope that you're getting all this on tape, gentlemen."

The XO sheepishly answered him. "I'm afraid not, Skipper. As I indicated in my latest systems status update, the recorder's still down."

"Then bring in the backup recorder," Mac responded icily.

"We already did, Captain," Matt Cox put in. "And that failed also, a good two hours ago. I've got two machinists scrounging around for spare parts even as we speak, but you know how old those reel-to-reels are, sir. They're dinosaurs!"

"Since we can't document those two subs without a recorder, what are we going to do about their presence here, Skipper?" the XO questioned.

Mac thought a moment before responding. "Though I'd love to teach the PRC a little respect, with a couple of well-placed Mk48s, I'm afraid that such a drastic course of action is out of the question at the moment. So I say let's give 'em a good lashing and put the fear of Mao in their godless hearts."

Peter Kraft dared to break in at this point. "What in the world's a lashing?"

"Doctor, as a marine biologist, I'm sure you understand the principles behind active sonar," Mac answered. "And a lashing involves just such an active sonic pulse, though in this particular case it will be aimed squarely at our two targets and amplified to maximum volume. Needless to say, when it hits 'em, those poor bastards are going to have some mighty sore eardrums. And since they still won't know precisely where we're positioned or who the hell we are, they'll be experiencing their fair share of uncertainty as well."

"'Uncertainty' is putting it mildly, Skipper," interrupted the XO. "Hell, those Chink bubbleheads will be scared shitless. I'll put a week's pay that they'll turn tail and run for home before we can even get a decent return on them."

Mac's mouth turned in a broad grin, and he reached up for the microphone that hung from the ceiling. Before speaking into it, he explained his next course of action to the men in the room.

"I'm going to put the crew at general quarters and prepare a full load of fish just to be on the safe side. Ever since Tiananmen Square, you never really know how the Chinese will react, though in this instance I'll put my money with the XO."

Seconds later a piercing electronic tone sounded throughout the ship, and Kraft accepted the captain's invitation to join him in the control room. With the call to battle stations, a new atmosphere of tenseness filled the dimly lit compartment. As several additional sailors appeared with sound-powered phones around their necks, Mac confidently strode onto the slightly elevated platform that lay beneath the periscopes, the XO close beside him.

"This is the captain. I've got the helm. Chief, make our depth two-five-zero feet at one-third speed."

"Two-five-zero feet at one-third speed, aye, Captain," the diving officer repeated.

"Lieutenant Bradley," Mac continued. "What's our weapons status?"

The weapons officer quickly answered, "Tubes one through four are loaded with wire-guided Mk48s, Captain."

"Skipper," announced the XO. "Estimate contacts Sierra four and five in the first CZ, with range down to one-seven-thousand yards. Course continues due east."

"They're comin' right down our throat," Mac whispered. "Weaps, how many ranges do you have on them?"

"Three, Captain."

"And how many legs?" demanded the XO.

"This is our fourth, sir," Bradley reported.

From Kraft's vantage point at the side of the weapons console, the captain's eyes seemed to light up with devilish glee as he shouted out for all to hear, "Sonar, Conn, lash those Red sons of bitches, Mr. Cox!"

"Conn, sonar, we're goin' active!" repeated the excited voice of the senior sonarman.

From the elevated speaker came a deeply resonant, hollow pinging noise. Kraft suddenly remembered the World War II submarine movies he had seen as a kid, when active sonar scans such as this one seemed to almost always be followed by a gut-wrenching depth-charge explosion.

"Conn, sonar, we've got 'em!" boomed Matt Cox's voice. "I show solid returns on both contacts, Captain."

From out of the blackness beside the navigation plot, Chop suddenly appeared at Kraft's side. The usually carefree supply officer looked tense as he quietly whispered into the civilian's ear.

"This is the hairy part, Doc. Those sub captains we just lashed will be furious about now, and all too soon we'll know whether or not they're going to answer our little wake-up call by taking a potshot at us."

The rapt faces of the young sailors surrounding them echoed this fear, and Kraft looked to the captain for reassurance. Mac McShane looked to be the image of resolute firmness as he stood on the bridge with his gaze locked on an elevated sonar repeater. Beside him, his XO held up a stopwatch and counted off the seconds that remained between the submarine full of men and possible oblivion.

"I show one minute thirty seconds since they received our ping," he reported.

"That repeater screen that the captain's studying says it all, Doc," whispered Chop. "Because if they launch torpedoes, that's where we'll first see 'em."

Kraft looked at this screen and struggled to make some sort of sense out of the numerous columns of thin, grayish lines. He assumed this was a visual representation of the sounds being relayed by the hydrophones, and he nervously jumped when two of the lines began quivering, like a seismograph during an earthquake.

"Is that movement it?" he asked, a little too loudly. "Are we under attack?"

"Hell, no," answered the captain. "That frequency you're seeing is way too low for a torpedo."

It was the joyous, amplified voice of Matt Cox that explained the true nature of this sonic modulation. "Conn, sonar, we're picking up an increased screw count on both submerged contacts! We're also showing a 180-degree course change. Captain, they appear to be turnin' tail and headin' back to the strait!"

A wave of relieved chatter filled the control room as these words sank in.

"Skipper, you sure were smart to put your money with me," the beaming XO exclaimed.

Mac allowed himself only the briefest of relieved grins before addressing his men. "Okay, gentlemen, keep those voices down and your minds on the business at hand. Because we're not done with those two subs just yet. Helm, bring us around to course two-eight-zero and crank up all ahead standard."

"Course two-eight-zero, all ahead standard, aye, Captain," repeated the diving officer.

Kraft watched as the planesman entered this new velocity request into the annunciator and then reached out with both hands to turn his airplanelike steering yoke. Responding almost instantly, the deck began canting over hard on its left side. The marine biologist had to reach up to grasp a ceiling-mounted handhold to keep from falling.

"Now where are we off to, Chop?" he muttered.

The supply officer was once again his normal relaxed self as he answered. "The captain is going to make certain that those two subs are indeed heading back into the Sea of Japan. Only after we monitor them transiting the Pérouse Strait will he let them off the hook."

"Then what?" Kraft wanted to know.

"Who knows?" said Chop. "Scuttlebutt has it that there are two 688s headed our way to relieve us. And then maybe *Chicago* can get on with the mission that you arrived to undertake. Just what is it that brought you to *Chicago* anyway, Doc?"

"Chop," Kraft replied, "I guarantee you that you wouldn't believe me if I told you. So hang in there for the department-head meeting the captain will be calling shortly. Then you can see for yourself just what I need from you."

"If that's the way you want it, so be it." Chop looked at his watch and added, "I don't know about you, but all this action has worked up a fierce appetite. I sure hope you like turkey, Doc, because as you'll soon enough learn, on this pigboat, every day's Thanksgiving!"

9

Liu Shao-chi proudly stood on the bridge of his vessel, glowing with the confidence of an ancient Chinese warlord. As long as they were at sea, the *Star of Linshu* was his exclusive realm—its forty-seven crew members faithful vassals to his law only.

Though there were certainly newer, more high-tech ships in the People's cargo fleet, he viewed his current command as a great honor. Born seventy-two years ago in the distant province of Gansu, in a tiny village overlooking a crumbling portion of the Great Wall, Liu came from humble beginnings. His father and his father before him were simple shepherds. This was the craft by means of which he had been expected to make his livelihood, until political events inside China altered his destiny.

While he absently gazed out at the deep blue, white-capped waters of the North Pacific, his mind returned in time to a spring morning in 1934. He had just turned thirteen, and knew little about the vast world beyond his village, when a ragtag group of strangers from the south visited them. How their eyes lit up when they told of the great struggle that their motherland was engaged in! Less than a week later the impressionable teenager joined the ranks of these strangers, and became a member of Mao Tse-tung's People's Liberation Army.

Six decades had passed since that day, and Liu never again returned to the village of his birth. He became a man during the great Long March that followed his enlistment, when Mao led his Communist faithful to the farthest frontiers of southwest China to escape the wrath of the ruling Kuomintang Nationalists under Chiang Kai-shek. In the bitter cold, desolate wilds of Shensi Province, he was indoctrinated in the basic tenets of Communism, and had been a faithful follower ever since.

It was the struggle with the barbarian Japanese that first brought him to the sea. Mesmerized by the ocean's vastness, he volunteered to be a lowly stoker aboard a tramp steamer. Hard work and dedication led him steadily up the chain of command, and by the war's conclusion he was a first officer in the newly formed People's Navy.

The decades that followed the war were times of great change for China. Mao's teachings spread the length and breadth of the land, culminating in the Great Cultural Revolution. A loyal member of the navy during these eventful years, Liu watched with pride as his country continued to gain in international stature, until it finally blossomed into a legitimate nuclear superpower.

At the age of seventy he had been forced to give up his commission, and rather then rot away in retirement, he decided to remain at sea as a civilian in the merchant marine. His many years of oceangoing experience gained him instant employment, and thus he found himself in his present command.

A large swell rocked the deck, but the white-haired septuagenarian barely flinched. No stranger to these fickle seas, he knew very well that the excellent weather they were presently enjoying could deteriorate in a moment. When a quick check of the barometer indicated the slightest of drops in pressure since his last reading, Liu decided it would be best to take advantage of this relative calm before the next low-pressure system arrived.

"All stop!" he ordered, his deep voice booming with authority.

"All stop, sir," repeated the helmsman, who alertly stood at his right side.

As the command was directed down into the engine room, the ship's massive dual propellers spun to a halt. Soon they were dead in the water, and Liu instructed the deck crew to begin the task that had brought them to this relatively isolated portion of the North Pacific in the first place.

With a whining roar, a series of powerful pumps were activated. From deep within the ship's hold, tons of syrupy sewer sludge were sucked up into a half-dozen tubular steel pipes, specially designed for this purpose. Liu himself gave the order to open the stopcock valves regulating the pipe's flow, and the sludge poured through the six outlets set into the outer hull well above the waterline.

A spreading gray stain colored the sea's surface immediately below these outlets. Liu watched this fan-shaped pattern widen from the exterior catwalk, and choked when a vile stench met his nostrils. Forced to return indoors, he realized that the smell out there was but a by-product of the accumulated body wastes of the people of Shanghai.

It would take a good hour to empty all of the sludge. Then they would pump out an adjoining compartment, which contained a mixture of toxic industrial and medical wastes. Only after emptying yet another hold filled with low-level radioactive waste would the *Star of Linshu* turn back for port.

Though it was a far cry from the exciting missions of his navy days, Liu knew he was providing an important service. It seemed that as fast as he could return home, the ship would be filled once again, and back to sea they'd go. This voyage marked their sixth such trip just this year.

With the landfills on the mainland packed to overflowing, the ocean's depths remained the sole solution to the motherland's serious waste-disposal problem. Proud to be a part of this effort, Liu was renowned for his ship's quick turnaround time. No one could get in and out of port quicker than he. And he would have had yet another trip under his belt if it hadn't been for an unfortunate encounter that occurred last spring.

The *Star of Linshu* had been three days out of Hangzhou at that time. They had just reached the western edge of the Ryukyus and were doing a routine dumping when a Japanese Maritime Self-Defense Force frigate appeared on the horizon. Confident that he was well within international waters, Liu was nonetheless concerned when this warship's captain had the audacity to challenge his right to be in this portion of the Pacific. An inoperable radio kept Liu from contacting his own fleet for protection, and he was forced to weigh anchor with half of the hold still full when the JMSDF vessel shot a five-inch shell across their bow.

Liu was genuinely surprised when his country's official protest of the incident was countered by the pathetic, whining cries of various worldwide environmental groups. It was evident that such extremist organizations were steadily gaining power in decadent capitalistic society. Western journalists by the dozens converged on Qingdao to interview Liu and tour his ship. Not the least bit interested in the valuable service to society he provided, they focused only on the negatives, accusing him and his men of poisoning the seas with life-threatening toxins. One of the organizations that these journalists represented actually threatened to take Liu to the World Court in order to prevent the *Star of Linshu* from participating in future voyages. Only then did the motherland step in to ban future interviews and send these confused Westerners back home.

Ever since that painful incident, Liu had been advised to operate more discreetly. No longer would he use the crowded waters of the Ryukyus for a dumping ground. Instead circumspection took precedence over convenience, and the entire operation was moved to the north, far from the public's ever-probing eye.

With the steady throbbing hum of the pumps in the background like music to his ears, Liu used his binoculars to scan the horizon. He saw nothing but the approaching dusk, with fiery hues of orange and red painting the western skies like an artist's brush on canvas.

As he lowered his binoculars the deck beneath him unexpectedly shuddered. The tremor was vastly different from that caused by a swell, and the elderly mariner looked over to examine the instrument gauges mounted in the nearby bulkhead. Again the deck plates shook, this time more violently. He could only guess that one of the pumps had somehow exploded.

"Comrade Captain!" cried the terrified voice of the ship's chief engineer from the elevated intercom speaker. "Our starboard hull has been penetrated amidships, directly below the main boiler, and we're taking in seawater!"

With the coolness of a longtime sailor, Liu addressed the nearest intercom handset. "Easy does it, Comrade. How can our hull become penetrated when we're not even moving? Check the status of the stopcock valves. Most likely, what you're experiencing down there is only an accidental backwash."

Satisfied that this crisis was only a minor one, and that the chief was only overreacting to it, Liu hung up the handset and left the bridge for the exterior catwalk. Outside, the stench of the sludge still pervaded the air. Ignoring the vile odor, he peered over the railing. Strangely enough, a frothing, saucer-shaped pattern of bubbling seawater surrounded the central portion of the hull. It appeared to emanate from well below the waterline, which meant that its source couldn't possibly be the stop-cock valves. With the sea itself veiled by encroaching nightfall, Liu turned for the bridge to get a battery-powered torch.

As he stepped through the hatchway the entire ship rocked with a violent concussion that sent him crashing to the deck below. The sickening sound of rending steel was accompanied by a sudden abrupt change in the ship's center of balance. The vessel rolled over steeply on its right side, sucking the sea into its collapsed bulkheads with the force of a whirlwind.

Trapped beneath an assortment of tangled debris, Liu vainly struggled to free himself. His back was broken. The last thing he was aware of before fading into unconsciousness was the putrid stench of Shanghai's sewers—a smell that would linger in his nostrils for all eternity.

10

Peter Kraft found it hard to believe that the excellent meal he had just completed was prepared and served at a depth of 150 feet beneath the cold waters of the North Pacific. The food and service were the equal of any restaurant he had ever frequented, and the pleasant wardroom atmosphere was an added bonus.

With the majority of the *Chicago*'s officers seated beside him and the sounds of Beethoven's Sixth Symphony playing on the stereo, the meal started off with a cup of tasty navy-bean soup, followed by a tossed salad complete with tomato and cucumber bits and a choice of three dressings. Next came the main course—turkey, giblet gravy, mashed potatoes, string beans, and cranberry sauce. Hot biscuits and honey were also served, with plenty of strong coffee on the side. Dessert was a hot pumpkin pie, accompanied by what the proud chief responsible for this feast assured them was a low-fat whipped-cream topping.

An evening wardroom ritual aboard the *Chicago* was the showing of a full-length feature movie. As a newcomer, Kraft was given a rather thick booklet containing an alphabetical listing of the titles in the boat's film library, and was asked to choose one. This was a great responsibility, and fortunately he didn't have to go far in his search. He picked *The Abyss,* an underwater science-fiction flick he had seen several years before. His shipmates seemed quite satisfied with his choice, and even the captain expressed his intention to watch it with them.

Bowls of hot popcorn magically appeared. Yet just when the XO was about to insert the VCR tape, the telephone growled. Captain McShane's handset was mounted into the table beside him, and he picked up the receiver and held the briefest of conversations. There was a thoughtful look on his face as he hung up the handset and addressed them.

"Hold the flick, XO. It seems that during our last Comm transmission, we picked up what appears to be a garbled Mayday signal on the playback tape. Triangulation shows it originating in the southern Kurils, a good two hundred nautical miles distant."

"Did it originate from another ship?" asked Weapons Officer Bradley.

"Can't say for sure," returned Mac. "But since there's nothing out there but water, I'd say that's a given."

Kraft couldn't help but wonder if this call for help was coming from the same area where the squidder had gone down. The captain's brief troubled glance seemed to confirm this suspicion, and Kraft carefully listened as McShane spoke.

"I don't know about you guys, but I've seen enough from those Chink subs to know that they're goin' back to the barn. XO, I want you to personally instruct the OOD to change course for the southern Kurils and prepare for a possible search and rescue."

"You've got it, Skipper," the executive officer replied as he slid the VCR tape back into its jacket.

"And Dr. Kraft," continued McShane. "I think it's time for that department-head briefing we discussed earlier. It looks like in approximately nine more hours you just might be getting a chance to earn your keep around here."

Kraft wasn't really looking forward to the briefing. Still uncomfortable with the bizarre nature of his mission, he was surprised at how readily the dozen or so officers and chiefs who attended the briefing accepted it. He had expected to hear more jokes and outright skepticism. Instead the men listened to his every word like eager freshmen and only broke their intense silence when the photographs from the *Koji Maru* were passed around. Amazed and astounded by these shots, they pledged their every effort to ensure the success of Kraft's mission.

Afterward Chop congratulated Kraft on a job well done. The amiable supply officer was rapidly becoming a genuine friend, and Kraft accepted his advice to get some shut-eye, as they weren't expected at the search site until daybreak.

Feeling more at home now, Kraft returned to his bunk and decided on a shower before bed. Like an old veteran, he properly flushed the urinal and obeyed Chop's instructions in using the shower. First, he turned on the water and adjusted the temperature with his outstretched hand. Then, after engaging the water restricter that was set into the shower head, he climbed into the stainless-steel stall, disengaged the restricter, and soaked himself in a torrent of warm, soothing water. The precious fresh water was then turned off while he covered himself with soap, and turned on again for a brief rinse-off.

It was while he was using the squeegee to scrape the remaining water and soap from the stall's sides that he noticed the deck begin noticeably tilting. It took a massive effort on his part to keep his balance and remain standing. With a towel wrapped around his waist, he managed to maneuver himself out into the passageway.

Two of the boat's junior officers were engaged in a hushed conversation and didn't seem to be the least bit affected by the odd angle of the deck beneath them. Somehow he was able to pass them without falling over, and after returning their nods of greeting, he headed straight for his berthing space.

The *Chicago*'s keel evened out soon after he climbed up onto his mattress and crawled beneath the sheets, still clothed in nothing but a white, terrycloth towel. He pulled shut his drapes and didn't bother flicking on the overhead light. Someone was snoring nearby, and in the distance he could just hear the sounds of several sailors conversing. Normally a light sleeper, Kraft all but ignored these sounds, the stress of the past twenty-four hours having finally caught up with him.

His sleep was sound, though filled with dreams. The most intense of these conveyed him back to Key Biscayne. He was taking his usual morning bike ride to work when somehow he ended up deep in a mangrove swamp. He remembered the sickening feeling as his thin tires sank into the soft, white sand, and the fear he felt at the thought of falling over and reinjuring his hip. Exposed mangrove roots provided yet another obstacle, and when his brakes inexplicably failed, he knew he was in real trouble.

Then, in a heartbeat, he found himself in a warm, watery environment. His bicycle was gone, and he was swimming in the wide channel of water separating Key Biscayne from Virginia Key. The current was fierce, and no matter how hard he struggled to escape the powerful riptide, his stroke failed to free him. Ever fearful of smashing against the abutments of the causeway and then being washed out to sea, he cringed when his foot brushed up against the cool, leathery skin of a submerged sea creature. A black, triangular dorsal fin broke the water's surface only a few feet in front of him. Its upper portion was pure white, indicating that it was a dreaded white-tip shark. This man-eater began to circle him, and his only salvation was a silver dog whistle that materialized between his lips. He blew into the instrument, and the familiar leaping forms of two dolphins appeared on the horizon. Unfortunately they were swimming away from him, and no matter how hard he blew into the whistle, they failed to respond.

"Dolly, Matilda, come back here!" he desperately cried into the gathering wind.

Instinctively he looked to his left and viewed the white-tip headed straight for him, its massive jaws agape, displaying row upon row of glistening, razor-sharp teeth. It was only then that he finally snapped awake.

Slowly the terrifying vision of the attacking shark faded from his consciousness. With his heart still pounding in his chest, he searched the blackness to reorientate himself. A cool, air-conditioned breeze brushed up against his cheek. The comforting sounds of someone snoring could be heard close by, and in the distance he could just make out the voices of men conversing. The cramped, coffinlike outline of his bunk gradually took form, and he groped beneath his pillow for his digital wristwatch. A check of the time revealed it to be 6:37 A.M. Surprised that morning had arrived so swiftly, he pulled back the curtains, carefully scooted off the mattress, and dressed in his blue coveralls and Rockport walking shoes.

After a quick visit to the head he stopped off at the wardroom. It was vacant, and he helped himself to a freshly baked powdered sugar doughnut and a mug of strong black navy coffee. Thus fortified, he proceeded to the deck above to check out the sub's current position at the navigation plot.

He entered the control room by way of the forward hatch. Unlike the previous evening, the compartment was brightly lit. He noticed the ever-present seated helmsmen, then spotted both the captain and his XO draped over the viewing lenses of the boat's two periscopes.

"That appears to be the extent of the flotsam, Skipper," reported the XO, without turning from the eyepiece.

Quick to intercept Kraft was the boat's smiling supply officer. "Good morning, Doc. I was just about to go down and wake you. How'd you sleep?"

"Except for some wild dreams that I'd rather forget, just fine, Chop," Kraft answered. "Where are we?"

Chop responded while leading him over to the vacant fire-control console. "We got some unexpected help from the current and reached the search site a bit earlier than anticipated. Only moments ago our periscope scan spotted some floating debris topside. We still don't know its exact origin, and the jury's still out on whether or not we're gonna surface to have a closer look at it."

"Any luck on sonar?" Kraft asked hopefully.

Chop shrugged as if he didn't know. "Why don't we go see for ourselves, Doc?"

They entered the nearby sound shack and found Matt Cox and his three-man team settling in for the first watch of the day. They were in the middle of some sort of discussion, and Cox warmly smiled upon spotting the newcomers.

"'Morning, gentlemen," he greeted. "I was just tellin' my boys about Dr. Kraft's briefing last night and exactly what we're to be listening for."

Cox placed his hands on the broad shoulders of the fair-haired sailor seated at the middle console. "Seaman Algren here was just askin' how we're supposed to be able to hear this giant ray if it don't make any sounds of its own. Can you help me with the right answer, Doctor?"

"I'd be glad to," Kraft said. "Unlike a dolphin or whale, the ray family as a whole isn't known to produce any audible vocalizations, though we still don't know if this is true when applied to the particular unknown species that I'm here to track down. Because of this creature's great size, I'd say our best shot at picking it up will be listening to how the other creatures of the sea react to its presence. If I'm not mistaken, they'll quickly flee for safer waters with the ray's approach, and even the usually vociferous shrimp will be abruptly silenced when it's around."

"Back at sonar school, they called such detection methods the black-hole approach," interjected Cox. "Because of the ultra-quiet nature of the newer generation of Soviet submarines, they taught us to be aware of the lack of normal sea noise, which could very well indicate an alien intruder in our midst. If I'm not mistaken, our very own Specs here was the champion black-hole detector."

The bespectacled sailor seated at the far left console blushed shyly, and Cox reached up into a fist-sized hole that had been cut into the overhead ventilation shaft. He proceeded to pull out several aluminum cans of Dr. Pepper. After handing one to each of his men, he asked Kraft and Chop if either of them was interested in an "ice-cold frosty one."

Both declined the offer, and listened as Cox readdressed his team.

"This first Pepper of the day is on me. The next one you're gonna have to *earn.* So apply yourselves, gentlemen, and let's give the doctor here our best effort."

"Sonar, Conn," called an amplified voice from the intercom. "Prepare to surface."

Cox grabbed the microphone and responded to this directive. "Conn, sonar, prepare to surface, aye, Conn."

Chop glanced at Kraft and whispered, "Looks like things are about to get real interesting around here for you, Doc. Let's return to the control room and see what the captain's got planned for us."

This observation proved to be true as the *Chicago* angled up to the surface, and Kraft was invited to join the sub's CO on its sail. A bright orange, one-piece immersion suit was brought out for his use. The marine biologist slipped the garment over his coveralls and tightly bound the Velcro wrist and ankle straps to make sure it was waterproof. With a pair of binoculars draped around his neck, he waited beside the aft accessway as the sail's two hatches were popped open. There was a slight flutter of air pressure in his eardrums, followed by a cool draft of sweet, ocean-scented air.

"Doctor, shall we see what the morning's got in store for us?" asked the captain, who, dressed in a similar immersion suit, led the way up the sail's interior ladder.

The water-soaked rungs were slippery, and Kraft was extra careful to climb with caution. Halfway up the ladder, he passed a sailor perched on a narrow platform, his lips to a mounted sound-powered telephone. A thin slice of deep blue sky seemed to beckon enticingly from above, and Kraft continued his climb with renewed anticipation.

At the very top of the sail was a rectangular opening. As he passed the final rung Kraft gratefully accepted a helping hand from above. He stood erect and found himself beside the captain in a space that could barely fit the two of them. From this lofty vantage point, he was able to look out over the *Chicago*'s spherical bow and view the surrounding sea.

The sun had just broken the eastern horizon, and the glistening waters sparkled with a diamondlike radiance. For the most part, low-lying gray clouds covered the sky, though a sliver of powdery blue was occasionally glimpsed. Flat, calm conditions prevailed on the sea, but the keelless submarine still rocked to and fro, set in motion by an evenly spaced series of passing swells.

"This is some incredible view, Captain," Kraft remarked.

"You should be up here when *Chicago* is cutting through the water at flank speed," McShane offered, scanning the nearby ocean with his binoculars. "When we're really truckin', the sea bubbles over the bow in a perfect sphere, which continues all the way to the base of the sail and beyond."

At the moment the sub was moving at the barest of perceptible speeds. This left the portion of the upper deck visible forward of the sail completely free of water. A single hatch was recessed into the deck here, almost halfway to the bow, and Kraft watched as it popped open and several sailors emerged. Each wore an immersion suit and carried a long, telescoping boat hook.

"Clamp on those safety lines, sailors!" McShane ordered the threesome.

They responded by unwinding the coiled nylon line attached to their waists and clipping the free end into a recessed rail that extended the length of the deck. Secured now from accidentally falling overboard, they spread out to search the sea for floating debris. Several pieces of timber were spotted, along with an empty wooden crate, a bent aluminum spar, a crushed barrel with no label, and a good portion of badly frayed rope.

"Is that a partially submerged launch over there, off our port bow?" McShane pointed a finger toward the sea.

Kraft looked in this direction with his binoculars and spotted the dim outline of what appeared to be a small white boat, just visible beneath the sea's surface. "I believe it is, Captain," he replied, trying hard to contain his rising excitement.

"Helm," McShane ordered into the bridge speaker. "Come around easy to course three-three-zero."

The *Chicago* gradually turned to port, and the sunken vessel took on additional details. It was about ten feet long and looked to be an abandoned lifeboat.

"Do you see it, Chief?" Mac shouted to the leader of the deck crew. "It's just off our port bow."

The sailor signaled with a thumbs-up and, together with his two shipmates, hooked the sunken launch by its gunwales. Two of the boat hooks were needed to lift the sunken craft upward while the chief utilized his hook to fish out a single, orange kapok life preserver. All eyes were on the chief as he picked up the vest, carefully studied it, and conveyed his findings to his CO.

"It seems to be Chinese, Captain! It's covered with stenciled lettering, but all of it is written in chicken tracks."

"Send it belowdeck, Chief," Mac ordered. "Ensign Lee should be able to make some sense out of it."

While the life vest was carried down into the access trunk Mac again raised his binoculars. "My gut tells me something tragic took place in these waters recently, Doctor," he whispered. "And who knows—just maybe that devilfish of yours was responsible. So keep a sharp lookout, and perhaps it'll return to take on somebody more its size this time."

Down in the *Chicago*'s sonar compartment, Matt Cox took advantage of their current stationary position to take care of some badly needed maintenance and statistical work. Since the sub's towed array couldn't be utilized while the boat was surfaced, he put one of his technicians to work on the broken recorder. This left only two of the consoles manned, Seaman Algren on the broad-band processor and Specs on the narrow. Cox also took this period of relative quiet to update his long-ignored log, but was soon interrupted by Specs.

"New submerged contact, sir. Designate Sierra eleven, biological."

"Sierra eleven, biological it is," Cox repeated with little enthusiasm, a feeling that was echoed when he passed this information on to the Conn.

Never one to get excited over paperwork, Cox realized that he'd have to get his act together if he wanted to be promoted to a higher pay grade. During his last watch he failed to record a single transient contact, and hadn't even bothered to log his team in or out. Such sloppy documentation could land him in hot water with the XO. So he did his best to recreate the night's activities from memory.

Meanwhile Specs had his attention focused on a completely different matter. The new biological he had been tracking had gone unexpectedly silent. One moment it was there, as clear as could be—a hollow, intense clicking noise that appeared to be generated by thousands of passing sea creatures. And then, just when the racket reached its loudest point, there was an abrupt swing to utter quiet. A quick check of the other frequency ranges on which biologicals were known to emit produced similar results, and Specs couldn't help but remember the words of Dr. Kraft.

"Hey, Algren," Specs whispered to his shipmate at the adjoining console. "Could you take a listen at ten thousand hertz and tell me if you hear anything?"

Algren's failure to respond to this simple request caused Specs to take a closer look at his normally helpful associate. It was evident that Algren had his own concerns at the moment, for his attention was riveted on his glowing CRT screen.

"What's so interesting, Eric?" asked Specs, with a polite nudge of his elbow.

"I'm either goin' bonkers," replied his perplexed shipmate, "or someone back in engineering has got his stereo turned up way too loud. Because I can swear there's a violin playin' out there at fifty fathoms off our friggin' stern!"

When word arrived on the *Chicago*'s sail of the unusual happenings in sonar, Mac allowed his gut instinct to take over. Without moving his amplified line of sight off the water near their stern, he addressed Kraft, his voice grim.

"Doctor, if I were you, I'd get down below on the double and get those bullets of yours ready. I'll notify Chop to pull an M-16 out of the weapons locker, and then escort you up the forward access trunk. I say this, Doctor, because though it hasn't shown itself just yet, I sense that something's out there on the prowl, and it's headed this way—pronto."

Without demanding an explanation, Kraft ducked down to transit the sail's interior ladder. Barely conscious of his surroundings, he breathlessly climbed down the iron rungs. Ignoring the slight twinge of pain that coursed through his right hip as he hopped down onto the deck, he looked to the left and spotted Chop quickly approaching him from the control room.

"Follow me, Doc," Chop ordered as he led the way to the deck below.

Barely able to keep pace with the supply officer, Kraft was limping slightly by the time they reached the wardroom.

"Doc, get those bullets of yours and meet me around the corner in the passageway beside the officers' head. That's where the weapons locker is located."

Kraft nodded in acknowledgment and headed straight for his nearby berthing compartment. Oblivious to any noise he might make, he ripped open his bunk's curtain, flipped on the fluorescent light, and yanked up the mattress. His hands were shaking as he pulled out his locked briefcase, and it took two attempts to dial in the proper access sequence. It finally opened with a sharp click, and he grabbed the loaded ammo clip and rushed back for the corridor without bothering to stow away the rest of his gear.

He found Chop beside the open gun locker. A variety of weapons were stored here, including several combat shotguns, .45-caliber pistols, and M-16 rifles, one of which Chop was in the process of removing from the storage rack.

"Are you familiar with one of these babies, Doc?" he asked.

Kraft carefully grasped the black metallic weapon and expertly checked its empty chamber, rammed in his ammunition clip, and pulled back the bolt to chamber the first of twenty specially designed rounds. Only after engaging the safety did he respond to the supply officer's question.

"Me and the M-16 go way back, Chop. I'm the one who first developed this method of fish tagging. And though I'm far from being an expert marksman, I've successfully tagged my fair share of bluefin tuna, sailfish, and marlin."

A red-faced sailor rounded the hallway and excitedly addressed them. "Lieutenant Walden, the captain says it's urgent that you get the doctor topside on the double, sir!"

Chop slammed shut the weapons locker and briefly met Kraft's gaze. "Sounds like we've got some action up there, Doc. Are you ready to rock-and-roll?"

"Lead the way, Chop," said Kraft, wiping the gathering sweat from his forehead with the sleeve of his immersion suit.

The climb up the forward access trunk was a good deal shorter than that up the sail, and Kraft emerged onto the *Chicago*'s exterior deck barely winded. Gray skies and calm seas continued to prevail, and he was looking up to the towering sail when the captain's deep voice boomed out.

"Look over there, Doctor, twenty yards off our port beam!"

Kraft anxiously followed McShane's pointed finger out to sea and almost immediately spotted a large patch of surface turbulence. It appeared to be moving rapidly, and when it rounded their stern, the startled marine biologist let loose a gasp composed equally of fear and wonderment. There was absolutely no doubt in his mind that the creature responsible for this turbulent wake was of incredible size, which only added to his fear of its apparently evil intentions.

"It's been circling us like that for a good couple of minutes now. I think it's trying to decide whether or not to take us on!"

As Chop emerged from the access trunk carrying the M16, he couldn't help but notice the marine biologist's startled gaze. Following Kraft's line of sight out to sea, he, too, spotted the bubbling white turbulence that was rounding their bow.

"Good Lord!" he exclaimed. "Will you just look at the size of that mother! Hang loose, Doc, while I hook up your safety line so you can get down to business."

Kraft accepted the rifle, and as Chop prepared to hook up a line to his immersion suit's waist clamp, the captain once more cried out. "It's changing course and looks to be headed our way! Doctor, plug that damn thing and let's get the hell out of here!"

Kraft watched the turbulence turn broadly until it was almost directly amidships. He was startled when Chop, who watched beside him, suddenly dropped the safety line without completing the final hookup and shouted, "Doc, it looks like it intends to ram us!"

Trying his best to retain his cool, Kraft took several deep, calming breaths before raising the rifle's laminated stock to his cheek. With trembling hands, he struggled to take aim at the fan-shaped swath of agitated seawater that seemed to be headed straight at him, no fewer than twenty yards away.

"Doctor!" the captain shouted from above. "I can see the damn thing. It's a ray all right. But my God, it's almost half as big as the *Chicago*! Shoot that implant of yours this instant and then clear the deck. I'm taking us down!"

Kraft clearly heard this frantic order, yet could not immediately obey it, his aim being obstructed by the stinging rivulet of sweat that poured off his forehead. Forced to lower the rifle barrel momentarily and wipe his forehead with the back of his hand, he heard the captain shout once more, "Damn it, Doctor, clear the deck! We're goin' under."

A warning klaxon began blaring, and Kraft felt a hand tug at his side. "Come on, Doc," Chop implored. "You'll just have to get that sucker the next time."

Impervious to this plea, Kraft reaimed the rifle. "Just give me a second, Chop," he insisted. "I've waited an entire lifetime to see something like this."

The frothing turbulence seemed to fill the entire sea before him as Kraft snapped off the rifle's safety and centered his aim. Just as he squeezed off the first shot the deck rocked beneath him, sending his round astray. He cursed and, without a second thought, pumped yet another round into the chamber.

"For Christ's sake!" shouted Chop. "It's just not worth it, Doc. The captain's pulled the plug, and we're goin' under, no matter how important this damn creature is to you."

In response, Kraft merely raised the rifle in preparation for another shot. Chop had reached the end of his patience and reached out to pull Kraft into the nearby access trunk. Not to be denied, Kraft yanked himself free from Chop's grasp, and in the process accidentally knocked the supply officer in the forehead with the M-16's stock. Temporarily stunned by the blow, the enraged Chop blew up.

"That does it, Doc. As of this moment you're on your own, my friend."

Chop turned for the access trunk, and with the oncoming water already lapping at the raised coaming, he climbed inside and sealed the hatch above him. As the last member of the deck crew still topside, Kraft ignored the cool seawater gathering at his feet. Certain that the submarine would return for him once his mission was accomplished, he knew that only one thing mattered now—this was scientific history in the making, and nothing would keep him from firing the implant that would track this remarkable beast wherever it roamed.

Newfound confidence guided his aim, and with his target only ten yards distant, he peppered it with three evenly spaced shots. Certain that one of these rounds had hit its mark, he watched with relieved eyes as the turbulence suddenly veered sharply to the left. Just as he realized that the creature wouldn't strike them after all, the deck dipped beneath the waterline with an unceremonious downward lurch.

The true consequences of Kraft's rash behavior became evident when he found himself alone in the water. Thankful for the calm state of the sea, he rolled over on his back and allowed the buoyant immersion suit to do all the work of keeping him afloat.

Because of the low water temperature, he supposed

that his greatest threat was hypothermia. Cold seawater was already seeping into his suit's loose seams, and he gave himself a quarter of an hour of survival time at best. Surely the *Chicago* would return by then, he thought, though given his foolish behavior, he wouldn't blame them if they abandoned him.

Kraft knew that this wasn't the first time that his own bullheadedness had got him into trouble. In fact, just the other day he had entertained similar thoughts while floating in the waters of the institute's shark channel. He knew that the risks were great at that time and that he could easily have found a substitute. But because of his highly competitive nature and his desire to see a job through to the very end, he had turned a deaf ear to the pleas of his associates. Whether dedication or sheer stubbornness, this trait could very well be responsible for ending his life.

He surely couldn't blame his current predicament on the *Chicago*'s captain. The senior naval officer was only acting out of prudence in order to escape an almost certain collision. And poor Chop couldn't be held accountable either, for he had wanted only to save Kraft's life.

As an icy tendril of water crept down his back, Kraft thought how ironic it was that only this past winter he had sworn to himself that he'd ease up and not take life so seriously. He had made this promise from a hospital bed, shortly after his bicycle accident. Having been blessed with excellent health, not even having broken a bone, Kraft realized after his accident that he wasn't immortal after all. Yet it had only taken him nine months to revert to his old ways. And now it might well be too late to try to change.

Silently cursing his obstinacy, Kraft desperately searched the surrounding sea for any sign of the *Chicago*'s return. The pancake-flat sea allowed for excellent visibility, and he followed a set of rippling swells as they arrived from the north. Since he had absolutely nowhere to swim to and was completely at the mercy of the sea, he allowed his thoughts momentarily to drift back to the dream he had had earlier that morning. Could that frightening vision have been an omen of his current dilemma? It certainly looked that way, he thought as he scanned the sea, looking for a dreaded white-tipped dorsal fin.

An inexplicable feeling that he was being watched caused him to inspect that portion of the ocean directly behind him. Awkwardly turning himself around, sure enough, he spotted the familiar turbulence headed straight for him, less than twenty yards away. He hoped it was the *Chicago* returning to save him, but dismissed the thought as ridiculous as soon as it occurred to him. No doubt about it—the massive, fan-shaped disturbance took on a particularly malevolent character when viewed from his current lonely vantage point in the middle of the ocean.

To be eaten alive by another living creature is one of every man's worst fears. Though rays aren't avid flesh-eaters, a species this size could easily swallow him in a single bite. As he faced the monstrous tidal wave head-on this was the fate he prepared himself for.

BOOK II

REVELATION

*It's time for a warrior society
to rise up out of the earth and
throw itself in front of the juggernaut
of destruction, to be antibodies against the human
pox that's ravaging
this precious, beautiful planet!*
—DAVE FOREMAN, EARTH FIRST! COFOUNDER

11

The stateroom was pitch-dark, the only sound a muted pulsating hum, reminiscent of the song of the womb. Jean-Louis Moreau lay still on his cot, adrift in the twilight state between sleep and waking. As he stared out into the darkness elements of his recurring dream slowly faded from his mind only to be replaced by a tortured soundtrack that never seemed to leave him. Not even the melting strains of a violin concert could drown out the tortured cries that haunted him night and day.

Two decades had passed since that fated day aboard the *Agosta*. The violent deaths of the two blue whales had been seared into his soul and changed the course of his life.

It had started out innocently enough. Fresh out of the naval academy, with the ink on his commission papers barely dry, Moreau sat at the *Agosta*'s sonar console, enchanted by the gay singing of the boisterous blues. With Michel Baptiste's invaluable assistance, a periscope sighting confirmed the presence of a pair of whales. Moreau was delighted to learn that the pair they had chanced upon was a mother and her offspring.

Moreau would take to his grave the distinctive hiss of the vessel responsible for their slaughter. In retrospect it seemed that the whaling ship's arrival signaled not only the end of the two blues but of his innocence as well.

Could he ever count the number of nights when disturbing memories of this incident kept him from sleep? And the nightmares, visions of harpoons striking flesh and bloodred seas, filled with anguished whale cries—could he ever exorcise them from his mind? In a way, it seemed as if the two blues were still alive inside of him, their restless spirits demanding justice, an end to the needless slaughter that was rapidly leading their species to the brink of extinction.

Well aware of the great responsibility that fate had passed down to him, Moreau stirred when a muffled knock sounded on his closed door, calling out in a deep, gravelly voice, "*Entrez.*"

A shaft of light split the blackness, and the silhouette of a tall, thin figure with long flowing hair appeared, accompanied by a Slavic-accented, female voice. "Commandant, I'm sorry to bother you, but while evading the Los Angeles–class submarine, a single American was thrown overboard. Per your standing directive, he's been pulled aboard, sedated, and placed in quarantine."

"*Très bien, mon amie,*" said Moreau matter-of-factly. "And the American warship?"

"It was last monitored running for the cover of the thermocline," she answered.

"Inform Monsieur Godavari to engage hydrodrive on course one-five-zero, and let's be gone from these waters," Moreau ordered. "We've more than proven our ability to disrupt the much-vaunted SOSUS network, and our work here is finished."

"As you wish, Commandant." The woman turned and left, quietly pulling shut the door behind her.

Alone in the darkness once more, Moreau sat up stiffly and reached over to switch on an overhead lamp. A halogen bulb illuminated the compact, luxuriously appointed confines of his private quarters. Thick, royal-blue carpeting with a border of golden anchors lined the floor, walls, and ceiling. Such a soundproof covering guaranteed his privacy and gave his cabin a soft, comfortable feel.

He yawned, and his weary eyes passed over the many framed photographs lining the bulkhead beside him. Most of these were of the different French warships he had served on. They included a variety of attack and strategic-missile submarines, a helicopter carrier, an oceanographic research vessel, and a sub tender. Also on the wall was his academy diploma and various official citations and awards.

Stretching his thin, five-foot, eight-inch frame, Moreau stood to dress himself in a black one-piece jumpsuit and a pair of black running shoes. Conspicuously absent from this uniform were military patches or rank insignias.

As he crossed over to the port bulkhead to which his desk was securely mounted, the padded flooring beneath him momentarily shuddered. He had to reach out for the edge of his desk to balance himself when the deck below tilted sharply to the right. There was a slight sensation of sudden speed, and he was able to let go of his handhold only after the angle of the deck gradually stabilized.

Without bothering to seat himself, he reached out for the nearby intercom handset and spoke crisply into its transmitter. "Number Two, I understand that *Ecowar* has an additional passenger. When he comes to, I'm certain his curiosity will be fully aroused. We've previously talked about this possibility, and now that it's happened, we'll just have to make the best of it. Have Annie ease his anxieties with a cup of bostrichia tea, and we'll deal with him later. Right now I need you to meet me in control."

Moreau listened to the briefest of replies before hanging up the handset and continuing on to the adjoining Pullman-style washbasin. A bracing splash of cool water awakened him completely, and he looked out at the familiar reflection that stared back at him from the mirror.

Moreau's smooth, hairless scalp—he was bald by the age of thirty—clean-shaven jaw, and wrinkle-free skin made it almost impossible to determine his age. Yet evidence of the passing years could clearly be inferred from a comparison of the current Moreau with the color photograph that hung beside the mirror. Taken over a decade ago, it showed a smiling, carefree, crew-cut naval officer, smartly dressed in the blue uniform of the Marine Nationale. Exuding youthful confidence, Moreau stood beside his wife, Suzanne, and his one-year-old daughter, Anne-Marie.

The tropical setting of the photograph was Tahiti, where Moreau had been stationed. His young family had just arrived from Paris. With her short dark hair and big brown eyes, his wife of two years radiated a warm, natural beauty. Little Anne-Marie was already favoring her mother, and the photo had caught her smiling broadly, a smile that promised to break many a young man's heart. Unfortunately, as it turned out, the only heart she ever broke was her father's. Both Anne-Marie and her mother were abruptly taken from him less than a year later.

From that dark day onward, a carefree smile never broke his lips. His family's premature death stripped him of any chance of tasting life's true sweetness, leaving him too cold, hollow, and numb to ever again experience love.

Moreau had placed the photo so he would never be able to start a new day without viewing it, without seeing this continual reminder that nothing in life was permanent. Several years earlier the two blue whales had taught him this painful lesson. It took the loss of his own family for the message to sink in completely. Now it was through daily mortification that their sacrifice was remembered.

A lonely, high-pitched, mournful cry sounded deep in Moreau's cold soul as he turned to exit his stateroom. Outside in the carpeted hallway, Wagner's overture to *Tannhäuser* softly emanated from the intercom. This soulful piece was a fitting accompaniment to his somber mood.

Thoughts of his immediate duty replaced personal concerns as he made his way forward. The same blue carpet he had in his stateroom completely encased the corridor, which was wide enough for two people to pass through shoulder to shoulder. Large posters of an assortment of sea creatures covered the walls; he passed a leaping orca, a pod of frolicking spinner dolphins, and a sounding humpback, its fluke raised. Moreau had taken this shot himself during a cruise to Antarctica. Not noticing the photos, Moreau continued to the end of the hall, where an open hatch conveyed him directly into the control room.

The dimly lit space was dominated by a huge, wraparound display screen. Set before it were five high-backed leather chairs that were anchored directly into the carpeted deck. Four of these seats were currently occupied, and Moreau headed for the vacant center position.

"What's our status, Number Two?" he asked as he seated himself and buckled his shoulder harness.

This question was addressed to the powerfully built man who sat on Moreau's right. Ezra Melindi, a forty-seven-year-old Kenyan who sported a short, salt-and-pepper flattop, regarded the miniature computer keypad built into the right-hand portion of his chair's armrest, holding back his response until the backlit screen began filling with a flashing series of coded data.

"We're currently cruising at a depth of 810 feet on course one-five-zero," he answered, the deep silken tone of his voice inspiring instant trust. "Hydrodrive has been engaged, and our forward velocity is seventy-six knots. Fuel-cell capacity is ninety-seven percent, and all systems are operational except for our defensive shield."

Moreau seemed to flinch as he heard this news, and he quickly addressed the wiry, brown-skinned individual seated at the far left position. "Monsieur Godavari, what's the holdup on those shield repairs?"

Raghib Godavari spoke with a clipped British accent, his hands never leaving the pair of joysticks built into each of his chair's armrests. "*Mon commandant,* you can see for yourself the results of our latest diagnostic."

A quick manipulation of Godavari's left joystick caused a detailed schematic drawing of their current means of transport to fill the screen. Simply labeled ECOWAR, the drawing showed a vessel shaped much like a manta ray, complete with two hornlike protrusions on its tapered bow. Despite its organic-looking appearance, one merely had to view the complex interior of the futuristic platform to see that it wasn't a living creature.

More complex than the space shuttle, *Ecowar*'s primary subsystems were represented on the schematic as a series of elongated compartments, which were accessed by a central bisecting corridor. The compartment marked ENGINE ROOM was the largest single space, occupying the entire stern half. It was here that an electronic cursor began blinking.

Godavari readdressed his left joystick and the transparent drawing of *Ecowar* was replaced by a detailed schematic of a single circuit. Appearing like a complex maze of twisting streets, the circuit was further amplified to show a series of individual microchips that flashed on the screen with lightning-quick rapidity.

"We've isolated the problem in the laser's pulsed focusing mechanism, sir," Godavari continued. "Since the entire system had to be stripped apart by hand to replace the malfunctioning component, all other essential maintenance had to be placed on temporary hold."

"As it should have been," Moreau replied bitterly. "Our defensive shield has been down for over three hours now. Such a dangerous delay is inexcusable!"

Godavari's efficient tone did not fluctuate. "I understand, Commandant. Chief Yushiro is personally handling the repairs, and hopes to have our defenses at one-hundred-percent capability within the hour."

Moreau shook his head disgustedly and shifted his gaze to the exotic-looking redheaded woman seated at the far right-hand position. It was she who, only minutes ago, had stopped at his stateroom to inform him of the American submarine's status. At present, Ivana Borisov was fulfilling her primary duties as *Ecowar*'s senior navigator.

"Ms. Borisov, what kind of bathymetrics do we have beneath us?" Moreau questioned.

The Odessa native fed numbers into her keypad, and the central portion of the display screen filled with a 3-D, holographic view of the surrounding seabed. An assortment of data graced the right-hand portion of the screen, prompting the navigator to observe in heavily accented English. "We've just passed over the Honshu Seamount, sir. The Kuril Trench lies behind us, with our latest sounding at 5,653 meters."

"Set a course for Moruroa in the Austral Seamount chain," ordered Moreau. "And determine an ETA at current speed."

Borisov's hand attacked her keypad, and a large-scale bathymetric chart of the Pacific Ocean was projected onto the screen. A blue star began flashing in the lower right-hand corner of the chart while a diagonal yellow line extended all the way across the Pacific to their current position, off the coast of northern Japan.

"Our estimated time of arrival at Moruroa is in seventy-six hours," Borisov stated.

Ezra Melindi shook his head in wonder. "A little over three days and nights to cross the entire length of the Pacific, *Ecowar*'s capabilities continue to amaze me."

"That's nothing, Number Two," interjected Moreau. "Once the new engine inlet ionizer is completed and our superconductors are upgraded, *Ecowar* will be able to travel at twice its current speed."

Studying the display screen to trace their computerized route, he added, "Just think, that would give us another day and a half to patrol the Central Pacific Basin. What's the latest test update from the DGSE, Karl Ivar?"

Blond-haired Karl Ivar Bjornsen, a communications specialist from Haugesund, Norway, was the youngest member of the *Ecowar*'s crew and one of its most personable. "It appears that we're going to have this extra time after all," he announced as he pushed aside his lightweight headphones. "The directorate's latest satellite communiqué reports yet another delay due to a mechanical problem in the detonator. The countdown has been put on hold for another ninety-six hours."

Moreau cracked the barest of smiles. "So the infamous Force de Frappe continues to have its troubles. Little do they realize that their worst problem has yet to come."

A loud electronic chime sounded, and the lower left portion of the screen filled with the face and upper torso of an attractive young Australian woman with curly brown hair, a warm smile, and big, green eyes. Annie Sawyer served several functions aboard *Ecowar*. A registered nurse, she served as the vessel's physician. Of equal importance was her culinary skill in the galley, and her vivacity and enthusiasm had earned her the unofficial title of crew morale officer. Neither of these qualities were in evidence at the moment as she spoke in an unusually serious tone.

"Sir, I'm afraid I'm gonna need a hand in sick bay. The Yank's come to, and he's demandin' to see the officer in charge."

"Did you give him the bostrichia tea, Annie?" asked Melindi.

"That I did, sir," she replied. "But when I refrained from answerin' him, he flung the mug to the floor and continued repeatin' his demands."

Moreau had no time for secondhand information. "We're on our way, Ms. Sawyer," he gruffly stated.

Annie nodded, and as the video link faded Moreau unbuckled his harness, stood, and addressed his second in command. "Number Two, will you join me in the infirmary?"

"Commandant," said Bjornsen. "What will you tell the American?"

"What else but the truth," retorted Moreau. "We have nothing to hide aboard *Ecowar*. So you have nothing to fear from this stranger, Karl Ivar. And that goes for the rest of you also. As a fellow submariner, the American will soon enough see things our way."

"And if he doesn't?" Ivana Borisov wanted to know.

Moreau stared at the redheaded navigator. "In that unlikely event, contingency plans exist. So relax, each and every one of you, and perhaps we'll soon have a new comrade to welcome into our midst."

Peter Kraft was no stranger to fear. His profession took him on many an expedition to the open seas, where he swam with such dangerous sea creatures as sharks, barracudas, and poisonous sea snakes. His recent bike accident had subjected him to a different type of fear— the fear of suddenly finding yourself alone in a hospital facing an emergency operation that could leave you permanently crippled. Yet never in his forty-three years had he experienced anything like the blind terror that had seized him while he faced the giant manta ray.

He supposed that it was the unprecedented size of this monstrous beast that led to his panic—that and the helplessness of his situation. Whatever the explanation, the last thing he remembered was being adrift in the Pacific watching the ray's approach. He could practically reach out and touch the frothing line of fan-shaped turbulence, and was counting off his few remaining moments of life when he lost consciousness.

He had no idea how long he remained unconscious, could only remember slowly awakening from a deep, trancelike sleep that reminded him of what he had felt on emerging from surgery. He found himself alone in a pitch-black room, stretched out on a full-sized bed that was much more comfortable than his berth on the *Chicago,* with lush Wagnerian opera music softly playing in the background. Hearing this music underscored the utter unreality of his environment, and for a frightening, confused moment he wondered if he was indeed dead, and if this lightless but strangely comfortable world he found himself in were some kind of purgatory.

His speculations were temporarily interrupted by another session of deep, dreamless sleep. For all he knew, he remained in this comatose state for days. When he finally awoke, he was staring into the angelic face of a remarkably beautiful young woman. Again he briefly wondered if he had died and was awakening into some kind of afterlife, only to have his illusion abruptly shattered when the curly-haired stranger smiled and said, "Hello, Yank. Care for a cup o' tea, would ya?"

Kraft lay there speechless. This angel, if angel she was, had a strong Australian accent. Slowly his eyes scanned the now dimly lit compartment, which reminded him of a normal hospital room, except for the absence of windows and the deep blue carpet that lined not only the floor, but the walls and ceiling as well.

The confusing veil that had clouded his thoughts gradually lifted, and he anxiously questioned his green-eyed companion. "Is this a hospital ship?" he breathlessly asked. "Who pulled me from the sea?"

His companion's only response was a cryptic smile and an offer of some more tea. Not about to let her go without getting more solid details, he pressed her to reveal what had happened to him. Once more she deflected his questions, refusing to answer him directly, and Kraft's frustrations intensified. His anger erupted after he demanded to see her superior and she had the gall to respond with yet another offer of tea. Enraged, he angrily flung the teacup to the floor. In reply, she smartly turned on her heel and left the room, locking the door behind her.

Finding himself alone again, Kraft took the opportunity to explore his carpet-lined cell. About the size of a normal bedroom, it had three Murphy-type cots built into the walls in addition to the bed that he had been laid out on. A check of the only cabinet in evidence revealed an assortment of first-aid supplies including Band-Aids, gauze, disinfectant, a digital thermometer, a stethescope, and a blood-pressure monitor. Since the supplies were labeled in French, he assumed that this was the nationality of the vessel's owners.

It was apparent that they were still at sea as periodically he felt the deck roll slightly. Except for the music, which continued to emanate from the intercom speakers, little else but a barely audible humming could be heard.

An adjoining closet turned out to be a small bathroom. A new toothbrush and unmarked tube of paste lay in the medicine cabinet, as well as an electric razor and a tin of waxed dental floss. As Kraft glanced into the small mirror above the sink, he realized that he was still wearing his blue submariner coveralls. At the sight, a wave of disturbing new thoughts washed over him.

Surely the *Chicago* had returned to the surface to look for him. Since the submarine was bound to spot any newly arrived surface vessels in the area, the *Chicago*'s crew had to know of his current location. Yet if that was the case, why didn't they transfer him back to the submarine so that he could get on with his mission? Except for a certain mental cloudiness, his general health seemed to be okay. And even if this mysterious vessel, with its carpeted walls and musical ambience, could provide better medical facilities than the *Chicago*, why hold him in a room like a prisoner?

A renewed urge to get some answers to these questions led him back to the room's only door. When a quick check of the knob revealed it to be locked, he began pounding on the heavily carpeted door frame in a desperate effort to summon some assistance.

When his effort failed to produce results, Kraft searched the room for an alternative escape route. Beside the doorway leading to the bathroom, a single vent was built into the wall. Though he would need a boost to reach it, the vent looked just wide enough for him to squeeze through. Hoping to remove the grille and follow the ventilation shaft to freedom, he decided to roll up a mattress and use it as a makeshift stepladder. As it turned out, the folded mattress provided him just enough additional height to reach the grille. Though his fingers alone were unable to loosen it, by slipping a wooden tongue depressor under the vent's metal frame, he was at last able to edge it away from the wall. Proud of his ingenuity, Kraft was removing the rest of the grille when the door to his room suddenly snapped open.

From his elevated vantage point, he looked somewhat abashed as a powerfully built black man in a dark, single-piece jumpsuit entered. As the latter spotted Kraft the slightest of grins turned the corners of his wide mouth. Following the man into the room was the curly-haired Australian who had initially greeted him and a distinguished, bald-headed gentleman, who quickly assessed the circumstances Kraft was in and smiled as he realized how Kraft had arrived in them.

"Don't bother, *mon ami*. It's sealed from the other side. Besides, is this any way to respond to our hospitality?"

"Hospitality?" Kraft was dumbfounded. "I'm thankful to have been pulled out of the sea. But why lock me in this room and fail to answer my questions? And more to the point, who the hell are you, and what kind of vessel is this?"

The bald-headed man graciously bowed and introduced himself. "Jean-Louis Moreau at your service, sir. Welcome aboard my submarine, the *Ecowar*. This is my second in command, Ezra Melindi. And I believe you've already had the pleasure of meeting our esteemed nurse, Annie Sawyer. Now please come down off that mattress before you fall and hurt yourself."

True concern was audible in this request, and Kraft felt ashamed for his belligerence. Deciding to give his hosts a proper chance to display their intentions, he pushed the grille back in place, climbed off his perch, and said, "I'm Dr. Peter Kraft."

The mere mention of this name caused Jean Moreau's face to light up. "The marine mammal expert?"

"That's me." Kraft was genuinely surprised to be so readily recognized here.

"I'm most pleased to finally meet you, Doctor," Moreau said sincerely. "We have all three of your superbly written textbooks in our library, and a complete collection of your research papers. Your treatise on cetacean intelligence is a masterpiece."

"When I was a marine-biology student in Kenya, I came across your research, Dr. Kraft." Now it was Ezra Melindi who spoke, his voice filled with admiration. "I read your book on interspecies communication while participating in my first dolphin autopsy. When we cut into the animal's head, I saw for myself its incredible mass of neocortal matter, and knew in an instant that its intelligence was far greater than our own."

"I'm most flattered that you know of my work," Kraft replied a bit hesitantly. "But I still have no idea precisely where I am and how I got here."

"Doctor, you can rest assured that all of your questions will be answered in due course," returned Moreau. "But right now I insist that you join me in some tea while we get better acquainted."

Moreau looked at Annie and nodded. Taking this as her cue to excuse herself, Annie Sawyer left the compartment for the galley, leaving Kraft alone with the two senior officers.

"You say this vessel is a submarine," Kraft said while surveying the richly carpeted room as if seeing it for the very first time. "It's certainly better decorated than the sub I just came from."

Moreau grinned before answering. "*Ecowar*'s interior design is only one of many major differences between this vessel and the rather crude warship to which you were assigned. Which brings me to a question of my own. What is a civilian like yourself doing aboard a Los Angeles–class attack sub?"

Kraft answered as honestly as he could. "I guess you could say that it was fishery research that brought me there."

"Fishery research?" Moreau retorted. "I thought such work was done under the auspices of the American Coast Guard. Surely this service doesn't have a nuclear attack sub at its disposal."

"You'll have to ask the bigwigs back in Washington to answer that, my friend," said Kraft. "All I know is that the navy asked for my help, and here I am. Speaking of the devil, I sure hope the crew of the USS *Chicago* knows that I'm safe."

Ignoring this concern, Moreau delicately probed in a direction of his own choosing. "May I ask what kind of fishery research it was that brought you to the North Pacific, Doctor?"

"I don't know if you saw it when you pulled me from the sea, but I'm on the trail of a giant manta ray," Kraft revealed.

"*Mon Dieu*, a giant manta ray, you say?" Moreau wore his best poker face.

"Then you didn't see it," Kraft said dejectedly. "I don't know how you managed to miss it, because it was out there in the water with me shortly before you apparently arrived to pick me up. Surely you crossed paths with the *Chicago*."

"Now the *Chicago* is a different story, *mon ami*," Moreau muttered. "But I want to know more about this giant manta ray of yours. You say you saw this creature with your own eyes? How big is it and why is the U.S. Navy so interested in this beast?"

Before Kraft could answer, Annie Sawyer returned pushing a silver tea cart. The odor of freshly cooked seafood filled the room. Like a true gourmet Moreau appreciatively sniffed the air and redirected the conversation to more mundane matters.

"Ah, what an enticing aroma, my dear," he observed. "What have you brought us?"

Annie lifted the silver cover of a large chafing dish, and a cloud of steam wafted upward, revealing an appetizing assortment of freshly cooked hors d'oeuvres. "I managed to throw together some pastry puffs stuffed with sea scallops, shrimp, and crab meat," she announced. "There's also a fresh potful of tea."

Kraft admired the delectable spread and watched as Melindi helped Sawyer pour the tea into delicate bone-china cups, with gold-encrusted starfish encircling the rims. Matching plates were filled with pastries and passed around.

"These are absolutely delicious, my dear." Moreau licked his lips. "Your talents were certainly wasted in Perth."

"Thank you, sir," Annie humbly replied.

Though food was far from his mind, Kraft couldn't resist sampling a small bite of pastry. He liked what he tasted, and readily devoured the rest of it.

"My, these are tasty," he admitted between bites.

"Now try Annie's tea, Doctor," Ezra Melindi suggested. "It's her own blend."

Kraft lifted up his cup, which was filled with a steaming, light gold liquid. Before taking a sip, he sniffed it curiously. The delicate scent of fresh herbs met his nostrils.

"Be forwarned, *mon ami*," Moreau said. "That tea is brewed from the sea algae bostrichia. It has a powerful tranquilizing effect."

Not certain if the Frenchman was pulling his leg or not, Kraft took a tentative sip of the tea. It had a light, delicate flavor, not at all unpleasant.

"Not bad for sea algae," he said, before consuming

another pastry and washing it down with the rest of his tea.

While the Australian nurse/cook attentively refilled his cup Moreau returned to the subject they were previously discussing. "Doctor, I believe that you were about to tell us all about that monster manta ray of yours."

The food and drink did much to relax Kraft, and he readily replied. "I first read about this creature several weeks ago in the Miami newspapers. Its existence was all rumor at that time, mere isolated sightings by various Japanese fishing vessels. To tell you the truth, I didn't give the reports much credence. Then the U.S. Navy approached me with actual photographs of the ray, taken by the captain of a squidder whose boat was sunk by the beast in these very waters."

"Hold on a moment, Doctor," Moreau interrupted. "You're telling me that the U.S. Navy has pictures of this creature sinking a surface vessel?"

Kraft nodded and continued. "Like yourself, I was skeptical, even after personally viewing the photos. Yet when the navy offered to fly me to Hokkaidō and give me the services of one of its attack subs, I knew at least someone in Washington was taking the reports most seriously."

"What did the navy want you to do once this creature was located?" asked Melindi. "Kill it with a torpedo?"

"If that had been the case, I would have never agreed to help hunt it down," Kraft admitted. "My instructions were simply to locate the ray and tag it with a homing implant. I've used such methods before to track migrating pelagic fish in the Gulf Stream. Since the ray had already been responsible for the sinking of at least one ship, the navy rightfully wished to be able to track it down should it again become a hazard to shipping."

"You never did say how you managed to locate the creature, and how you ended up stranded in the water?" Moreau asked.

Kraft's mouth was unusually dry, and he consumed

another cup of tea before responding. "I can't really say what tipped off the *Chicago* to the ray's presence. It was an SOS that initially drew us to the spot where the encounter took place. We were recovering various surface debris when I was ordered down below to ready my gear. Call it a hunch on the captain's part, or perhaps he had some kind of warning from sonar. All I can say is the next thing I knew when I returned topside was that the ray was out there, actually circling us. It was real weird, almost like the beast was trying to decide whether or not to take us on. When it abruptly turned toward us, the captain ordered the *Chicago* to descend. Like the stubborn fool that I am, I ignored him. The next thing I knew I was in the water, with the ray headed straight for me."

"*Mon Dieu!*" exclaimed Moreau, clearly impressed by Kraft's story. "How did you escape?"

Kraft's face expressed pure bewilderment. "That's the funny part, because I can't really tell you what happened next. All I can say for certain is that the next thing I remember is waking up in this very room."

Moreau traded a guarded glance with his second in command while Annie Sawyer refilled Kraft's cup and spoke with genuine warmth and sympathy. "No wonder you threw that fit earlier, Doctor. I didn't realize what a traumatic experience you had undergone. I should have been more understandin'."

Kraft was getting to like the attractive Australian, and he spoke to her softly. "It's not your fault, Ms. Sawyer. I'm the one who should have been better behaved. After all, you folks saved my life out there."

"Hey, what's with this 'Ms. Sawyer' nonsense?" she snapped. "The name's simply Annie to you."

Though Kraft would have liked to continue bantering with her, he directed his next question to Jean Moreau. "You never did explain if the *Chicago* has been notified that I'm safe and sound. I still don't understand how they could have possibly missed seeing you topside. I just know that they'll continue searching for me until they're informed otherwise."

"As you may very well know, communications among embarked submarines is difficult at best," Moreau explained cryptically. "To the best of our knowledge, the crew of the USS *Chicago* doesn't know of your presence here aboard the *Ecowar*. But rest easy, Doctor. Your navy will be notified of this fact during our next communications broadcast."

The deck momentarily shuddered, causing the tea cart to rattle noisily. Kraft watched as Annie Sawyer reached out to steady it, then he reexamined the room with wondrous eyes.

"I still find it hard to believe that these rather luxurious confines belong to a submarine. Are we currently submerged?" he asked.

"That we are, Doctor," answered Melindi.

"I gather that this isn't a military vessel."

This time it was Moreau who replied. "Your conclusion is a correct one, *mon ami. Ecowar* was primarily designed for deep-sea research."

"The name you picked is certainly intriguing," Kraft observed. "What flag do you sail under, and where's your home port?"

Again it was Moreau who responded. "*Ecowar* is sponsored by a private foundation, whose interests transcend national borders and encompass the entire planet. We have several home ports to choose from, one of which is located in the South Pacific, where we're currently headed."

"I thought I had a pretty good idea of the number of private submarines available for ocean research," Kraft said. "Why haven't I heard of *Ecowar*?"

"For various security reasons, it's been decided to keep *Ecowar*'s existence a secret until its current sea trials have been completed," Moreau explained. "Only then will a suitable press release be circulated, describing the ship in detail and announcing its mission."

"I'd sure like to have a look around," Kraft admitted, after trying his best to stifle a yawn.

"It would be my honor to personally give you a complete tour, Doctor." Moreau watched his guest yawn. "But before we do so, why don't you remain here and get some rest. You obviously need it. After a couple of hours of sound sleep, you'll be refreshed and alert, and all the better prepared to appreciate this remarkable vessel."

Not realizing until then the extent of his exhaustion, Kraft suddenly felt drained and weak. His limbs were leaden, and it took a maximum effort just to keep his eyelids open.

"I guess I could use a couple of hours of shut-eye," he mumbled, yawning again.

Ezra Melindi was quickly at his side and guided Kraft over to the nearby cot. Less than a minute later he was laid out on his back, sound asleep.

"I did warn you about that tea, Doctor," whispered Moreau, who caught the glances of his two shipmates and beckoned toward the doorway. "Come on, *mes amis*," he quietly added. "It's time for us to get back to work."

12

Dusk fell swiftly in the North Pacific. This was especially apparent on the sail of the USS *Chicago*, where the coming of night signaled the crew's despair of ever finding Dr. Peter Kraft alive. Mac McShane and his supply officer stood on the very top portion of the conning tower, directly forward of the dual raised periscopes. A removable, tubular steel frame encircled them, and an American flag fluttered from this sturdy structure in the stiffening wind. Oblivious to the gathering twilight, both officers scanned the rolling seas with their binoculars, as did the two sailors situated in front of them in the sail's cutout observation platform.

"It's hopeless, Captain," Chop said as he lowered his binoculars and smoothed down the edges of the large bandage that covered most of his forehead.

Mac replied while scanning the sleek Spruance-class destroyer that was slowly patrolling the waters some hundred yards off their port bow. "I hear ya, Chop. But I can't stop thinking that we owe the doctor our best effort and then some."

"Sounds like you're still blaming yourself for his loss," observed Chop. "If anyone's to be held responsible, it should be me, for not being more forceful in getting the doc belowdeck."

"Nonsense." Mac lowered his binoculars. "As the captain of this vessel, I take total responsibility for the entire incident. Never forget, I'm the one who ordered us to submerge, and the safety of the deck party was in my hands exclusively."

A large swell rocked the keelless warship, and Mac looked out to the western horizon. The low-lying gray clouds that had been with them all day momentarily parted, revealing a final glimpse of the setting sun.

"It's all a damn waste," Mac bitterly muttered. "Especially since the ray veered off and didn't even come close to striking us."

"And how were you to know that it wouldn't hit us?" Chop retorted. "Come on, Captain, you were only doin' your duty to protect *Chicago*."

"Tell that to the family and friends of that poor marine biologist that we left topside," Mac countered.

The last golden vestige of sunlight was swallowed by the horizon, and a sudden chill permeated the air. Mac had pulled up the collar of his windbreaker and was looking down to the recessed bridge when the intercom speaker growled: "Ensign Lee would like permission to join you on the sail, Captain."

"Send him up," Mac directed.

The *Chicago*'s CO was making a final 360-degree scan of the surrounding waters when the sub's junior-most officer squeezed himself into the sub's recessed opening. Ensign Joe Lee's features clearly revealed his Oriental heritage, though his accent was pure American.

"Captain, I've got those results you asked for," he said.

"Fire away, Mr. Lee," Mac ordered, without taking his eyes from the binoculars.

"I'm sorry this has taken so long, sir, but when I found nothing in *Jane's,* I had to search through the entire *Lewis* catalog of the world's surface ships. I'm positive that the life vest we took aboard earlier belonged to a vessel by the name of *Star of Linshu.* The *Lewis* catalog showed only a single such ship. She's a twenty-thousand-ton PRC freighter, registered at Qingdao."

Chop was the first to respond to this information. "I wonder what in the hell the *Star of Linshu* was doing up here in the Kurils?"

"Maybe they were transporting a load of cargo up to Kamchatka," Mac guessed.

"That's unlikely, sir," returned the ensign. "The catalog shows the *Star of Linshu* to be a waste hauler."

This revelation caused Mac to finally lower his binoculars and directly address the ensign. "You know, come to think of it, I believe I read something in *Sea Power* this past summer about that ship. The Japs caught her dumping a load of industrial waste off the Ryukyus, and the discovery almost sparked a serious international incident."

"Well, from all the flotsam that we managed to collect today, the Japanese sure won't have to worry about the *Star of Linshu* dumping any more garbage in their waters," Chop noted.

At this moment one of the sailors packed into the sail's recessed observation platform interrupted the conversation. "We've got a message on the way from the *Hewitt,* Captain!"

All eyes went to the destroyer's bridge, where a powerful signal light could be seen blinking. As a former surface-warfare signalman himself, Chop readily translated this coded sequence into English.

"It appears that the *Hewitt* just got a positive return from that sonobuoy field their chopper sowed above the Honshu Seamount. And get this, Captain. The contact's broadcasting a steady ultrasonic homing signal on NOSC's frequency band."

"Well, I'll be," Mac muttered. "I don't suppose that they've got a projected course bearing on this contact?"

"They sure do, sir," Chop replied, his gaze locked on the flashing signal light. "It was last monitored cruising straight and true on course one-five-zero."

The signal lamp stopped its mad blinking, and Chop turned to address his CO. "Don't that take the cake, Captain? Somehow the doc managed to hit that giant ray with a transmitter."

"It sure seems that way," Mac said.

"Too bad we're stuck out here on picket duty and can't head south to follow it."

"Who says we can't, Chop?" Mac responded emotionally. "Hell, now that the *Hewitt*'s up here, and the *Pasadena* and *Honolulu* due within the hour, I'd say that the hole in our SOSUS line is adequately plugged. And so that Dr. Kraft's loss isn't in vain, SUBPAC's gotta free us to finish the job that cost a good man his life."

It proved to be the soothing sound of music that awoke Kraft from his deep slumber. His eyes opened to comforting blackness, yet this time no fearful disorientation greeted him. Only the ethereal strains of a flute and an unknown string instrument filled the room with a calming, Oriental melody.

Surprised at how good he felt, Kraft sat up and reached over to activate the overhead light. The soft illumination he activated was easy on his eyes, and he proceeded straight to the adjoining rest room. The simple act of brushing his teeth and shaving felt like great pleasures.

With the hope that he'd be able to find a shower somewhere inside his current means of transport, he left the head and crossed to the room's sole doorway. Unlike his previous try of the doorknob, it opened with a click, and he allowed himself a long sigh of relief upon noting that his brief imprisonment was finally over.

Outside, he found himself facing a rather spacious, carpet-lined hallway. There was a noticeable absence of the snaking electrical conduits and cables that adorned the ceiling and walls of the *Chicago*. In fact, he had trouble distinguishing the corridor from that of a modern office building. Instead of mind-numbing Muzak, the celestial flute music that he had awakened to filled the hall. It seemed to be the perfect accompaniment to his exploration.

Random choice directed him to the right. Posters portraying various whales lined the wall, and he briefly halted to study them. The artist had superbly rendered the raw power of a pair of sounding sperms, and perfectly captured the six species of rorquals—the fin, Byrde's, sei, blue, minke, and humpback whales.

Though he had been caught completely off guard when he learned that Captain Moreau and his second in command knew of his work, he only had to see these drawings to know that their interest was sincere. It was evident that these men were trained scientists and took their work most seriously. Looking forward to speaking with them further, he continued his exploration.

Several closed hatchways bisected the corridor. Since there was no one around to ask for directions, he followed the hall to the end. Here, beside the picture of an Amazon river dolphin, was a partially open hatch. The muted hum of machinery drew him inside, and he soon found himself in a spacious compartment filled with equipment, a good five times larger than his quarters. Kraft was reminded of a high-tech Silicon Valley laboratory he had once visited as he walked over to examine what he supposed was a mainframe computer. He counted twenty-four interconnected drives, all operating on 8mm cassette tape. Such a state-of-the-art system could process trillions of tera-bytes of data.

Kraft was proceeding over to an adjoining console to have a closer look at a flashing display screen when, strangely enough, a pair of outstretched legs blocked his way. Thankful finally to have someone to talk to, Kraft knelt down and addressed a prone figure wearing a black jumpsuit, intently working on a pulled-out circuit board.

"Excuse me, sir. But could you tell me where I am?"

"Ah, you must be our honorable passenger," returned a male voice with a definite Japanese accent. "Hold on, and I'll be right with you."

Kraft watched as the technician expertly utilized a surgical tweezer to complete his repair. Then, after snapping the circuit board back in place, he sat up stiffly and smiled.

"That was the hard part," he said with a wink. "Now to see the results of my efforts."

With a bit of effort he stood. Barely five feet tall, with short gray hair and warm dark eyes, the delicate-boned Japanese technician displayed a prominent limp as he made his way over to a nearby keyboard. It was clear that any physical handicap he might have didn't affect his typing skills as his hands attacked the keypad with a furious flurry. When a soft electronic tone sounded, he abandoned the keyboard, focusing his attention instead on the monitor screen, which began filling with data.

"Excellent," he said with a hint of triumph. "Now that's more like it." A satisfied grin painted his gaunt face as he turned toward Kraft and reverently bowed. "So you're Dr. Peter Kraft, the famed marine biologist. It's a great honor to meet you. I am Mikio Yushiro, but please call me Chief, like everyone else on board."

Kraft returned this bow, saying, "I'm sorry to bother you, Chief. But I'm afraid I've gone and gotten myself lost. Where exactly are we?"

"Why, the engine room, where else?" he matter-of-factly answered.

Kraft found it hard to hide his puzzlement, and he carefully reexamined the spotlessly clean compartment, noting with confusion that spinning shafts, grinding motors, and complex reactor vessels were conspicuously absent. "But where's the engines?" he blurted.

The technician laughed. "It's apparent that Commandant Moreau hasn't explained our unique propulsion system to you. Come with me, Doctor, and I'll give you a quick tour."

Still limping, the chief slowly crossed the compartment with Kraft close at his side. "Please excuse the slow going, Doctor. This limp, which I have had my entire life, is the result of a genetic deficiency bequeathed to me by my mother. I was born in the ashes of Hiroshima, shortly after the conclusion of the Great War."

"Please take your time, Chief." Kraft, who knew what it was like to have difficulty walking, meant these words sincerely.

They halted in the center of the room, beside a clear Plexiglas floor plate. Beneath this nine-foot-long rectangular grid were dozens of equally spaced, glowing tubes that appeared to be filled with lava.

"Would you believe that *Ecowar* is currently cutting through the depths at a speed of seventy-eight knots?" the chief asked. "And just think—all of this incredible power originates here, in this single bank of rechargeable fuel cells."

Though Kraft's first impression was that Yushiro was pulling his leg, he decided to go along with him. "But where's the propeller shaft and reduction gears?" he politely asked.

"Such devices aren't needed on *Ecowar*," the chief retorted.

"Hold on a minute," Kraft countered. "Do you mean to say that this vessel is traveling at over eighty miles per hour, and it doesn't even have a propeller?"

The chief grinned knowingly. "Welcome to the magic of magnetohydrodynamic propulsion, or MHD for short. You see, Doctor, the principle behind MHD is extremely basic. When a conducting fluid moves through a magnetic field, it may induce an electric current. This current, in turn, interacts with the magnetic field to produce a body force on the fluid."

"But where are the engines?" Kraft wanted to know.

His gray-haired guide pointed to a pair of deck-mounted metallic objects that reminded Kraft of miniature turbines. They extended all the way to the rear bulkhead and emitted the low, muted hum that had originally drawn him into this compartment.

"Those are the extent of our engines, Doctor. In place of the standard compressor, we've incorporated an ionizer. The combustion chamber has been replaced by a linear magnetic pulser pump, and instead of a turbine, there's a simple deionizer. Thus the MHD engine literally pulls *Ecowar* forward, our speed only limited by the density of the ions and the magnetic-field flux."

"I wish now that I had paid more attention in college physics," Kraft said, clearly impressed by the uniqueness of the futuristic propulsion system.

"Schooling only gives one the basic tools for knowledge," returned the chief. "Wisdom is the result of applying knowledge to everyday life."

While Kraft pondered these words three soft tones sounded from the intercom. The chief limped over to the nearest display screen, and as Kraft joined him the monitor filled with an image of Ezra Melindi.

"Chief," said the serious-faced Melindi. "The commandant would like to test our defensive shield. Are you satisfied with the repairs to the laser's pulsed focusing mechanism?"

Yushiro replied directly into the display screen. "That I am, sir."

Melindi nodded. "Excellent, Chief. I see that Dr. Kraft has joined you. Why not send him up to Control so that he can witness the test firsthand?"

With this, the monitor went blank, and the chief gestured toward the forward hatchway. "I'm certain that you'll enjoy watching the test from *Ecowar*'s control room, Doctor."

"I'm sure I will," Kraft agreed. "But how do I get there?"

"Do you mean to say that you haven't even visited Control as yet?" Yushiro was surprised. "My, this certainly will be a day full of wonders for you. Just turn to your right and take the main passageway all the way forward. And please, Doctor, do come back and visit anytime you'd like."

"I'll do that, Chief," Kraft said, returning Yushiro's bow, and then exited through the hatchway.

All the way down the corridor, his mind was filled with the remarkable technological achievements he had just witnessed. Though his skeptical side warned him to remain cautious, another part of him gloried in the fact that fate had chosen him to share in *Ecowar*'s secrets before the rest of the world learned of its existence. So far this vessel was like a glimpse into the future, a vision of a day when man had truly mastered machinery. Excited with the idea that at long last the seas could truly be opened up to real exploration, he rapidly passed by the closed door to his quarters just as a loud crashing noise sounded from an adjoining compartment. On a whim he decided to check out the source of the racket, and he curiously peeked inside the closed hatchway.

Dominating the wood-paneled room was a large, circular table. As his glance angled down to the plush red carpet, he spotted Annie Sawyer on her hands and knees. The Australian nurse was picking up a tray of silverware that she had apparently just dropped.

"Can I help you with that?" he asked.

"That's all right, Doc," she replied. "I can manage pickin' up after my own clumsiness."

Kraft's attention was drawn to the colored photographs that hung on the walls. One was a close-up of a familiar curly-haired figure dressed in a pink wet suit in the process of orchestrating a marine-mammal show at an outdoor seaquarium. There were the usual shots of leaping bottle-nosed dolphins, as well as several showing a group of seals in action. Yet what really drew his attention was a photo of Annie sitting astride an orca. She wore a pink cowboy hat in this shot, and was riding the massive killer whale like a participant in a marine rodeo.

"Annie, is this really you in these photos?" Kraft asked.

"That it is, Doc," she said, picking up the last piece of loose flatware and standing. "Of course, there were quite a few less miles on the ol' odometer back then."

"Incredible," Kraft muttered. "Where were they taken?"

Annie held back her reply until she reached Kraft's side. "This entire sequence was shot at the Perth Marine Park. I was head dolphin trainer there for three seasons."

"But I thought you were previously a registered nurse," Kraft said. "How did you manage all that schooling while working as a marine-mammal trainer? Believe me, I know firsthand that handling a tankful of dolphins is a full-time job on its own."

"That's one of the prime reasons that I gave up nursin'," Annie explained. "I started workin' at the seaquarium as an undergraduate durin' the summers. And when it finally came down to choosin' between dedicatin' my life to either humans or marine mammals, I picked the latter."

"Good choice," returned Kraft. "Now how in the world did you ever end up on *Ecowar*?"

"In a nutshell, Doc, one afternoon between shows my conscience got the better of me, and I realized that my dolphins were no better than a bunch of convicted criminals, imprisoned against their wills. That same night I released the entire lot of them back into the sea. Needless to say, I was fired the next day. Commandant Moreau happened to read about me in a Sydney newspaper and offered me this job. I've been with him ever since."

Kraft snickered. "I believe I know what prompted you to release those dolphins, Annie. I've had the same urge."

"The commandant hopes someday to get the United

Nations to require all captive whales and dolphins to be released into their natural habitat after an agreed-upon time limit," Annie announced.

Kraft looked a bit dubious. "Do you really think that the owners of marine parks would allow that to happen?"

Annie's voice took on an enthusiastic fervor. "That's why it's so important to appeal to the world community as a whole. Only with their support can we teach humanity that dolphins and whales are intelligent, thinking creatures. And that marine parks should cease to be prisons and instead become interspecies schools, where both marine mammals and humans can learn about each other in a peaceful, sharing environment."

"That's certainly something to think about," Kraft admitted. At that moment he noticed the soft flute and string music that emanated from the room's intercom speakers.

"I must say that the more I see of this vessel, the more I'm impressed," he added. "That includes your choice of background music. I believe yesterday it was Wagner. And today's selection, though unfamiliar to me, is just as inspiring."

"I'm glad you're enjoyin' it, Doc. Each day the commandant allows one of the crew to pick out several discs from *Ecowar*'s audio library. You can thank our chief engineer for today's selection. This composition for koto and flute was written in his homeland."

"I just had the honor of meeting Chief Yushiro," said Kraft.

"We're very fortunate to have his expert services," Annie said while looking at her watch. "Say, Doc, I bet you didn't even have any breakfast this mornin'. That's no way to start off a day. So what can I get ya?"

"Thanks for the concern, Annie, but I'm not much of a breakfast person. Besides, I'd better continue on my way. I'm expected in the control room."

"As you wish, Doc. But be sure to bring along your appetite for lunch. In your honor, I'm servin' an old-fashioned New England–style clambake complete with fresh lobster."

"Sounds wonderful, Annie. See you then."

Kraft left the wardroom with a new appreciation for Annie Sawyer. She was not only one of the most naturally beautiful women he had ever met, but she was clearly a woman of principle as well. He thought about her brief discourse on the rights of marine mammals as he returned to the main passageway.

A single closed hatch was set into the forwardmost bulkhead. Crowning the entryway was a picture of a fully grown blue whale. Kraft briefly studied the detailed rendering before pulling open the hatch and stepping inside.

He found himself in a dimly lit compartment, dominated by a huge, glowing display screen that appeared to fill an entire wall. Set immediately before this screen were five high-backed, leather chairs. Each of these positions was currently occupied, with a familiar, bald-headed figure seated in the center spot.

"Ah, Dr. Kraft, at last," greeted Moreau. "Please join us."

Kraft hesitated a moment while his eyes adjusted to the dim illumination. Carefully he made his way over to the middle chair. Here Jean Moreau beckoned toward a vacant jumpseat, positioned on his right, between himself and his second in command.

"Do have a seat, Doctor," he urged. "And please fasten your restraining harness."

Kraft did as instructed and, after pulling tight his airplanelike seat belt, redirected his attention to the display screen. A detailed bathymetric chart was projected here, along with a constantly changing selection of digital data that made little sense to him.

Unlike the standard navigational charts that graced the *Chicago*'s navigation plot, this one provided a holographic, 3-D view of the ocean bed. He couldn't help but marvel at the sight of twisting subterranean valleys and rugged seamounts, features that were left to the imagination on charts that showed sea depth alone.

"We are just about to initiate a test of *Ecowar*'s defensive system," revealed Moreau. "You may proceed, Mr. Godavari."

There was a brief flash of light and the chart was replaced by a detailed schematic. It showed a see-through image of what Kraft took for a second to be a manta ray. Only after viewing the individual compartments outlined in this delta-winged object did a sudden disturbing thought dawn in his mind. He couldn't keep from voicing his astonishment.

"My God, there was no giant manta ray. It was *Ecowar* all along!"

"I'm genuinely sorry that I had to keep this fact from you, Doctor," Moreau admitted. "But I thought it best that you learned it on your own."

"I can't believe it!" continued the stunned marine biologist, struggling to come to terms with this incredible revelation.

Remembering his initial skepticism when he first read the reports of the giant-manta-ray sighting in the newspaper, he muttered, "Brother, just wait until Commander Lawrence and the folks back at NOSC find out that their sea monster has turned out to be a submarine."

Moreau was quick with a reply. "The U.S. Navy's Ocean Systems Command has been patiently working on altering the traditional albacore-shaped hulls of their submarines for some time now. They might not be so astounded as you think."

Kraft's astonishment grew. "But why choose a manta-shaped hull?"

Moreau looked to his right, and Ezra Melindi provided the answer to this question. "Doctor, such a revolutionary hull form was needed to control the high-velocity flow rate created by *Ecowar*'s hydrojet engines. You've already visited the engine room, and I believe Chief Yushiro has explained our MHD propulsion system to you. With speeds well over seventy knots, we possess both the cruise characteristics of a low-drag sailplane and the maneuvering capabilities of a supersonic fighter aircraft."

"Incredible," Kraft breathed as the reality finally sank in.

A satisfied smile on his face, Moreau turned his attention back to the screen. "As I was saying, Doctor. We are about to initiate a test of *Ecowar*'s defensive system. In the unlikely event that we should come under torpedo attack, this is how we will counter it."

Kraft turned his own gaze back to the screen. He watched as the computer-enhanced, transparent model isolated a narrow rectangular compartment on the port side of the rounded bow, directly forward of the engine room.

"We have programmed a laser-guided decoy to simulate the attack run of an American Mk48," explained Moreau. "Begin launch sequence, Karl Ivar."

The young blond-haired man seated on Moreau's left addressed the keypad set into his right armrest. On the screen a red light began blinking inside the isolated compartment, and the technician reported, "Attack sequence has been initiated, sir. Ten seconds to launch."

A digital stopwatch was projected on the screen beside the flashing red light as Karl Ivar counted down. "Five . . . four . . . three . . . two . . . one . . . Weapon away!"

The deck shook with the decoy's release. On the screen the model was replaced by a holographic view of the surrounding waters, with the decoy's course clearly marked in red.

"I show a firm blue-green laser lock, sir," Karl Ivar reported as the decoy could be seen making a sweeping turn away from *Ecowar*.

Moreau explained what was occurring to Kraft. "The weapon is initiating a preprogrammed, 360-degree turn at this point."

Kraft watched as the flashing red dot gradually altered its course and turned back toward *Ecowar*'s stern.

"Decoy has capture!" called Karl Ivar. "Range to target, six thousand yards and closing."

A digital display began rapidly counting off the distance left until impact. It was moving much too fast for Kraft's peace of mind, and he listened as Moreau calmly called out his next order.

"Mr. Godavari, shift power to the stern defensive shield."

Out of the corner of his eye Kraft watched the brown-skinned technician seated in the far left position abruptly pull back on one of the joysticks he was holding.

"Pulsers are charged and focused, sir," said the technician.

"Decoy has broken the four-thousand-yard threshold and continues to close," added Karl Ivar.

"Watch the screen carefully, Dr. Kraft," Moreau instructed.

An electronic cursor began highlighting the area of ocean immediately behind *Ecowar,* and Moreau continued. "On my order, *Ecowar*'s blue-green laser will be targeted on the waters behind us. The resulting explosion will leave a vapor void some three thousand yards in diameter, cutting the attacking decoy's umbilical and causing it to harmlessly destroy itself."

As the screen's digital counter passed below 3,500 yards Moreau ordered, "Light off the pulser, Mr. Godavari!"

Kraft looked to his left as the technician pushed forward on one of the joysticks. His glance returned to the screen just in time to see a bright blue line streak out from *Ecowar*'s stern and project itself out into that portion of the ocean that Moreau had previously highlighted with the cursor. He also noted that the digital counter was just about to break three thousand yards.

"Decoy has lost capture!" Karl Ivar exclaimed. "It's just gone active again."

At a distance of 2,983 yards the digital counter

abruptly stopped. Then it slowly reversed itself and began registering an actual gain in distance.

"It's lost us, sir. Attack is terminated," Karl Ivar reported unceremoniously.

The red light representing the torpedo blinked a single time, and as it permanently faded Moreau spoke. "Number Two, please announce a job well done to Chief Yushiro."

A satisfied smirk etched the Frenchman's face as he turned his attention back to Kraft. "Well, Doctor, what do you think of our little demonstration?"

Overwhelmed by this futuristic display, Kraft answered as honestly as possible. "It appears to be a most novel and efficient way of countering a torpedo attack. My only question is, do you really expect someone to actually launch a weapon at you?"

"You'd be surprised what man-made dangers await us out here, Doctor," Moreau replied.

As if to confirm the accuracy of this assessment, the woman seated to their far right suddenly cried, "We've got a high-frequency, passive sonar contact, bearing one-seven-five, maximum range!"

"Amplify this signal, Ms. Borisov, and pipe it through the intercom," Moreau ordered.

The sonar technician alertly addressed her keypad. Seconds later a series of shrill, screeching sounds broke from the compartment's elevated speakers. Oddly enough Kraft was the first to identify them.

"I've heard that sound before. It's coming from a pod of dolphins. And from the racket they're making, I'd say that they're in some kind of serious distress."

"Mr. Godavari!" Moreau called. "Come around crisply to course one-seven-five."

Kraft watched as the helmsman expertly manipulated his joysticks, and the deck canted over steeply on its right side.

"Ms. Borisov, I need bathymetrics!" Moreau demanded. Once again the display screen filled with a 3-D view of the surrounding waters. Kraft noted the rugged-looking appearance of the seabed below, and listened to the latest navigational update from Ivana Borisov.

"We just passed the Makorov Seamount, and are approaching the Marcus Island chain. Depth under keel is 5,150 meters."

The chorus of amplified clicks and whistles seemed to intensify. In the background a barely audible catlike cry could be heard; it sounded almost as if there were humans out there desperately calling out for help.

"Active sensors show several surface contacts dead ahead of us!" Karl Ivar announced.

"I've got these same contacts on passive," Ivana Borisov confirmed. "Signature ID analysis indicates that we've got three diesel-powered vessels topside."

On the right portion of the screen, a waterfall display broke down these sound patterns into individual frequencies. Kraft was reminded of similar displays he had viewed in the *Chicago*'s sonar room.

"How close are these ships to the dolphins?" Moreau wanted to know.

Ivana Borisov returned to her keypad before answering. "They appear to be right in the midst of the pod, Commandant."

Moreau thoughtfully glanced over to Ezra Melindi. "Let's have a look, Number Two. Mr. Godavari, bring us up to visual-scan depth. Karl Ivar, prepare Freddie for launch."

As *Ecowar*'s bow began angling upward Kraft asked, "Who's Freddie?"

"Freddie's the name we've given to our remotely operated vehicle," said Melindi. "When released into the sea, he remains tethered to *Ecowar* by a fiber-optic umbilical, and can be used to relay environmental data and to accomplish repair-and-salvage functions. In this instance, Freddie will be sent to the surface to relay video pictures of the situation topside since *Ecowar* has no traditional hull-penetrating periscope."

"Approaching visual-scan depth," interrupted Godavari.

"Launch Freddie!" Moreau ordered.

This time it was Karl Ivar who attacked his keypad. The deck slightly shuddered, and the entire display screen filled with a fish-eye view of the sea, as relayed by the ROV's bow-mounted video camera. A curious nurse shark swam by, followed by a quick-moving school of tuna.

"Freddie away. Data link secured. Ten meters to surface," Karl Ivar said dispassionately.

On the screen's upper left-hand corner, a digital depth meter displayed Freddie's progress. Amazed by how quickly the meter flew by, Kraft counted the seconds it took for the gauge to hit zero. He had barely reached ten when the video camera broke the water's surface. Their line of sight was momentarily obstructed as a wave slapped up against the lens, and the camera initiated a quick 360-degree scan. Only when he was certain that there were no obstacles close by did Moreau give his next order.

"Focus scan on bearing one-seven-five, magnification power ten."

Almost magically the screen filled with a large, rusted-out fishing trawler surrounded by a pair of smaller capture boats. A net, hanging from the trawler's stern, looked as if it was being pulled in.

"Isolate the trawler, magnification power twenty," Moreau instructed.

Kraft was startled by the incredibly detailed scene that next filled the display screen. Several grubby fishermen could actually be seen pulling dozens of flapping tuna out of the net with long pointed gaffs. Beside them, yet another deckhand was attempting to remove a baby dolphin that was partially wedged inside the net's winch mechanism.

Kraft instinctively winced on spotting the crowbar the man was utilizing to free the badly mauled dolphin. It seemed to take an eternity for him to accomplish his task, and as the blood-soaked dolphin slipped back into the sea, the deckhand joined a rifle-toting shipmate at the railing. Another rifle materialized, and with sadistic grins painting their beard-stubbled faces, they took aim at the ocean's surface and began firing.

"Close in on the trawler's waterline, maximum amplification!" shouted Moreau, his powerful voice quivering with rage.

As the order was carried out all of those assembled inside *Ecowar*'s control room could clearly see the deckhand's target—a circling pod of frantic dolphins, vainly attempting to nudge life back into the fatally wounded baby that had just been thrown back into their midst.

Over the shrill cries of anguish that continued to be conveyed through the intercom speakers, the infuriated voice of Jean Moreau shouted, "Retrieve Freddie! Prepare to attack!"

Though Kraft felt plenty of revulsion and anger himself, Moreau's last order caused the hair on the back of his neck to rise. While summoning the nerve to question Moreau, he watched the crew busily address their individual keypads.

"Target the trawler," Moreau continued. "Collision alert!"

A steady, electronic warbling tone began to sound in the background, overpowering the cries of the dolphins.

"I have a lock on Freddie," Karl Ivar stated. "Retrieval initiated."

Confused as to what was happening, Kraft shouted, "What in the world is going on here?"

At this emotional outburst *Ecowar*'s captain turned fiercely, his anger barely contained. "Why, it's only too obvious, Doctor. It's time to rid the seas of the two-legged, unenlightened vermin responsible for slaughtering our dolphin brothers!"

For a moment Kraft was at a loss. Then his mind flashed back to the photographs Commander Lawrence had shown him back in Florida.

"Oh, my God," he managed to whisper. "Do you

mean to say that you're actually going to sink that tuna boat?"

When his query went unanswered, Kraft took the crew's silence for assent. Unable to swallow the outrage such behavior caused him to feel, however, he blurted, "I'm just as sickened by this wasteful incident as any of you are. But what gives you the right to attack that tuna boat in response? Men's lives are at stake out there!"

"If you're going to speak to me of rights, Doctor, then please don't forget those of the innocent dolphins dying up there!" returned Moreau. "The world community told those fishermen to employ the dolphin-safe fishing methods the majority of the tuna fleet are already using. But their greed and stupidity are too great, and for that they must now pay the price."

"Freddie's home. Retrieval is completed," Karl Ivar announced at this point.

The calm voice of Ivana Borisov quickly followed. "We have a final lock on target coordinates."

"The ramming spars have been deployed. I show full hydrothruster charge available," Raghib Godavari put in.

"*Ecowar* is ready to eliminate the target, *mon commandant*," Ezra Melindi said with ringing finality.

Moreau's eyes gleamed as he turned to face Peter Kraft. "Now you're about to witness *Ecowar*'s true mission, Doctor. We are the self-appointed protectors of the sea. And we will fight this battle with every means available to us, including the extermination of those who pollute its depths, exploit its resources, and needlessly slaughter its innocent inhabitants!"

Turning his glance back to the display screen, Moreau fervidly added, "Initiate attack!"

Like a well-oiled machine, the crew snapped into action. With a practiced coolness, Raghib Godavari shoved his right joystick forward. Almost instantly *Ecowar*'s deck angled sharply upward.

"Hydrothrusters engaged," reported the helmsman. "Seven-degree up angle on the bow ramming spars."

"Range to target two thousand yards and closing," said Borisov.

This range was continually updated on the display screen. When the digital readout passed 1,500 yards, Kraft anxiously gripped his chair's padded armrests.

"Prepare to engage reverse thrusters immediately upon impact, Mr. Godavari," *Ecowar's* second in command called out.

"Target remains steady in the water," Karl Ivar noted. "Active sonar scan shows no sign of movement."

"One thousand yards to target and continuing to close," said Ivana Borisov with machinelike precision.

More interested in studying the intense facial expressions of the crew than the flashing display screen, Kraft wondered if they weren't in some sort of hypnotic trance. There could be no doubting the maniacal gleam that continued to glow in their leader's eyes. Nevertheless he decided to make one more desperate attempt to break the spell.

"This is sheer lunacy!" he shouted. "It amounts to nothing less than cold-blooded murder."

"This isn't murder, Doctor," Moreau retorted, a crazed grin twisting his lips. "It's war against the rapists of the sea!"

As if she were deaf to this exchange, Ivana Borisov mechanically reported, "Five hundred yards to target. Recalibrate impact zone."

"Recalibration completed," Karl Ivar quickly replied. "Impact to take place directly amidships, two meters below the target's waterline."

"Brace yourselves, *mes amis,*" Moreau piped triumphantly, "as we strike yet another blow in the battle to save our planet's oceans!"

The powerful concussion that followed this dramatic utterance was almost anticlimactic. Violently thrown forward, Kraft fought back tears. While the intercom speakers conveyed the gut-wrenching sound of rending steel he visualized the *Ecowar's* twin, steel-reinforced spars slicing into the trawler's exposed underbelly. As the *Ecowar* pulled itself free tons of seawater would pour into the two gaping holes in the trawler's hull, and the doomed vessel would quickly sink with most of its crew still trapped inside.

Unknown to Kraft was the fact that beside him, Jean Moreau was seeing a similar vision. Yet in the Frenchman's nightmarish version, the vortex of water left in the sinking trawler's wake was all too soon filled with the lifeless bodies of dozens of dolphins, their sleek, bullet-hole-riddled corpses still seeping blood.

"Target depth is one hundred meters and sinking," reported the mechanical, Slavic-accented voice of Ivana Borisov. "Bulkheads continue to buckle and collapse."

"Commandant, will we be returning to the surface to eliminate the remaining capture boats?" inquired Karl Ivar.

Moreau thought for a moment before answering. "No, Karl Ivar. We've more than made our point. And besides, what good is this lesson unless some survivors are left to return to port and repeat what they've seen here?"

Shocked into speechlessness, Kraft listened as the speakers continued to relay the hideous scene occurring outside. This macabre event was mercifully cut short by the voice of *Ecowar's* master.

"Ms. Borisov, terminate the passive speaker feed," Moreau directed. "And Mr. Godavari, return to course one-five-zero, at standard cruising speed."

The overhead speakers went silent, and the deck canted over slightly to the left. Still seething in anger, Kraft listened to Moreau address the crew.

"You've done well, *mes amis*. Because of your actions, the seas today are a safer place."

"Tell that to the families of those drowned tuna fishermen," Kraft interjected bitterly.

A flicker of humanity seemed to cross Moreau's tortured mask of a face as he responded. "Don't think that taking those lives was easy for any one of us, Doctor. Life is the most precious of all earthly gifts. Yet sometimes it must be taken away to set an example for the greater good."

Kraft had heard enough, and he disgustedly shook his head, unbuckled his restraining harness, and stood up. "If you'll excuse me," he said curtly, "I'd like to return to my quarters."

Moreau's indifference was all too apparent as he replied, "Please make yourself at home, Doctor. Lunch is at two sharp in the wardroom mess."

"I'm afraid I don't have much of an appetite after what I just witnessed," spat Kraft, returning the Frenchman's callous stare as he turned for the control room's exit.

"As you wish, *mon ami*," Moreau whispered, a hint of disappointment in his voice. "As you wish, my obstinate American friend."

13

Mac McShane began his customary afternoon walk through the *Chicago* in the forward torpedo room. The dimly lit compartment was quiet, and he momentarily halted beside the vertical launch tubes that gave the boat a unique offensive punch. Packed within the upright launch canisters were fifteen Tomahawk missiles. Each of these twenty-foot missiles was powered by a turbojet sustainer motor with a solid-fuel booster. They currently carried two separate versions, one for land attack, with a range of 1,400 nautical miles, and an antiship model, with a range of 250 nautical miles.

Proven to be a potent weapons system during the Gulf War, Tomahawk allowed *Chicago* to take the fight to the enemy's shores if needed. Because the missiles were stored in their very own launch canisters, *Chicago* could also carry a full load of Mk48 torpedoes and Harpoon antiship missiles. These weapons were stored on pallets beside the boat's four twenty-one-inch, midships torpedo tubes. This was the portion of the boat Mac visited next.

A weapons officer in the early days of his navy career, Mac felt right at home here. The majority of torpedoes—or "fish" as they were better known—were securely strapped to the compartment's steel storage racks and covered by green plastic caps. As Mac reached out to touch the cool metal body of one of these lethal fish, he noted the spool that was attached to the weapon's stern. Wrapped within this spool were several thousand feet of fiber-optic wire, which would be played out upon launch. Because of the wire, the torpedo could get constant updates from the boat's fire-control system, and adjust its attack run as needed.

The muted raspy sound of someone snoring caused Mac to look toward the pallet's bottom rack. A single sailor was stretched out here, peacefully cutting Zs. Because of *Chicago*'s tight confines, it was necessary to utilize every available spare inch for living space, and so several members of the crew made their home here in the torpedo room. Mac quietly walked past the sleeping sailor to have a look at the launch console.

A sole seaman was currently on duty here. Mac remembered the bespectacled sailor from previous visits. Seaman First Class Joe Carter was a serious fellow, with a quick intellect and a desire to please.

"Good afternoon, Mr. Carter," Mac greeted softly.

Involved as he was in reading a technical manual, the young enlisted man gasped in surprise, stood, and squared his shoulders. "G-good afternoon, Captain," he stuttered.

To put him at ease, Mac casually asked, "What are you reading, sailor?"

"It's a sonar spec sheet that Petty Officer Cox gave me, sir," he nervously replied. "You see, I hope to qualify in sonar by the end of the year."

"If your work here in the torpedo room is any indication of your capabilities, you'll qualify with no problem at all," Mac stated simply.

"Why thank you, sir, for your confidence."

"We're all proud of you, son. Especially that mother of yours back in Kansas City. You know, I still have that letter she sent me before our last embark. And when this cruise is over, she sure won't be disappointed. Why I wouldn't be surprised to see a set of silver dolphins on that chest of yours this time next year."

"That's the goal, sir," replied Carter, a bit more at ease.

"What's our weapons status?" Mac asked.

Carter was quick with his answer. "Tubes one and four are loaded with wire-guided Mk48s, sir. Tube two is still down for maintenance, with tube three presently vacant."

"When's tube two going to be back on-line?" continued Mac.

"Lieutenant Bradley hopes to have it operational sometime this evening, sir."

Pleased by the update, Mac prepared to leave. Yet before doing so, he again spoke.

"You know, Mr. Carter, there's one question that I always wanted to ask you. In that letter from your mother, she mentioned that you passed up a chance to pitch for the Royals when you enlisted in the navy. What prompted you to give up a career in baseball?"

"I know that this is gonna sound corny, sir. But I chose the navy because I wanted a chance to give something back to my country. My father died when I was only three. He served in Vietnam with honors. And the only thing he really left me was his uniform and a box of medals. My mom always said that though he didn't really believe in the war, he thought it important for every American citizen to do his duty. He really loved this country, regardless of its faults. And though baseball offered me the possible big bucks, the navy satisfied an even greater need for me."

"I hear you loud and clear, sailor," Mac said, and left the torpedo room with a new appreciation for the remarkable bunch of men that made up his crew.

In this age of selfishness, it was rare to find a group of men who dedicated their lives to a greater good. Like Joe Carter, Mac had been at a crossroads twenty years ago when he was forced to choose between preparing himself for a job in private industry or enrolling in NROTC. Though pursuing a military career had certainly not been fashionable in the seventies, he picked the navy. Shortly thereafter, he met his wife-to-be at an NROTC dance. A military brat herself, Nancy was extremely supportive of his career choice, and they were married a week before he received his commission.

For the next two decades he never really questioned his choice. He had worshiped John Paul Jones when he was a child, and attempted to pattern himself as a modern-day equivalent of Jones, going to nuclear-power school and learning the intricacies of running a nuclear attack sub.

During the Cold War, which had been especially active beneath the silent seas, he had taken long patrols into the frozen Arctic, where he and his shipmates encountered Communism on the very doorstep of the Soviet Union. Unable to share the details of these encounters even with his wife, he knew deep in his heart that his efforts weren't wasted.

Today's new world order proved this fact. No longer did Soviet subs threaten America's shores. Yet underwater deterrence was still vitally necessary, to check the ambitions of a whole new cast of power hungry dictators.

Adjusting to this vast geopolitical change hadn't been easy. Many of his countrymen questioned the continued need for sophisticated warships such as the *Chicago*. They argued that with the demise of the Soviet Union, America's nuclear attack subs had lost their primary mission, and for all effective purposes should be mothballed. Of course, one only had to look to history to prove them wrong.

On December 7, 1941, America had learned a painful lesson regarding the need for a strong peacetime deterrent. And even though the country swore never again to lower its guard, today the deceptive voice of pacifism was once more loose in the land.

Ever thankful that there were still patriots like Joe Carter who believed in doing their part in the defense of their country, Mac entered the crew's galley. The afternoon meal was long over, and there were only a handful of individuals seated at the red-checked-tablecloth-covered tables, watching as a rock video—minus the sound—played on one of the elevated monitor screens. Mac spotted Matt Cox and one of his sonarmen seated at a back booth, playing a portable Nintendo game. Still not certain whether or not the ship's sonar recorder was operational as yet, Mac was about to question the sonar technicians when a familiar voice spoke from behind him.

"Greetings, Captain. Would you care for an oatmeal-raisin cookie? They're right out of the oven."

Mac turned to face a plump, pink-cheeked, bespectacled face topped by a spiky crew cut. Smiling as always, Petty Officer Howard Mallott held a platter of cookies in his hands. The portly head chef took his cooking most seriously, and Mac didn't dare refuse his offer.

"Delicious!" he exclaimed, after sampling one of the warm cookies. "You've got to promise to give me the recipe so that I can pass it on to my wife."

Beaming with pride, Mallott readily replied, "The secret's all in the ingredients, sir. I use margarine, brown sugar, vanilla, flour, and baking soda, in addition to the oatmeal and raisins. And of course you've got to be careful to cook them for only eight minutes at 375 degrees."

"I'll take your word for it, Chief," Mac answered.

"By the way, Captain, how did you like today's lunch?" Mallott asked.

Mac lowered his voice. "The turkey hash was very tasty, Chief. But I believe that we could have a bit of a problem if we don't get a little more variety on the menu. Scuttlebutt around the wardroom table says that you're even planning to put turkey meatballs on our Saturday-evening pizza."

"I hear ya, Captain," said the cook. "I guess I've gotten just a wee bit fanatical. Of course, I was only doing it for the crew's health."

"We appreciate your concern," Mac returned. "But the key to keeping this bunch of pirates happy is variety."

A sudden idea popped in Mallott's mind, and he excitedly wiped the lenses of his wire-rims with his stained apron. "How does a nice honey-baked Virginia ham steak with pineapple garnish sound to you, Captain? And then I could whip up some yams, green beans, apple sauce, and a mess of hot biscuits on the side."

Mac grinned and reached out for another cookie. "Chief, it looks like there won't be a mutiny on the *Chicago* after all."

With his cookie in hand, Mac turned his attention back to the senior sonarman, who was still involved in a spirited Nintendo bout. "Excuse me, Mr. Cox. I sure hope I'm not interrupting a winning streak."

Cox did a double take upon identifying the captain. "Hello, Captain. Actually Specs here was beatin' the pants off of me. Thanks for comin' to the rescue."

"Let's just say we're even now," Mac returned. "I never got to thank you for volunteering to pull that double watch during our recent search-and-rescue op."

There was genuine humility in Cox's reply. "It was nothin', Captain. In a way, I kind of felt responsible for Doc's loss. I should have been quicker in pickin' up that ray when it altered its course and headed toward us."

"I seriously doubt whether another minute or so would have changed the outcome any, sailor," Mac observed. "You and your team did some remarkable work back there just to tag that creature. You never did say exactly how you knew it was out there."

Cox pointed at his bespectacled co-worker. "Sir, you can thank Specs here for sniffin' it out. Specs, go ahead and tell the captain how you knew it was out there."

The junior technician shyly began to explain. "I guess you could say that it was just a lucky hunch, Captain."

"Nonsense," Cox put in. "Captain, it was much more than that. Somehow ol' Specs here was able to locate that ray not from its noise level, but by its *lack* of noticeable sound. I've listened to my fair share of black holes before, and I gotta take my hat off to Specs for gettin' this one right."

"If only we had a working recorder," Mac said. "What's the status on those repairs?"

"We were able to cannibalize enough spare parts to get one of them going again, sir," Cox answered. "The only trouble is, we no longer have a working backup."

"At least we've got one of them going," said Mac. "Since there's nothing we can do now to get Dr. Kraft back, all I can ask of you is to keep an extra-viligant watch these next couple of days."

"Are we still goin' after the ray, Captain?" Cox asked.

Mac nodded. "That we are, sailor. And this time you won't have to be listening for black holes to find it. Because at last report, that ultrasonic homing beacon it's been tagged with is broadcasting loud and clear."

This news caused a broad smile to appear on Cox's face. "All you have to do is get us close, Captain, and it's as good as tagged."

"You've got yourself a deal, Mr. Cox." Mac looked at his watch. "You guys get back to your game, and I'd better get aft before the XO writes me up for tardiness. See ya in the sound shack, gentlemen."

At the rear of the galley was a closed hatchway, with a radiation decal prominently displayed. Entry to this part of the ship was limited to a specially trained portion of the *Chicago*'s crew. Mac ducked inside and sealed the hatch behind him.

A long, narrow passageway led him farther aft. Shining banks of stainless-steel piping and snaking, wire-filled cables hugged the walls and ceilings here. The waxlike smell of warm polythylene permeated the air, and his steps were muffled by green rubber matting. In the distance he could hear the low whine of the ventilation blowers and the roaring surge of the circulation pumps that directed high-pressure water through the reactor grid.

Here, in the very heart of the vessel, Mac halted. Recessed into the deck at his feet was an inspection window. Twenty feet below, a small, well-lit portion of the reactor itself was visible. This was where the vital, golfball-sized core of uranium was positioned. Mac solemnly paid his respects to that power source before continuing aft.

A sign reading CHICAGO POWER AND LIGHT greeted him as he entered the equipment-packed maneuvering room. Three sailors alertly sat behind a massive console, monitoring the propulsion plant. Dozens of gauges and dials showed the volume, temperature, pressure, and velocity of the water as it passed in and out of the reactor vessel. A fourth crewman handled a small pistol switch that adjusted the control rods and directly affected the level of power produced. The XO and the sub's engineering officer were intently watching this sailor at work. Both held clipboards, and were totally unaware of the newly arrived visitor behind them.

Mac cleared his throat. "How's she running, XO?"

Phil Moore turned his head and smiled with relief. "All systems appear to have returned to normal, Skipper. We've isolated the problem to a stuck valve in the water pump."

"Is there anything we can do about it?" Mac asked.

This time Lieutenant Ward answered. "Not until our

next refit, Captain. Initial test results show that the noise we heard was only an anomaly."

"I sure hope you're right, Lieutenant," said Mac. "Because I'd hate to be in an ultra-quiet situation and have that valve stick on us again. Damn, when I first heard it in my stateroom, I thought there had been an explosion back here."

"It hasn't made a peep since," interjected the XO. "So perhaps it was just a temporary deviation."

A dungaree-clad sailor entered the maneuvering room from the forward hatchway. He seemed pleased to spot the captain and handed him a folded dispatch.

"Sir," he said with a no-nonsense tone. "This just arrived for you from COMSUBPAC."

Mac quickly read the message and looked up to meet the curious gaze of his second in command. "You'll never believe it, XO. But it appears that our favorite sea monster is up to its old tricks once again. This time it took on a tuna trawler off Marcus Island, resulting in the loss of twenty-three fishermen."

Moore did some hasty mental calculations before responding. "Surely it can't be the same creature, Skipper. Marcus Island is a good three hundred nautical miles south of here. I seriously doubt that even a hundred-foot manta ray can travel at twice the speed of the *Chicago*."

"Maybe there are two of them," suggested the engineering officer.

"If that's the case, it only doubles our work," Mac said. "Because we've just been tasked to eliminate the creatures responsible for these sinkings with all due haste. It seems that not even the U.S. Navy can ignore such a hazard to shipping any longer."

Peter Kraft lay listlessly on his cot, trying hard to sort out his emotions. In the background, a Tchaikovsky symphony provided a fitting context for his melancholy musings.

He had left *Ecowar*'s control room seething with anger. On the one hand, Jean-Louis Moreau seemed to be a sincere advocate of the rights of marine mammals to live out their lives without fear of needless slaughter. On the other hand, he appeared to be completely amoral. Without batting an eye, he had the audacity to order an attack whose results took an untold amount of human lives. Certainly, there was no moral justification for such a rash act, and Kraft could only wonder how a cultured, intelligent man like Moreau could be guilty of it.

There could be no doubting that billions of dollars had been invested in *Ecowar*'s design and construction. This meant that other individuals were involved—powerful, wealthy men and women, who were also aware of how the sub was being utilized. This fact boggled Kraft's mind.

No stranger to the environmental movement, Kraft was a strong supporter of protecting the planet's oceans. He had participated in his fair share of public demonstrations, and even spent time in Washington lobbying for federal legislation designed to protect Florida's endangered manatee population.

He remembered a summer he spent in the Everglades monitoring the local manatee habitat. A speed limit had been set on the canal he was studying in an effort to keep the slow-moving herbivorous mammals from being accidentally run over by passing boats. One afternoon, while passing an inlet where large numbers of manatees were known to frequent, Kraft spotted a speedboat shooting up the canal at full throttle. He desperately waved his arms to slow down the driver, who, in response, showed Kraft his middle finger. Seconds later the speedboat plowed into the back of a full-grown manatee cow.

Kraft immediately guided his skiff over to the injured creature. The speedboat's prop had cut a seven-inch gash right in its back, and as it painfully thrashed about, blood poured into the surrounding water.

Never had Kraft felt such frustrated rage as he looked up to meet the gaze of the fool responsible for this needless tragedy. The long-haired driver of the speedboat couldn't have been more than twenty. As he restarted his stalled engine he called out to Kraft in a weak, remorseless voice.

"Hell, mister, that damn fool thing should have had the sense to get out of the way!"

As he sped off down the canal Kraft watched the manatee sink into the blood-soaked depths. For the first time in his life he felt real hatred for another human being, and wished he had a gun so that he could avenge this tragedy.

Of course, this desire for retribution soon passed. Deliberately killing the speedboat driver would have gained him nothing but a prison sentence and done nothing to help the manatees. Kraft knew the only way to make a difference was through increased protective legislation.

Jean Moreau and his followers had obviously taken the other tack. Like vigilantes, they had taken the law into their own hands. No matter how legitimate their motives were, their method of enforcement made them no better than the perpetrators they hunted down and eliminated.

As Kraft absently gazed at the blue-carpeted walls of his cabin, the somber strains of Tchaikovsky still emanating from the intercom speakers, he pondered that fine line between mainstream environmental advocacy and radicalism. He often wondered if, had a gun been nearby that day in the Everglades, he would have shot that speedboat driver, so great was his initial rage. Remembering this incident helped him to understand the reason for *Ecowar*'s attack on the tuna vessel and its earlier destruction of the squidder.

He also remembered Annie Sawyer's story about freeing the dolphins she had been working with. Kraft had often talked about doing the same thing, especially with newly caught dolphins that were not taking well to captivity. He supposed he just never had the nerve to act on these urges and, as a result, had to suffer the sight of many a dolphin death.

The one thing that he was certain of was the remarkable sophistication of the vessel he currently sailed upon. *Ecowar* was like a glimpse into the future, especially compared with warships like the USS *Chicago*. With its pollution-free propulsion plant and state-of-the-art sensors, *Ecowar* could unlock the great mysteries of the deep. Surely even the deepest trenches were within its operational realm. As a scientific research platform, it would have no equal, and with its aid man could, at long last, fully explore the final remaining earthly frontier.

A knock on the door interrupted his thoughts. Though he was still in no mood for human companionship, Kraft called out, "Come in."

With a bit of difficulty, Annie Sawyer entered the room carrying a covered silver serving tray. "Excuse me, Doc." She sounded somewhat timid. "We missed you at lunch, and I thought you might be hungry."

Kraft watched as she placed the tray on the bedside table. He sensed both her apprehension and concern, and since he had no specific quarrel with her, he remained polite.

"Thanks, Annie, but I don't seem to have much of an appetite."

"Are you sure, Doc?" she asked. "I know for a fact that you haven't eaten a thing in almost twenty-four hours, and you must be famished."

Without giving him a chance to say no, she lifted up one of the plate covers and a cloud of fragrant steam wafted upward. "Please, Doc," she pleaded. "At least give it a try. After all, I made this clambake in your honor."

Unable to resist the sincerity of her request, Kraft reluctantly sat up and sniffed the air. "That sure smells good, Annie," he admitted.

"Then quit bein' the typical stubborn Yank, and give it a taste," she ordered.

Kraft fought back the urge to smile and looked down at the plate, filled with an assortment of seafood and vegetables covered in a rich brown sauce. Well aware of the ache in his empty belly, he swallowed his pride and reached out for a fork.

"I guess that a little nourishment wouldn't hurt me," he said as he prepared to sample the dish.

Sure enough, it tasted as good as it looked, and Kraft commented appreciatively. "My compliments to the cook. What's in it?"

Annie's relief was obvious. "Lobster, clams, mussels, grouper, corn, and potatoes, among other things. Enjoy, Doc."

Kraft ate with increasing relish, even going to the extreme of sopping up the sauce with a piece of crisp French bread. Before he knew it, his plate was empty.

"I guess I didn't realize how hungry I really was," he said a bit sheepishly, embarrassed at his earlier churlishness.

"Like me mother always said, a good appetite is never somethin' to be ashamed of," Annie pronounced while handing him a light-green-colored tart. "Do you like Key lime pie, Doc?"

"You bet I do," he said, giving the dessert a try. A single taste caused him to exclaim, "Annie, I don't know how you did it, but this tastes just like the Key lime pie back home, and I was born and raised in southern Florida, where the recipe originated."

Annie waited for him to finish his dessert before replying. "Wardroom scuttlebutt has it that you didn't take too kindly to the idea of *Ecowar* eliminatin' those dolphin killers on that tuna trawler. I thought you'd be the type of bloke who supported the rights of marine mammals to coexist with man in peace."

"It's not the motive behind *Ecowar*'s actions that bothers me, Annie," Kraft stated. "It's the actions themselves. By sinking that trawler, *Ecowar* puts itself on the same moral level as those fishermen."

Annie was bristling as she took in these words. "I beg to differ with you, Doc. From what I hear, those cold-hearted bastards were indiscriminately shooting into the pod just for the sick fun of it all. And that's not even takin' into account the dolphins that were killed or maimed by their outdated fish-capture methods. No, as far as I'm concerned, they got just what they deserved."

"I wish I could agree with you, Annie. But I find no justification for taking justice into one's own hands. It would be much better to address the problem by appealing to the international community for assistance."

Annie's tone turned bitter. "Even with the support of the United Nations, how many innocent marine mammals would die before they got around to passing legislation with some real teeth in it? It could take decades. And in the meantime, countless innocent species would be pushed to the very brink of extinction."

"At least you'd be going about it in the proper civilized manner," Kraft offered.

"Not once in recorded history has there been an incident of a marine mammal willfully killing a human being," Annie retorted. "You tell me, Doc, which species is the civilized one?"

Before Kraft had a chance to respond, there was a knock on the door, and Jean Moreau entered. Quick to sense the tension in the air, the Frenchman spoke warily.

"Excuse me, *mes amis*. I hope that I'm not interrupting anything."

"Not at all, Commandant," returned Annie. "I was just clearing off the doctor's meal." She picked up the serving tray and gave Kraft an icy stare before turning for the doorway.

Genuinely sorry to have provoked her ire, Kraft tried to be conciliatory. "Thanks again for thinking of me, Annie."

She silently exited, and Moreau took a seat on the

chair at the foot of Kraft's cot. He extracted a meer-
schaum pipe from his hip pocket.

Before lighting it, he asked, "Do you mind, Doctor?
I mix my own tobacco. It's a soothing concoction of sea
grasses and sargassum, flavored with vanilla-scented,
West Indian rum."

"Be my guest," Kraft said absentmindedly, his
thoughts still on his emotional exchange with Annie.

Moreau put a match to the yellowed bowl of his pipe
and took several puffs before exhaling a cloud of thick,
flavorful smoke. "I know it's a nasty habit," he admitted.
"But it helps me to relax and digest my food."

Unable to coax the merest bit of conversation from
his distracted guest, Moreau was content to sit back and
enjoy his pipe. In the background, the symphony was well
into its final movement.

"Ah, the finale of Peter Ilich Tchaikovsky's famous
Pathétique. They say that during its composition,
Tchaikovsky was often in tears. Was it but a coincidence
that only nine days after the symphony's first public performance the composer died of cholera? Or was it true
that Tchaikovsky felt its composition to be a premonition
of his own death?"

Completely oblivious to this comment, Kraft stood
up and began pacing nervously from one corner of the
compartment to the other. "Have you notified the navy
of my safety as yet?" he demanded.

Despite Kraft's tenseness Moreau calmly answered,
"There's no reason to lie to you, Doctor. For the sake of our
security, there can be no such communication on our part."

This revelation stopped Kraft in midstep, and he
spoke angrily. "I should have known you'd break your
promise."

"Easy, *mon ami*. You know as well as I the dangers
faced by a submarine when ascending to communicate.
Even *Ecowar* is forced to the surface to accomplish this,
leaving us vulnerable to detection by surface units, passing airplanes, or even satellites."

"All I'm asking is that you inform the authorities that I'm all right," returned Kraft. "At the very least you owe that to my family and friends."

Moreau thoughtfully puffed on his pipe before replying. "Perhaps we can make arrangements to get word to the U.S. Navy once we reach port."

"And how long is that going to be?" Kraft wanted to know.

"Je ne sais pas," Moreau answered. "Who can say exactly, though our food supplies limit us to a maximum of fourteen more days."

"Fourteen days!" Kraft sounded disgusted. "That's just great. I've got to be held prisoner here for another two weeks?"

"Prisoner, *mon ami*?" Moreau was genuinely taken aback. "Your door is not locked, and our home is yours."

Raising his hands in disgust, Kraft resumed his frantic pacing. Moreau watched him, stifling the urge to laugh at his impatience.

"I'm sorry to hear that you're not happy with our hospitality, Doctor," he managed to say.

"It's not your hospitality that's the cause of my upset," Kraft tossed back.

"Of course it isn't, Doctor. It's the nature of our mission that bothers you so, isn't it, my friend?"

"Your damned right it is!" Kraft exclaimed. "The moment you rammed that defenseless trawler, I wanted no more part of this vessel."

Moreau shook his head sadly. "What a shame, Doctor. And here you've only seen a small sample of *Ecowar*'s capabilities."

"I've witnessed more than enough already," spat Kraft. "Though there's no doubting that *Ecowar*'s design is decades ahead of any existing submarine, it's how it's being utilized that bothers me."

"That's too bad." Moreau sighed. "I sincerely respect your work, Doctor. And I'm continually amazed that the hand of fate has brought you to us. There's so much that I want to share with you, so much that I know you'll find enlightening. This is especially the case with our current destination."

With the background music swiftly moving toward its moody climax, Kraft stopped pacing, his curiosity suddenly piqued. "And where's that?"

"Moruroa, in French Polynesia," Moreau answered.

Having taken the proverbial bait, Kraft continued his probing. "And *Ecowar*'s reason for traveling there?"

"We plan to halt a scheduled underwater test of an advanced French nuclear device, which is supposed to take place in three more days." Moreau's tone was blithe as he baited the hook of Kraft's curiosity.

"But France is a signatory of the Nuclear Test Ban Treaty," Kraft countered. "And I thought that such tests were strictly forbidden."

"They are," retorted Moreau. "And that's why *Ecowar* must stop this criminal madness before yet more poisonous plutonium is released into our waters and atmosphere."

"If what you say is true, I'd be more than willing to accompany you on this portion of your journey. Though one thing still bothers me. How do you plan to stop this test? Surely you can't take on the entire French Navy."

Moreau laughed. "No, *mon ami*. *Ecowar* won't be taking on the entire Marine Nationale. And you can rest assured that the loss of life, if any, will be kept to a bare minimum."

Already forgetting the doubts and concerns that had previously possessed him, Kraft found himself intrigued. Atomic-bomb tests belonged to the unenlightened past. In the 1950s, he had absorbed his fair share of strontium 90, released during the atmospheric nuclear tests of the day. Nuclear weapons were anathema to everything he believed in, and Kraft wondered why the French risked both international censure and possible environmental catastrophe to detonate one of these wasteful, dangerous devices.

With the realization that his headstrong guest was on the verge of becoming an ally, Moreau decided to share a personal story with him. Yet before doing so, he repacked his pipe and summoned the inner strength needed to tell his painful tale.

"*Mon ami,* please make yourself comfortable while I bare a small portion of my soul to you."

Curious in spite of himself, Kraft returned to his cot, sat down on the mattress, and focused his gaze on his bald-headed host, who suddenly looked old and very vulnerable.

"Doctor, please believe me when I tell you that I understand the anguished confusion that you've been experiencing today. Though you may think me a bitter, callous man, dare open your mind to that which I'm about to share with you, and perhaps you'll emerge with a better idea of the complex forces that motivate me.

"The environmental vigilante you see sitting before you spent his formative years as conventionally as possible. Two decades ago I was a lieutenant in the French Navy. As you might have guessed, I began my career as a submariner. Exciting as this duty was, I had a new wife and infant daughter to consider, and Paris approved my transfer request after ten long years as an undersea warrior.

"My first reassignment was in Moruroa, in the South Pacific, the very island to which we're currently headed. For many years this top-secret location was the home of the Force de Frappe's nuclear weapons range. A combination of atmospheric, surface, and underwater blasts took place here. Like many of our generation, I took these tests for granted as the price we had to pay to remain free from Communist aggression. But all this changed the fated morning I was sent to a neighboring island to test for contamination.

"On the previous day, we had detonated a monstrous fifteen-megaton hydrogen bomb, one thousand times stronger than the weapon dropped on

Hiroshima. Because our illustrious president was visiting at the time, the test took place as scheduled, even though an unexpected storm occurred minutes before detonation.

"As it turned out, because of this storm, the wind changed direction and the tiny island of Takutea was placed directly downwind from the blast. Though I and my men were protected by radiation suits, the native population of the island was going about their business barely clothed, oblivious to the lethal, invisible danger that completely surrounded them.

"Our Geiger counters went off the scale, and we saw with our own eyes the coating of pulverized coral debris that fell in a strange snow the previous day. Many of the children were putting the highly contaminated ash in their mouths, and one elder was rubbing in into his eyes, to see if it would clear up his cataracts.

"Needless to say, we rushed back to base to report this calamity. I requested an immediate evacuation of Takutea's inhabitants, which, much to my utter horror, was unequivocally denied. It seemed that Command wanted to take this unprecedented opportunity to observe the island's population as scientists observe guinea pigs in a laboratory. Sworn to secrecy, we were then sent back to Takutea to monitor the radiation's effects.

"By the time we returned, three days later, the radiation was already taking its toll. Almost everyone was experiencing an aggravating skin rash. And more than half the natives were suffering from severe nausea and hair loss.

"Again I returned to Moruroa insisting that the inhabitants be moved. This time I was officially reprimanded, and transferred to an administrative assignment — in Papeete, where my wife and daughter were living.

"My naval career was never the same afterward. With visions of the natives of Takutea succumbing to cancer, leukemia, and all sorts of horrible birth defects, I resigned my commission shortly thereafter."

Moreau paused at this point to relight his pipe, and Kraft, who had listened to his story with growing horror, spoke up. "That's some story."

"Wait, *mon ami*," said Moreau. "The most tragic part has yet to come." The Frenchman took another puff on his pipe, before continuing. "My environmental consciousness was fully awakened by this time, and instead of immediately returning to France, I remained in Tahiti. Breaking my sworn vows of silence, I publicly protested the military's inaction. When this rather feeble effort failed to generate any support, and I learned of another impending bomb test, I knew that there was only one course open to me—I would charter a boat, set sail for Moruroa, and do my best to sneak into the test range and disrupt the test.

"Like a fool, I allowed my family to accompany me. The voyage was rough, and we arrived at our destination badly battered by rough seas and strong winds. A daring piece of nighttime seamanship on my part guided us into the atoll where the bomb was to be detonated in twenty-four hours. When the military learned of our presence the next morning, they hastily sent a corvette to escort us away. Of course, I refused to budge. As my wife prepared to document the inevitable confrontation on film, which we had hoped later to share with the rest of the world, the unthinkable happened. Without even a warning shot, the corvette rammed us directly amidships and cut our fragile sailboat cleanly in half.

"I was on the fo'c'sle when they hit us and was merely thrown into the water uninjured. My wife, however, picked that inopportune moment to run belowdeck and get our daughter. I can only pray that the end for them was swift, for both were in direct line of the corvette's bow as it sliced into us."

With his voice quavering at this point, Moreau halted a moment to regain his composure. He looked out at

Kraft with tearstained eyes, and the marine biologist felt genuine compassion for this man, whose idealism cost him the ones he loved most.

"Mon ami," Moreau bravely added, "now you know the true reason I dare not compromise *Ecowar*'s presence until our current mission is over. Because, for the sake of the health of generations yet unborn, this time I will not fail!"

14

Peter Kraft awoke from his sound slumber to the exotic strains of an Indian sitar raga. He felt rested, and a quick check of his watch showed that he had slept well over nine hours. This was most unusual, and he supposed that the great stress of the last couple of days had finally taken its toll. His growling stomach indicated that his appetite had returned, but before heading for the wardroom, he decided to try to track down a shower.

After brushing his teeth and shaving, he pulled on his blue coveralls and headed into the passageway. As luck would have it, a member of the crew was just passing by as he stepped out of his doorway. He recognized the slightly built, brown-skinned individual from his previous visit to *Ecowar*'s control room. He had been seated to Kraft's far left at that time, and appeared to be the sub's helmsman.

"Excuse me," said Kraft. "But I was wondering where the bathing facilities were located."

The sailor stopped, and a broad grin crossed his studious face. "Of course, sir. *Ecowar* is outfitted with two standard showers. The most accessible one is located in the crew's berthing compartment. That's the first door aft on your right."

"Thank you," replied Kraft, then added, "By the way, I don't believe we've been properly introduced."

"No, we haven't," returned the man. "Though I have the advantage in knowing your name, Dr. Kraft. I'm Raghib Godavari, from Bombay, India."

"That's a fascinating part of the world," Kraft replied. "One that I hope to be able to visit one day soon. By chance, did you pick out our wonderful background music today?"

Raghib once more grinned. "That I did, Doctor."

"Well, you made an excellent choice, Raghib. It's most refreshing after the rather heavy music selection of the last two days. What exactly are we hearing?"

The Indian readily responded. "It's an original piece composed by Pandit Ravi Shankar. This particular recording was made in July 1988, inside the Kremlin's Palace of Culture in what was then the Soviet Union. The concert was the culmination of a yearlong Indian festival in the USSR. It was performed by over 140 musicians and singers, whose diverse elements included the Russian Folk Ensemble, Moscow's chamber orchestra, and of course, Ravi Shankar's talented ensemble."

"No wonder the mix of sounds is so interesting," Kraft observed.

"You are most perceptive, Doctor. For the piece is named *Swar Milan,* which means 'musical notes meeting,' to honor this coming together of vastly different cultures."

"From what I've seen, it's a bit like *Ecowar,*" Kraft reflected.

"That it is," said Raghib, smiling. "Now, if you'll please excuse me, Doctor, I must get back to the helm.

Please feel free to join me in the control room after your shower. If you'd like, I'd be willing to give you a driving lesson."

"I'd enjoy that," returned Kraft.

As Godavari resumed his way forward Kraft traveled in the opposite direction. The crew's berthing compartment turned out to be a suite of six individual cabins surrounding a central bathroom. The cabins themselves were rather small, and reminded him of standard accommodations aboard a cruise ship. Each offered a comfortably furnished, private living space, complete with a full-size bed and wall-mounted desk. They were kept spotlessly clean, with the ubiquitous posters of various marine mammals hung on their carpeted walls.

All of the cabins appeared to be vacant, and Kraft gratefully entered the bathroom. A closed, frosted-glass door apparently led into the shower itself. Before opening it, he pulled off his coveralls and, dressed only in scivvies, proceeded to yank open the stall's door.

Much to his surprise, he found a naked Annie Sawyer inside, in the process of drying her hair with a towel. Without the least embarrassment, she looked up to identify the intruder.

"I'm sorry, Annie," blurted Kraft, quickly shutting the glass door, but not before getting a glance at her long, smooth legs, curly brown pubic patch, tight waist, and firm, bulging breasts.

"Don't sweat it, Doc," came her voice from inside the stall. "I'll be out in a jiffy."

Kraft's pulse had yet to return to normal as the glass door swung open with a loud click and Annie stepped out. A white, terrycloth towel, wrapped around her body, barely covered her.

"It's all yours, Doc," she said matter-of-factly.

"I'm really sorry, Annie, for barging in like that," he nervously repeated.

"Like I said, don't worry about it, Doc. With living

space as tight as it is aboard *Ecowar,* we're all used to the perils of communal living."

Embarrassment still flushed Kraft's reddened cheeks as he shyly looked up into the woman's big green eyes. "I guess some things aboard *Ecowar* are still going to take some getting used to," he awkwardly admitted.

"Then you plan to be stayin' with us a bit longer?" she hopefully asked.

"It appears that way, Annie. And by the way, I'm really sorry if I upset you last night. Here you go to all the bother of cooking me a special meal and providing room service, and all I do to show my appreciation is argue with you."

Kraft, clothed only in a pair of flimsy, white cotton briefs, noted how Annie's eyes momentarily scanned his own body. Ever grateful that he had kept himself physically fit, he nonetheless instinctively tightened the muscles of his stomach and well-developed pectorals.

"What happened to your leg?" she asked, pointing to the fresh scar that lined his right thigh.

"Bicycle accident," he replied. "I went off my ten-speed this past winter, and really did a number on my hip and femur. In fact, I'll be carrying a couple of steel implants as a result of this accident for the rest of my life."

With the skill of a trained nurse, Annie reached out and tenderly traced the pencil-thin line of scarred tissue. "That must have been some fall, Doc. How long were you laid up?"

"I had to keep all weight off the leg for three months. But I didn't need a cast, and once I got used to getting around with a walker and crutches, it really wasn't that bad."

"You're lucky it healed so well," she said as her gaze returned to his eyes. "Did you sleep well?"

"Like a rock, Annie. I guess it was all that good food in my belly that put me out."

Annie smiled warmly. "I'm glad you enjoyed it. I gather that your conversation with the commandant last night went well."

"That it did, Annie. Jean-Louis Moreau is quite an interesting fellow."

Annie appeared relieved to hear this. "The commandant is one of the greatest men I've ever had the honor of meeting. He's a guiding light for all of us."

"Last night after you left us, he graciously allowed me an enlightening glimpse into his painful past. As a result, I think I have a better understanding of *Ecowar's* mission. And just perhaps I can help redirect you in a more positive direction."

"There's no doubting that your presence aboard *Ecowar* has greatly influenced us already, Doc. But just be careful that the roles don't get reversed, and it's your beliefs that end up being redirected."

"Sounds like it's going to be an interesting cruise together, Annie."

"It sure does, Doc. Now, why don't you get on with that shower, and I'll pull you some clean towels and a fresh uniform. Would you care for some breakfast afterward?"

"I thought you'd never ask," Kraft teased. "What's on the menu?"

"How does an omelet made from cholesterol-free eggs, smoked salmon, and onions sound, Doc?"

"You're making me homesick for Miami Beach just mentioning such a combination. You're a gem, Annie."

The shower turned out to have a hand-held European-style nozzle. There was plenty of pressure and an abundant supply of hot water to go with it. The hard, needlelike spray was especially welcome on the tense muscles at the back of his neck and along his shoulders. He found no evidence of a water restrictor, and took his time lathering his body with aloe soap.

He emerged from the stall feeling reborn. As promised, Annie had left him a clean towel, beside which hung a fresh pair of boxer shorts and a black jumpsuit.

His blue coveralls were nowhere to be seen, and he didn't miss them in the least as he dried off and dressed in this new attire. The one-piece jumpsuit reminded him of an air-force flight suit. It just fit him, and he was able to loosen the waistband by readjusting a pair of Velcro straps.

A particularly rousing, Oriental-flavored sitar raga accompanied him to the nearby wardroom. There, he found the sub's navigator seated at the round table sipping a cup of tea, a bathymetric chart spread out before her. Kraft was all prepared to introduce himself when Annie entered from the galley passageway.

She took a second to look him over approvingly before commenting, "Looks like I got the fit just right, Doc. You're a real member of the crew now. How about that breakfast?"

"Go for it, Annie," he returned.

As Ivana Borisov looked up to see what was going on, Annie diplomatically added, "Doc, have you met our navigator?"

"Not officially," said Kraft as he held out his hand and accepted a rather cool handshake from the navigator.

"There's plenty of hot tea in the samovar, Doc," Annie informed him. "Help yourself while I throw together that omelet."

Annie disappeared into the galley, and Kraft poured himself a cup of tea and took a seat beside the navigator. She seemed rather reserved, and he did his best to break the ice.

"That chart you're studying looks more like the type of old-fashioned bathymetric maps I'm used to seeing," he commented lightly. "It sure gives you a flat perspective compared to that 3-D, holographic view in the control room."

"That it does, Comrade," she curtly responded.

Wondering if this woman was incredibly shy or just plain uncommunicative, Kraft persisted. "Is that a chart of Moruroa?"

"No, Comrade. It is of the Marshall group of islands, which we will shortly be transiting."

Kraft scooted over to have a closer look at the chart and found a familiar name among the dozen or so tiny islands visible here. "How close to Kwajalein will we be getting?" he asked.

Borisov looked toward him curiously. "Why's that, Comrade? Have you been to Kwajalein before?"

Her question was delivered in a tone more appropriate for an interrogation than to a social conversation, but Kraft nonetheless answered her casually. "Not only have I never been there, but this is the first time I've ever seen it on a map. One of my colleagues was stationed there, at the missile-test-range facility, and was always raving about the gorgeous reefs in the area."

"That must have been quite some time ago," Borisov observed. "Because today those reefs are all but gone."

"What happened to them?" he asked.

"As far as we can tell, pollution of the seas is the number-one culprit. Just last year I got the opportunity to participate in an expedition whose primary purpose was to study the causes of the reef's demise."

"Was this aboard *Ecowar*?" Kraft questioned.

"No, Comrade. This submarine was still under construction at that time. The expedition I'm talking about was organized under the auspices of my former employer, the Black Sea Marine Institute, at Odessa."

Having formerly corresponded with one of the founders of this institute, Kraft eagerly inquired, "You don't happen to know Dr. Viktor Orlov, do you?"

His innocent question prompted an enthusiastic response. "Of course I do, Comrade! Dr. Orlov was one of my undergraduate advisers. How in the world do you know of him?"

"We first met at a symposium in San Diego several years ago," Kraft revealed. "Since my main interest is cetacean behavior, I was fascinated with his unique experiments in interspecies communications. I was especially intrigued by his parapsychological approach to breaking the dolphin-man communication barrier."

"I know those experiments very well, Comrade. In fact, I was tankside one day when I personally witnessed an amazing display of telepathy. A famous Gypsy clairvoyant was brought in from Moscow. A mask was put over her eyes, and without any hand or verbal signals on her part, she was somehow able to utilize extrasensory means to make contact with the tank's two dolphins.

"All Dr. Orlov had to do was whisper a certain command in her ear, such as a tail walk or leap. Then after a brief period of intense concentration, the dolphins miraculously responded, with a one-hundred-percent success ratio. All of us assembled there were really spooked. And we were so hopeful that a great scientific breakthrough would occur—when the break up of the Soviet Union, of all things, forced all of us at the institute into an early retirement after we lost our funding."

"What a shame," remarked Kraft, who was distracted by the reappearance of Annie Sawyer.

"You two are really somethin'," Annie said as she placed a covered platter in front of Kraft. "When I left a couple of minutes ago, the two of you were complete strangers. Now you're yakking away like a couple of long-lost cousins."

"Annie, do you remember those stories I was telling you about my institute's telepathy experiments with dolphins?" Ivana asked excitedly. "Well, Dr. Kraft here knows Viktor Orlov, the man responsible for them."

"You don't say," returned Annie.

More interested in satisfying his gnawing hunger than any further chatter, Kraft lifted up the plate's silver cover. Though it didn't quite rival the lox, onions, and eggs at Wolfie's Delicatessen, the omelet was tasty all the same. All he needed was a poppy-seed bagel to really feel right at home.

"Your chow is just delicious, Annie," Kraft complimented between bites. "How do you manage with no grocery store close by?"

"It can be a real challenge sometimes," she said. "And it certainly takes a lot of initial planning. Of course, the commandant's desire to have no red meat on the menu increases my work. Did you know that those eggs you're eatin' are made from veggies? And that goes for the milk and butter as well."

"Sounds like you run a real healthy kitchen aboard *Ecowar*," Kraft said as he polished off his omelet.

At this moment three soft electronic tones sounded from the intercom, followed by the deep, silken voice of Ezra Melindi. "Ms. Borisov, you are needed in Control."

Lifting her head, the navigator spoke into the ceiling-mounted transmitter. "Acknowledged, sir."

Getting up to leave, she turned to Kraft. "It was a pleasure talking with you, Comrade Doctor," she said while folding up her chart.

"Likewise," Kraft said as he watched her nod toward Annie and quickly exit. When the door closed, he took a sip of tea and commented, "She seems like an interesting lady."

"That's putting it mildly," returned Annie. "Ivana has many diverse talents. She's a superb photographer, and is responsible for many of the whale photos gracing *Ecowar*. She was also being trained as her country's first female aquanaut. If it wasn't for the dissolution of the USSR, she'd probably be living in the Black Sea in an experimental underwater habitat right now."

"Annie, what do you think about telepathic communication with dolphins?" Kraft asked on an impulse.

Annie looked at him to make sure he wasn't just trying to be funny. Assured of his seriousness, she replied, "You know, Ivana's asked me that very same question, and I really can't say. As a trainer, I spent many hours at the dolphin pool. The behaviors I was teaching were mainly based upon food rewards. And though I found my students amazingly bright, most of the time they reacted on the same behavioral level as a smart dog.

"Then, just when I'd start to take them for granted, they'd go and do something right out of the Twilight Zone. Like the time we invited some local children to swim in the pool. My dolphins loved to interact with humans in the water—except for one temperamental old-timer that we named Crusty.

"Crusty liked to play rough, and loved to bite and bump us. Worried about how he'd treat the children, I went into the tank to personally supervise his behavior. One of the visitin' lads was autistic. He was respondin' incredibly well to the dolphins, really comin' out of his shell and havin' a grand ol' time in the water pettin' them. Somehow Crusty picked up on him, butted me away with his snout, and swam up to the child. Expectin' the worst, I hurried over to the youngster's side and witnessed a truly astounding sight—ol' rough-and-tough Crusty was rubbin' up against the child as gentle as could be. Why, the brute even offered the lad a ride around the pool on his dorsal fin, something he never did for us!"

Kraft smiled at so warmhearted a tale, then looked at Annie pensively. "That kind of makes you wonder, doesn't it, Annie? Though I've never witnessed anything quite that dramatic, sometimes when I'm alone with the two dolphins I'm currently training, I sense in them a certain receptiveness toward me. It's almost as if they can pick up my mood, cheering me up when I'm down, and just being mellow when my nerves are frazzled. When I broke my leg and couldn't visit them for several weeks, they were irritable and uncooperative. Their fish intake dramatically dropped, and my team had to discontinue any attempts to teach them new behaviors."

"How did they react when you first visited them again?" Annie asked.

Kraft smiled. "That was a morning I'll never forget. I'm told they began excitedly chattering away soon after the car I was being driven in entered the institute grounds. By the time we reached the parking space at the side of their tank, they were going positively crazy—leaping and tail walking almost nonstop. I had serious second thoughts about climbing the small flight of steps leading to the tank's edge. But I could clearly hear the excited squeals and whistles and didn't dare disappoint them. Thank goodness I didn't, because the joyous reunion that followed was as thrilling as anything I've ever known."

"That's a wonderful story, Doc," Annie said dreamily. "And it's experiences like these that really make me a believer in dolphin intelligence. Even though we still can't sit down with them and have a real conversation, we have somehow managed to build a bridge between our two species. And if man would only accept that there's a very good possibility that dolphins are our intellectual equals, it would be a big step toward seeing them as free beings, who have a right to live without fear of being captured, brutalized, or harassed."

Kraft couldn't argue with her view, and he suddenly found himself staring into Annie's deep green eyes. There could be no doubting the rapport that was developing between them. Confident and intelligent, Annie wasn't afraid to stick to her convictions, no matter the consequences. Kraft thought her a wonderful cook, an admirable nurse, and a woman of great physical beauty. Seeing her naked in the shower stall had only confirmed this, and he felt a strange tightening in his stomach as he fought the urge to kiss her.

The exotic strains of Ravi Shankar's sitar wove an erotic spell in the background, and Annie, too, felt herself entranced. The headstrong Yank certainly had possibilities. He was unquestionably bright and confident. He could be charming and quick with a compliment one moment, and deadly serious the next. Yet despite his obstinacy, he seemed sensitive and vulnerable, just the combination of traits she found attractive in a man. His rugged good looks were an additional asset, Annie thought, feeling the first stirrings of physical longing as she remembered her encounter with him beside the shower—his broad shoulders, the rippling muscles of his flat stomach, his narrow hips, and long, well-proportioned legs, strong from years of bike riding.

It had been much too long since she had given herself to a man. She barely remembered what it was like to feel real desire, to be touched and to share her deepest secrets with another. Well aware of the awkwardness of the situation, and the commandant's strict policy in such matters, she summoned her will to break this spell.

"A penny for your thoughts, Doc," she teasingly whispered.

Kraft sighed. "Annie, there's so much more I'd like to know about you. But I'm not sure if this is the proper time or place."

Annie smiled knowingly and put her fingers to his lips to silence him. "I hear ya, Doc. And I feel likewise. For now, let's just continue as friends, and let the future take care of itself."

With the spell broken, Kraft reached up his arms and stretched. "I guess I'd better let you get back to work, Annie. Raghib offered to give me a driving lesson, and I'm going to take him up on it."

"You won't be sorry," she replied. "Driving *Ecowar* is like playin' a computer game." When Kraft stood up, she added, "I sure hope you'll be joinin' us for dinner this evening. Afterward, there's goin' to be a discussion session and slide show."

"I wouldn't miss it for anything," returned Kraft,

who felt strangely empty as he excused himself and left the wardroom.

As it turned out, he arrived in the control room just in time to witness an extraordinary event unfolding on the compartment's central display screen. It took a moment for his eyes to adjust to the sudden red-lit darkness, but when they did, he found the entire screen filled with hundreds of large, darting, silver-flanked fish. The details were so lifelike that he felt as if he were in the very midst of this giant school. As he carefully worked his way over to the line of command chairs that faced the screen, he heard the deep voice of Ezra Melindi.

"Welcome, good doctor. You arrived at a most auspicious moment. Only seconds ago our bow-mounted video camera captured this school of albacore tuna, with whom *Ecowar* currently shares these waters. Do you know much about the albacore, Doctor?"

"I'm afraid my knowledge of this particular species is limited to enjoying them in a salad," Kraft admitted.

"I, too, enjoy a good tuna-fish salad," replied Melindi. "As I was just telling my shipmates here, the tuna is a most elusive, misunderstood animal. Because of its economic importance, I was privileged to spend some time with my country's ever-expanding tuna fleet. I learned then that creatures such as those before us can swim as fast as fifty-five miles per hour. Many swim up to a million miles by the age of fifteen, and weigh over fifteen hundred pounds, living on a diet of squid, crabs, eel, and shrimp. Interestingly enough, at full speed those fins of theirs retract into recessed body cavities, allowing the albacore to rocket forward with a minimum of flow restriction. Like a shark, if they were ever to stop swimming, they'd suffocate."

Ivana Borisov began now to speak. "The Black Sea Institute was one of the first organizations to study the world's tuna fisheries," she said from her customary position on Melindi's right. "At that time we learned that the Asians were responsible for pulling in seventy percent of the earth's tuna catch. For the most part, they utilized longlines, many stretching over eighty miles and holding up to two thousand baited hooks. The Japanese alone set over twelve million miles of longline, enough to circle the globe five hundred times!"

"In Kenya, they use the purse-seine method," Melindi interjected. "My people long ago learned the secret of locating the tuna under schools of dolphin. Once they are spotted, heavy skiffs are used to deploy a massive wall of floating net. A speedboat is then utilized to herd the dolphins into this net. On my first day out, I saw this wasteful method round up over two thousand rare spinner dolphins. The roiling sea was white with their explosive spray as the panicked dolphins vainly struggled to escape. And sadly enough, half this herd was doomed to die, with the result being one measly yellowfin tuna."

The immense school of fast-moving tuna continued to fill the display screen. Feeling as if he were swimming among them, Kraft continued to marvel at this fish-eye view. "Such needless dolphin deaths have been well documented in America's tuna industry as well," he revealed. "Two decades ago U.S. purse seiners in search of tuna killed nearly a half-million dolphins. Today, in response to public outcry, that number is down drastically."

His remark generated a passionate response from the blond-haired Norwegain, who was seated to the left of Ezra Melindi. "It's still way too many!" said Karl Ivar disgustedly.

"For once, I commend the Americans for at the very least trying," offered Ivana Borisov. "Because the other tuna fleets of the world have yet to be so enlightened, and are responsible for killing hundreds of thousands of dolphins each and every year."

"So much for enjoying my next tuna salad," Melindi muttered softly.

A moment of silence followed. All eyes remained

locked on the screen, where the darting tuna seemed to go on forever. Yet as suddenly as they appeared, they vanished, and *Ecowar* had the blue depths all to themselves once again.

"Dr. Kraft, would you like to drive?" asked Raghib Godavari from his position at the far left command chair.

Still apprehensive about taking the helm, Kraft found himself seeking permission from *Ecowar*'s executive officer. "Is it okay with you, Mr. Melindi?"

"Why, of course, good doctor," replied the grinning Melindi.

Kraft tentatively crossed over to the helm and watched as Godavari unbuckled his shoulder harness and stood up. "Please make yourself comfortable, Doctor," he said, gesturing toward his vacant chair.

Kraft uneasily settled into this new perch. A slight adjustment was needed to get the chair's shoulder restraints to fit properly. Once this was completed, he did his best to calm himself by taking a series of deep breaths.

"Doctor, go ahead and gently grasp the two joysticks that are set into each of your armrests," Godavari instructed. "And please make certain not to press the buttons set into the top portion of the pistol grip."

Kraft obeyed these instructions. He found the joysticks cool to the touch, their grips readily conforming to the shape of his hand.

"The right stick controls the vessel's pitch and yaw. By shoving it forward, we will dive and gain depth. Moving it in the opposite direction will cause us to ascend and lose depth. Course changes are achieved with sidewise pressure on the same stick, moving it in the direction in which you desire to turn."

"What functions does the left stick control?" asked the nervous student.

"For the most part, it determines our speed," Godavari answered. "The throttle is opened by pulling it back, and closed when shoved forward. But for right now, we'll concentrate exclusively on the right joystick, and start you off with a minor depth change. Doctor, carefully feel for the pistol grip's topmost button."

With his right index finger, Kraft cautiously isolated this button from two others. He nodded when this was achieved, and his instructor continued. "Go ahead and press this button a single time, Doctor. Then look to the lower left portion of the display screen."

Kraft did so, and watched as a digital display counter popped up onto the screen. One of the displays was in the shape of a bar graph, with increments in meters. The other was circular, and appeared to be a compass. A third digital counter displayed the numerals "73."

"Doctor, you have just accessed our current depth, course, and speed," the helmsman explained. "To isolate the depth gauge alone, press the top button twice."

Kraft did as instructed, and the bar graph greatly expanded. The digital counter beside the graph now registered 150, a fact Godavari immediately explained.

"The graph shows our current depth to be 150 meters. I would like you to take us down another one hundred meters. But before doing so, is there any additional information you'd like to know?"

Kraft thought a moment before replying. "It sure would be nice to know the depth of the ocean in these parts."

"Precisely," Godavari responded. "And to access those all-important bathymetrics, press the bottom button a single time."

Thankful he had given the right answer, Kraft depressed this switch and watched as the central portion of the display screen filled with a holographic view of the surrounding waters. At present, they were following the meander of a wide undersea valley, whose distant walls were formed by a succession of jagged seamounts. The depth of this valley ranged from 5,470 to 4,956 meters, and offered them plenty of water to work in.

"It looks all clear to me," Kraft observed.

"Then what are you waiting for, Doctor? Take us down to 250 meters."

With one eye on the depth gauge, Kraft took a deep breath and shoved the right joystick forward. Almost instantaneously *Ecowar*'s bow lurched downward, and Kraft's restraining harness bit into his shoulders while the depth counter swiftly dropped.

"Easy on that stick!" warned Godavari, who had to grasp a ceiling-mounted handhold to keep from tumbling forward.

Kraft immediately inched back the joystick, and their angle of descent leveled out dramatically.

"That's much better," said Godavari. "Remember, we're cutting through the water at over seventy knots. It doesn't take much angle on our planes to alter our depth, so address that stick gingerly."

Concentrating his efforts on getting a proper feel for the stick, Kraft momentarily averted his glance from the display screen. Only a few seconds passed before his instructor's voice once more cried out in warning: "Doctor, you'd better watch our depth!"

Kraft's startled gaze returned to the screen, and he found it hard to believe that they were already down below 280 meters. To bring them up to ordered depth, he took the helmsman's advice and carefully inched back the stick to reverse this descent.

This time when *Ecowar* changed direction, the angle upward was barely noticeable. Before he knew it, the depth gauge broke 255 meters, and with the slightest of manipulations, he was able to achieve a perfect "250" on the digital counter. Only then did he allow himself a relieved sigh.

"And I thought driving my ten-speed was fun," he joked. "Did it take you long to get the feel of *Ecowar*'s helm, Raghib?"

The Indian stifled a grin and humbly replied. "Not really, Doctor. You see, I was the one who originally developed this fly-by-wire system while a graduate student in Bombay."

"May I ask why you didn't keep this technology inside India?" Kraft asked.

This time Godavari hesitated a moment before responding. "I offered it to the Indian Navy. But they were content to continue importing their outdated submarine technology from the Soviet Union. Thus I had no choice but to offer my designs on the international market."

"And that must be where you met Commandant Moreau," Kraft concluded.

Godavari nodded, then pointed back to the display screen. "You've got it, Doctor. But let's get back to the subject at hand. Now that you know how to control our depth, it's time to try a course change. So that we don't go too far out of the way, change course to bearing one-five-five. But don't neglect to check those bathymetrics first."

In this fascinating way, the morning passed. By the time Godavari replaced him at the helm, Kraft's pleasure and confidence in his driving had increased to the point where he practically had to be dragged out of the Indian's command chair.

Soon afterward Jean Moreau joined them, and the light mood that prevailed quickly turned solemn. Kraft sat in the jumpseat to Moreau's right, and noted how his presence altered the crew's personalities. There were no longer any spontaneous comments or small talk. The atmosphere was all business as Moreau strapped himself into his chair and scanned the screen to determine their progress.

"It appears that we should be able to get a visual on the Bikini Atoll from this distance," Moreau observed. "Mr. Godavari, bring us up to visual-scan depth. Karl Ivar, prepare Freddie for launch."

Kraft watched the helmsman expertly pull back his right joystick, and *Ecowar* initiated a barely perceptible ascent that halted at a depth of twenty-five meters. On the center portion of the display screen, the bathymetric chart showed them to be on the easternmost edge of the undersea valley they had been following steadily southward. A large seamount capped by a circular atoll rose to the surface off their port bow. Kraft assumed that this was Bikini.

"We have attained visual-scan depth," Godavari stated.

"Launch Freddie," ordered Moreau. "And summon the chief."

The deck shook slightly as Karl Ivar addressed his keypad. "Freddie away. Data link secure."

As the ROV's video camera activated, the entire screen filled with a fish-eye view of the surrounding sea. The bright afternoon sun illuminated an expanse of crystal-clear blue water. Yet any sea life was conspicuously absent.

"Ten meters to surface," Karl Ivar reported.

Seconds later Freddie completed its ascent. A gentle chop rippled the sea's surface; the horizon was cloudless and the sky a striking blue. Quickly now, the video lens made a hasty 360-degree scan.

"Focus scan on bearing zero-four-eight," Moreau directed, after determining that there were no surface vessels in the area. "Magnification power twenty."

A snaking gray line of distant land flashed onto the screen. The profile took on additional detail when Moreau ordered the lens to maximum amplification. It proved to be a barren piece of low-lying, sand-filled land, devoid of even a palm tree. A tall antenna and a small concrete hut were the extent of its habitations. Kraft could only wonder what the reason was for the barbed-wire-tipped, chain-link fence that encircled this structure.

"So this is the infamous atoll of death," said a Japanese-accented voice from behind.

Chief Mikio Yushiro slowly limped over to Moreau's left side and continued. "I have waited many years to see this legendary place."

"So have we all," remarked Moreau. "*Mes amis,* feast your eyes on this barren expanse of volcanic, coral-encrusted sand. This cursed place witnessed sixty-six separate nuclear tests from 1946 to 1958."

"I wonder if we'll ever know the true amount of radioactive fallout released into the atmosphere as a result of those useless tests." The gray-haired chief sounded bitter as he unconsciously massaged his deformed leg. "The development of nuclear weapons as a so-called deterrent to war was a curse on generations yet unborn. And all of us alive today are paying the price in the form of the planet's skyrocketing rates of cancer, leukemia, and related illnesses."

"What truly bothers me is that such testing continues to go on even today," observed Ezra Melindi.

This comment elicited an emotional response from Jean Moreau. "At least we can all take some satisfaction in knowing that in another forty hours, *Ecowar* will be in position to strike a crippling blow to the test ambitions of one member of the world's nuclear club. And perhaps the international community will finally—"

"Surface contact, Commandant!" Karl Ivar interrupted. "I've got an active sonobuoy in the water, bearing two-six-zero."

"Retrieve Freddie!" Moreau firmly ordered. "Mr. Godavari, take us down to three hundred meters. And carefully, *mon ami.* We must not cut Freddie's umbilical."

Not certain what was going on here, Kraft watched the helmsman guide them back into the protective depths. Noting the concern of all those assembled beside him, he worriedly questioned, "Are we in some sort of trouble?"

"Have no fear, Doctor," Ezra Melindi whispered. "It appears that these waters have just been visited by an aircraft of some sort, which dropped a sonobuoy nearby. Believe me, it will be of little consequence."

Though Kraft wished he could share the second in command's optimism, he only had to scan the worried face of Jean Moreau to know the seriousness of the situation. Wondering if the aircraft was American, Kraft found himself hoping for a safe escape as *Ecowar* continued its gradual dive.

15

Captain Mac McShane spent most of his day in his cabin, trying to put a dent in a pile of paperwork. His first priority was his report regarding the loss of Dr. Kraft. An official inquest of the unfortunate accident would take place upon *Chicago*'s return to port. Mac wanted to make certain that he had included all the details of the incident while they were still fresh in his mind. Prepared to take full responsibility for the marine biologist's death, he somberly reread his account of the tragedy before turning his attention to more mundane matters.

After he read over the crew's proficiency report, the result of many long hours of work on the part of his XO, Phil Moore, there was the usual stack of memos from BUPERS to peruse, as well as several technical reports. He also spent some time planning an article he intended to write for the Naval Submarine League's quarterly journal. Though he had been a member of the league for four years, this would be his first literary contribution.

With both military and civilian members, the Naval Submarine League had been created to support the need for a strong U.S. submarine force. Although submarine operations were for the most part kept hidden from the public eye for security reasons, the league attempted to keep the public informed about modern-day submarine warfare.

Mac's article was to be about the danger of prematurely pulling the plug on projects such as the upcoming Seawolf class of nuclear attack sub. As the first new class of American submarine in over two decades, Seawolf incorporated the latest technology, including an array of vastly improved sensors in its hull and a propulsion plant that gave it a seventy-five-percent improvement in tactical speed compared with vessels such as the *Chicago*. Canceling the project would threaten a vital national strategic asset. The facilities and engineering capabilities needed to sustain continued development could not be switched off and on again at the government's whim.

Maintaining a stable, highly trained work force was also a concern, and would directly influence America's high-technology capabilities far into the next century. Because there was no predicting the future, the United States had to be prepared to deploy the best submarines available. And vessels such as Seawolf were the cutting edge of undersea warfare.

After an hour or so spent outlining the article, Mac was transcribing the results into his laptop when the intercom growled.

"Captain, here," he said into the nearest handset.

"Skipper," returned the familiar voice of Phil Moore. "I think you'd better join me at Navigation. We've just received word of another sighting of our target."

"I'm on my way, XO," Mac replied, then hung up the handset and headed for his cabin's door.

Mac noticed that normal daytime illumination prevailed in the control room as he passed by the seated helmsmen and briefly addressed the *Chicago*'s current OOD. "It appears that you were right, Mr. Ward, and that stuck water valve was just an anomaly after all."

"That looks to be the case, sir," returned the engineering officer from his perch beside the periscopes.

"Please pass on a job well done to your men back in *Chicago* Power and Light for allowing us to run at flank speed these last couple of hours," Mac added, proceeding past the vacant radar console.

Several individuals were anxiously gathered around the adjoining navigation plot. Lieutenant Len Matson, their balding navigator, was using a pencil and ruler on the topmost chart. Beside him, Phil Moore pointed to the chart with the well-chewed stem of his corncob pipe.

"What have you got, XO?" Mac asked as he joined them.

A look of puzzlement crossed Moore's face as he replied. "I sure hope you can help us figure this one out, Skipper. Because our latest VLF comm transmission from SUBPAC is a real humdinger. Approximately an hour ago, a P-3 Orion out of Kwajalein tagged our monster ray again. Its ultrasonic homing beacon was broadcasting loud and clear only a mile or so off the Bikini Atoll. Which means that it's continuing its southeastern course, at a speed twice that of *Chicago*!"

Mac didn't need to look at the chart of these waters to know that his XO's calculations were correct. As he searched Moore's confused face he came up with the best explanation that he could think of.

"There must be one hell of a southernly current down there that we don't know about," he surmised.

"At this rate, we'll never catch up with him." The XO's frustration was obvious.

"The only thing we've got going for us is the persistence of our nuclear reactor," Mac thought aloud. "That ray's bound to eventually tire, and when he does, we'll be right there on his ever-lovin' tail."

A sudden, loud, gut-wrenching noise put an end to this speculation. As Mac heard it his expression turned to pure disgust.

"Shit!" he cursed. "So much for that stuck water valve being an anomaly. Damn it, XO. I sure hope we won't have to rely on our stealth when it comes time to hunt that sucker down."

As it turned out, Ezra Melindi's observation proved correct, and the sonobuoy drop that had surprised them off the Bikini Atoll proved to be of little apparent consequence. Even during their emergency dive, Freddie was successfully retrieved. And with their short but stirring visit to the nuclear test site but a memory, they returned on course for far-off Moruroa.

Kraft got a chance to deepen his acquaintanceship with Karl Ivar Bjornsen when the latter invited him on a tour of *Ecowar*'s weapons compartment. Situated in the stern half of the vessel, immediately forward of the engine room, it was barely the size of Kraft's stateroom.

His personable, blond-haired guide explained the reason for this. Simply put, *Ecowar* carried no offensive torpedoes or missiles, its weapons being exclusively defensive and limited in scope to the laser shield that Kraft had already seen tested and an assortment of noise-makers and decoys for close-in defense.

After a quick look at the laser, Kraft learned that Karl Ivar was from Haugesund, Norway. In the tradition of his Viking forefathers, he went to sea as a mere child on his uncle's fishing boat. At sixteen he joined a sealing ship bound for distant Newfoundland. When Karl Ivar invited Kraft to the evening's after-dinner discussion, during which he would be showing slides of this expedition, Kraft instantly accepted.

Invigorated by the day's busy events, Kraft returned to his cabin to freshen up and was surprised to find it close to dinnertime already. He allowed himself the briefest of naps before washing his hands and face and then heading for the wardroom.

As planned, he arrived in the wardroom at 6:00 P.M. sharp to find his four dinner companions already gathered around the table. Invited to take a place between Jean Moreau and Ezra Melindi, Kraft was impressed by the formal table setting. A white linen tablecloth, with tiny embroidered anchors covered the circular table. Dolphins were carved into the gleaming silverware, and the bone china was decorated with delicate sea horses. The elegant ambience was enhanced when Karl Ivar lit the white tapers in a pair of large silver candlesticks.

Annie made her appearance and filled their crystal goblets with golden wine. She met Kraft's gaze with a wink and then bowed her head as Moreau began the evening prayer.

"Tonight's reading is from the book of Isaiah," he said, and then proceeded to recite from memory. "'The earth mourns and withers. It lies polluted under its inhabitants; for they have transgressed the laws, violated the statutes, and broken the everlasting convenant. So be forewarned that on that cursed day, the Lord with his great sword will punish Leviathan. And he shall slay the beast that is in the sea.'"

He paused at this point to meet the gazes of his crew, then resumed: "Lord, may all those at my side be an instrument of your will, to turn the wicked tide and counter the vile ways of the transgressors. For thine is the Kingdom, and the Power, and the Glory, forever and ever. Amen."

Almost on cue, background music began playing. The lively strains of Grieg's *Peer Gynt Suite* did much to lighten the pall Moreau's benediction had cast over the company. And as the conversation turned to more mundane matters, Ezra Melindi raised his wineglass and graciously welcomed Peter Kraft to their table.

Dinner arrived in a large silver tureen. Kraft identified it as cioppino, a rich bouillabaisse made with tomatoes, grouper, and calamari. With the addition of some crispy French bread, it proved to be a simple, hearty meal, which was consumed with a minimum of conversation.

Afterward, while Karl Ivar helped Annie clear the table, Ezra Melindi uncorked a cherished bottle of Portuguese sherry. Moreau pulled out his pipe and raised his glass in a toast.

"Dr. Kraft," he said. "I realize that we still have many differences between us, but let our current friendship be a bridge to future understanding."

"I'm all for that," returned Kraft, watching as Karl Ivar pulled down a picture screen from the ceiling beside the forward bulkhead.

Using a remote-control device, the Norwegian dimmed the lights and, after returning to the table, utilized the remote to activate a slide projector. The screen filled with the image of a large, yellow surface vessel, a crane and a helipad on its deck. The ship lay at anchor in harbor, with an assortment of quaint, brightly colored buildings visible in the background.

"This first photo was taken in Haugesund, my hometown," explained Karl Ivar. "The ship you see here is the *Nordkapp*. It's one hundred meters long and fully capable of ice operations."

The next photo was a close-up of the ship's exterior bridge. Taken at sea, it showed a smiling Karl Ivar flanked by two older men, who shared his height, build, and coloring.

"That's my father on the right and his brother to the left. Uncle Yngve was the one who got us jobs on the *Nordkapp*. He had sailed on the ship the past two years, and his hard work on it had made him a wealthy man."

A series of slides flashed onto the screen, showing the *Nordkapp* plowing through a rough, whitecap-topped sea. It was during this sequence that Annie returned again from the galley. She silently took a seat as Karl Ivar continued.

"It took us a little over a week to reach our destination, the Labrador Sea ice floes off the coast of northern Newfoundland. We arrived during a howling gale, and it wasn't until the next afternoon that I first laid eyes on the creatures we had traveled these thousands of miles to hunt down."

The screen filled with a close-up of a white-faced seal pup. It had dark, inquisitive eyes, a black button nose, and stiff whiskers jutting out on each side of its face.

As Annie exclaimed in delight Karl Ivar explained the slide. "What you are viewing is a two-week-old harp-seal pup. Weighing only fifteen pounds at birth, the pup's white coat provides camouflage during the first, vulnerable days of life. They can weigh up to one hundred pounds by the age of three weeks. When they add additional blubber, the coat darkens."

The next slide showed Karl Ivar's uncle standing on the ice, smoking a cigarette. He held a thin wooden club with a spike at its end. The young Norwegian's voice slightly quavered as he commented on this slide.

"I realized that something distasteful was about to occur when Uncle Yngve joined me on the ice and handed me what he referred to as a hak-a-pik. This crude device was nothing more than an ax handle with a six-inch steel hook on the end. Little was I prepared for what happened next."

The series of photos that followed began with a shot of several dozen harp-seal pups innocently lying on the fractured ice, with the *Nordkapp* visible in the background. It was followed by a picture of a skinned seal-pup carcass.

"I could hardly believe my eyes when Uncle Yngve,

my father, and several other men that I had known since birth approached the unwary pups with their hak-a-piks. With few natural enemies to speak of, the seals did not flee. I remember almost dropping my camera and wanting to cry out in warning when the first spike hit a pup's skull.

"After this first kill, the hunters proceeded to cut open the pup's chest cavity and drink its warm blood with their cupped hands. I was truly sickened by this revolting sight, as well as the horrible slaughter that soon followed."

When a photo of a heap of seal pelts on the blood-stained ice appeared, Karl Ivar had to halt a moment to regain his composure. This time when he again began his commentary, the deep emotion he felt was apparent to all his auditors.

"The slaughter continued unabated for the rest of the afternoon, with a pup killed every thirty seconds. I'll never get their horrified cries out of my mind. Like human babies in distress, they frantically squealed out in horror as the sealers methodically chopped and skinned their brethren. Many of the pups did not die, even after repeated blows, so the impatient hunters simply skinned them alive.

"That evening I couldn't bear to look my own father in the eyes. He had betrayed me by participating in this butchery, and alone in my bunk, I schemed to interrupt the next day's hunt. The way to do so came to me in the wee hours of the night. Since it was the pure white pelts that the hunters were after, I decided to find a way to ruin the skins while the pups were still alive.

"Below, in the *Nordkapp*'s engineering spaces, providence led me to a case filled with bright yellow spray paint. Armed with a knapsack load of these cans, I anxiously waited for the dawn. Then while the hunters were having their breakfast, I scrambled onto the ice and began my traitorous deed."

"Good for you, Karl Ivar!" Annie cheered, leading a rousing chorus of applause.

"I sincerely respect your bravery," added Chief Yushiro. "But surely the other hunters must have been furious with you."

"Furious isn't the word for it, Chief," said the grinning Norwegian. "When they saw the hundreds of seals whose skins I had managed to color lying there on the ice before them, I first feared they'd kill the pups just for spite. But then one of the hunters focused his fury on me, and for a second there I thought that I'd be the next victim of their hak-a-piks."

"What kept them from killing you?" Annie asked. "Was it your father's intervention?"

Karl Ivar looked directly at Jean Moreau. The Frenchman returned his gaze and nodded for him to continue.

"I guess you could say that my savior is sitting right here at this table. Because just when the mob began taunting me, a helicopter descended from the sky. And that's when I first laid eyes on my guardian angel, Commandant Jean-Louis Moreau."

The Frenchman was quick to interrupt at this point. "Actually it was pure chance that brought me to that particular ice floe on that cold March morning. I had arrived in Newfoundland the previous day, hoping to witness my first harp-seal hunt. When I learned of the *Nordkapp*'s presence in the frozen waters off St. Anthony, I chartered a helicopter. We were only minutes away from having to turn back because of low fuel when I spotted the bright yellow vessel in a sea of ice. A blood trail led us to the hunters, and we landed, totally ignorant of the drama that was being played out before us."

Karl Ivar added, "Though I don't remember the exact details of the confrontation that followed the commandant's arrival, I do know that he shared my horror when he saw for himself the heap of blood-soaked pelts. Harsh words continued to be exchanged. And when a hunter prepared to kill a pup that I had missed, the commandant rushed to the poor creature's defense with a can of paint from my knapsack."

"That's when I realized the true precariousness of our situation," Moreau interjected. "The Norwegians were outraged, and when one of the hunters produced a pistol, I knew it was time for a hasty strategic retreat."

"Karl Ivar, surely your own father wouldn't have let them harm you," Annie remarked.

"To tell you the truth, I didn't wait around long enough to find out," Karl Ivar said. "And the next thing I knew, I was climbing into the helicopter's cockpit, with the commandant at my side. The last I ever saw of my father and uncle was as we took off for St. Anthony."

"Do you mean to say that you haven't seen your family since?" Kraft asked.

Karl Ivar shook his head. "I haven't seen anyone in my family, but at the commandant's insistence, I wrote my mother shortly after we returned to the mainland. We have kept in touch ever since, though she knows little about my current whereabouts."

"I sure hope that your father and uncle still aren't hunting the harp seals," Annie interjected at this point.

"I was happy to learn from my mother that both of them lost their taste for the hunt shortly after I abruptly left them. In her last letter she reported that they were about to begin another venture together, one just as distasteful as the slaughtering of innocent baby seals."

"What's that?" Annie asked.

Karl Ivar's disgust was obvious. "Both of them have signed on to crew a whaling ship."

"Perhaps we shall yet meet up with your father and uncle," said Melindi.

A moment of silence was broken by Annie's hopeful voice. "I don't suppose that anyone's in the mood for dessert?"

Finding no takers, she watched as the commandant reached over and took the remote-control device from Karl Ivar's hand. "Thank you, Karl Ivar, for that thought-provoking presentation," said Moreau. "Unfortunately I must sadly report that the harp-seal slaughter continues, and a population that once reached 20,000,000 is today below 500,000. Ecological groups the world over have appealed to the Canadian government to at least limit the hunt. Yet while Ottawa debates, the seals still die, and we can only pray that a more enlightened policy will result.

"But enough of this somber subject, *mes amis*. So that Dr. Kraft doesn't get the idea that all of our discussions are so melancholy, with Annie's help, I've put together a little slide show of my own. So if you'll just bear with me, here we go."

Moreau flicked the remote control, and the screen filled with a pair of colorfully drawn dolphins on a light pink background. The snouts and dorsal fins of these creatures were stylishly exaggerated, as was the wavy brown stripe along their grayish bodies.

"I photographed this fresco in the Queen's Chamber at the Palace of Knossos. It dates back to 1600 B.C."

The next picture, depicting a harnessed dolphin pulling a small fishing boat, was a mosaic. "This amazing artifact also originated in ancient Crete," Moreau continued. "It almost certainly proves that the Cretans had succeeded in taming dolphins for such tasks as piloting their ships. Interestingly enough, the Roman historian Pliny documented the Cretan custom of immediately freeing a dolphin accidentally caught in a fisherman's net."

A picture of an ancient coin flashed up onto the screen. On the surface was the bust of a woman, wearing a crown of laurels. Encircling this bust were four sleek dolphins.

"*Mes amis*," remarked Moreau. "What do you think of a culture such as that of ancient Syracuse, which makes the dolphin a part of its mythology, here shown with the mereid Arethusa, beloved of the river god Alpheus."

The slide of the coin was replaced by one showing the bottom of a large cup. Painted here in faded orange, black, and yellow was a charioteer driving four rearing stallions. Leading them was a single leaping dolphin.

"This is one of my very favorites," admitted Moreau. "I found this fourth century B.C. Italian cup in the Louvre. Represented here is the god Apollo and the animal which he found most sacred of all—the dolphin!"

A quick series of slides showed a variety of ancient coins, shields, vases, and cups. In each instance, their surfaces were etched with a dolphin motif. "The Aegeans, Etruscans, Greeks, and Romans also used the dolphin in their art," Moreau explained.

"Has it ever been determined what they were meant to symbolize?" asked Kraft, impressed with the quality of the presentation.

Moreau seemed pleased with Peter's question, and he readily replied. "That's a very good question, Doctor. And perhaps this next slide will help answer it."

Next to fill the screen was the image of an urn, whose lip was decorated with a series of leaping dolphins. Each of the creatures had a fully armed Greek warrior on its back, with a single figure playing a set of Pan pipes leading the strange procession forward.

"From the time of Homer, it's been suggested, the Aegeans believed that it was the dolphin that carried the soul of the departed to the Isle of the Afterlife," explained Moreau. "According to the Greeks, dolphins were actually men who had been transformed into marine mammals by the God Dionysos. This urn, which I photographed in Boston's Museum of Fine Arts, documents this transformation process, and hints at a mystical process modern man has absolutely no knowledge of.

"And of course, there's this fresco that I captured during a visit to Rhodes," Moreau added, in reference to a slide showing a young girl playing a flute to an attentive dolphin listener. "Once again it's Pliny who mentions that the dolphin is friendly to man and is charmed by his music, particularly the sound of the flute."

"I know that fact for certain," interrupted Kraft. "My head dolphin trainer is a classically trained flutist. One day she just happened to bring her flute to work so she could practice her scales. Little did she expect the reaction she got from our two bottlenoses. They went wild when she began practicing, and even showed their appreciation by singing when she played them some Mozart."

"My dolphins used to like rock music," revealed Annie. "Whenever they seemed lethargic, all I had to do to pep them up was play something by the Beatles. That never failed to get them stirred up."

"Speaking of your dolphins, Annie," said a slyly grinning Moreau as he pressed the remote control and a picture of a bikini-clad Annie riding the back of a dolphin popped up on the screen. "As this last slide so aptly displays, the close bond between man and dolphin continues to this day. Yet I can't help but come to the conclusion that we are on the verge of unveiling a great secret concerning our friends in the sea that our ancestors were aware of long ago."

To a smattering of applause, Moreau snapped off the slide projector and turned up the lights. Annie rose to return to the galley, and Chief Yushiro excused himself for the engine room. While Karl Ivar refilled their glasses with sherry, Moreau repacked his pipe.

"I hope that our little show didn't bore you, Doctor," said the Frenchman as he tamped down his tobacco.

"Not at all," Kraft said. "I found the subject matter most stimulating."

"What really upsets me," said Ezra Melindi, "is the fact that creatures such as the harp seal and the dolphin are rapidly facing extinction, unless drastic measures are taken to save them. Here we have life-forms, known to exist from the very beginning of recorded history, about to be wiped out by modern man's stupidity."

"It is said that our generation alone will witness the disappearance of one half of the earth's rich and subtle forms of life, which have been evolving for billions of years," said Moreau, before putting a match to his pipe's bowl.

"Mark my words," warned Melindi. "Today it might be the harp seal, the dolphin, or the whale that we might be seeing for the last time. But if the trend continues unabated, tomorrow will witness the end of humankind as well!"

"Man already wipes out his own," added Karl Ivar. "Look at the conquistadores. They were responsible for destroying entire civilizations."

Moreau exhaled a stream of fragrant smoke. "Just as the conquistadores led to the extinction of dozens of native human populations, modern man has destroyed the culture of the marine mammal. As Dr. Kraft here will attest, cetacean brains are unique. Their massive, highly centralized neocortical regions prove that they are just as advanced a species as Homo sapiens. And here we're being given this once-in-a-lifetime opportunity to actually communicate with a species not our own. Who knows what ancient knowledge our brothers in the sea can pass on to us. All of this will be lost for eternity with the death of the last dolphin or whale."

Stimulated by Moreau's remark, *Ecowar*'s second in command spoke up. "From a moral point of view, the mere possibility that marine mammals might be rational, thinking creatures with something valuable to teach mankind is enough to make it unethical to kill them. For they are the people of the sea, and harvesting them for their skins and meat is nothing but murder!"

"What do you think of this argument, Doctor?" asked Moreau. "In your esteemed opinion, are marine mammals on the same evolutionary level as man?"

Kraft attempted to answer the difficult question as

logically as possible. "In my own studies, I have found cetaceans to have many unique physiological characteristics that separate them from lower forms of animal life. As you previously mentioned, the sheer size of the cetacean brain, its convolutions, connectivities, and massive associational areas, point to the sheer bulk of information being processed. Cetaceans also demonstrate cerebral control of breath, body functions, and emotions, and have incredible acoustic abilities, allowing them to both send and receive with great speed and complexity. But putting them on the same evolutionary level as man still bothers me."

"As it does me," admitted Moreau. "Because in my opinion, dolphins and whales have evolved way beyond man. Once, in the Indian Ocean, I witnessed a miraculous event that opened my eyes to their true place on this planet. At that time I saw a pod of fifty killer whales, spread out over an area of ten square miles, all turn around at exactly the same moment as they took a collective readout from a single echolocation train. If mankind could demonstrate such collective interdependence, just think of the great advancements we could make!"

"I've also seen a pod of orcas attacking and fatally wounding an adult whale just for a bite of its tongue," Kraft revealed. "Such behavior hints at the creature's true bestial nature, and makes me seriously question these evolutionary advances that you speak of."

Before Moreau could argue, three soft electronic tones sounded from the intercom, followed by the concerned voice of Ivana Borisov. "Commandant, passive sensors are picking up an unusual biological disturbance in the seas directly before us. It's unlike anything I've ever heard before."

"I'm on my way, *mon amie*," Moreau said to the ceiling-mounted transmitter.

"What do you suppose that's all about?" Melindi asked, before finishing his sherry and pushing his chair back to stand.

Moreau stood and beckoned toward the wardroom's exit. "Shall we see for ourselves, Number Two?"

Kraft briefly met Karl Ivar's puzzled stare and accompanied him into the passageway. The ship's two senior officers led them into the control room, which was lit by a dim red light to protect the crew's night vision. Kraft momentarily halted inside the hatchway and waited for his eyes to adjust. The others were already securely buckled into their safety harnesses by the time he reached his jumpseat.

A quick scan of the display screen showed them to be at a depth of 165 meters with a forward velocity of eighty-one knots. The bathymetric chart showed them transiting the Gilbert Islands, with Tarawa, some fifty miles to the west, the nearest landmass. There was a good five thousand meters of water beneath them, with a bare minimum of seamount activity in the area.

As Ecowar's senior sonar technician, Karl Ivar was responsible for analyzing the mysterious sound signature. With a practiced fluidity, he addressed his keypad, and a variety of waterfall displays were projected onto the screen. Several minutes were needed before the analysis was completed and he could convey the results.

"The dominant sound is a sharp clicking noise at thirty thousand hertz. Yet I'm also picking up an indecipherable disturbance at twenty hertz, which leads me to believe that there are two separate entities out there somehow occupying the same portion of ocean."

"Hit them with active and get us an exact depth and range," commanded Moreau.

"Proceeding to go active," said the Norwegian as he readdressed his keypad.

Seconds later a loud, hollow pinging noise sounded inside the compartment. The active sonar pulse could also be seen as a series of fast-moving, rippling waves on the display screen.

"We've got a solid return!" Karl Ivar called out excitedly.

"Hit it again, and see if it's moving," Moreau directed.

Another ping rang out inside the dimly lit control room, and this time the sonic waves on the display screen momentarily parted, a mere thousand yards off their starboard bow.

"I've got it, Commandant!" Karl Ivar adjusted his compact headphones. "One of the creatures is definitely a whale, with a length of some sixty-five feet. And whatever it may be that's swimming alongside it, both creatures have just crossed the layer and appear to be headed straight toward the ocean's surface."

"Ms. Borisov," said Moreau firmly. "What are the environmental conditions topside?"

"We have a flat calm on the surface, Commandant, with full moon illumination," she efficiently reported.

"Excellent." Moreau looked to his right and anxiously addressed Melindi. "Number Two, if I'm not mistaken, we're about to witness a sight few mariners have ever been privileged to see."

"Aye, Commandant," returned the Kenyan. "The battle of the giants of the seas!"

"Disengage hydrodrive, Mr. Godavari," Moreau ordered. "And take us to the surface!"

Kraft didn't know what to expect as *Ecowar*'s bow angled sharply upward, and his pulse quickened with anticipation. When the vessel finally broke the water's surface, his eyes went straight to the display screen as Moreau ordered, "Engage bow video camera, Karl Ivar. Maximum magnification, on-target course bearings."

The entire screen seemed to come alive with roiling, bubbling seawater, lit by a radiant full moon. Kraft's first impression was that he was viewing the results of an underwater volcanic eruption. But then the true source of this tempest became visible in the form of a huge sperm whale, a monstrous giant squid wrapped tightly around its thrashing body.

"Just as I hoped!" Moreau shouted. "It's cachalot

versus Architeuthis, the legendary kraken, in a battle royal of the two greatest predators the oceans have ever known!"

The boxlike head of the sperm was engulfed in a network of writhing arms. Even from this distance, Kraft could make out the squid's tubular-shaped, phosphorescent-lit body and a single enormous eye that glistened with the alien glimmer of a distant star.

Well aware that they were indeed seeing an event only a handful of men had ever witnessed before, Kraft mentally recreated the hunt that proceeded this epic struggle. He knew that a fifty-ton male sperm consumed up to a ton and a half of squid daily. Most of these squid were of a vastly smaller variety, only two feet long and weighing a mere five pounds each.

To reach the realm of the giant squid, the sperm would have to have essayed a dive of up to an hour in duration. In these black depths, the blinded whale would have had to rely solely on echolocation to find its prey. Then the struggle would have begun, against a creature thought to grow over fifty feet long and weigh nearly half a ton.

Even with his greater size, the whale would be in for the fight of his life. The huge cephalopod that he had picked for his meal wielded ten wreathing tentacles bristling with hooked suckers as big as dinner plates. In addition, the squid sported a beaklike jaw, poisonous saliva, and an ink sac, all controlled by the largest, most complex brain of any invertebrate.

"Mon Dieu," exclaimed Moreau, his glance locked on the display screen and the thrashing combatants. "Truly we're seeing the most spectacular sight in all of nature. It only goes to show that reality is the most visionary world of all. Never fear to wonder, mes amis. This is the one trait that will yet lead to our species' salvation."

Like jackals around a feeding lion, ready to share in the feast, numerous sharks could be seen impatiently circling. Then just as suddenly as the combatants appeared, the conflict ceased, and the sea resumed its placid calm.

"Au revoir, mes amis," Morceau whispered in a reverent tone. "You return to the depths where death awaits. And now it is up to us to share your valiant struggle, in poetry and song, and tales for generations not yet born.

"Let's be gone from this place, Mr. Godavari," he added pensively. "Moruroa awaits us!"

16

Peter Kraft stirred restlessly. No matter how hard he tried, sleep would not come. Every time he attempted to clear his mind and relax, myriad haunting visions would disturb his thoughts. There was Karl Ivar on the blood-stained ice, and a line of dolphin-borne Greek warriors on their way to the afterlife. And could he ever erase the memories of the great battle between the sperm whale and the giant squid?

Something was happening deep inside his soul. Though he knew he should be longing for home and demanding to be released, such thoughts were far from his mind. Jean Moreau and the others were challenging him to come face-to-face with his inner self and testing the strength of his convictions.

The members of *Ecowar*'s crew shared a very special sense of purpose. They were readily willing to share this spirit with him, a virtual stranger who had come to them on a whim of fate.

Already, the evolutionary change was starting to take place. With enlightened eyes, Kraft could see his past and the small circle in which he did his work. His studies in behavioral science used to be the extent of his world. Now, with the assistance of Moreau and his followers, the veil had been lifted, and a vision of a larger life dawned in his mind.

In this new world, everything was interrelated, from the tiniest microbe to the largest of whales. And man was but a piece of this chain. The occupants of *Ecowar* had selflessly dedicated themselves to protecting the integrity of the cradle of life itself. For it was from the oceans that the ancestors of man evolved, and without the seas and their rich web of life, mankind as we know it could not be sustained.

How blind he had been to this simple reality! As a scientist, he had surrendered himself to the demands of academic success and, in the process, had wasted precious time, the greatest gift of all. The clock was ticking, and with each second's passing, another species was gone for all eternity.

Kraft had seen the warning signs. In the Florida Keys alone, he had witnessed the destruction of entire reef communities by the uncontrolled encroachment of man. Dead dolphins were washing up upon their beaches in unprecedented numbers, the cause of death an AIDS-like virus spawned in the polluted waters in which they lived. Whether it be endangered sea turtles choking on plastic bags, or seabirds poisoned by pesticide-filled runoff, the oceans were in need of man's attention. With *Ecowar*'s invaluable assistance, Kraft could finally hear their supplications.

In their zeal for making a difference, the men and women of *Ecowar* had picked the outlaw path of militancy to enforce their ideals. This was one thing that Kraft could not condone. Somehow or other, he hoped to impose a more moderate, mainstream approach during his remaining days as a crew member.

The manner in which Karl Ivar went about painting the skins of the harp-seal pups was a perfect example of Kraft's own approach. By ruining the fur, the Norwegian was able to save the seals and get his point across with one pass of his spray can. No human lives were lost in the process, whose next logical step should be lobbying for the enactment of strict legislation to outlaw future hunts.

There had to be some way to apply such nonviolent strategies to other ecological threats, such as the pirate tuna trawler *Ecowar* had recently sunk. Kraft hoped to discuss such alternatives with the crew.

With this goal in mind, he finally surrendered to a deep slumber. His dreams were not long in coming, and he found himself riding his ten-speed over the Key Biscayne causeway. The rushing waters of the channel below beckoned dangerously, but unlike his previous nightmare, this time he made it to Virginia Key without incident.

Gustavo Martinez was waiting for him at the institute's security gate. As Kraft crossed the alleyway leading to the dolphin tanks, he suddenly found himself climbing into the equipment-packed bowels of the USS *Chicago*. Chop was there to greet him, and as the personable supply officer led him into the submarine's wardroom, he encountered Jean Moreau seated at the head of the table, calmly smoking his pipe, with a glass of sherry before him.

Annie Sawyer entered the compartment, a silver serving tray in hand, and his pulse quickened as he noticed that she was completely naked. Ignoring Moreau, she threw herself into Kraft's arms. Their lips met with a shock of electricity, and with hungry tongues madly probing, he stroked the silken skin of her back and buttocks. His need for her was great, and his manhood had grown stiff with expectation. But before he could consummate this desire, his glance returned to the head of the table, where Raghib Godavari sat in full lotus position, deep in meditation, the seductive strains of a sitar filling the room with intoxicating sound.

His tantalizing dream faded at this point. And it was almost completely forgotten by the time he finally awoke, seven and a half hours later. He lay in bed for another quarter of an hour, trying to piece together the more sensuous portions of his dream. The curly-haired Australian woman was still on his mind as he got up to shave and brush his teeth.

There wasn't a soul in the crew's head, and he allowed himself a long, soothing shower before dressing and continuing to the wardroom. Much to his dismay, this portion of the ship was also vacant. Kraft poked his head into the galley, and got his first look at the fairly cramped space where Annie worked her culinary magic. The stainless-steel counters were immaculate, with not a crumb visible.

Disappointed to find himself alone, he returned to the wardroom and poured a cup of tea. A platter of crisp graham crackers sitting beside the tea service provided him with a hasty breakfast. Annie and the rest of the crew, he supposed, were in the control room, and it was to this portion of the sub that he next headed.

As he stepped through the hatchway he indeed found his shipmates gathered here. Strangely enough, night-vision conditions prevailed, even though his watch showed it to be half past ten in the morning. After several seconds his eyes adjusted to the dim lighting, and he noticed eerie sounds emanating from the intercom speakers. What began as a deep, cowlike bellow became a high-pitched chirp, a boisterous roar, and a long, mournful moan that Kraft could actually feel in his gut.

"*Bonjour,* Doctor," Moreau greeted from his command chair. "I was just about to send Annie to collect you. Please join us—the symphony has only just begun."

Kraft found Annie seated in the jumpseat on Moreau's left. As he took his customary position on the Frenchman's other side, Ezra Melindi explained what they were listening to.

"Good doctor, you've joined us at a most fortuitous moment. Have you ever heard the song of the Pacific humpback before?"

"Actually I've only heard the Atlantic variety," Kraft answered, amazed by the variety of sounds that continued to be relayed into the control room.

"I believe that I can offer you one more piece of evidence to support my view of the complex intelligence of our cetacean friends," interjected Moreau. "As the crew will validate, we passed this same pod of whales during our trip up to the Kurils three weeks ago. Though we initially encountered them at a more northerly latitude, the last time we heard of the humpbacks, they were singing this very same song, down to each individual phrase."

"If you'd like, Doctor," Karl Ivar offered, "I have a copy of the original tape that I can play back for you. You'll hear for yourself the incredible similarity of the two songs."

"Do you realize what such a thing means, Doctor?" Moreau continued. "It is certain proof of an organized whale culture. Each thirty-minute-long song is repeated note for note."

"I wonder what they're saying to each other?" Kraft said.

This time it was Melindi who replied. "My people have a legend which says that the song of the humpback is a kind of oral history of the whales, an epic poem of sorts, which the pod adds onto with each passing year."

"While studying humpbacks off the coast of Bermuda, Dr. Roger Payne proved that the whales were actually repeating these complicated rhythmic sequences," Moreau said. "He found that new songs were added each year. And it's even been determined that when repeating each other's songs, the whales breathe at the same point, pausing just like well-trained choir singers!"

At this moment the whales tackled a particularly complex phrase, and Kraft finally understood why the lights had been dimmed. Like good concert goers the world over, the crew of *Ecowar* wished to maximize their pleasure in the underwater arias and so sought to reduce extraneous sensory input.

As he listened to the complex, unearthly cries Kraft found their effect on him to be soothing. It was almost as if he could open himself to the whales' plight, feel their loneliness, adrift as they were in the great ocean.

He wondered if the humpbacks were aware of *Ecowar*'s presence among them. If the legend that Ezra Melindi spoke of proved true, perhaps one day the whales would sing of the strange, manta-ray-shaped object that arose from the depths to defend them from mankind's evil ways.

Kraft briefly scanned the faces of the crew members. It was evident from their tranquil expressions that they, too, were entranced by the whales' singing. Annie seemed to be especially affected by the unwordly sounds, her serene smile giving her an almost angelic appearance.

Memories of his recent dream flooded his consciousness, and he guiltily remembered the moment when their lips first met. This thought was quickly followed by a surge of physical longing. At the exact same moment Annie turned her head and gave him a warm, inviting look.

"Pretty remarkable, isn't it, Doc?" she whispered, as if they were the only two persons in the room.

He could only nod in agreement, allowing the whales to speak for him. As if in response to his wordless request, a deep, yearning cry arose from the sea, filling the compartment with intense feeling, a yearning almost palpable. It was in this way that Kraft conveyed his desire for Annie, a need that was as primal as the voices calling to them from the black depths.

There was a shared sense of melancholy when the whales eventually left them. As the last lonely song faded no one seemed to be in a hurry to break the spell. Several minutes of thoughtful silence passed before Moreau cleared his throat.

"What a fitting sendoff for *Ecowar*'s most important mission to date," he expounded. "Mr. Godavari, engage hydrodrive, flank speed. Ms. Borisov, what's our current ETA to target?"

The overhead lights suddenly went on, and Kraft watched the helmsman push his left joystick forward to open the throttle. The deck shook, and the display screen filled with a detailed bathymetric chart that showed their current location to be immediately south of the Samoan Islands. Various data began filling the screen's right portion, prompting a quick response from their navigator.

"ETA Moruroa at zero-three-zero hours, Commandant."

"That will give us plenty of time to get into position by daybreak," Moreau said to his second in command.

"Then we'll be crossing the reef at night?" Melindi asked with a hint of concern.

"Our sensors can easily handle the transit, Number Two," Moreau reminded. "And besides, that reef is the least of my worries."

"Sonar contact, Commandant," Karl Ivar reported matter-of-factly. "I've got a single surface vessel bearing two-eight-five, maximum range, and heading away from us."

"Get used to sharing these waters with others, Karl Ivar," Moreau advised. "As we continue southward the seas will be crowded with surface traffic. You will be required to be supremely alert to the one threat that truly bothers me—the presence of another submarine."

Annie was unbuckling her harness, and as she rose to

exit, she passed by Kraft and softly addressed him. "Some morning, huh, Doc? Did you sleep well?"

Kraft grinned. "What I lacked in quantity, I more than made up for in the quality of my dreams."

"How about some breakfast?" she asked. "I could whip you up some seafood crepes."

"Does that offer go for me as well, Annie?" Ezra Melindi interjected. "I don't know about you, good doctor, but hearing all those whale songs has given me a wicked appetite."

Annie smiled. "Then come on, the both of you. If you behave, I just might brew up some fresh cappuccino."

Melindi looked at Kraft and winked. "I believe that we can summon the willpower to behave ourselves, Annie." Slapping Kraft on the back, the Kenyan chuckled. "Come on, Doctor. I'm anxious to learn about the project you were involved in before fate dropped you on our doorstep. And perhaps afterward I can show you some more of the ship."

Though Kraft would have preferred some time with Annie alone, he accepted the good-natured offer and accompanied Melindi back to the wardroom. The second in command proved to be excellent company, and after a delicious brunch Melindi took him on the promised tour.

Kraft had seen most of *Ecowar*'s major compartments by now, and he soon learned that much of the ship's operational systems were hidden from view. Starting in the engine room, Melindi showed him the actual working components of the equipment that Chief Yushiro had initially explained. Although Kraft was not able to grasp the details of the complex technology, not being trained in this area, his guide patiently tried to simplify the operations of the vessel's propulsion plant so he could understand.

Afterward Kraft got his first close-up view of the enigmatic subsystem known affectionately as Freddie. The ROV—Remotely Operated Vehicle—was reached through a watertight hatch set into the floor of the weapons compartment. Freddie turned out to be larger than he expected, its square yellow body approximately the size of a subcompact automobile. From its blunt bow a pair of articulated manipulator arms extended. A series of mercury-vapor lights surrounded the all-important, centrally placed video camera, and a ring of thrusters encircled the ROV's body.

To launch Freddie, the storage well was sealed and the pressure inside equalized to that of the surrounding sea. Once this was accomplished, an accessway cut into *Ecowar*'s bottom hull was hydraulically opened, allowing the ROV to be released, with the fiber-optic "umbilical" its only contact with the mother ship.

A quick stop at Melindi's stateroom allowed Kraft to see how *Ecowar*'s senior officers lived. Not much larger than the small cabins reserved for the crew, each stateroom was comfortably furnished with the usual wall-mounted desk and dark blue carpet. What distinguished Melindi's from the rest of the ship, though, were the photographs hung on the carpeted walls. Displayed here were various shots of Melindi's homeland.

Kraft recognized Mt. Kilimanjaro in one of these photos. But it took Melindi's help to identify a portion of Lake Victoria, the steel-and-concrete skyscrapers of downtown Nairobi, and an inspiring shot of the Rift valley, where Louis Leakey searched for the earliest remains of ancient man.

When Kraft learned that Moreau's cabin was on the other side of a shared bathroom, he asked his guide if he could have a quick peek inside. Melindi saw nothing wrong with this and led Kraft into the adjoining stateroom, which proved to be an exact duplicate of his own cabin, except for the pictures on the walls. Those in Moreau's cabin were of warships— several submarines, a helicopter carrier, and two large surface ships. All flew the French tricolor and were positioned beside official-looking citations and awards.

"These are the warships the commandant previously served on," Melindi explained.

While passing by the Pullman-style washbasin, Kraft spotted a five-by-eight-inch photograph hung beside a small mirror. It showed a young, smartly uniformed, crew-cut naval officer in a lush tropical setting. Beside him was an attractive woman with short dark hair, and a little girl with a wide, devilish smile.

"I assume that's the commandant with his wife and child shortly before they were killed," surmised Kraft.

A surprised look crossed Melindi's face. "How did you know about them?"

"The commandant told me of the tragedy soon after I arrived here," Kraft answered.

"You should be honored, good doctor. That's a story he rarely shares."

On the ledge beside Moreau's cot, a violin case could be seen. Surprised, Kraft voiced his curiosity. "Is there a violin inside that case?"

"Not just any violin, good doctor, but a priceless instrument handmade by Antonio Stradivari of Cremona in 1833."

Impressed, Kraft continued his probing. "I gather that the commandant is an accomplished musician."

"If you stay with us long enough, hopefully you'll hear for yourself," said Melindi.

"No wonder music is such an important element aboard this ship," Kraft observed. "Personally I think it's a great idea having *Ecowar*'s passageways filled with song. But tell me, why is there no music today?"

A wide grin lit up Melindi's face as he answered. "But there already has been, good doctor. Today the music was selected—and performed by—our good friends the whales."

The tour continued, extending well into the afternoon. It ended in the control room, where Kraft found only two of the command chairs occupied. Karl Ivar was at the helm, and Ivana Borisov took on the dual roles of navigator and sonar technician. Kraft learned from Melindi the reason for this reduced staff.

"Because our destination will be reached in the early hours of the morning, the commandant and the others have turned in early to get as much rest as possible. There will be no formal evening meal, and I suggest an early retirement for yourself as well."

Since Kraft didn't want to miss any of the action, he took this advice. He spent the rest of the afternoon in his cabin, reading a worn copy of Rachel Carson's *Silent Spring*. It had been many years since he had last read this excellent farseeing book, which had described the dangers of pesticide pollution over three decades ago.

A trip to the galley to get himself an evening snack found the vacant passageways eerily silent. The wardroom was empty as well, and he helped himself to a bowl of leftover cioppino that had been kept warm in a silver chafing dish. He soon returned to his cabin, where Rachel Carson kept him company until he finally fell asleep.

This time he dreamed of bloated, dead fish lying belly-up in the stagnant water. In another dream he was deep in a mangrove swamp, where DDT-deformed baby chicks desperately waited in their nests for parents that would never return to feed them. He was in the midst of just such a horrific vision when a hand on his shoulder gently nudged him awake.

"Doc," said a soothing female voice. "Doc, wake up. It's Annie."

Not knowing if her voice was dream or reality, he opened his eyes. Sure enough, kneeling beside him was the curly-haired Aussie who had been the subject of his much more pleasant dream of the previous night.

"Good morning, Doc," she added with a warm smile. "The commandant asked me to awaken you."

Inside the darkened confines of his cabin, Kraft had

no idea of the time, and he groped for his watch. Failing to locate it immediately, he groggily asked, "What time is it, Annie?"

"Five twenty-seven A.M. to be exact," she stated. "It will be dawn soon, and we've already taken up position inside the atoll."

This news awakened him completely. "Do you mean to say we've reached Moruroa already?"

Annie nodded. "We've still got a half hour or so before the first light of day, so you've got time to wash up if you'd like. Also, there's hot tea and muffins in the wardroom. Now I'd better get back to Control myself. See ya shortly."

Kraft responded with a wide yawn and an appreciative wave as he watched Annie exit. He yawned once more, and as he sat up and swung his feet off the cot, the book that he had been reading the night before tumbled down onto the carpeted deck. Without taking the time to pick it up, he hurried over to the washbasin to complete his morning regime.

He finished in time to have a muffin and some tea. Though he'd have loved nothing better than a hot shower, he plodded on to the control room to see for himself the reason for this early wake-up call.

As he expected, all of the command chairs were filled as he entered the hushed compartment. He quietly made his way to his jumpseat and peered up at the display screen. Lying at anchor in a deep blue lagoon were a trio of sleek warships, all flying the French tricolor. In the background could be seen a flat, sand-filled strip of beach as well as a couple of scraggly palm trees.

Noting the newcomer's presence beside him, Moreau hastily briefed Kraft. "Welcome to Moruroa Atoll, Doctor. As you can see for yourself, Freddie has already been launched. The two frigates before you are the *Suffren* and the *Duquesne*. Both are armed with a full complement of missiles and torpedoes. Anchored between them is our target, the hydrographic research vessel *Triton*."

Kraft spotted a bright orange, torpedo-shaped object hanging from a crane on *Triton*'s center deck. "Is that a mini-sub of some sort?" he asked.

Before answering, Moreau addressed the blond-haired man on his left. "Karl Ivar, isolate *Triton,* magnification power twenty."

As the Norwegian input the order into his keypad, the screen filled with a close-up view of *Triton*'s deck. The bright orange object that had piqued Kraft's interest could now be seen clearly. It dangled from a hydraulic hoist mechanism, its stern and bow secured by a sturdy steel restraining strap. Kraft noticed several white-uniformed sailors working close by.

Only now did Moreau answer Kraft's question. "That's Griffon, the submersible responsible for positioning the nuclear device in a hole drilled into the atoll's coral crust. In theory, this hole is supposed to contain the blast, entrapping the plutonium and residual radiation in a glassy cocoon for all eternity. Yet it's widely known that a blast of this magnitude risks fracturing the atoll's fragile crust, resulting in a dangerous amount of radiation seepage."

On the screen, three individuals dressed in hooded biohazard containment suits approached Griffon. They began working on the mini-sub's skirted undercarriage, prompting Melindi to continue the commentary.

"Those technicians are most likely connecting the device's detonator."

"Now's the time to act, *mes amis,*" Moreau announced. "Karl Ivar, take Freddie down and initiate the approach. Number Two, project a schematic of our target."

The display screen's video link was terminated, to be replaced by a transparent scale model of the *Triton*. Seventy-four meters long, the hydrographic research vessel had a helipad on its stern, with a single funnel set forward of the vacant landing platform. Directly amidships hung Griffon, with the bridge located farther toward the angled bow. Melindi utilized an electronic cursor to highlight the area of hull directly below the deck-mounted submersible.

"We will place the limpet mine here," he explained. "This will severely damage not only Griffon, but the vital test-monitoring equipment stored in this section of the *Triton.*"

"And Dr. Kraft," added Moreau. "You'll be pleased to know that we've timed our attack to coincide with the serving of the morning meal. Thus the majority of the crew will be congregated forward, in *Triton*'s bow, and the loss of life should be kept to a minimum."

Though Kraft would have liked to speak up and question the need to attack this ship in the first place, he held his tongue and listened as Karl Ivar calmly reported, "Freddie has reached the bottom of the lagoon, and is making his way toward target."

This was followed by a somewhat concerned report from Ivana Borisov. "Both frigates have just gone active, Commandant!"

"Pipe this scan through the intercom," directed Moreau.

The hollow ping of an active sonar search sounded in the background. Kraft knew that normally such an unwelcome racket was a submariner's worst nightmare, and he voiced his confusion. "What keeps their sonar from discovering Freddie?"

Melindi answered him. "The same sonar-absorbent, anechoic tiles that cover *Ecowar*'s hull also line the hull of Freddie. No matter how hard they try, their search will fall on deaf ears."

"A thousand yards to target and closing," Karl Ivar reported.

The constant, monotonous pinging sound of the active sonar had an almost hypnotic effect on Kraft. He was in the process of visualizing the sonic pulses as they rippled through the water when a barely audible, alien buzzing noise diverted his attention.

"We've got some sort of battery-powered submersible approaching from the direction of the *Suffren,* Commandant!" Ivana called out.

Moreau's answer was succinct and vehement. "Put Freddie on the bottom and open video link!"

The tension in the control room was rapidly intensifying. Kraft wiped a thin line of sweat from his forehead and watched Karl Ivar attack his keypad.

His glance returned to the display screen, when seconds later Freddie's video link was reestablished. Kraft watched as a brightly colored reef fish swam by, followed by a distant, flickering light that steadily grew in intensity, as did the buzzing whine that had initially distracted him.

It seemed to take forever for the source of these disturbances to show itself. And when it did, Kraft couldn't help but sigh out loud in wonder. Passing almost directly in front of the video camera was a torpedo-shaped sled, with a pair of speargun-toting scuba divers perched securely on its back.

"My, the legionnaires are being most thorough with their security precautions this morning," Moreau lightly observed.

"I wish them luck," said Melindi. "Because not even the legendary French Foreign Legion will be able to locate our Freddie."

Sincerely hoping that this was the case, Kraft breathlessly watched the sled disappear into the black depths. It took several more minutes for the characteristic whine of the single propeller to dissipate, and only then did Moreau signal the all-clear.

"Continue on, Karl Ivar," he directed.

Freddie lifted off the seabed and passed over a bleached clump of fan-shaped coral. Kraft knew that ordinarily such a tropical reef should be swarming with sea life. Yet except for the single fish that they had previously viewed, the waters were conspicuously empty.

"Eight hundred and fifty yards to target," Karl Ivar reported.

On the right-hand portion of the display screen, a

digital counter appeared, rapidly updating the distance between Freddie and the *Triton*. When it passed five hundred yards, Kraft stirred with the realization of just what is was they were about to attempt.

According to the tenets of international law, this act was terrorism pure and simple. His brow furrowed in concern as he wondered if murder would soon be added to these charges.

"Don't look so glum, Doctor," advised Moreau, who couldn't ignore Kraft's worried frown. "Generations yet unborn will look to this day with the greatest of appreciation."

Kraft's frustrations were most apparent as he replied. "I just wish there was a less violent way to stop them."

Moreau answered directly. "If you can think of one, I'll be the first to listen. But right now I have no other alternatives. Because the narrow-minded bureaucrats responsible for this test and others like it don't give a damn about taking responsibility for their selfish actions. Regardless of the fact that they're irrevocably poisoning this fragile planetary vessel on which we all live, they'll continue testing their weapons of mass destruction for the sake of satisfying their pitiful egos."

"One hundred yards to target and closing," interrupted the machinelike voice of Karl Ivar. "Spot illumination activated. Initiating up angle."

Freddie's bow-mounted mercury-vapor lamps suddenly snapped on, and the display screen filled with a barnacle-encrusted portion of *Triton*'s hull. A complicated series of coordinates appeared on the bottom of the screen. Several additional seconds passed as Freddie traveled alongside the hull, then abruptly stopped.

"Freddie should be directly below the Griffon, Commandant," the Norwegian reported.

"Very well, Karl Ivar," said Moreau. "Place the limpet."

Kraft's gaze was locked on the display screen, where

one of Freddie's articulated manipulator arms inched its way toward the barnacle-covered hull. Tightly grasped inside the pincerlike hand was a shoe-box-sized plastic tray with magnets set into each of its corners. With a deliberate, cautious movement, the mine was successfully secured to the hull. Only then did the manipulator arm retract. The bow lights snapped off, and Freddie smoothly returned to the blackened depths.

"*Mon commandant,*" Melindi whispered. "Prepare to purge from your heart the bitterness that you have carried these past years."

Moreau responded by snapping open his right armrest. He slid aside a protective cover plate, and a single red button was revealed.

"Umbilical retrieval continues smoothly," Karl Ivar informed. "Another 250 yards and Freddie will be home."

Moreau's voice rang with conviction. "That's enough, Karl Ivar. Surface Freddie and initiate visual scan of target."

Once again the sleek profile of the *Triton* filled their display screen, some 750 yards distant from Freddie's probing eye. The vessel's stern-mounted blue, white, and red flag fluttered in a stiffening breeze, and a deceptive state of calm seemed to prevail.

A full minute of anxious silence passed, and Kraft looked to his left to see what was keeping Moreau from proceeding. Oddly enough the Frenchman's eyes were tightly shut, his rigid expression focused totally on the muffled utterances that were passing his trembling lips. Kraft's first impression was that he was viewing a man lost deep in prayer.

But then Moreau's eyes suddenly opened and he called out in an anguished tone, "This is for you, *mes amours*!"

Moreau's right index finger depressed the red button, and Kraft's glance quickly returned to the screen. The first indication that the mine had detonated was a seemingly insignificant puff of smoke at the *Triton's* waterline.

The true force of the explosion became evident when the entire vessel was lifted up out of the water. Then down it came in a frothing splash that caused the Griffon to go crashing to the deck below. A secondary explosion rocked the warship, and the bright orange submersible tumbled into the sea and sank into the roiling depths bow-first.

"That should seal the fate of both the detonator and the test-monitoring equipment," Melindi announced with finality. "Surely we've succeeded in setting back their program for a good year at the very least."

Moreau appeared to be in a world of his own and failed to react to this comment. His eyes were riveted to the display screen, where smoke could be seen pouring from the *Triton*'s belowdeck spaces.

Well aware of their exposed position, Melindi was quick to take charge. "Karl Ivar, pull in Freddie and let's get out of these waters."

Even when the ROV's data link was cut and the screen promptly went blank, Moreau continued staring at it like a man possessed. The sound of Ivana Borisov's voice, crying out in warning, soon broke this spell.

"Both the *Suffren* and *Duquesne* have started their turbines, Commandant!"

This was all the Frenchman had to hear to return to the land of the living. "Mr. Godavari, prepare to engage hydrodrive on course three-zero-zero the second Freddie's been retrieved," he directed.

"Sonobuoys in the water above us, Commandant!" Ivana excitedly reported. "The frigates must have launched their helicopters."

"Karl Ivar," barked Moreau. "Sever Freddie's tether."

"But Commandant," the Norwegian pleaded. "Without Freddie we'll be blinded. Just give me thirty seconds more."

A digital counter appeared on the screen. The rapidly descending numbers showed Freddie less than one hundred yards away as the intercom speakers began broadcasting a series of ever-quickening sonar pings.

"Karl Ivar, sever that umbilical this instant!" ordered the enraged captain. "Mr. Godavari, prepare to get under way."

This was the first time Kraft had ever seen a member of the crew dare to disobey Moreau. Karl Ivar appeared to be deliberately stalling, and Kraft wondered what the consequences would be as the digital counter passed ten yards.

"Storage bay is open and final retrieval initiated," said the Norwegian, who was forced to wait another ten seconds before triumphantly adding, "Freddie's home!"

With a lightning-quick movement Raghib Godavari manipulated his joysticks. The deck canted over steeply to the right, and Kraft could feel his restraining harness bite into the skin of his shoulders. There was the slightest perception of forward speed, and he could visualize *Ecowar* rocketing through the blackened waters.

"Something's just entered the water topside!" warned Borisov. "I think it could be a—"

The Russian's words were cut short by a trio of ear-shattering blasts. Ecowar violently shook and rocked from side to side. His breath squeezed from his lungs by the force of this concussion, Kraft looked ominously upward as the lights blinked off, on, then permanently off.

"Mr. Godavari, activate emergency lighting!" Moreau shouted. "Number Two, get me a damage-control diagnostic!"

Several nail-biting seconds passed before a series of red battle lanterns snapped on. The display screen weakly flickered alive with a barely visible see-through scale model of Ecowar, and line after line of confusing data filled the right-hand portion of the screen. As he interpreted it for the others Melindi's relief was obvious.

"Hull integrity remains intact. Damage is limited to the electrical distribution grid."

"Page Chief Yushiro!" Moreau ordered.

Melindi readdressed his keypad and the lower left-hand portion of the screen projected a static-filled video image of the engine room. In the background, Mikio Yushiro and two assistants could be seen feverishly working on a flashing computer console.

"Chief, can the electrical grid be rerouted to get the primary systems back on-line?" Moreau called out.

Yushiro breathlessly answered without taking his eyes away from his console. "We're doing our best to do just that, Commandant. But until we have time to replace all the shorted circuits, power is going to have to be diverted from the defensive pulsers."

"So be it," retorted Moreau. "And notify me at once should you experience the least bit of difficulty along the way."

No sooner did the video feed terminate than the control room's lights popped back on at full capacity. A sigh of relief was shared by all, and no one was happier than Raghib Godavari.

"All helm functions back on-line," he reported. "Hydrodrive reengaged on course three-zero-zero."

Unfortunately Ivana Borisov's news was not as heartening. "The *Suffren* and the *Duquesne* continue following us out to sea."

Moreau didn't seem overly concerned by her report. "*Ecowar* will have no trouble outrunning them, though their helicopters could still be a bother."

Kraft was somewhat encouraged by this response, but still had trouble comprehending the true seriousness of their situation. With all its flashing digital counters and holographic images, *Ecowar* seemed more high-tech video game than actual warship. Thus he was little prepared for the next round of bad news delivered by Borisov.

"Underwater contact, bearing two-seven-six, range ten thousand yards!"

"Analyze the signature, Number Two," Moreau directed in a cool, calm manner.

Melindi attacked his keypad with fury, and the screen filled with an assortment of waterfall displays and analysis projections. The Kenyan quickly scanned this data, and when he voiced the results, his tone was far from reassuring.

"Computer indicates that there's an eighty-three-percent probability that this contact is a French Rubis-class nuclear-powered attack sub."

"Damn!" cursed Moreau. "If that's the case, that would make her the *Casabianca,* under the command of Jules Renard. I know that old fox well, and it would be just like him to shoot first and ask questions later."

This remark all too soon came true when Borisov called out forcefully, "Torpedoes in the water! I count two separate weapons, bearing two-seven-six, range ninety-five hundred yards and rapidly closing."

Now the reality of their predicament really struck home, and Kraft felt the first stirrings of fear gathering in his stomach. Before, it all seemed to be just a game. Now their lives were on the line.

"How can we counter those torpedoes with our defensive shield inoperable?" he cried.

"Easy does it, *mon ami,*" Moreau urged coolly. "Have you lost your faith in *Ecowar* already? Karl Ivar, prepare to launch decoy. Mr. Godavari, come around hard to course one-two-zero!"

Kraft was barely aware of the restraining harness biting into his shoulders as the deck angled over steeply to the right. A wave of fear-induced claustrophobia engulfed him, and for the first time he wondered what would happen if one of the torpedoes were to strike them. Surely not even *Ecowar*'s revolutionary hull could deflect such a blow, and they'd be crushed to death by tons of onrushing seawater.

"Decoy ready for launch, sir," Karl Ivar announced.

"Launch decoy on bearing one-nine-zero," ordered Moreau.

The deck shuddered. And from the elevated intercom speakers a new sound was relayed—the grinding, high-pitched whine of their decoy.

"Good doctor, have a look at the display screen," Melindi suggested, in an effort to distract Kraft from his panic.

With the sweat pouring off his brow, Kraft did as instructed. Projected before them was a directional targeting chart, showing constantly updated, electronic representations of *Ecowar,* its decoy, and the two oncoming torpedoes.

"Soon you'll see why your fears are unfounded," Melindi continued softly, his confident tone sounding a bit forced. "Our decoy is designed to simulate *Ecowar'*s sonic signature. With a little luck, the torpedoes will attack the wrong target."

"Mr. Godavari," Moreau interrupted. "Come around crisply to course three-four-five."

The deck angled over sharply to the left. Struggling to keep his eyes on the screen, Kraft noted how their position changed in response to the captain's orders. The two oncoming torpedoes didn't appear to be the least bit fooled by this tactic, as Ivana Borisov's next update indicated.

"Torpedoes continue their approach," she reported. "Range is eight hundred yards and closing."

For the first time Moreau's firm tone momentarily faltered. "Karl Ivar, why isn't that decoy emitting?"

The Norwegian answered while frantically inputting his keypad. "The data link seems to be jammed, sir. I'm switching over to the auxiliary umbilical."

All eyes were on the display screen as the solid red line representing the decoy's course began rapidly blinking. When one of the attacking torpedoes veered off toward it, a brief outburst of relieved chatter broke out in the compartment.

"There goes half our threat," Melindi observed.

Any continued celebration was quickly forestalled by Borisov's next update. "Only a single torpedo continues on course. Range is seven hundred yards and closing."

"Why don't you launch another decoy?" Kraft asked with a bit more control.

Melindi shook his head, worry etched on his features. "I'm afraid, good doctor, that there's no time for that."

Not expecting an answer with such chilling implications, Kraft was engulfed by another wave of fear. "Then how are we going to counter that remaining torpedo?"

To his immediate left, Jean Moreau was contemplating this very same question. With his intent glance glued to the targeting chart, the Frenchman weighed his rapidly dwindling options.

"Karl Ivar, what's the depth of the reef that lies due east of us?"

Without having to access his keypad, the Norwegian answered. "It's approximately twenty-five feet beneath the surface, sir."

"You'd better pray that those bathymetrics are accurate, *mon ami,*" returned Moreau. "Because that reef offers us our last chance."

Having personally seen the damage a coral reef had inflicted on the hull of the institute's capture boat, Kraft dared to question Moreau's decision. "You're not going to try to cross over it, are you?"

"Why not, Doctor?" Moreau asked. "With a draft of just over twenty feet, *Ecowar* should have a whole five feet to spare."

If he had any doubts about his decision to attempt a risky course change, Borisov's excited report—"Torpedo has capture!" she exclaimed—laid them to rest.

"Bring us up to the surface, Mr. Godavari!" Moreau firmly ordered. "On course zero-nine-zero."

By a complicated manipulation of his right joystick, the Indian literally flew the *Ecowar* through the water like a jet fighter on afterburners. Upward they shot, with the deck tilted sharply on its right side and MHD engines pumping out maximum power.

"Reef dead ahead, sir," enunciated the mechanical voice of Karl Ivar.

"Torpedo has just crossed the six-hundred-yard threshold," added Ivana Borisov.

As he worriedly scanned the flashing data on the display screen, Kraft didn't know which threat he feared more—being struck by the torpedo, or impaled on the awaiting reef.

"Relax, Doctor, and make the most of this moment," Moreau said calmly. "It's only in times of risk that man's truly alive."

Though Kraft would have liked nothing better than to argue otherwise, his apprehensions kept him from speaking. His throat dry with fear, his heart racing, and sweat pouring down his forehead, he began to count off his remaining seconds of life.

The strained expressions of the crew around him showed that most of them shared his concern. Only Moreau seemed to thrive on this anxiety. Like a child in the front seat of a roller coaster, the Frenchman was anxiously bent forward, his eyes wide with a wonder beyond mortal fear.

A quick check of the screen showed Kraft that the moment of judgment was upon them. The jagged bathymetric line representing the reef was directly in front of *Ecowar,* with the flashing blue light of the pursuing torpedo only inches from their squared stern. Nervously tightening his grip on the jumpseat's armrests, he began silently praying to a God he was just now rediscovering as *Ecowar's* rounded bow crossed over the first portion of the reef.

His worst fears seemed to be realized as a nerve-tingling, scraping sound reverberated through the tension-packed compartment. The deck shook, and the abrasive racket intensified to the point that Kraft could visualize the jagged coral heads ripping into Ecowar's exposed underbelly. As the terrifying din reached its climax, an ear-shattering, booming explosion abruptly overrode it. The deck wildly vibrated, the lights blinked off, and in the blackened darkness a piercing electronic alarm began ringing.

Any second now Kraft was prepared to hear the roar of the onrushing sea as the sub's bulkheads collapsed. Again he attempted to pray, but his great fear made the necessary concentration impossible. But then two surprising things occurred—surprising and, at first, puzzling. The deck stabilized, and then the lights snapped back on. This was followed by the relieved voice of Ivana Borisov.

"Torpedo has impacted the reef and is destroyed. Attack terminated."

"Clear water ahead of us, Commandant," said Karl Ivar, as if absolutely nothing out of the ordinary had just occurred.

The familiar scale model of *Ecowar* flashed onto the display screen. Only after Melindi completed his analysis of the data that accompanied it did Kraft realize that they had somehow prevailed.

"Damage-control diagnostic indicates a tear in our exterior hull alongside the port ROV housing. All primary subsystems remain on-line, though I'm afraid that the collision did in Freddie."

"No matter, Number Two," replied Moreau. "We have successfully completed our mission as planned, and now we have the time to return to Phoenix base and properly initiate repairs. Besides, it appears that Dr. Kraft here is in sore need of a little R and R."

"Phoenix base?" Kraft repeated, his pulse still beating madly.

Moreau directly answered him. "That's our home port in the Pacific, *mon ami*. And there's no need for any additional worry on your part because Phoenix base is only a day's sail from here. I'm certain you'll find it a most fascinating place. And besides, it's located near American Samoa, where we'll gladly drop you off once *Ecowar* is completely seaworthy once again."

Looking to his left, Moreau added, "Mr. Godavari, come around to course three-two-five and engage hydro-drive. *Mes amis,* it's time for *Ecowar* to return home!"

17

Some three thousand nautical miles northwest of Moruroa Atoll, the USS *Chicago* continued its patrol. Despite the unusual nature of their current mission, a business-as-usual atmosphere prevailed as the crew went about their daily work.

In the hushed confines of the sub's torpedo room, Seaman First Class Joe Carter spent the majority of his watch participating in a torpedo-loading drill. When the number-three tube went down with a minor malfunction, they were forced to cut the exercise short. The tube had since been sealed, and it would be up to the next watch team to repair it.

Throughout the drill, Carter noticed the nervousness of his shipmates. Most of their anxiety was centered around the recent loss of their civilian passenger. Scuttlebutt had it that Dr. Kraft needlessly drowned after refusing to obey Captain McShane's order to clear the deck. Of course, what really bothered them was the unusual nature of the threat that had precipitated this command.

When Carter learned that they were on the trail of a giant manta ray, he was incredulous. Yet the moment he heard of the civilian's tragic death, he was ready for action. Rumor had it that the sea creature was as big as the *Chicago* and could be a genuine threat in the event of a collision.

Since he and his cohorts had been trained to utilize their torpedoes exclusively for attacking other submarines, Carter wondered if they could handle this new danger. Surely this was an unprecedented challenge.

In another portion of the *Chicago,* a watch team had more immediate concerns. There never seemed to be enough hours in the day to complete the all-important work of the men assigned to *Chicago* Power and Light.

As the boat's engineering officer, Lieutenant Paul Ward had for a long time insisted on his fair share of eighteen-hour workdays. His area of responsibility was vast. Monitoring the reactor alone was a full-time job, and he could count on one hand the number of times he had been allowed an undisturbed night's sleep.

Their current operational status was another of the challenges that seemed to arrive on a daily basis. For hours on end, the *Chicago* had been traveling at full speed. This meant operating with the throttle wide open, regardless of the noisy cavitation that might be left in their wake.

In addition to the need for top speed, the captain had tasked him to correct a peculiar problem in the reactor's water pump. On two previous occasions, a valve in the device had stuck momentarily, resulting in an unwanted banging racket that echoed through the *Chicago* like a rifle shot. Figuring out how to fix such a malfunction without drastically reducing their forward speed was his current dilemma.

Never one to complain, Paul Ward knew what he was getting involved in when he enlisted in the navy back in 1983. Picking submarine duty for the express purpose of learning how to operate a nuclear reactor, he completed his initial two-year training as a reactor technician aboard the USS *Will Rogers,* which had been designed as a launchpad for the Poseidon C-3 missile and thus was the perfect place to learn his craft. His hard work caused him to be chosen for the Navy Enlisted Scientific Education Program. Upon graduation, he was commissioned an ensign in the United States Navy.

His current assignment was his first as a department head. If all went well, his next promotion would lead him one step closer to the most coveted position in the entire submarine force—skipper of his very own fast-attack sub. Such openings were few and far between and required a spotless service record.

Yet this was only one of the reasons why solving the mystery of the noisy valve was important to him. For Paul Ward was a perfectionist, and he'd have no inner peace until this problem was history.

In the space directly forward of *Chicago* Power and Light, Chief Petty Officer Howard Mallott was facing his own version of a career crisis. It all started when Captain McShane diplomatically confronted him and questioned his menu selection. This was the first time that the personable CO had ever voiced a negative word regarding the chow, and Mallott took it most seriously.

When he first ordered stores for this patrol, his intention was to serve healthy, low-fat meals, a rarity in the navy. He went to great lengths to secure foodstuffs that would provide such a diet. He demanded skim milk, margarine, and yogurt instead of the usual ice cream. He even changed from their normal cooking oil to a canola-based product. That request alone put him deeply in debt to his shore-based supply officer.

Though he heard the usual rumbles of discontent among the men, especially when they learned that their burgers were made from turkey, Mallott ignored them. He really thought that he was making progress in getting them to accept this new, healthier diet when Captain McShane unexpectedly burst his bubble.

Mallott respected the captain's opinion. Unlike many COs he had previously served under, Mac McShane was a fair man, who wouldn't voice a complaint unless it was valid. Thus, to get back to his good graces, Mallott would have to make some fundamental menu changes.

Variety was his biggest problem. Since the majority of meat in the freezer was still turkey, he'd have to plan each meal with utmost caution. The extra care he took in preparing tonight's menu was a prime example.

To deliver the variety that the captain had asked for, this evening's dinner theme would be a Mexican fiesta of tacos, enchiladas, and chili served with copious amounts of spicy salsa. And little would the crew know that the ground meat in these dishes was turkey.

Having sworn his cooks to secrecy, Mallott was already focusing on tomorrow's meal. Just to be on the safe side, he decided to defrost the remaining beef briskets and satisfy the crew's craving for red meat with a rip-roaring Texas-style barbecue.

Completely ignorant of the machinations of the *Chicago*'s head cook, Mac McShane had withdrawn to his stateroom to work on his article for the *Submarine Review*. For once, the writing was going smoothly and he was just about done with the first draft.

Since his preliminary outline, he had decided to shift his argument supporting the maintenance of a strong U.S. submarine industrial base. Keeping the shipyards in business was, it was true, cost-effective, but he had neglected something more important: worldwide geopolitical instability.

Though the Cold War was over, life inside the former Soviet Union was far from stable. With the collapse of Communism had come runaway inflation and general economic chaos, which threatened to tear the new Russia asunder. Added to this were the ethnic battles in the republics and the reappearance of a strong left-wing movement that had the full support of the military. Given its history of revolution, Russia's current instability provided an important example of why America needed to be prepared for strategic threats.

Even with the Russians' talk of peaceful cooperation, submarines continued to be produced in Russian shipyards. Unlike the crude, noisy models of the former Soviet Navy, these high-tech vessels were quiet, capable warships on a par with the earlier 688-class models. Code-named Akula, Sierra, Pantera, and Typhoon, they demanded respect. To prepare itself for any potential future conflict, the U.S. Navy had to be in a position to produce submarines such as the new Seawolf.

If the industrial base needed to construct boats like Seawolf was shut down, it could take decades to reestablish. And even then, it would be but a shadow of its former self, as new workers would have to be retrained and plants retooled. Many high-technology capabilities would be lost forever.

Satisfied with the cogency of his argument, Mac remained at his laptop, completed the draft, and decided to stow away the disc awhile before taking a fresh look at it. Then, checking his calendar, he saw that he had one more piece of writing to attend to before he could turn off his computer. In six more days, his son would be eleven. Before leaving on this patrol, Mac had gone out and bought him a full-size telescope and tripod. His wife would give it to Mac Jr. at his party, scheduled to take place at Sea World.

Unable to pick up a telephone and convey his love and best wishes, Mac had only one alternative. The familygram was a submariner's only contact with the outside world while on patrol. Limited in both space and content, a familygram provided assurance that a sailor's loved ones were all right. It also told of births and deaths and could be used to convey anniversary or birthday wishes.

Sadly enough, Mac had only been home for three of his son's past birthdays. Mac Jr.'s childhood was passing quickly, and his father had missed so very much. The advent of the video camera helped fill in some of the missing pieces. But film was no substitute for the look on a child's face on Christmas morning or that feeling of joyous expectation before the birthday cake was brought in.

Reaching into his desk drawer, Mac fondly pulled out a white envelope. Inside was the birthday-party invitation Mac Jr. had given him the day the *Chicago* left San Diego. He wondered if somehow his son was hoping he'd be able to make the party after all. Little did the boy realize that his father would be halfway around the world, and would be fortunate to make it home by Thanksgiving.

As Mac looked at the leaping golden dolphins that decorated the invitation, a disturbing thought came to him. Only a few short days ago Dr. Peter Kraft was sitting in this very cabin. Now he was dead. Did Kraft have a son or daughter of his own? he wondered. He had arrived on the *Chicago* so abruptly and he and Mac had had little time to get to know each other. Now it was too late.

An official inquest of Kraft's death was to be held upon *Chicago*'s return to port. Though Mac blamed no one but himself for the accident, the testimony of Chop and the others who were topside that fated day would surely absolve him—in everyone's eyes but his own. As far as the captain of the *Chicago* was concerned, Peter Kraft was lost because of an order that he had given. Regardless of the court's verdict, this was the judgment Mac's inner court had handed down. And there would be no appealing it.

Sobered by this thought, Mac suddenly found himself in no mood to work on his boy's familygram birthday message. He returned the invitation to his desk drawer and snapped off the halogen lamp. Darkness engulfed him, and he leaned back in his chair, visualizing for the thousandth time the last time he had laid eyes on Dr. Peter Kraft.

In the adjoining control room, Lieutenant Vic Bradley was the current OOD. The boat's weapons officer stood on the elevated bridge, a dark green woolen sweater over his coveralls and his hands behind his back. Positioned slightly behind the two helmsmen sitting on Bradley's left was the boat's present diving officer, Chief of the Boat Joe Hoffler. The COB had the unlit stub of a cigar in his mouth, and his eyes were locked on the dials and gauges of the main control panel.

Vic Bradley had great respect for the COB. Hoffler was an experienced sailor, the kind of man you wanted around when there was trouble, and Bradley had learned to overlook many of his social deficiencies. He wasn't at all surprised when Hoffler leaned forward and tweaked the ear of the outboard helmsman.

"Wake up, Green!" he called. "Damn it, son. Watch that course of yours!"

The burly sailor he had been addressing sat up straight and double-checked their compass heading. He made a slight course adjustment, then slumped back down in his chair, one hand casually draped around the steering yoke.

Bradley stifled a laugh when the COB once more tweaked the helmsman's ear.

"And put both those hands of yours on that steerin' yoke, son!" Hoffler commanded. "Jesus H. Christ, you're sittin' there on that fat ass of yours, holdin' that yoke like you was drivin' your pappy's Ford. Don't forget, sailor, you're steerin' a billion dollars' worth of submarine through the water. So wake up, boy, and take some pride in that job of yours!"

"Conn, Sonar," an amplified voice broke in over the control room's intercom. "We have a new contact, bearing two-two-zero, designate Sierra seven, biological."

The OOD reached up for the ceiling microphone beside him. "Sonar, Conn, designate Sierra seven, biological, aye, Sonar."

Bradley quickly checked this new contact on the repeater screen mounted directly before him. Satisfied that the classification was correct, he returned his attention to the diving console to check on the COB's next move.

"Good work, Algren," said Matt Cox, referring to the report that the young sailor had just passed on to the control room. "We'll make a qualified sonarman out of you yet."

Reaching up into the overhead ventilation shaft, Cox pulled out a small box of raisins. "Consider yourself properly rewarded," he announced as he tossed the box to the blond-haired sailor seated at the far left console.

Specs, who sat at Algren's side, briefly removed his wire-rims to rub the bridge of his nose, then turned back to the repeater screen. Currently responsible for monitoring their towed array, he isolated individual hydrophones by manipulating the thin black joystick mounted into his console.

On Specs's right was Marvin Johnson. A professional jazz musician before a minor run-in with the law sent him packing for the navy, the streetwise Bronx native was right at home in the sound shack. He especially enjoyed listening to the natural noises of the sea and was, at the moment, monitoring the syncopated rhythm section of a family of chattering shrimp.

Noting Johnson's preoccupation, Cox playfully punched him in the left shoulder to get his attention. "What's so interesting out there, Marvelous Marv?" he asked.

Johnson pulled back his left headphone and answered, all the while struggling to keep the irregular beat of the shrimp with his hand. "It's nothin' but a biological, my man. Ya know, there's some really hot sounds happenin' down there, bro."

"Well, save the musical critique for your next jam session," returned Cox. "Right now there's only one sound I want you to be groovin' on, and that's the beat of that ultrasonic homing signal."

"Shit, man, you don't really think we've got a chance of taggin' that sucker," countered Johnson. "I said it before and I'll say it again, there's a lot of ocean out there, and this whole thing's nothin' but a wild-goose chase."

"I agree," Algren put in. "Sniffin' out another sub is difficult enough. But this is like searchin' for that proverbial needle in the haystack my granny was always tellin' me about."

In the past, Cox had always encouraged his men to speak their minds, and this occasion proved no different. As he reached out to gently massage the neck of the technician who had yet to voice his opinion, he asked, "What do you think, Specs? Is this whole thing only a waste of time?"

Specs hesitated a few seconds before voicing his opinion. "I don't see how this operation is any different from the other exercises we've participated in. In my book, duty is duty. Whether it be sitting up in the Kurils waiting for Ivan, or sprinting into the South Pacific on the trail of a monster ray, it really doesn't matter to me."

"Then you really think we've got a decent chance to tag that ray?" Cox continued.

Specs shrugged his skinny shoulders. "I don't see why not, sir. If the coordinates Command has passed down to us are accurate, and that beacon keeps transmitting, I say that if it's out there, we'll tag it."

Cox look most pleased with this response as he turned to address Specs's skeptical shipmates. "Now that's the type of attitude that I like, gentlemen. And in honor of Specs's clear thinking, he gets today's grand prize."

With these words, the senior sonar technician reached up into the ventilation shaft and pulled out a cherished box of Cracker Jacks. He solemnly handed it to Specs as if it were nothing less than the Holy Grail.

"Here you go, Specs," he intoned. "You're now the lucky owner of the only box of Cracker Jacks on the entire USS *Chicago*!"

At the *Chicago*'s navigation plot, Lieutenant Commander Phil Moore intently studied a bathymetric chart of the waters surrounding the Marshall Islands. With the scarred stem of his corncob pipe, he pointed out a tiny atoll located in the central portion of the chain. Close beside him, Lieutenant Len Matson listened as the XO explained the significance of this minuscule circular landmass.

"We're just a stone's throw away from Kwajalein now. Too bad we can't pay the folks there a quick visit."

"I didn't realize that the atoll had been settled," said the navigator.

"The air force keeps a small weather station there, in conjunction with the Pacific Missile Test Range," the XO revealed. "It's hard to believe that the center of the atoll is bull's-eye for warheads launched from Vandenberg, some four thousand miles northeast of here."

"That's a hell of a missile shot," Matson said.

"I'll say it is," Moore agreed. "And you can really appreciate the incredible technology involved if you ever get the chance to visit Vandenberg. My brother-in-law was stationed there in the late eighties. I had some time off in between tours back then, and while me and Connie were driving up to Big Sur, we decided to stop off in Lompoc and see what duty on an air-force base was all about.

"I don't know if you've ever visited that portion of California, Lieutenant, but the scenery up there is just beautiful. Rolling green hills, thick oak woods, and right smack in the middle of it all, one of the most sophisticated missile-launch facilities on the planet."

"Weren't they planning to launch the space shuttle from Vandenberg at one time?" interjected Matson.

The XO nodded. "That they were, Lieutenant. We even spent over a billion dollars getting a site prepared, until Washington inexplicably pulled the plug on the project. We got to tour the partially completed pad and, strangely enough, encountered a bunch of archaeologists working on a dig nearby. It seems the site the air force picked was smack dab in the center of a Chumash Indian burial ground. And even stranger was the rumor that the local Indians cursed the site when they learned that we intended to utilize it for our launchpad."

The navigator grinned. "Maybe that curse cost us taxpayers the billion dollars that you mentioned they wasted on the site."

"Who knows?" said the XO in all seriousness. "But fortunately the other launch sites on the base have been a great success. We got to climb down into a Minuteman silo and visited a subterranean control room where SAC launch crews were trained. An actual launch was scheduled for that evening, but it was scrubbed because of bad weather."

"Too bad you missed it," said Matson. "I once saw a Minuteman test shot while on duty at Cape Canaveral, and it was a sight I'll never forget. That gleaming white rocket shooting into the blue heavens—the roar of its boosters practically cut right through me."

The XO returned his attention to the chart; while circling the atoll with his pipe's stem, he continued: "Though I missed that opportunity to witness a launch, I did learn something interesting while having dinner at Vandenberg's officers' club. Several months before, a Minuteman with an advanced MIRV'd warhead was launched from the base, with its destination here at Kwajalein. The shot went off perfectly, and several eyewitnesses viewed the reentry bus as it scored a direct hit in the waters of the lagoon. Yet the next morning when they went to retrieve it, the warhead and its vital telemetry package was nowhere to be found.

"Divers were sent down to scour the seabed, and it was reported, though never officially verified, that they found something that sent shock waves all the way back to the Pentagon. My brother-in-law's usually booming voice decreased to a bare whisper as he described the tractorlike treads the divers supposedly spotted, embedded in the sandy floor of the lagoon."

The navigator's eyes widened in astonishment. "Sounds like it could have been a mini-sub of some sort."

"That's what I thought," said the XO. "And the particular model I had in mind was the Soviet Sea Devil, a submersible craft whose design was copied from the Germans at the end of World War II."

"Did they ever find our warhead?" asked Matson.

"Not that I know of, Lieutenant. Though if you ask me, its disassembled components are sitting in a Russian warehouse somewhere gathering dust."

"Lieutenant Commander Moore," interrupted a sailor assigned to the *Chicago*'s radio room. "We're receiving an extensive VLF message from COMSUB-PAC that I thought you'd like to get a preliminary look at, sir."

The XO turned his gaze away from the chart and met the glance of his navigator. "Perhaps there's been another sighting of our favorite sea monster," Moore quipped. "Shall we see for ourselves if this is indeed the case, Lieutenant?"

Both officers took off expectantly for the nearby radio room. A bank-vault-type lock protected the sealed compartment, and the XO hastily dialed in the proper combination. Once inside, he went straight to the decoder, where the newly received message awaited his perusal.

"Will you get a load of this," he said while skimming the page-long dispatch.

"Does it concern the giant ray?" asked the curious navigator.

"In a matter of speaking." The XO slowly reread the entire dispatch before he went on. "It looks like you'd better be drawing us up the quickest route to Moruroa Atoll in French Polynesia, Lieutenant. Because as of this moment, we've been temporarily relieved from our monster hunt and have been ordered further south to assist the French Navy. It seems that they've been the victim of a terrorist incident that resulted in the loss of a warship and several deaths. And get this—the suspected culprit is a mini-sub of some sort, whose country of origin is yet unknown. Brother, wouldn't it be something if this phantom sub turned out to be the same one that stole our warhead back at Kwajalein!"

18

Commandant Jules Renard anxiously paced the padded deck of the *Casabianca*'s control room. Like a caged animal, the forty-seven-year-old, silver-haired senior officer was attempting to project his will in order to effect the outcome of their current hunt. From station to station he roamed, passing the sole seated helmsman, the knot of concerned sailors gathered around the navigation plot, the fully manned fire-control console, and last but not least, the all-important sonar station. It was this latter station that Renard especially concentrated on. The three sonarmen currently on duty were his most experienced watch and, not surprisingly, were commonly referred to as the A-Team. It would be from their lips that first word of their prey would come.

"Initiating sprint sequence, Commandant," reported the rough voice of the diving officer. "All ahead full," he added to the helmsman.

As this directive was passed down to the engine room, Renard visualized their 48MW pressurized water-cooled reactor activating. The resulting superheated steam would then pass through their dual turbines, in turn powering the boat's five-bladed propeller. In only minutes, the smallest nuclear-powered submarine ever built would be cutting through the depths at a speed of over twenty-five knots.

They would continue in sprint mode for the next five minutes. Then the engines would once again go silent, and the 237-foot-long vessel would soundlessly drift, to allow the sonar team a noise-free background for their hydrophones.

Such a search mode was called sprint and drift. It was first taught to Renard at the naval academy by none other than Admiral Michel Baptiste. Surely the Marine Nationale's most infamous submariner would take great satisfaction in seeing this novel tactic being utilized two and a half decades later. Renard doubted that Admiral Baptiste would be so pleased with the *Casabianca*'s initial attack— since its failure had precipitated their present search.

Renard had been at fire control himself and had seen the DUUX 5 Fenelon passive sonar get an exact range on the phantom submarine responsible for the cowardly attack on the *Triton*. Even with the element of surprise in *Casabianca*'s favor, their salvo of advanced F17P wire-guided acoustic homing antisubmarine torpedoes failed to hit their mark.

When these weapons originally detonated, Renard had been so certain that his ambush had succeeded. It was only after the roiling depths calmed that he learned otherwise. The last they heard of their quiet prey was a jetlike surge as the phantom sub disappeared into the blackened depths beyond the now fractured reef.

Such utter incompetence on Renard's part could not be excused. Patience was definitely not one of his virtues, and his Basque origins showed themselves in his sworn desire to make good his mistake. For he was a fast-attack captain and, as such, was the best that France could offer. And ever true to the tradition of the Marine Nationale, failure was something he could not permit!

Jean Moreau sat behind his desk in his darkened stateroom, a single white candle flickering before him. The slender taper provided just enough illumination to see the button-sized, gold-plated pin in his palm. Given to him over a decade ago, when he received the rank of commandant in the Marine Nationale, the pin was circular in shape; on it was a compass topped by two crossed swords with a submarine positioned above them.

He had worked a lifetime to win the pin. The desire had inspired him to try just a little bit harder during those difficult days at the academy, and was the reason he sacrificed the best years of his life in the defense of his native France.

How very proud he had been to wear the golden insignia on his chest! It indicated that he was one of a chosen few, selected because of his integrity, trust-worthiness, and ability to be the commander of the most lethal attack platform in the French fleet.

That he would someday break his vows and become an enemy of this same fleet would have been unthinkable back then. But during this morning's attack the unthinkable had come to pass.

The moment the charges went off on *Triton's* hull, Moreau took the final, fatal step in a process that had begun long before. Accountable now to no one but himself, he had at long last transcended the constraints of nationalism.

Surely French blood had been spilled on Moruroa Atoll. Less than two decades ago he would have been on the other side, leading the hunt to track down and destroy *Ecowar*. But fate had since intervened, and now ex-shipmates such as the *Casabianca's* Jules Renard had taken his place in defending France's honor.

Now that the elation of combat had dissipated, Moreau finally realized the significance of the encounter. It was the final break, the test of his deepest convictions, proving that he had been reborn. Because of his act today, he would never again be allowed in his homeland, except as an acknowledged traitor and a prisoner of the state.

This realization was frightening, and Moreau needed courage to overcome the doubt that momentarily possessed him. Concentrating his inner sight on the flickering flame, he visualized the ghostly apparitions that had led to this fated day. New purpose flooded into the abyss; he heard anew the cries of a blue-whale calf, saw anew the imploring black eyes of a baby harp seal, delighted again in the boisterous vocalizations of a pod of leaping dolphins. To defend these creatures, he had been reborn in this life. And though he had tragically lost his family and been forced to abandon his homeland along the way, he had gained an entire planet in their place.

To properly mourn this passing, Moreau put down the golden pin that had triggered these thoughts. He reached out into the darkness and grasped the smooth wooden body of his violin. With his bow in hand, he tuned down the violin's top string by a semitone and prepared to play a piece of music proper to his solemn mood.

Saint-Saëns's *Danse Macabre* was a stirring tone poem evocative of a graveyard at midnight, when death summons the skeletons from their coffins with the haunting, funereal strains of his fiddle. Moreau learned the piece as a child. Since then, his soul had transgressed, and in celebration of his miraculous rite of passage he raised his Stradivarius in homage.

The mournful sounds of Moreau's violin seeped into *Ecowar*'s control room. The compartment's only two occupants barely paid it any attention, their ears attuned instead to the distant, pulsating tones of a homing beacon that emanated from the seafloor several thousand yards before them.

"That's the Nova Canton Trough transponder all right," Ivana Borisov announced as she cupped her headphones over her ears. "It looks like we've made it home, Karl Ivar."

"That we have," responded the Norwegian from his position at the helm.

On the display screen, the projected bathymetric chart showed *Ecowar* to be following the east-west meander of a wide undersea canyon. A red light began flashing on the easternmost edge of the trough, indicating the position of the transponder Ivana had just identified.

"Once you get our exact fix, we'll have no trouble at all picking up the transponders that follow," said Karl Ivar. "And then it will be as easy as setting the automatic pilot and allowing the sonic glide path to guide us through the lava tube straight into Phoenix base."

With the transponder's guidance, Ivana accessed the computer to determine this positional fix. A series of longitude and latitude coordinates flashed up onto the right-hand portion of the screen, and she removed her headphones and rubbed her sore ears. Only then was she fully aware of the distant violin sounds.

"Ah, Karl Ivar," she whispered. "He's at it again."

The Norwegian removed his own headphones, and he, too, concentrated on the mournful chords. "What a sad tune the commandant's playing. As excited as he was when he left us, you'd have thought he would pick a rousing anthem."

"You never know with that one, do you, Karl Ivar? One moment he's up, full of dreams and grand visions, and the next he goes off to a far darker place—a world where all is cold, distant, and lonely. Our commandant is indeed a complicated man, Comrade."

"In all the years I've known him, he still puzzles me," Karl Ivar admitted. "When I left Newfoundland with him, the commandant readily assumed the responsibility of providing me with a home. He allowed me into his secret world without question. Much more than my friend, he became my substitute father."

"I, too, felt his warmth when I first met him, Karl Ivar. But I guess it's taken the tight confines of *Ecowar* for us to see the commandant's darker side, as that tune he's playing so aptly demonstrates."

Karl Ivar's forehead creased with sadness as a particularly somber series of minor chords sounded from the violin. "Don't think it's been easy for him to accept the consequences of our attack on the *Triton,* Ivana. I'm sure you've heard all the stories about the tragic loss of his wife and daughter at the hands of the French Navy, and his hunger to get even. But now that he's gotten his revenge, it's the commandant who has to live with the blood of his countrymen staining his hands."

"What he needs is something to get these dark thoughts out of his mind," Ivana suggested.

"We'll be at Phoenix base shortly. And there will be plenty of work for all of us, including the commandant, if we are to get *Ecowar* completely seaworthy again. If I'm not mistaken, that will be the perfect medicine for his depression."

"I hope we can find something to keep the American occupied," remarked Ivana. "Our esteemed guest appeared to be badly shaken by that torpedo attack."

Karl Ivar put his headphones back on before replying. "Dr. Kraft has every reason to be scared. Put yourself in his place, and you'd feel exactly the same. After all, he didn't volunteer to serve aboard *Ecowar* like the rest of us. We knew the risks from the very beginning. But the poor doctor is just now realizing the many dangers involved with our mission. His nervousness will go away eventually, though I doubt he has the stomach to become a permanent crew member."

Ivana also put her headphones back on and turned her attention again to the screen just as another red light began blinking at the far eastern edge of the trough they continued to follow.

"We're picking up the second transponder, Comrade," she excitedly observed. "We'll be attaining glidepath coordinates in precisely fifty-nine minutes and counting. Phoenix base, here we come!"

Peter Kraft had just managed to fall asleep at last when the moody chords of a far-off violin broke his light slumber. For a few moments he lay there in the confusing blackness, unable to tell whether the sounds he was hearing were part of a dream or were real. Finally he realized that the violin he was hearing was probably the same one he had seen in Moreau's cabin. As he came more fully awake he noticed that what he was hearing was an expert rendition of Saint-Saëns's *Danse Macabre*. The music evoked images of brisk Halloween nights and witches' sabbaths. It had always been one of his favorite pieces of mood music.

As it turned out, the *Danse Macabre* was perfect background music for his current pensive mood. The traumatic events of the morning had left him emotionally drained, and not even a cup of Annie's bostrichia tea succeeded in relaxing him. Kraft had experienced his fair share of frightening encounters, but never had he felt the blind terror that overcame him during the escape from Mororua Atoll. He supposed it had a lot to do with the unique nature of his current environment. *Ecowar* was still an alien place to him, where he felt totally powerless to influence the course of external events.

His reliance on others for protection really bothered him. At least in the past, when he found himself in a dangerous situation, his own responsibility for getting into the situation was clear. It had been his own decision to risk life and limb by riding his bike, immersing himself in the institute's shark channel, or even daring to remain topside while the *Chicago* descended. In each instance, he remained accountable to only himself.

His stay aboard *Ecowar* was another matter. Here he was totally dependent upon his shipmates. This became all too obvious as he sat in the control room, watching his fate being played out on the compartment's display screen. This was no video game that he was viewing, but a life-and-death struggle whose purpose continued to elude him.

Did *Ecowar*'s crew really believe that by damaging the *Triton,* France would abandon nuclear tests? And this went for the tuna fisherman and squidders they had previously challenged as well. As sure as the sun would rise, other boats would replace the ones that had been sunk, and the slaughter of marine life would continue.

It was still Kraft's belief that the only way to make a real difference was to pass binding international legislation. To work, such laws would have to be rigidly enforced; in this capacity, as oceanic policemen, *Ecowar*'s crew could be of real service. If the day ever came when man finally united to protect the seas, Kraft would have no trouble at all supporting the use of *Ecowar* as an enforcement tool. For once the enemies of the ocean found out what they were up against, only the most foolish of souls would dare risk incurring *Ecowar*'s wrath.

As it stood now, they were nothing but seagoing vigilantes, no better than the men whose lives they were taking. An international pariah, *Ecowar* would be relentlessly hunted down, and the true nature of their mission would be lost in a cascade of sensational tabloid headlines. The crew's blind idealism promoted this fate, their attack on Mururoa sealed it.

The mere thought that a powerful consortium existed and shared these warped ideals disturbed Kraft even more. A costly vessel of this complexity could not exist without a concerted effort. Surely the individuals financing this effort would recognize that as it stood now, they were doomed to lose their great monetary investment and much more.

What a waste that would be! A vessel with *Ecowar*'s capabilities was an ideal research platform, able to bring scientists into the uncharted depths. Its advanced propulsion plant could revolutionize sea travel, while its advanced life-support and sensor systems could be applied elsewhere.

Kraft knew that their next scheduled stop offered his last chance to get his message across. At Phoenix base he would have an unparalleled opportunity to determine the nature of *Ecowar*'s support base. If luck was with him, Kraft would be able to present his argument to the men responsible for the vessel's development and support.

In an adjoining compartment, the mournful strains of Moreau's violin also provided the background music for Annie Sawyer. Her entire day had been spent in the galley, attempting to clean up the shambles that were left in the wake of *Ecowar*'s mad dash from Mururoa Atoll.

Her first concern had been the foodstuffs that were tossed onto the deck from their sprung storage bins. She planned to have a word or two with the repair staff at Phoenix base in order to avoid future messes of this sort.

As expected, the rest of the debris gathered on the carpeted deck was a combination of cooking utensils and silverware. Fortunately the cabinet holding their china collection wasn't affected, and she only had to contend with a minimum of broken glass at her feet.

She was well into her cleanup when Ezra Melinda entered the galley. *Ecowar*'s second in command briefly scanned the unusually cluttered counters before saying, "My, my, Annie, you have quite a mess on your hands. Why didn't you ask for some help?"

"It's nothing I can't handle on my own, Ezra," she replied, scooping up a pile of spilled sugar and returning it to a canister.

"Any other damage to report?" he asked.

Annie looked up and swept back a loose strand of hair from her forehead before answering. "Nothing appears to be broken that can't be readily replaced."

"That's good news, Annie. And I'm sure you'll be happy to hear that we've already initiated our glide path into Phoenix base. When we arrive, I'd like you to be the one to escort the good doctor topside. He'll inevitably be full of questions, and we're relying on you to answer them while we get on with the job of coordinating the repair effort."

"I'd be more than happy to act as Dr. Kraft's escort, Ezra. Is he still in his cabin?"

Melindi nodded. "We haven't heard a peep out of him since his morning visit to the control room."

Annie completed filling up the sugar canister and stood. "I sure hope he's feelin' better, Ezra. I understand he took our escape pretty badly."

The Kenyan grinned. "My nerves weren't exactly in tip-top condition after that torpedo chase either, my dear. So go easy on our guest. And let's give him a visit to Phoenix base that he'll never forget."

Annie offered Melindi a mock salute and scrounged up the ingredients for a peanut-butter-and-jelly sandwich, his favorite snack. A series of five soft electronic tones sent him scurrying out of the galley with his sandwich in hand. The deck briefly shook, and as the bow began to tilt, Annie rushed back to her stateroom to clean up before continuing on to Kraft's cabin.

She knocked on his door and found the marine biologist propped up in bed, reading a well-worn paperback. His greeting was neutral, so Annie knew she'd better proceed diplomatically.

"What's ya readin', Doc?" she asked.

"It's a book by Rachel Carson I found in the wardroom library," Kraft replied, barely looking up from the page he had been reading.

"Ah, *Silent Spring*," she returned. "Good choice. Did

you know that Rachel Carson is a national heroine back home in Australia? Though she's been dead for some time now, her books still sell well and are often quoted in the media. I read her book *The Sea Around Us* when I was just a teenager, and it made me see the oceans as a single ecosystem. What do you think of *Silent Spring* so far?"

Though he was in no mood for company, he couldn't ignore Annie's persistence, and he laid the open book on his lap. "Her message that the natural world is dying, poisoned through corporate greed, is just as relevant today as it was when it was first published. I first read *Silent Spring* in high school. Reading it again, I'm impressed with Carson's incredible foresight."

"I sure wish her message had been better heeded," said Annie. "As a kid, I remember one spring day when a mosquito control plane flew over our house sprayin' pesticide. I thought it was great fun as the pilot criss-crossed the billabong in our backyard, showering the stagnant pools of water with fine spray. Then the next morning we found three small songbirds dead around the birdbath. Those birds were my friends. They built their nests in our trees year after year and had learned to trust us completely. And here the government went and wiped them out with DDT in a single afternoon."

Kraft nodded in understanding and found he was glad after all that Annie had visited him. "We've sure managed to make a real mess of things in our mad rush to gain control over nature."

Annie sensed his change of mood and eagerly replied, "Rachel Carson warned about unrestrained pesticide use. What really scares me today is the way scientists are manipulating the genetic makeup of plants. They say they will produce a new generation of hearty, disease-resistant crops that won't need herbicides. But by fooling around with DNA, who knows what type of horrible Pandora's box the researchers could be opening."

"It sounds to me like a game of ecological Russian roulette, Annie. I sure hope that some strict international controls are set up in this new industry, especially in the less developed Third World countries."

Five soft electronic tones sounded in the background, followed by a shudder of the deck below, and a teasing grin broke out on Annie's face. "Doc, I've got a surprise that's gonna make you awfully happy. Come on, and I'll show ya."

Unable to resist this offer, Kraft placed his book on the bedside table, stood, and followed her out into the passageway. They headed forward, where a ladder had been pulled down from a ceiling-mounted storage well beside the control room.

"Be my guest, Doc." Annie gestured toward the ladder and the open hatchway above it.

Kraft needed no more prompting. The climb was a short one, and with the blessed sweet scent of fresh air filling his nostrils, he emerged onto *Ecowar*'s outer deck.

His astonished glance went straight upward, where a cathedrallike, chiseled-rock ceiling formed the roof of an immense subterranean cavern. Banks of powerful lights set into the cave's smooth rock walls illuminated the five-hundred-foot-wide lagoon in which they floated. A gangway on the deck led to a dock area where several individuals were gathered, all dressed in black jumpsuits. Dozens of modular shipping containers lined the walls behind them, where other workers drove to and fro in battery-powered forklifts.

"Welcome to Phoenix base," Annie said as she emerged onto the deck beside him. "Well, Doc, what do ya think?"

Kraft struggled to find the words to express his amazement. "Incredible, Annie! Where the hell are we?"

"Would ya believe in the hollowed-out cinder core of an inactive volcano?" she replied.

"You've got to be kidding me." Kraft couldn't believe this place was real. It seemed like something from a movie.

Annie shook her head. "It sure isn't any joke, Doc. And wait until you see this."

Kraft watched as she pulled an elongated silver dog whistle out of her pocket and put it to her lips, emitting a series of blasts that were inaudible to their ears. As Kraft scanned the flat blue waters a line of turbulence broke the surface near the far wall. Seconds later two bottle-nosed dolphins emerged from the depths. The sleek creatures appeared excited as they rushed over to *Ecowar* and greeted Annie and him with animated clicks and whistles. Annie bent down to address them.

"Hello Eno, hello Pelee. Did ya miss me?"

The dolphins reacted with emphatic shakes of their heads and another burst of chatter, and Kraft couldn't help laughing at their response as he knelt down at Annie's side.

"You know, your friends here remind me to two very special dolphins back home. What exactly are they trained to do?"

"For the most part, they're lookouts for uninvited visitors," she answered. "Their watery beat includes this lagoon, the lava-tube entryway, and a portion of the open Pacific directly outside this tunnel."

"So that's how we got in here," Kraft commented, searching the darkened recesses of the cave for any sign of the accessway to the outside world.

"Though we don't expect any trespassers here, both Eno and Pelee are on the job twenty-four hours a day, seven days a week," Annie continued. "They haven't been taught any aggressive behaviors—like your navy's sentry dolphins, who have been trained to pull the air hoses out of enemy divers' mouths. They're merely here to sound the alert should a worst case scenario come to pass."

"I'm embarrassed to say that I'm responsible for training many of those U.S. Navy dolphins you speak of, Annie. My understanding is that their dolphin sentry program really wasn't that successful. Only one location really lent itself to such a program. That was in Bangor, Washington, at the Trident submarine base. The year-round cold water temperatures there led to an abrupt termination of the project when the dolphins came down with severe viral infections."

Once more looking up to the cave's expansive ceiling, Kraft hopefully added, "Now, I don't suppose there's an island up there somewhere and an easy way to get to it?"

"Come on, Doc," said Annie with a playful wink. "You haven't seen anything yet."

They left the dolphins, and Annie led the way over the gangway. This allowed Kraft to get his first good look at *Ecowar* from a distance, and he readily saw why the vessel had been mistaken for a living creature. The revolutionary design of its hull did strongly resemble a giant manta ray, down to the twin ramming spars in its rounded bow. He saw no evidence of any visible damage to the outer skin, except for several missing rubberized tiles. Suspecting that this was the sonar-absorbent covering that he had been told about, Kraft climbed down off the gangway and took his first step on solid land.

He had grown accustomed to the gentle rocking motion of the submarine, and his first step onto the dock was a bit tentative. His inner ear had yet to adjust to the change, and he had to fight off a wave of dizziness. Annie sensed his discomfort and grabbed him by the arm. Together they continued toward the group of jumpsuit-clad figures Kraft had spotted from *Ecowar*'s deck.

He could soon identify two of these individuals as Jean Moreau and his second in command, in spirited conversation with an older, bald-headed gentleman, who could easily have passed for Moreau's father. Standing at his side was a well-built, brown-skinned young man with long dark hair cascading over his shoulders. His handsome face lit up in a smile when he spotted Annie, and Kraft felt a twinge of jealousy.

Ezra Melindi announced their approach with a good-natured greeting. "Annie, good doctor, welcome."

As the two newcomers joined the foursome Moreau introduced them. "Dr. Kraft, I'd like you to meet my dear friend and mentor, Admiral Michel Baptiste, who like myself is a veteran of France's Marine Nationale."

Kraft accepted a firm handshake from the distinguished-looking man standing at Moreau's side.

"*Enchanté,* Doctor," said Baptiste, his blue eyes boring deep into Kraft's with the intensity of an X ray. "It's an honor to meet you. Jean-Louis has been telling me all about the fortuitous circumstances that brought you to us. And you can rest assured that whatever humble conveniences this base has to offer are yours for the asking."

"Thank you, sir," Kraft replied, sensing the power the elder Frenchman exuded.

"Dr. Kraft," added Moreau. "I'd also like you to meet Matthew Amanave. Matthew's tribe are our hosts here at Phoenix base."

Kraft did his best not to wince as he shook the native's hand and felt his viselike grip.

"On behalf of my people I'd like to welcome you to our island, Doctor," Matthew said in perfect English. "Please make yourself at home here."

Kraft looked up to the ceiling. "So there's land on the other side of these walls," he said, without hiding his delight.

"That there is, Doctor." The handsome native turned to look at Kraft's curly-haired companion. "And welcome to you, Annie," he said with an adoring grin.

"*Ma chérie,*" interrupted Michel Baptiste as he stepped forward and kissed Annie on each cheek. "You are looking more beautiful than ever. We've missed that smiling face of yours."

"It's wonderful to be back, Admiral," Annie sincerely replied.

"Well, good doctor." Ezra Melindi was speaking now. "What are your first impressions of Phoenix base?"

"I think the only word to do it justice is incredible," Kraft said quickly. "This place must have cost a fortune to build."

"Actually Mother Nature did most of the excavation for us," Baptiste explained. "You see, the cavern was already hollowed out by lava when I first chanced upon it two decades ago."

"It suits our needs most adequately," added Moreau. "Offering us a secure base of operations far from the prying eyes of the world's navies."

As Melindi had predicted, Kraft was full of questions. "Is this where *Ecowar* was originally assembled?"

Baptiste briefly met Moreau's glance before answering. "Yes, it is, Doctor. If you'd like, I'd be more than willing to share all the details of her development and construction during tonight's luau."

"I'd most appreciate that, sir." returned Kraft. Karl Ivar could be seen approaching them from one of the modular buildings with a clipboard in hand.

When Moreau saw him as well, he said, "If you'll please excuse us, Doctor, we must get on with coordinating the repair efforts. Annie, why don't you escort our guest outside."

This was all she needed to hear to grab Kraft's arm. "Come on, Doc. Like I was sayin' before, you ain't seen nothin' yet."

Kraft accepted a curt nod of good-bye from Baptiste and Moreau and followed Annie into the cavern. They passed Karl Ivar, who greeted them with a hearty thumbs-up, and passed by the modular building from which the Norwegian had just emerged. A quick glance into the structure's window showed a fully stocked office, walls lined with filing cabinets, and a trio of women busily typing at computer keyboards. The modular structures that adjoined this office appeared to be storage spaces; equipment-packed pallets filled their smooth rock floors.

Kraft and Annie had to halt briefly at one point when a forklift buzzed by. The brown-skinned driver of the vehicle appeared to be from Matthew Amanave's tribe; he waved to them before disappearing into one of the larger storerooms.

Though Kraft would have liked to have a closer look inside, he allowed his escort to guide him to a nearby wall of solid rock, embedded in which was a rectangular portal. When Annie pushed a white plastic button in the panel, a portion of the wall slid open with a hiss, and Kraft found himself facing a large freight elevator, padded with the same blue carpeting that graced the interior of *Ecowar*.

Now Annie pressed the top button of a stainless-steel control panel, and the doors hissed shut. As the elevator rocketed upward she squeezed his right hand. "It sure beats walkin', Doc. And wait until you see the view."

Even with this warning, Kraft was little prepared for the vista that greeted them when the elevator halted and its doors slid open. The first thing to meet his eyes was a vivid blue, cloudless sky, and a warm gust of air hit him full in the face. As they left the elevator he found himself on a wide ledge built into the side of a perfectly formed volcanic mountain. Five hundred feet below was a spacious, palm-tree-lined, white sand beach, and beyond it, as far as the eye could see, were the aquamarine waters of the Pacific. Kraft noticed a group of naked children playing in a shallow tide pool beside two young men in loinclothes, who were launching an outrigger canoe. The narrow wooden vessel looked quite fragile from Kraft's height, but it proved most seaworthy as its occupants guided it through the curling surf with powerful strokes of their paddles. Watching the outrigger's progress from the beach were a trio of native women dressed in colorful muumuus. A large basket filled with pineapples and coconuts lay at their shoeless feet.

Kraft sighed in wonder. "Annie, you'd better pinch me right now so that I know for sure that this isn't a dream."

She grabbed his forearm and did as directed, causing Kraft to yelp.

"Hey, that was only a figure of speech, kiddo," he said, rubbing the skin of his arm.

"You'd better watch what you say and think on this island, Yank," she cautioned. "Because the natives call it the place where desires come true."

Kraft looked back to the ocean, where the two natives had just raised the outrigger's small sail. "I'll tell you one dream that's certainly come true, Annie. This place is a paradise!"

"For once I perfectly agree with ya, Doc. Now, how about a nice long walk along the beach to get our land legs back?"

Her suggestion suited Kraft just fine, and together they followed a lava-rock roadway down to the sand. Here they stripped off their shoes and socks and began their hike. The fresh salty air was like a tonic, and Kraft felt like a new man as they passed the playing children and waved to their mothers.

The wet sand was cool beneath his feet, and he had to hurry to keep up with Annie's brisk pace. He hadn't properly stretched his legs in a long while, and for the first half mile or so his right hip bothered him. Then his muscles loosened and he forgot about his injury.

From the jungle beyond the slapping surf, tropical songbirds cried out. The beach soon narrowed, and they passed a broad clearing, where they saw a collection of grass shacks with palm-frond roofs and walls. Natives of various ages had gathered outside the simple structures, preparing food and attending to their children. Several of the youngsters, their small dogs yapping away at their feet, ran out to greet the two jumpsuited newcomers. It was an idyllic scene, right out of a Gauguin canvas.

They continued following the beach for another

quarter of an hour before reaching a dilapidated wooden pier and turning inland. A narrow dirt trail led them deep into the dense jungle. It was cooler here, and all too soon the sound of the surf was swallowed by shrill bird cries and the incessant hum of insects.

Another type of earthly paradise showed itself when a small bubbling brook led them to a deep, crystal-clear pool formed by a cascading waterfall. Quick to test the waters with her outstretched foot, Annie ahhed in delight.

"Ever take a dip in a thermal hot springs before, Doc?" she innocently questioned.

Not waiting for an answer, she pulled down the zipper of her jumpsuit and began disrobing. Shocked, Kraft looked away as she peeled off her bra and panties and sat down at the edge of the pool.

"Don't be so shy, Yank. After all, you've already seen me in the buff. Join me. I don't know about you, but I can't remember the last time I had a decent soak."

The sound of splashing water indicated that she had entered the pool, and only then did Kraft look back to Annie. Her back was turned toward him, and the water was just over her shoulders. Curiosity got the better of him, and he knelt beside the pool and checked the temperature with his hand, finding it much hotter than he expected. He could see its soothing effects on Annie as she turned around and once more pleaded.

"Come on, Doc. It's no fun in here alone. And I'll tell ya what. I promise to close my eyes while you get undressed and climb in. And for bein' a good sport, I'll even throw in one of my famous back rubs."

"You just made yourself a deal, kiddo," Kraft said, losing his inhibitions quickly as he peeled off his clothing.

He slid into the pool completely naked, and the near-scalding water covered his skin with a pinpricking heat. He needed to stand on tiptoe to keep from submerging, but once his body adjusted to the temperature, he let himself go under.

When he came up for air, a pair of warm hands grabbed his shoulders from behind. With an expert touch, Annie began gently kneading the tight muscles at the back of his neck. Instantly captivated by the massage, Kraft allowed himself to go limp as her touch released wave after wave of tension into the waters of the pool.

"That does it," Kraft mumbled dreamily. "Now I know that I've died and gone to heaven."

"Remember, Yank," Annie whispered. "You've got to watch what ya wish for on this island."

She gradually increased the pressure of her hands, massaging his broad shoulders and back. Knot after knot of tightness melted in her grasp, and as she reached down to take in his hips and upper thighs, he felt her brush up against his back.

What happened next was beyond her control. Kraft spun her around and took her body tightly in his grasp. One glance was all she needed to see the hunger in his eyes, and she found herself powerless to resist his moist, trembling lips.

Somehow they managed to work themselves directly under the cascading waterfall, and with the heated torrents consecrating their union, she felt his stiffening manhood against her thigh. She traced the muscles of his abdomen downward, and grasped for his crotch, working his erection to fullness with her hand.

Kraft tenderly traced her nipples with his tongue, then nursed them until they, too, were erect. At the same time his fingers found the moist recesses of her womanhood. As they brushed up against her sensitive clitoris she arched her hips forward, telling Kraft that she was ready, and as she wrapped her legs around his slender hips, the two became one.

Her silken depths greedily accepted him, and their lips once more met hungrily as Kraft pulled his hips back and then plunged forward smoothly. Time after glorious time he repeated this blissful thrust, until Annie felt a wave of intensity gathering deep within and then crashing like the tide on the rocks. Kraft's quickening thrusts signaled the arrival of his own fulfillment, and she greeted his shooting seed with another quivering spasm.

Afterward she lay in her lover's strong arms, spent and satisfied. Only then was she aware of the force of the waterfall that continued to soak them from above. Slowly she guided Kraft to the edge of the pool, and once again their lips met. This time their kiss was long and tender, and they could hear the exotic hum of the jungle creatures around them.

"I told ya you had to watch what ya wished for on this island," she teasingly whispered into Kraft's ear. "Because if you're not careful, it just might come true."

"That's an understatement if I ever heard one," Kraft replied. "Because my every wish came true the moment that fate brought me to you, kiddo."

"You Yanks are so damn sentimental," she said, staring deep into his eyes.

"I had a feeling that this place was paradise the moment we stepped out of that elevator. But only now do I realize how true that observation was. Tell me, Annie, do you treat all of *Ecowar*'s passengers like this?"

"I can't really say," she cooed. "Because you're our first one."

"Good," he retorted. "And let's keep it that way."

"Aye, aye, Captain!" she said with a mock salute.

Kraft replied with another kiss. Just when their embrace was heating up, Annie pulled herself back.

"Oh, no ya don't, Yank. One more romp in the bush with you, and I'll never be able to make it back to camp."

"Who needs to go back to the others, Annie? I'm quite content to camp out right here."

"Sounds invitin', Doc. But I wouldn't want you to

miss tonight's luau. As a first-time guest here, the kava ceremony will be held in your honor."

"Kava ceremony?" he repeated.

Annie rolled her big green eyes and grinned. "Doc, this is gonna be a day you won't long forget—and for more reasons than one. That I can guarantee ya!"

19

Eleven hundred and forty nautical miles southeast of Phoenix Island, the *Casabianca* quietly cut through the black depths of the South Pacific. A full day of sprint and drift took its crew to the very northern edge of their current search grid, with absolutely nothing to show for their efforts. With each passing hour, Captain Jules Renard knew that the odds against a successful hunt were drastically increasing. Since their quarry could have gone in any number of directions, Renard had nothing but instinct to guide him. But he was not accustomed to failure, and relied on his many years of naval experience to see him through.

With no time to rest, Renard allowed himself a precious half hour to freshen up and grab a quick bite. He felt guilty as he left the hushed operations center for his stateroom, where his empty cot seemed to beckon him to lie down. Though he'd have liked nothing better, he couldn't afford the luxury.

In the nearby wardroom, a long-anticipated meal served to refresh him, and a mug of strong black coffee inspired a renewed effort on his part. He restlessly charged out of the wardroom, fully prepared to continue his hunt.

As he strode back into the red-lit operations center, he ordered, "Take us up to periscope depth!"

"Periscope depth, aye, Commandant," repeated the sole helmsman.

Renard reached up for a handhold and watched the helmsman pull back on his control yoke. The digital depth gauge on the bulkhead displayed their decreasing depth. A soft creaking of the bow plates signaled a change in water pressure, and Renard expectantly turned for the adjoining periscope well when the tilt of the deck began to stabilize.

"Periscope depth, Commandant," reported the helmsman.

"Up scope," Renard directed.

As the periscope shot up from its storage well in the sail, Renard pulled down the viewing lens, snapped the focus handles in place, and switched on the unit's infrared lens.

A rapid 360-degree scan showed no threatening surface traffic topside, where a full moon lit the night. He began a slow, intensive search of the surrounding seas, paying particular attention to the northwestern horizon, from which direction the American 688-class fast-attack sub, USS *Chicago* would be arriving to assist the Marine Nationale in their hunt.

His initial reaction upon learning of his government's decision to ask the United States Navy for help was far from positive. American submariners were a cocky, egotistical lot who would try to control the search. Renard had worked with them during NATO exercises and knew that the only way to get along with them was to give them their own search grid.

Still, he knew he could use the *Chicago* to expand the scope of his own area of operations. The *Casabi-*

anca was the only French submarine currently in the Pacific, and Renard planned to give it the lion's share of responsibility—the waters to the west, south, and east of Moruroa. Together with the *Duquesne* and the *Suffren,* they would saturate the area with their sensors, and if the phantom submarine they were pursuing had picked this avenue of escape, they would know it.

Meanwhile the *Chicago* would be given responsibility for the sector of sea immediately north of the Manihiki Plateau. Beginning in the Phoenix Island chain, the Americans would bring their sophisticated sensors into play in the unlikely event that their quarry was hiding in this isolated portion of the Pacific.

Satisfied with his plan, Renard completed his scan, stepped back from the lens, and snapped down its dual handles. "Down scope," he ordered. "Helmsman, return to operational depth, on course one-four-zero."

The *Casabianca* angled back down into the cool depths and swung around on a southeasterly heading. Renard had made his decision, and now it would be up to fate to determine if it was a correct one.

Gripping an overhead handhold to keep from falling, the veteran mariner wished only one thing. If he had a squadron of French attack subs at his disposal, he could guarantee the success of this search. But alas, budget constraints had shrunk the Marine Nationale's submarine fleet to a shadow of its former self. The glorious days when Renard and ex-shipmates such as Jean-Louis Moreau roamed the high seas were gone forever.

With the arrival of night, Phoenix Island was transformed into a Polynesian paradise. As the full moon rose above the watery eastern horizon, the beachside bonfire was lit, signaling the beginning of the luau, and the island's inhabitants excitedly gathered around the crack ling embers. Included in this group were Peter Kraft and *Ecowar*'s crew and support staff.

Earlier in the day, a pit had been dug into the beach and lined with red-hot lava rock. An entire suckling pig was then lowered into the hole, along with an assortment of freshly caught seafood and native vegetables. The pit was then covered, and for hours on end, its contents were slowly steamed to a mouthwatering consistency.

To the accompaniment of softly pounding drums and the ever-present crashing surf, the feast was distributed. Kraft was especially famished, and with Annie close at his side, he dug into his meal. The roast pig was perfectly cooked, with a smoky-sweet flavor. Annie introduced him to taro, a local tuber, which was ground into a white paste and tasted much like a potato.

Seated in the sand beside them, Jean Moreau and Michel Baptiste conversed quietly while consuming their platters of steamed fish and vegetables. The rest of the crew was gathered in a tight semicircle to Kraft's right. Of this group, only Ezra Melindi joined Kraft in eating the succulent pork.

There was little talk as they ate. Seconds were offered, and Kraft was among those who readily refilled his plate, making sure to leave room for a dessert of fresh pineapple spears covered with macadamia nuts and shredded coconut.

By the time the evening's entertainment began, he was stuffed. The pounding drums increased in rhythm, and out of the darkness and into the flickering light of the bonfire arrived a line of grass-skirt-clad hula dancers. With a sensuous grinding of their hips, the half-dozen long-haired native beauties "sang" a song by means of hand gestures rather than words.

The song abruptly changed when four fierce-looking warriors arrived. Dressed only in loincloths, their muscular, oiled bodies shimmering in the firelight, they raised their spears and shields and broke out in a low, guttural chant. The hula dancers gracefully weaved between them, softening their warlike presence with a peaceful, gentle grace.

Spellbound by the exotic performance, Kraft was caught by surprise when Moreau leaned over and whispered into his ear.

"This dance celebrates the tribe's arrival here ten generations ago. It describes their long voyage of discovery by sea, and tells of the sea goddess, Mu, who took the form of a white killer whale to lead them to this place."

"What's the significance of those spear-toting warriors?" Kraft asked.

Moreau readily replied. "Soon after their arrival here, they realized that they weren't alone. An aggressive, bellicose tribe lived at the base of the volcano, and a classic struggle between good and evil ensued, with our hosts eventually prevailing."

The drumbeat increased to a frenzied tempo. Somehow the hula dancers managed to keep up with the frantic pace, and the chants of the warriors intensified in volume. Just as the rapid beat reached a crescendo the drums went silent. The dancers halted in midstep while the warriors released one more high-pitched, deafening shout and hurled their spears into the sand.

A round of applause greeted the dance's conclusion. Kraft watched the dancers take their bows, feeling stimulated and appreciative of their efforts.

"What do ya think of that, Doc?" Annie asked from her position on Kraft's left side.

"That was a wonderful presentation, kiddo," he replied sincerely.

Moreau and Baptiste walked over to join them. "I hope that you're enjoying yourself, Doctor," Baptiste said.

"That I am, Admiral."

"I'm glad to see you're making the most of our landfall," said Moreau. "Life beneath the seas can be quite nerve-racking, and there's nothing like shore leave to properly unwind and relax."

"How did you ever find a place like this?" Kraft asked.

It was Baptiste who answered. "Eighteen years ago the winds of fortune blew me to this island while I was running from an approaching typhoon. Well removed from the nearest trade route, Phoenix Island was virtually untouched by modern man, and the native population was most accommodating. Together we sat out the storm, and afterward I was led up the slopes of the volcanic mountain and shown the extraordinary cavern that nature had carved inside it. I remember thinking to myself at that time what an ideal secret anchorage such a site could provide. Little did I dream that less than two decades later I would put the cavern to just such a use."

"Is this where *Ecowar* was built?" probed Kraft.

"More or less, *mon ami*," Baptiste replied. "Though all of her diverse parts were manufactured elsewhere, this is where the final assembly took place."

"You must have had a hell of a time getting all these parts to such an isolated corner of the world," Kraft speculated.

Baptiste shook his head. "It really wasn't all that difficult, Doctor. The majority of *Ecowar*'s components were designed and manufactured in France. We leased our own fleet of cargo vessels and transported the materials in complete secrecy."

"I find it hard to believe that you could tap into the industrial base of such technologically advanced components without being discovered by the French government," Kraft said, a note of challenge in his voice.

Baptiste grinned. "You'd be surprised at how much anonymity a few well-placed francs can generate, *mon ami*. And fortunately for us, money has never been an obstacle. *Ecowar*'s patrons are as diverse as her crew. They come from the highest ranks of society, and all share a single unwavering desire to protect the planet's endangered oceans."

Sensing an opportunity to air his views, Kraft cautiously spoke. "I've seen the way *Ecowar* enforces this doctrine, and though I share your concern for the sea's preservation, I find myself unable to condone the taking of innocent human lives. What gives you the right to be judge, jury, and executioner all in one?"

"Ah, *mon ami*," said Baptiste with a sigh. "The one thing you have yet to understand is that we are not dealing with a tribunal of justice here. As far as we're concerned, the verdict is already in, and we have no choice but to declare total war. What you witnessed out there was nothing but a skirmish, compared to the battle we'll soon be waging!"

Before Kraft could respond, the tall muscular native he had met in the cavern approached them. A large coconut in his hands, Matthew Amanave sat down in the sand in front of them.

"Aloha, my friends," he greeted. "I sincerely hope that everyone's having a good time."

"That we are, Matthew," replied Moreau. "As always, your gracious hospitality is most appreciated."

After acknowledging the compliment with a nod, Matthew turned to the only American in their midst. "You honor us with your presence this evening, Dr. Kraft. As is the custom of my people, I'd like to share with you the secret of the kava ceremony."

Since Kraft had failed to learn anything more about this mysterious ceremony from Annie, all he could do was sit back and listen to the handsome native.

"Kava is the sacred substance given to my ancestors by the goddess Mu. Its consumption will open your soul to the sacred flame. If you are found worthy, the goddess will descend in a vision and show you the true path of your earthy life."

Able to make little sense out of this, Kraft was grateful when Baptiste said, "Do not worry, *mon ami*. The drink that Matthew is about to share with you is derived from the root of a plant indigenous to these islands. It tastes a bit like milk flavored with pepper and cloves, and is considered sacred because of its mild hallucinogenic properties."

"Before taking a drink," added Moreau, "it's customary to spill out a few drops and say the word 'manuia.' Then consume the remaining kava in a single gulp. And have no fear, Doctor. Its soothing effects are similar to Annie's infamous bostrichia tea and will harm you in no way."

Now that he had drawn the attention of all of his shipmates, Kraft didn't dare protest. He watched as Matthew removed the upper portion of the coconut and handed him the lower half. His hand shook slightly as he noticed the milky liquid in the shell cup. Briefly looking over at Annie for moral support, he decided that he had no choice but to drink it.

Following Moreau's instructions, he poured several drops of kava out onto the sand before him, then cleared his throat and softly said, "Manuia." He lifted the coconut cup to his lips and drained it dry with a single long sip.

The kava went down smoothly. It was tastier than he anticipated, and he smacked his lips and handed the coconut back to Matthew. "Not bad," he said, accepting a smattering of applause from those gathered around him.

"Sit back now and relax, good doctor," advised Ezra Melindi, who sat beside Ivana Borisov. Raghib Godavari was beside Ivana, with Karl Ivar between the Indian and Annie.

"Dr. Kraft, I understand from Jean-Louis that you're on the staff of the Rickenbaker Institute of Marine Sciences," said Baptiste. "You wouldn't happen to know a Dr. Charles Kromer, who, I believe, is also affiliated with that distinguished institution?"

Taken aback by this unexpected comment, Kraft replied, "Dr. Kromer is not only the institute's director, but he's my boss as well. May I ask how you happen to know him?"

"Of course, *mon ami*," said Baptiste. "We met at a conference in Monaco several years ago. Dr. Kromer presented a fascinating paper on the relationship between phyto-plankton blooms and the vast decrease in the South Atlantic commercial fishery stocks."

"I know all about that paper," Kraft admitted. "It was one of the last studies Dr. Kromer completed before accepting the institute's directorship."

"I am sorry to hear that, *mon ami*," said Baptiste. "Dr. Kromer showed great promise, and for him to waste his intellect on administrative chores is a sad commentary on the state of marine-biological research."

"I fully agree with you, Admiral," said Kraft. "Now that I think about it, Dr. Kromer was a much more likable person back in the days when that paper was written. His current responsibilities allow him little time for hands-on research, and lately he seems more concerned with budgets than with science."

"Dr. Kraft, is it true that your latest work involved the training of dolphins to repel sharks?" Matthew Amanave asked.

"It's true all right," Kraft answered. "And my initial tests were just starting to show some promise when I was called here to the Pacific for a vastly different purpose."

"Pardon me for saying so, Doctor," interrupted Baptiste. "But when Jean-Louis first told me about your reassignment to the Pacific, I couldn't help laughing. Yet I should have realized all along that *Ecowar*'s unique hull shape would lead to just such a misunderstanding. Though for your navy to actually believe that they were on the trail of a giant manta ray is a little too much."

"I'd like to go on public record as saying that I was skeptical of such a creature's existence from the very beginning." Kraft felt a strange tingling sensation in the pit of his stomach as he spoke.

Matthew Amanave still had Kraft's dolphin research in mind as he continued. "Doctor, I, too, have thought about using our marine-mammal brothers to ward off sharks. As a people who rely on the ocean for our livelihood, we've had too many deaths and serious injuries due to marauding sharks. Perhaps you could tell me more about your work at a later time."

Kraft liked the young native's directness and he replied sincerely. "I'd be more than willing to share all that I know about the subject."

"By the way, Matthew," said Ezra Melindi. "Have you been fishing in Vanua Cove lately?"

"As it turns out, we'll be going out there tomorrow morning," Matthew answered. "And all of you are most welcome to join us."

"That's an invitation you shouldn't pass up, Doc," said Annie. "If you think we know somethin' about trainin' dolphins, wait until you see the way Matthew's people use them to drive fish into their nets."

A disbelieving look crossed Kraft's face and Moreau quickly picked up on it.

"No, Doctor, what Annie says is quite true. And it's but another example of the dolphin-man cooperation that's been documented here for well over a century."

Still not certain whether or not they were playing with his mind, Kraft said, "Sounds to me that like that giant manta ray, this is something you've got to see with your own eyes to believe. So I'd be happy to accompany you on tomorrow's fishing trip, Matthew."

A gray-haired man who Kraft supposed was part of *Ecowar*'s support staff approached Baptiste from the direction of the jungle. Kraft heard a rapid exchange of French, after which Baptiste stood and addressed the crew.

"I'm sorry, but the party is over, *mes amis*. All of you are needed back at *Ecowar* for a preliminary test of the electrical grid."

With a bare minimum of complaints, the crew stood.

Kraft joined them and was pleasantly surprised when Moreau walked up and addressed him.

"Doctor, there's no reason that your evening should be wasted. Stay here with Annie and relax. You've more than earned this respite, and I insist that you take full advantage of it."

In no mood to argue, Kraft looked at Annie and accepted the request for both of them. Good-byes were exchanged with the rest of the crew, and soon they were standing alone beside the raging bonfire.

"A penny for your thoughts," Annie whispered.

A Cheshire-cat grin turned the corners of Kraft's mouth. "I don't know about you, kiddo, but I can think of nothing better than a nice long midnight soak in our favorite jungle hot tub."

Without a second's hesitation Annie responded, "Then whatever are ya waitin' for, Yank? Lead the way!"

Several wooden torches were set into the sand near the waterline, and Kraft borrowed one to provide illumination for their hike. They followed the beachside route they had used earlier in the day. It seemed different at night, with the sound of the crashing surf prevailing over birds and insects. The wet sand was cool between their toes, and they linked hands under a crystal-clear canopy of twinkling stars.

"Annie," said Kraft, his stride less than urgent. "I hope you're not mad at me for how I acted earlier today. Believe me, I haven't hit on a girl so fast since high school."

"Cut it out, Yank," she returned. "There were two of us in that pool, remember? I'm just as much to blame as you. Besides, who's to say that you did anything wrong? I'm sure not complainin'."

"I don't know, Annie. It's just that we barely know each other, and I want your respect as well as your love."

"Boy, are times ever a-changin'," Annie reflected aloud. "Ten years ago that would have been my line."

Pulling him to a halt, she looked Kraft full in the

eyes. "I certainly don't want you to think I'm a pushover, Peter. The fact is, I find it hard to remember the last time I gave myself to a man. And that only goes to show how very much I want you."

"I can't believe it!" Kraft exclaimed.

Confused by his reaction, Annie anxiously inquired, "What can't you believe—that I really desire you?"

"No," said Kraft. "For the first time since we met, you actually called me by my first name!"

"I always heard you Yanks were daft, and now I know for sure!"

Kraft reached out to embrace Annie. This time when their lips hungrily met, he felt a shock of electricity pass between them. Never before had he wanted a woman as much as he wanted this headstrong, curly-haired Aussie. Rising desire inflamed his loins, and he was wondering if he could hold himself back until reaching the pond when a series of high-pitched squeals sounded from the direction of the sea.

Annie broke their embrace and cried, "Dolphins, Peter! There are dolphins somewhere close by."

Kraft somewhat reluctantly joined her in her search. In the light of the full moon he planted his torch in the sand and felt the warm, salt-laden breeze on his face. As he looked past the first set of waves, he spotted several triangular dorsal fins breaking the surface.

"There they are!" he called, pointing to a spot less than three hundred feet away. "They're dolphins all right, and there appears to be quite a few of them."

Annie also spotted the bobbing dorsal fins. "I wonder if that's the pod from whose ranks I recruited Eno and Pelee? Come on, Doc. Let's go out there and have a swim with 'em."

Though Kraft had second thoughts about the safety of such a dip, Annie was already zipping off her jumpsuit. Not about to let her go out there alone, he began undressing.

Her nude body was already plunging into the surf

by the time he peeled off his underwear, and he proceeded into the tepid sea as quickly as possible. The
sandy underfooting conveyed him past the first breakers. The seafloor dropped off steeply, and he dived
beneath the waves and began swimming. He had to
admit that it felt wonderful to be out in the ocean once
again. His brisk crawl stroke took him beyond the surf
line, where he rendezvoused with Annie, and joined her
treading water.

"Lord, will you just look at that gorgeous moon!"
She sighed, rolling over on her back and staring up into
the heavens. "It's shinin' so brightly you can see its
craters."

Kraft also began floating on his back, and as he
searched the sky he marveled at its utter clarity. Myriad
twinkling stars met his awestruck gaze, and he completely
forgot any anxieties he had about this swim when a
shooting star streaked through the sky.

"Did you see that shooting star, Annie?"

"Don't forget to make a wish, Doc," she reminded,
her gaze still locked on the moon.

Kraft glanced over to check on his companion and
found Annie's face and body aglow in the radiant moonlight. Seeing her full breasts and luscious lips, he realized
that the only wish he would make upon the shooting star
was to have her beside him. His penis began to slowly
swell, and he swam to her side and took her hand.

"What do you say about swimming back to shallow
water?" he whispered seductively. "There's something I
want to give to you."

Annie's eyes twinkled like stars as she spotted
Kraft's stiffening member. Not a word was spoken
between them as they briefly kissed and quickly headed
back to the shallows.

They halted at the spot where the waves began to
form, and Kraft set his feet down on the sandy bottom.
He stood, and the water just reached his shoulders.

Annie was quickly in his arms. With a passionate

urgency, their lips met, and she wrapped her slender legs around his waist, anchoring their embrace. There was a new tenderness to their kisses, a sensuous probing of tongues, unrestrained by guilt or doubt. Fulfilling each other's deepest physical needs was their only concern.

Placing his right hand on Annie's ripe bosom, Kraft kneaded the firm flesh and traced the tips of her nipples. She purred in response and reached for his erection, more than ready for him. Slowly at first, Kraft pushed his hips forward, then gently pulled himself back before plunging forward again. Gradually he increased the rhythm of his stroke, rising need guiding him onward. With a renewed urgency, Annie's lips met his in frantic kisses.

Just then a familiar high-pitched squealing noise sounded close by. Without breaking their connection, their lips parted, and they scanned the surrounding seas for the noise's source.

It was Kraft who spotted the first dolphin, less than ten feet away from them. Curiously enough, its head was out of the water and its gaze locked right on them. Annie also spotted the dorsal-finned voyeur, who was soon joined by an equally enthralled compatriot.

"What do you think, Annie," Kraft teased. "Are we setting a bad example?"

Annie laughed softly. "You've been around dolphins long enough to know that they're the most libidinous of all mammals. So don't stop now, Doc, because they're already naturally horny."

As they eagerly returned to their lovemaking, Kraft noticed that the dolphins had begun to circle them in ever-tightening spirals, until he saw that one of them had a distinctive notch cut into its dorsal. He shared this information with Annie, who had other, more pressing concerns, and her kisses all too soon caused him to forget about their two curious visitors. Once more his hips moved in frantic rhythm, and together they rode the pleasurable crest of a wave of their own making.

An unusual numbness seemed to course through his body. The bounds of his physical self seemed to disappear magically, and he was lifted into a new realm, free from all tensions and anxiety. It was all so clear now. To give love was everything!

Annie's embrace seemed to strengthen this realization. Without stopping his hips, he felt her rising pulse, the urgency of her breathing, and knew without a doubt that this was the woman he had waited a lifetime for. Entering her was like making love to the sea.

As he felt the first stirrings of her orgasm, his own seed rose in response, and they climaxed together. Only then, as his seed pumped deep inside of her, was he again aware that they were not alone.

Less than a foot away, the dolphin with the notch in its fin lay still in the water, its knowing, black gaze directed at Kraft. Its stare seemed to unlock a mystery, projecting a panoramic vision deep inside Kraft's mind. The subject of the vision was friendship and understanding, and Kraft knew in that instant that this creature of the sea was his equal.

"Will ya just look at that!" said Annie, who also spotted the nearby dolphin. "He's a bottlenose all right, and quite a big bull. Ya know, I think he's gonna let us touch him."

Following Annie's lead, Kraft cautiously reached out and stroked the dolphin's smooth, rubbery body. It reacted with a squeal of delight and moved in to gently nudge its snout up against the intertwined bodies of the two lovers.

"I think we've got a new friend," Kraft whispered.

"Peter," Annie whispered back, her voice tinged with emotion. "I hope this day never ends. It's been the most wonderful twenty-four hours of my entire life."

"By the looks of that moon overhead, I'd say we have a couple of hours left until midnight, kiddo. So if you don't mind leaving our new friend here behind, how about spending the remaining time in our thermal pool?"

Kraft followed his offer with a long kiss. When they finally broke for air, both of them noticed that the dolphin was gone.

"That's a date, Yank," said Annie as she unwrapped her legs and stood. Guiding him by the hand, she led the way back to the beach, where their torch flickered like a welcoming sentinel.

20

Captain Mac McShane awakened earlier than usual, and greeted the new day with a ravenous appetite. His sleep had been sound, and as he washed up, bits and pieces of a dream flashed into his mind. Much of it had been about his son. They were sailing together on the ocean, and a very grown-up Mac Jr. was comfortably seated at the helm of their twenty-eight-foot sloop. Mac remembered rigging the vessel's single headsail jib and looking out to sea, where a sole dolphin with a distinctive notch in its dorsal fin was riding their bow wake. Oddly enough, the dolphin appeared to be determining their course; whenever it decided to turn, Mac. Jr. obediently turned the wheel and they followed.

Mac supposed that the dream was a subconscious by-product of the familygram birthday greeting he had completed before going to bed. The dispatch, he hoped, would be broadcast during their next Comm transmission, and Mac knew it would be well received back in San

Diego. Content with the knowledge that a complete video of Mac Jr.'s. Sea World party would be waiting for him upon his return, Mac zipped up his coveralls and headed straight for the wardroom.

He found both his XO and navigator at the wardroom table, well into their breakfasts. A bathymetric chart was spread out before them, and as he headed for his customary seat at the head of the table, he briefly halted to have a closer look at the chart.

"Good morning, Skipper," said Phil Moore. "You're up with us chickens this morning. Did ya sleep well?"

"Like a rock, XO," Mac returned. "I see you've already pulled the chart of the Phoenix Trough."

"I thought that would be the best sector to start our search in, Captain," volunteered Len Matson. "The trough directly joins the surrounding islands, and its depth would provide another submarine plenty of cover to hide in."

"When's our ETA?" Mac asked.

"At current speed we should be arriving in the trough sometime after lunch, Skipper," Moore answered, between sips of his coffee.

"Good," Mac said as he sat down. "I'd like to be able to complete an intensive periscope scan of the sector before dark."

No sooner had he taken his chair than *Chicago*'s portly cook burst through the galley door. Howard Mallott anxiously placed a covered dish in front of Mac.

"I see that you're an early bird this morning, Captain," he remarked. "I hope you brought along your appetite."

Mac nodded. "As a matter of fact, I did, Chief. What's for chow?"

Mallott's eyes flashed as he lifted up the silver plate cover. "Your favorite breakfast, sir—Virginia-ham steak, biscuits, hash browns, and two eggs cooked sunny-side up, with plenty of hot joe on the way."

"Looks delicious, Chief," Mac remarked sincerely, pulling off the silver napkin ring that had his name engraved on it.

"Enjoy it, sir," Mallott said, as he handed him a full mug of steaming hot coffee.

"By the way, Chief," Mac said, before digging into his meal. "I want to commend you on your excellent menu selection lately. That Mexican fiesta of yours was a real winner. And your barbecue brisket couldn't have been better if I cooked it myself."

His red face beaming with pride, Mallott said, "Thank you, Captain. And you ain't tasted nothin' until you dig in to tonight's prime-rib feast."

As Mallott rushed back into the galley to relish this long-awaited compliment, Mac took his first bite of ham. "Now this is more like it, gentlemen," he commented, finding the pinkish meat grilled to perfection.

"We all thank you, Skipper, for having that little talk with the chief," offered the XO. "Since he stopped serving all that turkey, morale around here is on the rise. Why, I bet not even the French submariners we'll soon be working with are eating as good as this crew."

"You've got that right, XO," Mac added while breaking the bright yellow yokes of his eggs with his biscuit. "And a fitting way to cap off tonight's red-meat binge is to go ahead and tag that phantom sub we've been tasked to hunt down. That would make it a real celebration!"

Under a cloudless, powder-blue sky, the dawn broke over the Pacific. From a sandy, sea-grape-covered hillside overlooking Vanua Cove, Matthew Amanave watched a half-dozen brown-skinned fishermen ready their nets. A line of rippling surf crashed onto the white sand beach. Seven miles away over a blue channel of water, the hazy green outline of Atafu Island could be seen.

Redirecting his gaze to the sparkling clear waters of Vanua Cove, Matthew spotted several leaping mullet at the far side of the surf line. His guests were late. This was most unusual for the punctual Frenchmen. Matthew could only assume they wouldn't be able to join him this morning, and he decided to return to the beach and get on with the fishing.

Matthew helped his men carry their coil-lined mesh nets down to the water. Although he had not spotted a single dolphin, he gave the order to deploy the nets.

They proceeded into the cove until the water was well up to their waists, and began unraveling the nets, which had been carried on long wooden staves. Once fully deployed, they created a formidable barrier. Matthew called his men back to the beach to begin the ceremony to call forth the mullet. The sacred chant was uttered, and the men returned to the waterline, where they began loudly slapping the water with the open palms of their hands.

Matthew scanned the waters of the channel for any sign of their divine helpers. Another mullet leaped in the distance, and as Matthew repeated the sacred chant his grandfather had taught him, the grinding roar of an outboard motor sounded in the distance. When a Zodiac raft rounded the breakwater, Matthew realized that his friends would be joining him after all. Hoping that their arrival would bring luck, he proceeded to the beach to greet them.

The Zodiac held four individuals. Matthew identified Ezra Melindi at the helm, along with Jean Moreau, Annie Sawyer, and the American, Dr. Peter Kraft. It was the bald-headed Frenchman who threw him the mooring line while Melindi cut the engine.

"*Bonjour,* Matthew," said Moreau. "We're sorry to be late."

Matthew did his best to pull the loaded Zodiac up onto the beach. Melindi jumped off the raft to assist him, and together they easily pulled the inflatable vessel halfway out of the water.

"Actually I'm the one who caused us to be late this morning," admitted the American, who sported a beard-stubbled face and bloodshot eyes. "I'm afraid I over-slept."

"I hope it wasn't the kava's fault," returned Matthew.

Kraft briefly looked to Annie Sawyer before responding. "That among other things, my friend."

Matthew helped them out of the Zodiac as Melindi said, "I see that you've got the nets deployed. How's the fishing?"

Matthew shook his head. "It appears that we've somehow gained Mu's disfavor. The mullet are out there, but so far no dolphins have arrived to herd them to shore."

"I believe we spotted the reason for this when we rounded the breakwater," Morcau announced. "And it has nothing to do with Mu's disfavor. It seems you've got a pod of killer whales in the channel, gorging themselves on your prospective catch. Not even the bravest dolphin is going to run that blockade to assist you."

"Why not use the Zodiac to scare them off?" Kraft suggested. "The roar of the outboard motor will deafen them, and they'll move off to more peaceful waters."

"Sounds good to me, *mon ami*," returned Moreau. "Come, Doctor. Let's you and me give it a try."

Annie appeared concerned as Kraft returned to the Zodiac. But she didn't dare express her displeasure as he helped Melindi and Matthew place the raft in the water. Moreau joined Kraft inside the inflatable and took up a position at the helm. Kraft knelt in the bow, leaving Annie with a wide yawn and a brief wink as the engine roared back to life.

Moreau displayed enviable seamanship as he crisply turned the Zodiac around and pointed its blunt bow toward the open waters of the channel. A deafening buzz-saw whine emanated from the outboard motor as the Frenchman opened up the throttle. Kraft was forced to reach out and grab the nylon rope threaded through the gunwales when the Zodiac catapulted off a swell and smacked back down into the water.

A massive, triangular black fin broke the channel's surface to their right, some one hundred feet distant. Kraft anxiously pointed in this direction and shouted, "Orca, Commandant!"

Moreau also spotted the distinctive dorsal fin, and the Zodiac angled sharply starboard. At first, the killer whale seemed to ignore their presence. To get its attention, Moreau began rapidly circling the twenty-eight-foot, eight-ton creature in ever-tightening spirals. The boat was less than three feet away from it when the orca yanked up its blunt black-and-white-striped head. Kraft could clearly see the line of razor-sharp teeth and its large, black eyes set well back on the head, near the jaw.

The orca looked directly at them with a hint of annoyance. Appearing more aggravated than afraid, it sounded. And the next they saw of it, it was well out into the waters of the channel.

"That's one down!" Moreau cried triumphantly. "Now let's get the message across to the others."

This tactic was successfully repeated two more times on a pair of smaller females. As Kraft searched the waters for their next candidate, he spotted the entire pod moving off into quieter waters. He signaled to Moreau, and the Frenchman joined him in a high five, then guided the Zodiac back to shore.

Melindi helped them pull the raft up onto the sand. Kraft climbed out and was immediately met by Annie.

"How did it go, Doc?" she asked.

Exhilarated, Kraft replied, "That's the last we'll be seeing of those orcas for a while."

"Good," put in Matthew Amanave, who stood at Annie's side. "Now we can get on with the fishing!"

Moreau joined them on the beach, and together they walked over to the group of fishermen huddled near the waterline. Matthew turned to the waters of the cove and began singing a low, guttural chant in his native tongue. His shiny black eyes seemed to glass over as his chanting grew louder, until he was almost shouting.

"Now call forth our brothers in the sea!" he finished.

Without hesitation, the fishermen waded into the surf. When they were waist-deep in water, they began slapping the sea with the open palms of their hands. Their empty nets still floated before them, and all eyes were focused on the waters beyond.

A few minutes after they began beating the water, Annie pointed out a leaping mullet close by. Though Kraft thought this was an isolated sighting, Annie excitedly shouted, "Here come the mullets!"

It turned out that she was right when, seconds later, the waters of the cove began to boil over with thousands of leaping, silver-flanked fish. Quickly the natives waded forward to attend to their nets. Moments later the booming voice of Ezra Melindi was heard shouting, "And here come the dolphins!"

Kraft followed Melindi's outstretched finger and witnessed a miraculous sight. A hundred or so feet away, dozens of small black fins appeared in the water. Soon the individual bodies of these dolphins could be seen as they surrounded the leaping mullet and began moving in toward the beach.

"My God!" Kraft exclaimed. "They really do herd those mullets into the nets. This is simply incredible!"

"According to legend," explained Moreau, "the dolphins have been assisting Matthew's people in this manner from the very first day his ancestors arrived here. They thus consider the dolphin a holy animal, and it is expressly forbidden to kill one."

"I can certainly see why," Kraft added.

The fishermen had already succeeded in encircling a large school of leaping mullet. As the net was pulled in, the first of many wriggling fish were carried ashore by their gills. Meanwhile, on the far side of the net, the dolphins were doing a bit of fishing themselves. With practiced ease, the sleek marine mammals could be seen throwing the mullet high in the air, then catching them in their mouths. This amazing sight prompted Moreau to speak again.

"Whether or not it turns out that the dolphins are intentionally collaborating with man here, this proves that the two species can work together for each other's mutual benefit. Perhaps one day the dolphin will truly become man's helper in the sea, consciously sending schools of fish into our nets."

"Looks like we've got some company comin'!" reported Annie, who pointed out a single vessel headed toward the cove from the channel.

The vessel proved to be a compact outrigger canoe. Its two native occupants furiously stroked the water with their paddles.

"That's my cousin Amanu," Matthew Amanave said. "We sent him to Atafu Island to check out the identities of several boats recently spotted on the far side of the island. Come, let's get his report firsthand."

Kraft felt the first stirrings of apprehension as he followed the group down to the water. The outrigger canoe continued its rapid approach, and Kraft got his first clear view of the muscular native seated in the vessel's bow, who could easily have passed for Matthew's brother. As the canoe shot past the leaping dolphins and plunged through the surf, Kraft saw the rivulets of sweat that ran down his bare, heaving chest.

Matthew was the first to grab the pointed bow of the canoe. With Melindi's help, they pulled it ashore. The sweating native in the forward position spoke between deep gasps of air.

"Pirate whalers, cousin! We spotted five of their vessels anchored in Atafu Cove."

"Are you sure they're whalers, Amanu?" questioned Matthew.

"Positive!" Amanu panted. "They displayed no flag, and each was outfitted with a bow-mounted harpoon gun."

This was all Moreau had to hear. "This certainly warrants further investigation on our part, Matthew. Though with *Ecowar* laid up for repairs, we'll have to cross the channel by Zodiac."

It was clear that Matthew wasn't the least bit concerned by this fact. "That should be easy enough to do, Commandant. When do we leave?"

Moreau looked over to catch Ezra Melindi's glance. "If they're indeed whalers, it will be to our advantage to first return to Phoenix base and properly outfit ourselves."

"I'm almost afraid to ask," interrupted Kraft. "But what do you plan to do to these whalers once you locate them?"

"Why that's only too obvious, Doctor," Moreau shot back. "Because now's the time to eliminate this entire nest of vermin before they can slaughter one more innocent creature of the deep!"

It took them a full hour to return to Phoenix base. The support staff was well into their repairs of *Ecowar*'s hull. With Michel Baptiste close at his side, Moreau rushed off to the weapons locker.

It was decided to utilize two Zodiacs to carry a nine-person assault team. Kraft found himself having practically to beg to be included, and it was with some reluctance that Moreau finally agreed to take him along.

The sun was high in the sky when they finally began to cross the channel. Kraft was assigned to Ezra Melindi's raft. The Kenyan instructed Karl Ivar to take the helm, with both Matthew and his cousin Amanu perched in the bow. Kraft sat amidships, alongside a sealed weapons container with Melindi positioned directly behind him.

They were traveling with the engine throttle wide open, and the resulting ride was far from smooth. Following Melindi's example, Kraft braced himself against the gunwale with his feet. Even then, the ride was bone jar-ring, and at one point he feared for his right hip.

The lead Zodiac under Moreau's command was posi-tioned to their port. Moreau himself was at the helm, with Michel Baptiste, Ivana Borisov, and Annie as his passengers.

It took a little less than a quarter of an hour to com-plete their passage. The shores of Atafu island were far from welcoming. Formed from another extinct volcano, Atafu's shoreline was littered with lava rock and thick vegetation, and Amanu had to point out the safest place to make their landing.

They had to cross an area of rough surf before they finally reached a narrow stretch of beach lined with coconut palms. They hurriedly left the Zodiacs, and as the equipment was unloaded Amanu explained the next portion of their journey.

"The cove where the whalers lay anchored is another mile further inland. I know a trail that will take us most of the way, and should get us to the cove without being discovered."

Several Uzis appeared from the weapons container. Backpacks were distributed and filled with the rest of their armory. As it turned out, Kraft was given a knap-sack filled with grenades, and he felt somewhat uncom-fortable as he draped it over his back. Annie seemed to sense his discomfort, and she flashed him a smile before joining the others beside Moreau.

"We'll let Amanu and Matthew take the point. The rest of us will follow. And please, *mes amis,* keep as quiet as possible," he urged.

Michel Baptiste appeared particularly delighted as he shouldered his backpack and stuffed a 9mm pistol into his waistband. "Hey, Jean-Louis, this is just like old times," he whispered. "It's good to be on the front lines once more and see a little action for a change."

Moreau nodded politely in response and put his right index finger to his lips, then pointed to the tree line. At this, Amanu immediately began the march inland. Matthew followed close on his heels, with Melindi leading the rest of the group.

Kraft was content to be the last one in line, with Annie directly in front of him. The trail was narrow, barely as wide as Kraft's foot, and led them into the thick stand of palms. Before he knew it, the crashing surf was no longer audible. Replacing it was the incessant, pulsating hum of jungle insects, interspersed with the high-pitched cries of tropical birds.

The underbrush thickened as soon as they left the last palm tree behind. Massive ferns dotted with brightly colored flowers sprouted along the trail, and in the distance Kraft could just hear the babble of a brook. The humidity made the mere act of breathing difficult, and sweat poured off his forehead and dripped down his back. He swatted at a mosquito on his neck and prepared himself to ford a good-sized stream that cut the trail up ahead.

He was wondering whether or not he could cross over the stream without getting his feet wet when a sudden piercing squeal caused him to freeze. The underbrush to his right violently shook, and out of the jungle shot a full-sized boar. As the snorting beast crossed the path only inches from Kraft's body, he fought back the urge to scream. With his heart pounding away in his chest, he looked up and saw Annie on the far side of the stream facing him. Her smile alone gave him the strength to continue.

When he eventually caught up with the group, they were gathered at the foot of a steep embankment, with Amanu at the tail end of a briefing.

"We will be able to see the cove from the top of this rise," Amanu whispered. "So you must proceed most cautiously."

No trail was visible on the embankment, which was formed from a solidified lava flow. "How ya doin', Yank?" Kraft heard Annie ask as he got ready to climb.

He flashed her his most determined glance. "You haven't lost me yet, Annie. Though that boar back there almost gave me a heart attack."

"Well, keep a stiff upper lip, Doc. Amanu says we're real close now."

Kraft answered with a thumbs-up, and Annie grinned and led the way up the rise. As he expected, he made the climb without difficulty, and soon found himself lying on his stomach beside the others on the embankment's flat summit.

From this lofty vantage point, he could see a small, tree-lined cove less than a quarter of a mile distant. Three rusted trawlers lay at anchor beside a rickety wooden pier. Kraft's stomach began to tense as he noted that the cove's clear blue water was stained red alongside the pier, and he soon enough ascertained the cause. Gathered on the dock was a group of grubby individuals engaged in butchering a baby dolphin. Several dozen bloody dolphin carcasses, already skinned, lay in a heap nearby. Kraft tried hard to control his rising anger upon spotting a submerged capture pen beside the dock, where a collection of thrashing dolphins awaited their turn to die.

"Those brutes aren't even takin' the time to kill that poor baby dolphin before they skin him!" Annie whispered in horror.

Moreau lay beside Annie, and Kraft could hear the Frenchman angrily ask, "Amanu, are you absolutely certain that you saw five vessels here earlier?"

"As Mu is my witness, I'm positive!" answered the native.

"Two of them must have gone out to sea to ply their illegal trade, Commandant," Melindi offered by way of explanation.

"We must finish our work here quickly, then return to Phoenix base and get *Ecowar* seaworthy with all due haste!" added Michel Baptiste.

Ivana Borisov came up with a plan of action. "The most efficient way to scuttle those ships would be to place a limpet mine on their hull, directly below the engine room."

"Can you manage to place these charges on your own, Comrade?" asked Baptiste.

"Don't worry, Admiral," the Russian replied. "While I was training to become a member of Soviet Special Forces, my Spetsnaz courses included underwater demolition. Though I can't move in with the stealth of a Freddie, the underwater breathing apparatus I brought along should allow me to get close enough to do the job."

"That's all I ask, *mon amie.*" Moreau regarded her with admiration. "Because while you're placing the mines we'll be working to free those dolphins from that pen."

"I know a trail that leads to the far side of the cove," Amanu said. "One could enter the water there without being seen from the pier."

Moreau responded immediately. "For the sake of your sacred God Mu, lead on!"

They located the trail at the bottom of the embankment. It was a narrow, twisting affair that took them through a dark, menacing stand of ancient teak trees. Kraft now traveled close to the front of the group, and he was one of the first to spot an abandoned lean-to near which the waters of the cove were visible.

Amanu halted beside the dilapidated structure, and the rest of the team followed suit. Ivana wasted no time stripping off her jumpsuit, displaying a lean, fit body. Her black underwear had to serve as her swimsuit. Karl Ivar helped prepare her equipment, pulling three hand-sized, light plastic trays out of one of the knapsacks. Each tray had a D-shaped handle and was fitted with a timing device and four magnets.

Kraft found her portable breathing device particularly interesting. It was not much larger than a fat fountain pen, and had a rubber mouthpiece in its side.

"Tell me, Doctor," inquired Moreau. "Do you still disapprove of our methods?"

Kraft hesitated a moment before answering, unable to condone the Frenchman's actions, yet unable to condemn him wholeheartedly either. There could be no denying his disgust on first viewing the baby dolphin being butchered. But did this cruel, merciless act demand physical retribution on its perpetrators? In this isolated setting, merely confronting the dolphin killers with the illegality of their actions would gain nothing. So to protect the remaining dolphins, Kraft found himself leaving the moral high road behind.

"I guess under these circumstances, we really don't have much of a choice but to take the law into our own hands and stop those murderers ourselves," he muttered.

Moreau replied while managing the barest of grins. "There's hope for you yet, Dr. Peter Kraft. Now, what do you say about helping me open that pen and saving as many of the remaining dolphins as possible?"

"How can I help?" Kraft asked.

"We'll slip into the water and head for the pen while the others provide a suitable diversion," Moreau answered. "By the way, *mon ami,* how's your swimming?"

Kraft glanced over at Annie as he answered. "I can hold my own in the water, sir."

Having overheard the entire exchange, Annie broke in: "Commandant, please let me take your place in the water. No offense, sir, but my swimming is much better than yours. And besides, both Dr. Kraft and I have more experience handling dolphins at close range."

Moreau was all set to object when Michel Baptiste interceded. "She's right, Jean-Louis. Let her go with the doctor. You can help us with that diversion."

Moreau reluctantly yielded, but not before leaving the two volunteers with a last piece of advice. "Very well, *mes amis.* But keep low in the water. And for goodness' sake, be careful out there!"

Before he had a chance to change his mind, Annie led Kraft to the far side of the lean-to. "Come on, Doc," she said while unzipping her jumpsuit. "We're those poor dolphins' only chance!"

Kraft followed her lead and also pulled off his clothing. Dressed in his scivvics, he watched as Ivana Borisov rapidly made her way into the water with a satchel draped over her shoulders. Annie grasped his hand, and together they also took off for the cove.

The water was warm and motionless. From the cover of a twisted mangrove root, they spotted the three rusted trawlers, and beside them, the dock containing the submerged pen. A quarter-mile swim lay before them, and they decided to take advantage of the thick mangrove forest that lined this portion of the cove for as long as possible.

As he prepared to push off, Kraft took one last look at the jungle from which they had just emerged, glimpsing the two bald-headed Frenchmen who could be seen kneeling beside a fallen tree trunk. The elder of the two gave him with a crisp, appreciative salute.

Ivana Borisov had disappeared beneath the water when Kraft realized that they had to move fast. Annie took the initiative, swimming as powerfully as she had last night—under much different circumstances. It took total effort on his part to keep up. Establishing a steady pace, they passed the last protective mangrove root. With half the distance covered, Kraft swam forward to take the lead.

As he scanned the distant pier he realized how exposed and vulnerable they were. A lone, beard-stubbled sentry manned the dock, a rifle draped over his slouching shoulder. Another rifle-toting sentry strolled the deck of the nearest trawler. This individual seemed to be fascinated by something in the water beside the ship, and Kraft thought the worst when he began to unsling his weapon. Had he spotted Ivana?

As the sentry was ramming a bullet into his rifle's chamber, a geyser of water erupted on the opposite side of the pier, accompanied by a booming blast that Kraft could actually feel in his chest. The staccato crackle of small-arms fire sounded from the direction of the jungle. The pier's occupants went scrambling for cover, and Kraft knew that the promised diversion was under way.

A new urgency guided his swimming. Trying his best to ignore the booming explosions topside, he made a last-ditch sprint for the dolphin pen.

He heard the dolphins long before he saw them. The panic-stricken creatures were crying out in hysterical, high-pitched squeals. Forgetting all about his own gathering fear, Kraft took a deep breath and swam the rest of the way to the pen underwater.

The enclosure proved to be little more than a squared off nylon net, kept afloat by Styrofoam buoys. Dozens of terrified, madly thrashing dolphins were packed within a space no larger than a small closet.

Kraft was determining the best way to release them when Annie joined him. She was clearly winded as she said, "Someone up there was shooting at me!"

"Are you all right?" asked Kraft.

Nodding, Annie was quick to direct her attention to the plight of the dolphins. "Thank God that we got here in time. Now, how are we gonna get them out of there?"

Kraft answered while examining a portion of the net beneath the buoys. "Give me a hand, kiddo. This part of the net appears to be tied with nylon rope, and we should be able to open a hole here."

A thundering explosion sounded nearby, and both of them hurriedly went to work unraveling the net. Kraft fought to control his trembling fingers. Adding to his anxieties were the frantic cries of the dolphins, the crackling bursts of small-arms fire, and the rapid pounding of his own heart.

What seemed to take an eternity only took a few minutes, and they gratefully peeled back the net, exposing a gaping hole. Yet the scared dolphins refused to budge, and Kraft could think of only one thing to do.

"Keep the net open, Annie. I'm going to have to go in there!"

Without a moment's hesitation Kraft entered the net and found himself in a swirling mass of slithering dolphin bodies. Trying his best to ignore the painful bites and bruises he received, he grabbed the nearest dolphin and forcefully shoved it out the hole. One by one, he guided the others to freedom, until only a single large bull remained. Kraft was all set to force him out of the net as well when he spotted a distinctive notch cut into the dolphin's dorsal fin. He realized with a start that this was the dolphin that had watched them intently the night before.

With great satisfaction he guided their old friend to safety. Yet before he could tell Annie, a bullet ripped through the water directly beside him. He fought his way out of the net and found Annie tightly pressed up against the adjoining pier.

"There's a man up there on the dock with a rifle, Peter! We'll never get out of here."

Several more bullets shot past them and Kraft feared the worst. He supposed that their only chance of escape was to fill their lungs with air and swim underwater for as long as possible—though it was doubtful that either one of them could outswim a bullet.

When another round of shells ripped into the water, Kraft's desperation grew. In his preoccupation he almost ignored a strange biting sensation on his foot. Puzzled, he ducked his head underwater. Much to his surprise, the notch-back dolphin had returned. The creature proceeded to gently rub the side of his twelve-foot-long body up against Kraft's right thigh. Beyond conveying his thanks, the dolphin seemed to be trying hard to tell Kraft something. As Kraft reached out to touch the creature's dorsal fin, he understood just what it was.

"Annie!" he exclaimed after surfacing and regaining his breath. "Don't ask me how or why, but our means of escape is waiting for us down below. Take a deep breath, and follow me!"

Kraft allowed no time for questions, and Annie filled her lungs with air and followed him down into the depths. As anticipated, the dolphin was calmly waiting for them there. Kraft pointed toward the creature's dorsal fin, and made a grasping motion. Annie quickly got the message, and together they grabbed onto the dolphin's upper back.

A single motion of the dolphin's powerful fluke was all that was needed to send them rocketing through the depths. Bullets that continued to rip into the water above were of absolutely no concern to the dolphin, who in less than a minute had them safely out of harm's way.

The dolphin finally surfaced in the middle of the cove, and as they filled their lungs with blessed air, Annie shook her head.

"How in the blazes did you ever manage to get us that lift, Doc?"

"Did you check out that notch in our savior's dorsal fin, kiddo? Believe it or not, this is our voyeur friend from last night!"

"You're spookin' me, Doc," Annie said.

Kraft laughed and, while stroking the dolphin's flanks, noted that the bursts of gunfire in the distance had become sporadic. "I believe that we can make it the rest of the way on our own. Thanks again, ol' buddy," he added, affectionately petting the bottlenose on his snout.

The dolphin responded with an animated squeal and, after accepting a pet on the snout from Annie, headed for the open ocean.

"Come on, Annie. Let's get the hell out of here."

She needed no more prompting to head for the cover of the nearby mangrove swamp. Kraft swam right alongside her, and only when they reached shore did he realize the full extent of his exhaustion.

He allowed himself barely a minute to catch his breath. With Annie's help, he found the path leading to the lean-to. Waiting for them were Moreau, Ezra Melindi, Karl Ivar, and Ivana Borisov. Ivana was already dressed, and was readying a radio-controlled detonator when they entered the clearing.

"Ah, *mes amis!*" exclaimed Moreau, his delight most evident. "We didn't know if you'd ever return to us."

"Good doctor, Annie, you're a sight for sore eyes," added the smiling Melindi. "What happened to you out there?"

Kraft glanced at Annie and replied, "You'd have had to been there to believe it."

"And the dolphins?" Karl Ivar wanted to know.

"They were last seen swimming for the open Pacific," Annie proudly reported. "What kind of luck did you have with the mines, Ivana?"

"We'll know the answer to that question once I complete this final connection," Ivana replied.

With the assistance of a wire stripper, she exposed an inch-long strand of copper filament, which she wrapped around the detonator's vacant terminal, then delicately handed the entire device to Moreau. The Frenchman scanned the faces of all those assembled around him before passing the detonator on to Peter Kraft.

"It's only fitting that you do the honors, Doctor," he solemnly remarked.

"I don't know if I can," returned Kraft.

"Nonsense, *mon ami.* You must, for the sake of those dolphins!" Moreau urged.

Kraft also scanned the faces of those gathered at his side, and his confused glance locked onto Annie's. A look of firm determination shone in her big green eyes, and he could feel her powerful will imploring him to take this step.

His mind suddenly flashed back to the moment he had first laid his eyes on the baby dolphin being skinned alive. As he visualized the heap of skinned dolphin carcasses scattered on the dock, anger—the indignation and outrage of a full-fledged eco-terrorist—burst inside of him. Without giving a second thought to the human lives he might be endangering, he held up the detonator and pressed the first of three toggle switches.

A muted crack exploded in the distance. Kraft's hand was shaking so badly that he didn't know if he'd be able to hit the next switch. But then his mind seemed to fill with the hysterical cries of the trapped dolphins he had just freed. To avenge their slain brethren, he flipped the remaining two toggle switches simultaneously.

It was almost anticlimactic when the next two bursts sounded. A series of secondary explosions followed, and Kraft wearily dropped the detonator and looked over at Moreau.

"Well done, *mon ami*. Now you have an idea of the blind fury that motivates us. And to properly close this dark chapter, it's time to return to *Ecowar* and hunt down the two vessels that have managed to escape us!"

At this moment Matthew Amanave emerged from the jungle. Bright red blood stained his body, and he appeared close to tears as he turned back toward the thick underbrush and watched his cousin appear. Also covered in blood, Amanu could be seen holding the limp, blood-splattered body of Michel Baptiste.

"*Mon Dieu*, Michel!" Moreau howled like a wounded animal, and rushed to his friend's side. One look was all he needed to see that Baptiste was dead. "Michel! Michel!" he cried as he cradled the limp corpse in his arms.

"There was nothing we could do for him, Commandant," offered Matthew. "The admiral gave up his life to save ours when he threw himself on a grenade that landed in our ambush site."

Collapsing on his knees, Baptiste's body still firm in his grasp, Moreau continued to wail, oblivious to those around him. "Ah, Michel! Michel! So far we have come, *mon ami*. So far we have come for you to die in this distant land in such a needless manner. Just as *Ecowar* was your dream from the very beginning, so it was in the end.

And we shall take this final cruise together, *mon ami,* and only then will your soul be at rest, knowing that revenge is finally ours."

Moreau looked up with tear-filled eyes. "Back to the *Ecowar, mes amis*! For we have yet more murderers to hunt down!"

21

The USS *Chicago* entered the deep waters of the Phoenix Trough shortly after 3:00 P.M. To get their search off on the right foot, Captain Mac McShane made certain to have Matt Cox and his watch team on station in sonar. Cox was well aware of this great responsibility, and motivated his troops with a round of ice-cold Dr. Pepper that he had safely stashed away in the overhead air-conditioning duct.

It was with great expectations that Cox watched his men go to work. To his far left, he saw Specs deploy the sub's towed array. Eric Algren scanned the narrow-band processor from the center console while, on his right, Marvin Johnson monitored the broad-band frequencies.

From his position behind them, Matt Cox randomly monitored each of these consoles with the assistance of a pair of headphones. His glance was currently locked on Algren's CRT screen, where the submarine they hunted would, they hoped, show itself. Cox paid special attention to the narrow-band processor's spectrum-analysis graph.

"It sure would be nice to know exactly what it is that we're listenin' for," commented Marvin Johnson as he routinely accessed his console's keypad. "At least with our last assignment, we knew where we stood."

Cox readjusted his right headphone and responded to this comment. "Though we've got no ultrasonic homing signal to lead us to our target this time, I'm kinda glad we're gettin' back to what we do best—huntin' down other submarines."

"That's all fine and dandy," returned Johnson. "But is this new target a nuke or diesel-electric? And more importantly, what's so damn important about trackin' it down in the first place? Shit, man, since when have we gone and got uptight and personal with Frenchie anyway?"

"Maybe this is nothing but a NATO drill," Algren offered.

"No way," replied Cox. "When the captain and XO briefed me earlier, both of them stressed the fact that this wasn't an exercise. Scuttlebutt says it has somethin' to do with a terrorist attack on a French warship, and that's why we were called in to help."

"It's kind of scary knowin' that terrorists have somehow gotten their hands on a submarine," Algren said.

Cox grunted. "It was bound to happen sooner or later, babe. And let's just pray that we can do our bit in huntin' them down."

"What the hell?" Specs mumbled as he pressed his headphones to his ears. "It sounds like there's a baby crying out there!"

Cox quickly switched over to monitor the towed array console, and as his eyes scanned the flashing repeater screen, he heard a series of low-pitched cries through his headphones. They had an eerie, mournful quality to them, and Cox excitedly addressed the only trained musician in their midst.

"Hey, Marvelous Marv, take a listen, babe."

Johnson wasted no time redirecting his scan to the towed array. He, too, heard the distant cries, and a wide smile turned the corners of his mouth. "Hot damn, it's an undersea rap group!" he joked. "Just listen to those suckers. From the racket they're makin', I'd say we've got a group of humpbacks topside."

The sounds continued to intensify, and Cox angrily cursed. "Damn! Just what we needed to make our job even more difficult. Get a firm fix on 'em, Specs, and I'll spread the word to Control."

A disgusted expression crossed his face as he reached up for the overhead microphone and spoke into the transmitter. "Conn, Sonar. We have a new contact, bearing one-six-zero. Classify Sierra eleven, biological."

The trip back to Phoenix base was a solemn one. Moreau had insisted upon bringing his dead countryman back with them for an eventual burial at sea. Michel Baptiste's bloody corpse was wrapped in a tarp and reverently laid out on the floor of the Zodiac at Moreau's feet. Still too distraught to take the helm, Moreau sat by himself and vacantly stared out into the waters of the channel while Ivana Borisov replaced him at the throttle of the outboard motor.

Annie switched places with Matthew and was able to make the return trip at Kraft's side. Both of them sat on the bow of Melindi's Zodiac. Discretion was no longer a concern for them, and they displayed their affection by holding hands.

Few words passed between them as the raft rocketed over the waters of the channel. Much like Moreau in the other Zodiac, Kraft's vacant gaze was locked on the sea, his thoughts a tangle. He had been deeply moved by his shipmates' response to Baptiste's death. That wasn't the problem. The problem was that when they climbed the volcanic embankment on their way from Atafu Cove, he viewed firsthand the destruction to which he had directly contributed.

Suddenly he saw the extent of the damage. Their mines had led to the destruction of all three trawlers. Two of the vessels were completely sunk, only their twisted superstructures visible. The third lay on its side with thick clouds of oily black smoke pouring from the jagged hole in its hull.

On the pier, the surviving fishermen were attending to their wounded. Two of the bloodstained bodies laid out on the rickety dock appeared to be corpses, and a rescue effort of some sort was being attempted on the boat that had yet to sink.

Unable to forget his participation in the attack that led to this tragic scene, Kraft desperately attempted to come to terms with himself. He had crossed the line, of this he had no doubt. And with this realization, his conscience was demanding an explanation.

Noticing the skinned dolphin carcasses on the dock and the floating remnants of the capture pen he and his cohorts had destroyed, he was reminded of the dolphin lives he had helped save. But was their freedom worth the spilling of human blood? This was the question that continued to haunt him, and Kraft scanned the surging waters for an answer.

Their arrival back at the subterranean cavern holding *Ecowar* generated a flurry of activity. Moreau snapped out of his mournful reverie and took control of getting the submarine seaworthy once more.

Still determined to eliminate the two pirate whalers that had escaped them, he ordered the dry dock flooded. Kraft was pierside when the Frenchman informed Chief Yushiro of his intentions. *Ecowar*'s head engineer took these new orders in stride and calmly explained the various subsystems that would remain inoperable during this rushed cruise. Kraft intently listened as Yushiro rattled off a list that included a serious electrical distribution problem and a malfunctioning defensive shield. Regardless of these problems, Moreau remained adamant, and all too soon the water was pouring into the dry dock as the support crew hastily did last-minute repairs to *Ecowar*'s interior.

"Conn, Sonar," called the amplified voice of Matt Cox over the control room's intercom speaker. "We've got another surface contact. Bearing one-seven-five, range twenty thousand yards. Classify Sierra thirteen, trawler."

From his central command position on the bridge, Mac McShane reached up for the ceiling microphone. "Sonar, Conn, designate Sierra thirteen, trawler," he said into the transmitter. "Any idea what's going on up there, Mr. Cox?"

The senior sonar technician's voice hesitated a moment before responding to this query. "The whales continue to sound all around us, sir. My best guess is that we've tagged a fishing vessel of some sort in their midst."

"Aye, Sonar," Mac said as he hung up the microphone, and turned to face the diving console. "Helm, take us up to periscope depth," he firmly ordered.

Phil Moore stood close at Mac's side, the stem of his trusty corncob clenched between his teeth.

"What do you think, Skipper?" the XO softly asked. "Could that trawler be a whaler?"

The deck began angling upward by the bow, and Mac answered while reaching up for a handhold. "It sure appears that way, XO. Let's have a peek and find out for ourselves."

"Periscope depth, Captain," informed the diving officer.

"Up scope," Mac directed, as he snapped down the periscope's dual grips and anxiously peered into the eyepiece.

His first view was a watery one as the scope rose toward the surface from the sub's sail. Mac scanned the seas for obstacles as the lens broke the water's surface.

A deep blue cloudless sky greeted him. The ocean was almost flat, with just an occasional swell rippling its surface. Only when Mac was confident that there were no surface threats in the area did he turn the lens to bearing one-seven-five. Sure enough, the vessel of which his sonar team had warned was just visible here. Mac increased the magnification, and the ship took on additional detail. Approximately two hundred feet long, it sported an unusual boxy superstructure that was in sore need of a paint job. By increasing the lens amplification to its maximum level, he could see a wide opening in the vessel's transom near the waterline. A large, black, bloated object was being pulled from the sea here.

"It's a whaler all right, XO," Mac announced. "From the look of her, she's a factory ship, and they're in the midst of pulling in a whale even as I speak."

Mac backed away from the scope and allowed his XO to have a look. Phil Moore was momentarily speechless as he watched the massive sea creature being pulled up onto the ramp by its tail and then disappearing into the ship's hold.

"That's one humpback that will never sing its song again, Skipper," he said with a disgusted shake of his head. "You know, I thought that particular species was protected."

"There's not much we can do about it now, XO," Mac observed.

"What a waste." Moore backed away from the eyepiece. "I realize that whaling's an old, established industry, but you'd think it would be an anachronism in this modern age."

"I hear you, XO," said Mac. "And personally, nothing would give me more satisfaction than putting an Mk48 into the hull of that rust bucket. But right now that's far from our main concern."

"What's next, Skipper?" Moore wanted to know. "With all this traffic topside, we sure don't have optimum conditions to continue our search. Maybe we should leave the trough and patrol elsewhere."

Mac thought about this for a moment before responding. "That's a tempting suggestion. But if that sub we've been tasked to track down is indeed in the area, you can bet it's going to make the most of these noisy conditions to hide in. No, my gut says to remain in the trough, and perhaps we just might get lucky."

Kraft was impressed with how quickly the support staff was able to get *Ecowar* ready to sail again. As soon as the dry dock was refilled, Ezra Melindi ordered the crew aboard. Kraft was given the option of joining them or remaining on the island. Though he was tempted to remain, his curiosity got the better of him. He somewhat reluctantly said his good-byes to Matthew Amanave and his cousin Amanu and boarded the ship with the others.

Michel Baptiste also joined them, in a manner of speaking. The elder Frenchman's corpse was laid out in Moreau's stateroom. The captain hoped to bury him at sea once they carried out their primary mission.

As it turned out, Kraft had just enough time for a quick shower and uniform change before a slight shudder of the deck indicated that they were on the move. He arrived in the control room and found it fully occupied. A tense atmosphere prevailed as he took his customary position between Moreau and Melindi.

"Initiate preprogrammed exit procedures, Mr. Godavari," Moreau directed.

Kraft finished buckling his shoulder harness and looked up to the display screen. The schematic on the middle panel reminded Kraft of a runway view from an airplane's cockpit during takeoff. A line of flashing red lights ran through the center of the drawing, and Kraft assumed that he was looking at an animated version of the lava-tube tunnel they were currently transiting. His assumption was verified by Moreau's next words.

"Karl Ivar, how are you picking up the tunnel's transponders?"

The Norwegian responded without removing the compact headphones that cupped his ears. "Loud and clear, Commandant. Glide path is locked in and departure sequence activated."

"Pipe the active sonar signal through the ship's intercom," Moreau ordered.

Karl Ivar addressed his keypad, and a distinctive, hollow pinging sound reverberated through the compartment. It seemed endless, its constant rhythm synchronized with the flashing red lights on the display screen. The strobelike sequence had an almost hypnotic effect on Kraft, and he wasn't at all disappointed when the sonar feed began to fade.

"We just passed the last pinger," Karl Ivar informed. "Departure sequence completed."

"Mr. Godavari," snapped Moreau. "Engage hydrodrive on course one-eight-zero. If there are whales in the area, we'll most likely find them due south of us, beneath the deep waters of the Phoenix Trough."

Kraft watched Raghib Godavari expertly manipulate his joysticks. He shoved the left one forward to open their throttle and sent the deck angling over steeply on its starboard side with the right joystick.

Ivana Borisov accessed the bathymetric chart that next filled the screen. It showed the wide undersea valley they were about to penetrate, with Phoenix and Atafu islands barely visible on the northernmost quadrant. The latest sounding showed over five thousand meters of sea beneath their hull. Everyone was caught by surprise when an electronic chime began ringing. All eyes went to the lower left portion of the screen, which was suddenly filled with the image of their very disturbed chief engineer.

"Commandant," Yushiro announced, "I understand the urgency of our current mission, but I must remind you of the fragile state of our electrical system. The engine inlet ionizer shows signs of overheating, and I request permission to stand down from hydrodrive."

Moreau's response was quick and firm. "Permission denied. We've got hundreds of square miles of ocean to search, and speed is one of the only factors that we have on our side. So do whatever's necessary, Chief, but keep that entire power train on-line!"

"Aye, Commandant," Yushiro retorted.

As the video intercom link was terminated Melindi spoke carefully. "Commandant, you're certainly asking a lot of the chief. I peeked into the engine room before we cast off, and it was a mess of loose cables and torn-apart consoles."

"There's no time for cautiousness, Number Two," Moreau replied passionately. "Our mission is much too vital to be held back by fear of mechanical failure."

A moment of hushed silence followed. For the first time Kraft sensed serious disagreement on the part of Ecowar's second in command. The strain of their rushed departure was finally showing itself. Kraft could only wonder what would break first, the crew's nerves or Ecowar's mechanical systems?

"Surface contact, Commandant!" Karl Ivar exclaimed. "Bearing one-nine-five, maximum range."

"By all means, share it with us," Moreau directed.

Kraft briefly met Melindi's worried gaze as Karl Ivar input this request. The furrows on the African's brow seemed to magically disappear when a deep throaty growl emanated from the intercom speakers.

Beside him, Jean Moreau's spirits also lightened as he absorbed the familiar racket that continued to intensify in volume. Closing his eyes to focus solely on this sonic signature, he expertly picked out the surging, cavitational hiss of a single prop screw, which was badly nicked and thus "singing." The diesel power plant that powered the propeller was definitely not built for stealth, and its steady roar indicated a full flank throttle. Somewhere in the recesses of his mind, Moreau knew that he had heard this distinctive signature before. As he searched his memory the intercom projected a muted soulful, high-pitched cry that was in vast contrast to the steady roaring growl that continued in the background.

"Humpbacks!" cried Karl Ivar. "We've got whales topside!"

Suddenly Moreau flashed back two decades in time to the sonar console of the *Agosta*. They had been patrolling these very seas, and Moreau was monitoring the gentle cries of a mother blue whale and her baby when fate interceded in the form of a pirate whaler. Never would he forget the distinctive racket this vessel made as it cut through the seas. And now, twenty years later, like an undead spirit from the past, the same ship had returned.

"It can't be!" Moreau cried as his eyes popped open and he jerked forward.

"Whatever's the matter with you, Commandant?" asked Melindi. "You look like you've seen a ghost."

"In a way, I have, Number Two," Moreau reflected aloud. Gathering his composure, he added, "Bring us up to visual-scan depth, Mr. Godavari. Karl Ivar, prepare to launch Freddie!"

"Conn, Sonar," reported the amplified voice of Matt Cox. "We've got another surface contact, bearing two-two-zero, range seventeen thousand yards and closing. Designate Sierra fourteen, trawler. And this one's comin' in with a bone in its teeth, sir!"

Phil Moore was on the periscope, doing a mock-torpedo-attack work-up on the whale factory ship anchored to their southeast when this latest sonar update was received. He quickly turned the scope to a southwesterly bearing and locked in the contact of which Cox had just informed them.

"What have you got, XO?" Mac asked, rushing over from the navigation plot.

"We should have been expecting this one, Skipper," said the XO while backing away from the eyepiece. "Have a look for yourself."

Quick to replace Moore at the scope, Mac identified the new contact as the factory ship's hunter vessel. It was cutting a white swath through the blue sea and had a formidable-looking harpoon gun on its prow. As it advanced, several sailors could be seen gathered beside the gun, anxiously pointing to the water ahead of them, and Mac focused his line of sight to this portion of the sea. Less than a minute passed before he spotted the slender, five-meter-tall blow of a spouting whale, only five hundred yards away from the rapidly approaching trawler.

"There she blows!" Mac reported. "Barring a miracle of some sort, the Pacific will shortly have one less whale swimming in it."

The infuriated occupants of *Ecowar*'s control room were watching this same scene unfold on their display screen. The view from Freddie's video camera was strikingly realistic, and even included the fleeing whale's triangular fluke as it desperately sounded for safer waters.

"This time the hunter shall become the hunted," whispered Moreau. "Retrieve Freddie! Prepare to attack!"

With a concerted effort, the crew busily addressed their individual keypads. The first to report in was Karl Ivar: "I have a lock on Freddie. Retrieval initiated."

"Targeting sequence has been inputted," stated Ivana Borisov.

A steady electronic drone began in the background. Kraft stirred uneasily and turned when Moreau quietly addressed him.

"Less than a week ago, you condemned us for such an attack. Do you feel the same today, Doctor?"

Unable to answer this question immediately, Kraft struggled to sort out the emotions that continued to bewilder him. Once again he found himself torn between the lesser of two evils, and when he finally voiced his opinion, it was with a hint of reluctance.

"Don't get me wrong, Commandant Moreau, I still think it's wrong to kill in cold blood like this. But I guess that someone's got to draw the line if whales like those humpbacks up there are going to have a chance to survive."

"You've come such a very long way, Dr. Peter Kraft," Moreau said, a hint of fondness now in his voice. "And speaking for all of us aboard *Ecowar,* I'd be honored to have you as a permanent crew member."

Kraft was shocked by this offer, and he responded sincerely. "I'm truly flattered, sir. But I'm afraid that my place is still up there, in society's mainstream."

"Freddie's home. Retrieval completed," Karl Ivar reported.

"We have a final lock on target coordinates," added Ivana Borisov.

"The ramming spars have been deployed," said Raghib Godavari. "I show seventy-three-percent hydrothruster charge available."

"*Ecowar* is ready to eliminate the target, Commandant," Melindi matter-of-factly observed.

Moreau's mood abruptly changed, and a zealous gleam glowed in his eyes as he sat forward and shouted, "For the sake of our whale brothers and the soul of Michel Baptiste, initiate attack!"

Specs hated to admit it, but this afternoon's watch was turning into one of the most difficult sonar sessions of his naval career. The constantly singing humpbacks were distracting enough. Added to the grinding roar of the whaling ship topside, it was all but impossible to hear. He was about to give up on his headphones and concentrate solely on his monitor's waterfall display. If there was another submarine out there, he'd see its sound signature long before he'd ever hear it in their current clamorous conditions.

Though he really wasn't anticipating any results from the scan, he gave it his best effort anyway. With practiced ease, he isolated the towed array's various hydrophones. When a minute flutter caught his attention, his first impression was that it was an anomaly. Only when the slight distortion repeated itself did he gather his courage and speak up.

"Sir, there's something strange on the array's low-frequency band."

Cox was quickly at his side, and Specs pointed out the two flutters on his waterfall display.

"You know," Cox said, "it does look like something just popped up through the thermocline, directly beneath that trawler. Could it be a whale?"

"It's possible, sir," returned Specs, still not one hundred percent sure of himself. "If it's not some kind of weird anomaly, that is."

Having just come to the same conclusion, Cox took the gamble and reached up for his direct line into the control room. "Conn, Sonar," he barked into the microphone. "We've got a possible submerged contact, coming up through the thermocline, directly beneath Sierra fourteen!"

"Range to target thirty-five meters and closing," reported Ivana Borisov. "Recalibrate impact zone."

A visual of the whaler was projected on the display screen. Currently passing the hull was a detailed cross hair, similar to that on a rifle scope. As the cross hair halted on the central portion of the hull, Karl Ivar calmly spoke out: "Recalibration completed. Impact to take place directly amidships, two meters below target's waterline."

Kraft was amazed to realize that *Ecowar* could accurately hit a moving target like this. He tried his best to make some sense out of the confusing assortment of data on the screen. And he expectantly grasped his armrests when the digital distance-to-target indicator passed the twenty-meter threshold.

"Brace yourselves, *mes amis,*" warned Moreau. "For the battle to save a species from extinction continues!"

"Conn, Sonar!" exclaimed Matt Cox from the control-room intercom. "Something big, possibly a whale, is coming up directly beneath Sierra fourteen, and it's comin' up quick!"

Mac noted the senior sonar technician's abandonment of normal operating vernacular, and hastily redirected the periscope from the spouting Humpback he had been following back to the whaler. The bow gunner was preparing for a shot and could be seen gripping the harpoon gun's trigger.

With no other data to go on, Mac accepted Cox's conjecture that the mysterious underwater contact was indeed a whale. The creature was apparently taking a page right out of Melville's *Moby Dick,* and was about to ram the whaler. Not wanting to miss this once-in-a-lifetime sight, he fine-tuned the lens focus on the harpooner.

The first indication of something unusual occurred when the gunner suddenly crashed to the deck. The entire ship violently shook, and Mac redirected the lens to take in the vessel's rust-covered hull. He began his scan at the still-quivering bow, and as he moved aft he could see that the brunt of the collision had taken place directly amidships.

Sweeping the lens down to focus on the waterline, he witnessed a shocking sight. The trawler's hull had been penetrated, not by a charging whale, but by a huge, black, saucer-shaped creature sporting two prominent horns. Looking on in disbelief as the creature disengaged its horns from the punctured hull's interior and sank back into the frothing sea, Mac finally found the words to express his astonishment.

"Holy Mother Mary, XO! If I just hadn't seen it with my own eyes, I'd never believe it. That was no whale out there. It was our good friend the monster ray, and it just took out that trawler!"

"Aw, come on, Skipper," countered the XO. "That's impossible."

Mac shakily stepped back from the scope and beckoned his XO to have a look himself. Moore got to the eyepiece just in time to see the whaler capsize and then sink.

"But how in the hell did that creature travel all the way down here?" he mumbled. "And why didn't we hear its ultrasonic homing beacon before it struck?"

"Who knows—maybe it shook the beacon, or perhaps it malfunctioned," Mac guessed. "Or it could be that there's more than one of 'em."

"That's all we need," said the XO as he turned to face McShane. "Now what, Skipper?"

The *Chicago*'s commanding officer firmly answered. "That's only too obvious, XO. Load torpedo tubes one and two with wire-guided Mk48s. If it returns for the factory ship, we'll have the sucker right in our sights!"

In *Ecowar*'s control room, the intercom speakers rang out with the gut-wrenching sound of rending steel and rushing water as the sinking whaler's bulkheads imploded. Kraft wondered how many men had already died as a result of the attack, and he was fighting back the urge to protest when he heard Moreau's next order.

"Target the remaining surface vessel."

"Initiating retargeting sequence," Karl Ivar reported.

As the Norwegian addressed his keypad the intercom chime sounded, followed by a video image of Chief Yushiro in the lower left-hand portion of the screen.

"Commandant," said the weary engineer, "I'm unable to recharge our hydrothrusters. I recommend returning to Phoenix base at once, sir."

Moreau reacted as he had before. "There will be no retreat now, Chief. I don't care how you do it, but you've got to redirect enough power to allow us to disengage just one more time. Do whatever's necessary, and then I promise you we'll turn for home."

Yushiro sighed heavily. "The only way to summon enough power is to shut down all primary sensor systems. That would leave us completely defenseless."

"What need is there for defensive systems," countered Moreau, "when it's *Ecowar* that's doing all the hunting?"

To see for themselves the manner in which the giant ray first showed up on their sonar screen, Mac and his XO headed straight for the adjoining sound shack. They found Matt Cox huddled over the bespectacled sonar-man.

"Mr. Cox," Mac greeted. "I want to see just what it was that initially gave away that submerged contact's presence."

Cox calmly pointed toward the waterfall display he had been examining. "I was just highlighting it myself, sir."

Pointing to the second of twelve bar graphs projected on the screen, he encircled a minuscule aberration in the sound-analysis curve. "This tiny flutter on the low-band spectrum is it, Captain," Cox said. "And you can thank Specs here for discoverin' it."

"Then that's all you'll have to listen for, gentlemen," Mac instructed. "The second it shows itself again, lock its signature into fire control, and we'll send in an Mk48."

Surprised by the aggressiveness of this order, Cox looked up from the screen. "Sir, you never did say exactly what it was that we tagged out there. Are we shootin' at a whale, or did we happen to stumble upon that sub we've been tasked to locate?"

Mac's answer shocked all four members of the sonar watch. "Neither, Mr. Cox. As strange as it may seem, that underwater contact you just tagged is none other than our old friend the giant manta ray!"

"Concluding final approach, Commandant," Karl Ivar reported.

"Hydrothrusters engaged, with a forty-one-percent charge available," added Raghib Godavari. "Seven-degree up angle on the bow ramming spars."

Kraft scanned the display screen in disbelief as they prepared to begin their second attack of the day. He could see from the image on the screen that their current target was stationary, and appeared to be a factory ship. As the all-too-familiar cross hairs scanned the vessel's square hull, he tried his best to visualize the poor whales being butchered inside the ship. Only by constantly reminding himself of this sober fact could he deal with the reality of their actions.

"Range to target one thousand yards and closing," reported Ivana Borisov.

"Bring us to the surface and initiate the attack, Mr. Godavari," Moreau ordered. "At long last a mother's needless death will be avenged!"

Inside the hushed confines of the *Chicago*'s torpedo room, Seaman Joe Carter assisted his shipmates in loading the second wire-guided Mk48. Much to his dismay, this was no drill. From what little they understood, the captain intended to fire these weapons at a live target. If this shot really meant war, he would do his best to make both his mother and his country proud of him.

In *Chicago* Power and Light, Lieutenant Paul Ward went about his business regardless of their current alert status. Even in battle, the vessel's propulsion plant needed attending to, since a sudden burst of speed could be the difference between life and death.

To prepare for any contingency, he had a relief team anxiously waiting in the maneuvering space to spell the reactor operators should there be a casualty. Hoping that this damage-control team would never have to be utilized, Ward studiously scanned the gauges of the main engineering console. As his eyes passed over the digital knot counter, a deep crack thundered through the compartment. He knew in an instant the racket's source, and he angrily cursed, knowing that there could be no worse time for the reactor's water-pump safety valve to once more malfunction.

"Underwater contact, Commandant!" Karl Ivar announced as he cupped his headphones over his ears. "There could be another submarine out there on bearing two-four-zero."

This disturbing news brought forth an instant query from Ezra Melindi. "Commandant, shall we break off our attack?"

Moreau sat there unmoving, his eyes locked on the display screen. "Whatever for, Number Two? At long last the sword of judgment is in our hands, and we shall slay the killers of Leviathan without fear of retribution!"

Unaffected by the exchange, Ivana Borisov's voice rang out. "We are penetrating the thermocline, Commandant. Range to target five hundred yards and closing."

This time when the familiar flutter appeared on his waterfall display, Specs did not hesitate to report, "Submerged contact, bearing zero-six-zero!"

"All right!" Matt Cox exclaimed as he reached up for the microphone to inform Control.

In the *Chicago*'s control room, Mac absorbed this

exciting news and calmly addressed the redheaded officer at the fire-control console. "The ball's in your court now, Mr. Bradley. Initiate sonar interface."

The weapons officer was already well into this process, and his reply was quick in coming. "Interface completed, Captain. We have a firm lock on target."

"Fire one!" Mac ordered.

Even from the control room, they could hear the resounding whoosh of compressed air as the Mk48 shot out of its tube. The deck shuddered with the sudden loss of weight, and as seawater ballast poured back inside the now vacant tube, the crew anxiously awaited the attack's results.

"Incoming torpedo!" alerted Karl Ivar. "I show a single weapon headed our way on bearing two-two-zero, at twelve thousand yards."

This news hit Kraft with all the force of a fist to the stomach, and he fought back the first rising wave of panic.

"So we are no longer the only hunter, Commandant," Melindi observed. "Surely you must call off the attack now."

Kraft turned to check Moreau's reaction. Unbelievably the Frenchman seemed completely deaf to it, his attention instead locked on the display screen.

"Target range three hundred yards and closing," Borisov said in her usual rote manner.

"Number Two," said Moreau pensively. "Compute the difference between the amount of time it will take for us to attain our target and disengage versus that torpedo's ETA."

Melindi appeared ready to protest, then reluctantly addressed his keypad. An assortment of new data flashed up on the screen, and he was quick to interpret it.

"If our disengagement is clean, we will have two minutes and seventeen seconds before torpedo impact."

Satisfied that his hasty mental calculations had been correct, Moreau confidently replied, "That's more than enough time to initiate evasive maneuvers. Mr. Godavari, prepare to engage reverse thrusters immediately upon striking our target, and then take us deep at flank hydro-drive speed."

"But Commandant," Godavari dared to interject. "Our hydrothrusters show less than a forty-percent charge."

"Mr. Godavari!" Moreau shouted. "You will do as ordered!"

Ecowar's helmsman sheepishly nodded. "Aye, Commandant."

"Range to target one hundred yards," Borisov announced with seeming unconcern.

"Torpedo has just broken the ten-thousand-yard threshold, Commandant," Karl Ivar reported.

Displaying a remarkably calm demeanor, Moreau met Kraft's troubled glance and whispered. "Remember, Doctor, it's only times like these when man lives life to its fullest extent."

"Brace yourselves, *mes amis*!" Moreau said forcefully. "The moment of truth is upon us!"

Kraft was absolutely certain now that he was in the presence of a madman. With no alternative but to accept his fate, he turned back to the display screen. Their target was clearly projected here, the cross hairs locked on the factory ship's waterline. As the digital distance-to-target counter was breaking fifty yards, Kraft grasped his chair's sweat-stained armrests.

His thoughts were of Annie as they passed within thirty yards of the whaler. She was currently assigned to the engine room, and all he prayed for was one last chance to feel the touch of her lips. To have found love after so long, and then to see that love threatened like this was more than Kraft could accept. Yet he knew he had to do his best to face this situation in a manner that would make Annie proud.

It was almost anticlimactic when the digital counter reached zero and *Ecowar*'s twin ramming spars sliced into the whaler's exposed underbelly. Tightly gripping his armrests in a vain effort to counter the violent shaking of the deck, Kraft waited to hear the reassuring growl of the sub's reverse thrusters. When they finally activated, the resulting whine was barely audible.

At Kraft's side, Moreau was also aware of this unwanted lack of sound, and he shouted into the intercom, "Chief, the only way you're going to get enough power into those thrusters is to temporarily shut down all the other support systems!"

A chime sounded, and Yushiro's frantic image flashed onto the screen. "But then we risk not having enough power to restart them," he warned.

"Sufficient power will be there, Chief," Moreau answered. "Have faith, *mon ami,* for only you can free us from this impasse."

The video link was abruptly terminated, and seconds later the overhead lights unceremoniously blinked off. Even the display screen became a wall of black as the distant bubbling growl of the thrusters gradually intensified. A loud, rending sound signaled that the ramming spars had finally wrenched themselves free. No longer having the crippled whaler to support it, *Ecowar* angled over sharply on its rounded bow and began plunging into the depths.

It seemed to take an eternity for the emergency lighting system to activate. Even then, the compartment was only feebly illuminated by a series of red battle lanterns. Once more, Kraft struggled to control his rising panic, which only increased as the crew began reporting in.

"All defensive sensors are inoperable, sir," Karl Ivar reported.

"Commandant, the helm is totally unresponsive," added Raghib Godavari.

Kraft had heard enough, and his distress was obvious as he spoke. "Does that mean that we're just going to keep sinking, and there's nothing we can do about it?"

Moreau was the picture of composure as he turned to Kraft. "Have faith, Doctor. *Ecowar* is designed to take a remarkable degree of punishment, and we shall yet prevail."

The hull seemed to moan ominously in response to his comment. Kraft had all but given up hope when the main lights suddenly snapped on, and an assortment of data began flashing on the screen.

"I've got the helm back!" Raghib Godavari cried out triumphantly. With a backward yank of his right joystick, the angle of their descent lessened.

But Kraft's relief was only of a moment's duration as Karl Ivar reminded them of another deadly concern. "Defensive sensors back on-line. Torpedo continues its approach. Range three hundred yards and closing."

What with all the other frenzied goings-on, Kraft had almost forgotten about this weapon, and his terror reached the breaking point as Karl Ivar went on to say, "Torpedo has capture, Commandant!"

"Take us up, Mr. Godavari!" Moreau screamed. "Emergency surface!"

Kraft found himself thrown backward into his chair as the bow angled steeply upward. His eyes desperately searched the confusing data on the screen in a futile attempt to understand their new threat. His effort was abruptly curtailed as the Mk48 detonated twenty-five yards behind *Ecowar*'s stern.

The aftershock sent a surge of seawater crashing into them. Almost torn from his shoulder restraints by the force, Kraft blindly looked out into the violently shaking compartment as the lights failed again. The terrifying sound of rending metal overhead was accompanied by an icy spray of seawater, and several pieces of loose equipment smashed into the still-vibrating deck as the emergency battle lanterns popped on.

Completely soaked, Kraft heard the deep, authoritative voice of the vessel's commanding officer: "Karl Ivar, repair that valve! Mr. Godavari, blow emergency ballast and get us topside! Number Two, how bad have we been hit?"

It took a full minute for Melindi to coax a faded damage-control diagnostic onto the display screen. "It doesn't look good, sir," he reported. "We took the brunt of the blow in the engine room. Though the inner hull's holding, I show flooding in the propulsion core, and a fire raging in the MHD generator."

The roar of venting ballast sounded, and thus lightened, *Ecowar* shot upward.

Raghib Godavari revealed the extent of the rapid ascent. "We've surfaced, Commandant. But without power, I don't know how long I can hold us here."

This was all Kraft had to hear to rip off his shoulder harness and stand up. "Come on!" he yelled. "We've got to abandon ship!"

Much to his horror, the crew didn't budge.

"What's the matter with all of you," he added frantically. "Now's our only chance to escape!"

It was only then that Moreau unbuckled his own harness and calmly stood up. With a reverent solemnity, he slowly scanned the concerned faces of his crew. "As previously discussed, we shall all remain on *Ecowar* to the very end."

"You people are crazy!" Kraft raged, his eyes wide in disbelief.

"Don't worry, Doctor," Moreau said. "This pact wasn't meant to include you. If you'll be so good as to accompany me to the main access trunk, we can get on with your evacuation."

Hardly believing what he was hearing, Kraft watched as Moreau began to make his way across the flooded deck to the hatchway. By this time Karl Ivar had completed his hasty repair of the sprung valve. As he passed by Kraft to return to his seat, he offered the American his hand.

"It was a pleasure sailing with you, sir," he said, without any sign of concern for his own fate.

Kraft returned his handshake and gazed around the room, taking one last look at his seated shipmates. As the finality of the moment sank in he felt almost guilty about the polite nods and salutes they gave him.

"Good luck with your future dolphin studies, Comrade," Ivana Borisov offered.

"Take care, Doctor," said Raghib Godavari.

"Yes, good doctor, do take good care of yourself," Ezra Melindi added with a fond grin. "We are relying on you to continue the battle, and to tell the children that we made this sacrifice for them!"

There was a loud tearing sound in the background, and the deck momentarily shuddered.

"Come on, Dr. Kraft!" Moreau urged from the hatchway. "We must hurry now!"

Unable to find the words to express the great fondness he felt for these brave sailors, he left them with a simple wave and eyes filled with tears. Thick smoke filled the central passageway as Moreau guided him to the access trunk. The Frenchman pulled down its ladder, and handed Kraft an orange life jacket and a thin, metallic object about the size of a small spark plug.

"Here, *mon ami*. We found this ultrasonic homing implant embedded in *Ecowar*'s hull during our recent repairs. May it lead to a quick rescue."

Kraft hastily strapped on the life preserver, and as he shoved the homing beacon into his jumpsuit's top pocket, he returned Moreau's resolute stare. "Thank you, Commandant Moreau," he whispered emotionally. "Thank you, sir, for everything."

Again the hull shuddered, and as Kraft anxiously reached up for the ladder, an anxious female voice sounded from the veiled passageway. "Doc!" shouted Annie as she rushed up to the access trunk. "Oh, Doc, thank goodness I got here in time!"

His own selfish desire to survive had made him forget about Annie, and he shamefully accepted her warm embrace. Their lips met in a kiss that lasted barely a second before Moreau urged him onward.

"Please, Dr. Kraft. You must leave here at once!"

The distant sound of tearing metal underscored his urgency, and Kraft reluctantly broke their embrace. "Get a life jacket, and join me, Annie," he pleaded.

The Australian looked into his frantic gaze with tear-filled eyes and spoke with firm conviction. "Peter, I can't join you. My destiny is here, aboard *Ecowar*. So please, darling, understand this, and know that the love we shared will live on with you."

The deck suddenly seemed to settle beneath them. When a small explosion sounded from the direction of the engine room, Moreau stepped between them and cried, "Doctor, you must go this instant!"

"Yes, my love," pleaded Annie. "You must go, and live to tell the others."

Though his heart begged him to stay, Dr. Peter Kraft made the most difficult decision of his life. Knowing full well that he'd pay the price in many lonely nights to come, he turned for the ladder and began the short climb to safety.

EPILOGUE

A jubilant atmosphere prevailed inside the control room of the USS *Chicago,* where the crew celebrated their successful attack with a chorus of relieved cheers and a round of high fives. Mac McShane was particularly delighted with the outcome, this being the first time he had shot a torpedo other than as a practice round. Making a mental note to pass on a job well done to the rest of the men during tonight's prime-rib dinner, he was taken by surprise when the agitated voice of Matt Cox broke over the intercom.

"Captain, I hate to be the bearer of bad news, but we've got an ultrasonic homing signal squawking up a storm topside. Its frequency matches that authorized by NOSC, which means our monster ray is still up there in one piece, on bearing three-two-zero."

"Damn!" Mac cursed as he joined his XO at the periscope well.

"Easy does it, Skipper," Phil Moore advised. "All this means is that the taxpayers are gonna have to lose one more Mk48 so we can get the job done properly. I'll furnish the final bearing."

Without a second thought, the XO engaged the *Chicago*'s attack scope. He snapped the retractable arms in place and peered into the eyepiece while checking for nearby surface obstacles. Only when he was assured that they had the waters to themselves did he turn the lens to the southwestern horizon.

The late-afternoon sun illuminated a gorgeous blue sky. The sea was almost dead flat, and as a curious gull flew by he increased the lens magnification tenfold.

"We've got that torpedo ready to fire, XO," McShane reported from close by. "Can you see it?"

When an extensive scan failed to uncover anything out of the ordinary in the vicinity, Moore increased the lens magnification to its maximum. A small bright orange object bobbing on the water's surface caught his attention, and as he fine-tuned the focus Phil Moore gasped in astonishment.

"You're not gonna believe it, Skipper," he managed to splutter as he backed away from the eyepiece, "but will you take a look at this!"

Not having the foggiest idea what his XO was referring to, Mac replaced him at the scope. The bright orange object was clearly visible, and Mac could see that it was a life jacket. But it was the identity of the man in the preserver that provided the real knockout blow.

"X . . . O," he stuttered. "It can't be!"

"Tell me about it, Skipper," Moore replied. "I could have sworn that the doc was shark meat, some five thousand miles north of here!"

"Join the crowd, my friend," Mac returned. "Let's get up there pronto. You can bet your pension that Dr. Peter Kraft is gonna have one hell of a story to tell!"

If you would like to receive a HarperPaperbacks catalog, please send your name and address plus $1.00 postage/handling to:

HarperPaperbacks Catalog Request
10 East 53rd St.
New York, NY 10022

CAMPBELL ARMSTRONG

Agents of Darkness

Suspended from the LAPD, Charlie Galloway decides his life has no meaning. But when his Filipino housekeeper is murdered, Charlie finds a new purpose in tracking the killer. He never expects, though, to be drawn into a conspiracy that reaches from the Filipino jungles to the White House.

Mazurka

For Frank Pagan of Scotland Yard, it begins with the murder of a Russian at crowded Waverly Station, Edinburgh. From that moment on, Pagan's life becomes an ever-darkening nightmare as he finds himself trapped in a complex web of intrigue, treachery, and murder.

Mambo

Super-terrorist Gunther Ruhr has been captured. Scotland Yard's Frank Pagan must escort him to a maximum security prison, but with blinding swiftness and brutality, Ruhr escapes. Once again, Pagan must stalk Ruhr, this time into an earth-shattering secret conspiracy.

Brainfire

American John Rayner is a man on fire with grief and anger over the death of his powerful brother. Some say it was suicide, but Rayner suspects something more sinister. His suspicions prove correct as he becomes trapped in a Soviet-made maze of betrayal and terror.

Asterisk Destiny

Asterisk is America's most fragile and chilling secret. It waits somewhere in the Arizona desert to pave the way to world domination...or damnation. Two men, White House aide John Thorne and CIA agent Ted Hollander, race to crack the wall of silence surrounding Asterisk and tell the world of their terrifying discovery.